Adventu

-

GW01043926

Pegasus m

Adventures with Pegasus
- Book One

Pegasus makes an entrance

by Scout P Walker

*This story is dedicated to all curious children
who question what is real and what is not;
and who never believe anything just because
an adult tells them it is so*

Series title: Adventures with Pegasus
Title: Pegasus makes an entrance
Number in the series: 1
Copyright © Scout P Walker 2021
Published by Erik Istrup Publishing
Cover art by Stella de Burca
Published through Ingram Spark
Font: Palatino
ISBN: 978-87-94110-21-1

Genre: Fantasy

This is book one in the series

Erik Istrup Publishing
Jyllandsgade 16 st. th., 9610 Nørager, Danmark
www.erikistrup.dk/publishing/ • eip@erikistrup.dk

Contents

Turn a page
and the story
begins!

1 - A Small Brown Pony

The two children were hanging over the five-bar gate opening from the lane into Farmer Grubble's field. They were trying to attract the attention of a rather scruffy brown pony grazing in the middle of the thistle-filled grass.

The pony however, was totally ignoring them, even though they had called out his name several times and had held out handfuls of lush grass picked from the ditch by the side of the lane.

"Are you sure Mr Nibbs is his name?" Esme asked her brother.

"Yes! I've told you. I heard Dad say so to Mum when he got back from doing that harvesting job for old Mr Grubble."

"Well, he's not taking any notice," Esme commented, pointing out the obvious. "So we might as well go home. He's not a very pretty pony anyway. And he looks quite old."

"**I'm** not going home." Reuben wondered to himself if his sister would have been more enthusiastic if the pony had been 'pretty'. Girls always seemed to want things to be pretty.

It was halfway through the summer holidays and ten year old twins, Esme and Reuben Montana had run out of exciting things to do.

This was unusual.

The children's parents ran a smallholding where they grew things in pollytunnels. The summer was their very busiest time, which meant that the family never went away together on holiday during the summer. Apart from making sure they were well fed, had enough clean clothes and cleaned their teeth regularly, the twins' parents left them to amuse themselves most of the time.

And the twins were very good at keeping themselves happily occupied. They just loved living in the countryside and ... they had loads of imagination, so boredom was not something they experienced very often.

They were very happy spending time in each other's company – even though they did argue a lot. Reuben thought his sister was a bit of a sissy sometimes; and she though he could be a bit stupid sometimes. But of course, woe betides anybody else who tried to criticize one or the other!

But today ... they **were** - bored that is! So this had seemed like a good time to make the acquaintance of this new pony that had appeared a few days earlier in the field.

They were pony mad and had permission to ride several local ponies when the owners weren't needing them. But much to the twins' annoyance they didn't yet have a pony of their own. Their parents never seemed to get any further than 'seriously looking into the possibility' ... something to do with the twins showing they were responsible enough to take care of a pony of their own.

Esme swung her leg backwards and forwards, kicking her foot against the bottom crossbar of the gate. Then she sighed loudly, dropped off the gate onto the dried-out mud below and started to walk away down the lane towards their house.

"I'm going to ride him!" Reuben's voice stopped her in her tracks. Esme swivelled around to look back at her brother. "Don't be silly!"

"I am. I'm going to ride him." Reuben insisted stubbornly.

"Oh come on Reuben, you know we're not allowed!"

"I don't care. I'm going to ride him."

"Reuben!" Esme stamped her foot in annoyance. "You **know** we can't ride him. Mum said he's never been properly broken."

"She doesn't know that for sure; she's only guessing. You've just said he looks quite old. He must be broken. Why would Mr Grubble buy an unbroken pony?" Reuben frowned and then added quietly: "Anyway ... who wants to a pony that's 'broken'. I'm going to be a Horse Whisperer ... I won't need to 'break' ponies to train them!"

Esme shrugged. She too much preferred the idea of horse whispering than horse breaking! But that didn't mean she was convinced that riding Mr Nibbs right now was a good idea.

"You don't know where he's come from. That farmer buys all sorts of things and then sells them again. Like that old bicycle he sold Dad. That was pretty useless until Dad fixed it. Come on Reuben, let's go home. I'm getting hungry!"

"No!" Reuben stuck his chin out and shook his head stubbornly, "You go if you want ... scaredy cat!"

That hurt! Esme was furious. "I am not scared! You know I'm not. And anyway I ride better than you do! **You** are just being stupid!"

Reuben glowered at his sister, climbed over the gate and started walking towards the pony. She **was** a better rider than he was and he didn't like being reminded of it. But he was bored and fed up, and now he was angry with her as well ... he'd show her!

But he did feel his heart beginning to thump a bit. Ponies can be horribly unpredictable and there was no guarantee that this pony would want a small boy clambering onto his back.

Esme returned to the gate and climbed reluctantly over into the field as her brother approached the pony. She didn't like being called a scaredy-cat and wanted to leave him to get on with it. But ... sometimes her brother did the stupidest things just to prove how brave he was, and somehow she felt responsible for him even though he was fifteen minutes older than she was.

The stocky little pony had lifted its head as the boy walked purposefully towards it. Its dark brown coat was covered with a layer of dust. Burrs and grass seeds were attached to its tangled mane and tail, and long strands of summer grass dangled from its mouth. It looked quite comical – and perfectly harmless.

Or did it?

Esme suddenly realised that there was something slightly odd about Mr Nibbs!

'*Something is going to happen!*' The thought just popped into her head. She tried to run and call out a warning to Reuben. But she found she couldn't move. And her voice wouldn't work.

All she could do was watch.

Reuben was talking to Mr Nibbs, flattering him with silly remarks about how handsome he was. Mr Nibbs' lips and nose twitched and several grass stalks dropped to the ground.

"Good pony… look what I've got." Reuben soothed. He reached into his trouser pocket and pulled out a couple of grubby sugar lumps. He knew that sugar was as bad for ponies' teeth as it was for children's teeth. But he also knew that horses and ponies really like it, just like children do. So he always kept a few lumps handy in case they were needed for making friends with a new horse or pony.

The pony inspected the offering held out to him on the palm of Reuben's hand. He shuffled the sugar lumps around a bit with his lips – probably in an attempt to get rid of the fluff – then drew them into his mouth and crunched them up.

Having got the formalities over with, the boy and the pony looked each other straight in the eye as though saying: "OK … what next?"

"Right." muttered Reuben to himself. He patted the pony's neck, drew a deep breath grabbed a handful of mane and threw his right leg upwards. He just managed to propel himself onto the pony's back.
Mr Nibbs was only about twelve hands high, and Reuben who was skinny and agile, had managed quite a presentable vault first go.
The boy heaved a sigh of relief. The vault had been more difficult than he had thought it would be, and it would have been embarrassing to have failed in front of his sister.

"See!" he called out to Esme as he gently wriggled around on the warm broad back to find a comfortable position, "He's as quiet as … " The word 'anything' was shoved back down Reuben's throat as the pony exploded into an impressive display of bucking.

Reuben didn't stand a chance. He flew high, sailing up and out, way ahead of the pony's bucketing form.

Esme, still voiceless and rooted to the spot, watched her brother's body come rushing down towards the ground. She was both horrified and enthralled by what she was seeing. Because for the flash of a second it had looked just as though her brother and the pony were moving around inside a rainbow. And Mr Nibbs … **he** looked quite different – much bigger and sort of transparent.

Then, in the same moment Reuben hit the ground with a thump, the vision disappeared. Esme was able to move again, running immediately towards her brother. The pony was standing over Reuben, nostrils close to his face as though examining the boy. But as Esme reached them the pony snorted, gave a surprisingly agile jump sideways over the boy's still form and raced away towards the corner of the field where he disappeared into a small clump of trees.

Esme stood looking down at her brother. She didn't know what to do.
A part of her wanted to run home and get her mother. But another part of her was saying not to do that; to just stay with Reuben. It was as though a voice – her own voice – was talking to her from inside her head. The voice was saying to her over and over again, very loudly: "*It's all right. Reuben is not hurt. Stay with him. It's all right. Reuben is not hurt. Stay with him.*"

She could see that her brother was breathing normally. But he was so still. She stared at him, feeling rather dazed herself. Her eyes ran over the scruffy jeans and torn tee-shirt he refused to let their mother throw away. One of his ancient trainers, laces undone, had been dragged off his sockless foot by the force of his acrobatics. Filthy foot, she noted. Yuk!

Then her eyes moved to his face. Funny how he looked so different from her. Other twins she had seen looked really alike. She knelt down beside him and tugged at his mass of dark curly hair, hoping this might wake him up.

It did. His strange pale green-grey eyes stared up into the dark brown ones of his twin for several seconds.

The blankness of his gaze frightened Esme. It was as though he didn't see her.

"Reuben ... Reuben?" she queried hesitantly.

At that, Reuben jerked bolt upright and grabbed hold of his sister's shoulders, and his gaze switched from blankness to intensity as he peered into her eyes.

She was really startled now. Something **was** the matter with her brother!

He opened his mouth but no words came out. He shut it again and swallowed, all the time keeping a tight grip on Esme's shoulders. He closed his eyes and opened them again very wide. "Esme ..." he breathed.

"Yes Reuben, what **is** it?" Now that she could see that he wasn't hurt, Esme was beginning to get cross with her brother. His fingers were digging into her shoulders.

"Esme, I've got to tell you. I've got to tell you now. You've got to listen to me!" He took another swallow. "Do you understand … you've got to listen to me! They said I'd got to tell you right away, otherwise I'd forget."

"Reuben … are you all right?"

"Yeah … all right…?" Reuben looked puzzled. Then slowly he relaxed, removed his hands from Esme's shoulders and glanced around. He looked all around the field and then he looked down at himself, suddenly shoving his hands under the seat of his jeans, pulling them back again and peering at them intently for a moment. "Errr … hm, yes. Yes, I'm all right … I think. I mean, I'm not hurt." He knelt up and peered over his shoulder, trying to see the seat of his jeans at the same time as he asked Esme: "Where is he; Mr Nibbs? Where has he gone?"

"He's in the corner of the field. He galloped away after he bucked you off. But Reuben, what did you mean? What have you got to tell me? And what's the matter with your jeans?"

"Have I got glue on my jeans? … tell you…?" Reuben looked blank. "Oh heavens! I **am** forgetting. They said I would!"

"They? Who's 'they'?"

"Old Woman, and … and … and the um … the other Mr Nibbs. It's very important I tell you. They said if I told **you** it wouldn't matter if I forgot because **you** would remember for me. Will you Es?" Reuben grabbed one of his sister's hands.

"Yeh … I expect so; I usually remember things you tell me."

"Esme … I've been somewhere!" Reuben was almost whispering.

Esme looked at her brother intently. She knew that sometimes funny things happen to people when they get a bang on the head. But at the same time she was recalling the strange way her own voice had spoken to her - inside her head. And she was remembering the rainbow and the large transparent horse she thought she had seen. The 'other' Mr Nibbs, Reuben had just said.

"OK then. Go on, tell me. Where have you been?"

2 - Cloud Nine

Esme moved away from the prickly thistle she had been sitting on and settled herself more comfortably on the grass. She nodded encouragingly at her brother.

"Go on then, tell me where you've been."

"Promise you'll listen. Promise you won't interrupt?"

She promised.

Reuben grabbed at his hair with both hands, leant backwards, squinched his eyes tight shut and screwed up his nose. He took an enormous deep breath, blew it out noisily '*phwhooooh!*', leaned forward, opened his eyes and began his story.

"When I opened my eyes – not just now with you but 'before' – there was this enormous horse standing over me. It was his breath on my face that woke me up." Reuben paused before continuing and regarded Esme with such intensity that she shivered.

"This horse spoke to me!" He raised his hand at Esme as he saw her begin to open her mouth. "Honest Es, he did, he spoke to me ... I mean ... hmm ... you'll see what I mean." He hastened on to his next sentence, not giving Esme the slightest chance to prevent him from continuing his story.

"So anyway, this horse said: '*At last! Thought you were never going to wake up Boy. You're late you know. School started yesterday.*'"

And so Reuben told his sister about 'where he had been'.

School … yesterday! Reuben felt his mind beginning to race, confused. It was the middle of August and school wasn't due to start for weeks!

The horse spoke again: '*No, no, you silly boy, not **that** school. I'm referring to The School of How It Really Is.*'

Reuben was still lying on the ground. But he could tell that the horse was probably looking quite exasperated in that way horses can when their humans are being particularly stupid. It's the same way children can look at their parents when the adults can't understand something really obvious.

'Help, what's happening?' thought Reuben to himself. 'I must be dreaming.'

'*Not dreaming in the way you mean it. Come on now, we must be going. Stand up and get on my back and we'll be off.*' The horse's very large soft muzzle was so close that its long stiff whiskers were tickling Reuben's face.

Reuben's body obeyed the gruff voice and scrambled him to his feet as the horse lifted its head. But his mind was yelling at him: 'this horse knows what I'm thinking!'

'We'd be in a right mess now if I didn't wouldn't we? You don't speak Equus, and I don't speak Human.' The horse tossed his head powerfully and snorted loudly with what almost appeared to be laughter.

At this point Reuben had a chance to take a better look at the huge silvery grey animal that was like no other horse he'd ever seen.

It must have been twenty hands high or more, and it had a wonderfully arched neck like those famous 'dancing' Spanish horses he had seen on television. Its eyes were so bright that sparks seemed to be flashing from them, and every time it breathed out Reuben could see the breath all misty, like you can on cold mornings. And its body was just … spectacular! Not exactly transparent so you could see through it, but sort of … quivery all over … as though it wasn't really solid. 'Shimmery' was the word that popped into Reuben's head.

But the weirdest thing was that most of its shoulders and flanks seemed to be covered in feathers.

As she heard this part of the story, the boy's sister let out a little tiny gasp and shivered slightly. She crossed her arms and held them tight against her belly.

This incredible animal stamped a front leg impatiently. *'Stop gawping Boy!'* it snorted, huffing out a stream of smoky breath. *'And would you mind shutting your mouth. There are lots of insects around and getting caught inside your throat would be the death of most of them.'*

Reuben hadn't realised his mouth was hanging open in amazement. He shut it quickly, still gazing up at the huge silver-grey animal.

'Come on ... I've told you ... you're late! You've got an appointment with Old Woman, and she's really hot on time keeping. It's been arranged for you to meet her on Cloud Nine ... and you know what clouds are like.'

Before Reuben had a chance to say that 'no', he didn't really know what clouds are like, the horse continued: *'Can't trust them. They never stay in the same place for very long. I waste more time looking for clouds than almost anything else! If we don't get there soon, 'Nine' might have moved to somewhere else ... and then where would we be? I'll tell you, my boy. We'd be in the middle of no-where, that's where we'd be, the middle of no-where ... because no-where only become somewhere when there is some-thing there to make it a some-where. So will you please hurry and get onto my back.'*

"Get onto your ... "

'Ye-es ... that's right ... up ... on ... to ... my ... back.' said the horse with exaggerated patience. *'All you have to do is **thinkthink** yourself there. You can **think**, can't you? Most humans are so busy thinking they never have time to **feel** anything.'*

"Um ... er ... yes ... but ... "

*'Oh my goodness, you humans are so slow … because you spend so much time thinking **useless** thoughts. Ha ha ha!'* The horse snorted out laughter at its own joke. *'I can see I'll have to do it for you this time. But you'll have to learn you know, to think-think that is.'*

Reuben had just about time to prevent his mouth from falling open again when he found himself upon the animal's back. He was surprised – and pleased - to find it felt really solid.

'Make sure you're nice and secure. You might come unseated if we meet up with a fast corner – they often bounce up unexpectedly just to catch you off guard – nasty habit of theirs. And we'll be travelling fast too. Not breaking any speed limits of course, just fast enough to catch up with the time we're losing.'

A quick thought flitted into Reuben's mind that this really was a 'jaw-dropping' experience! A small giggle began to arise in his throat as his boggled mind saw the funny side of things.

But before that thought could develop, Reuben was taken aback yet again when he looked down at his legs and saw them resting on a mass of … feathers! How on earth was he supposed to make himself secure? Perhaps this strange animal had a safety harness attached to it.

'No need to worry Boy, you'll soon get the hang of things,' huffed the horse in gentler tones as he realised Reuben was frightened. *'Humans are always frightened the first time, but you'll eventually find the most comfortable position and develop perfect balance. For now*

though … just think-think what you need to feel safe. Er, let me see … I know. Think-think glue onto the seat of your pants. That should fix you!' He gave a horsey chuckle.

*'Oh wow. **Glue** on my jeans … what will Mum say!'* The deep horsey 'voice' cut through Reuben's image of his Mother's look of disbelief as he tried to explain why there was a gluey patch on the seat of his jeans.

'Use think-think - that's the magic form of think - for when you want things to happen instantly. Think-think it on … think-think it off … easy as pie … or cake if you prefer. Now come on, make it snappy otherwise we'll never catch that lost time.'

Reuben, whose mind was now so boggled he couldn't think straight anyway, wondered how on earth he was supposed to think-think. Nonetheless, he crouched forward a bit and tentatively imagined smearing the contents of a tube of glue over the seat of his trousers … and then he wriggled around on the horse's back. At least, he did a couple of wriggles and then found he couldn't move his bottom at all. He was stuck fast to the horse's back!

He gulped.

'Ouch, that hurts! No need to test quite so vigorously!' The horse twitched its shoulder muscles in protest. *'Right then, we're off.*

The feathers beneath Reuben's legs began to ruffle up and the boy felt his legs being pushed upwards as the giant wings (for that is what they were) began to unfurl. Having his backside immobilised by the glue prevented him from shuffling around and dropping his legs down the animal's sides behind the wings as these expanded to their full width. He felt a real idiot with his legs stuck out straight in front of him, and just for a moment he forgot to feel frightened.

The wings were ... absolutely HUGE. Reuben was mesmerised.

There was a noisy rush of air as these great wings began to beat slowly and strongly, lifting the horse and its young rider straight upwards ... just like a helicopter.

Fear returned! Reuben was terrified now! But there he was, stuck on this creature's back as it moved higher and higher, up into the sky.

Slowly, as he managed to overcome his fear, he found he was able to wiggle his legs around just enough for them to drop down behind the place where the horse's wings joined its shoulders. He thought he heard another muttered protest of pain.

This was a better position though, it felt more balanced. He was able to lean forward, almost lying down, and reach out to grab a fistful of the horse's long wavy mane in each hand. He buried his head into its hairy warmth and found himself noting that it was a bit odd that this 'shimmery' creature felt ... and smelled ... like a real horse!

His mind was working overtime, trying to sort out what was happening to him. The only horse he had ever heard about that had wings was the one he had been told about in school … was it a history lesson? Some of the children had done a project on those weird old stories from Greece: Greek Myths, the teacher had called them … or maybe it was an English lesson? Anyway … they had been told that myths were stories that people had invented about things that weren't really true: stories about Gods and Goddesses, and strange animals and monsters. Dragons even! And in one of them there had been a winged horse that had acted as a messenger for all those Gods and Goddesses. What was its name … Peg … Peg something.

'Pegasus!' the creature's voice interrupted the boy's thoughts. *'That's me! Still running errands and ferrying folk around. Taxi service is what I feel like these days with more and more humans starting their Cosmic education.'*

The horse's 'words' came swirling faintly back to Reuben on the rushing wind and at that point he began to relax a little as he decided this was all a dream after all. Myths weren't real and Pegasus was a character from a myth, so this horse with wings wasn't real either … therefore it **was** a dream! He and his sister were good at dreaming. They remembered lots of their dreams and often spent breakfast telling each other about them. And best of all they were able to wake up if a dream got too scary.

'Not from this one, you won't!' The words drifted back to Reuben. 'No waking up from this dream until you've done the 'dreamwork' Old Woman gives you.'

Reuben hadn't managed to catch all that Pegasus had 'said' because the wind kept snatching the words away. But, no ... hang on a minute, thought Reuben, the 'words' weren't 'spoken-out-loud' words ... just thoughts that popped into his head ... so the wind couldn't snatch them away!

But even though he sort-of-understood that ... he still yelled loudly, wondering if the horse could **hear** him: "What did you say?"

'No need to shout. I know what you're thinking. That's one of the things **you'll** have to learn – to know what others are thinking. Not yet though. **So**, for the time being if it's easier for you, just act **as if** I am actually speaking to you and you are actually listening to my words. If you **want** to listen, that is. Many humans don't want to listen to anything I have to say.'

"Yes, I ..." Reuben immediately began to yell out loud again before he recalled that Pegasus knew what he was thinking. Wow... this was confusing! Aaagh ... oh help, he'd better be careful he didn't think anything that would offend the horse.

For a moment he tried to stop thinking altogether to be on the safe side. But he soon found this was impossible. Thoughts kept rushing into his mind one after the other ... he just could not stop them!

'Don't worry; none of your thoughts will offend me whilst you're still learning how to control them. You will, you know ... eventually ... be able to control your thoughts. It's 'Uncontrolled Human Thoughts' (UHTs we call them) that have got humans into such a mess you know. Pesky things they are, amazingly troublesome once they've been let loose... especially considering they don't **really** exist; if you know what I mean.'

Reuben didn't. But he didn't bother saying so because he didn't understand **anything** of what was happening to him.

'Beautiful, this planet,' continued the horse. 'Very special actually... used to be favourite holiday spot for all sorts of Cosmic Beings ... that was before Humans forgot why they'd come here in the first place and messed it all up with wars and pollution. It's a good thing Earth, as you humans call her, is a patient planet. Imagine a planet like Mars putting up with humanity's tricks and abusive behaviour. You've really gone too far you know! Not **you** personally Boy!' The horse hastened to add. 'Though of course that could change, depending upon the choices you make as you grow up!'

Pegasus paused, as though he was expecting Reuben to say something.
But Reuben's mind was too stuffed full of questions that kept demanding answers. One of these was: 'what does he mean by 'cosmic beings'? And the answer that had crept into his mind and snuggled up to this question had frightened Reuben. It was 'aliens'.

When he didn't receive a response from Reuben, Pegasus continued talking: *'This latest thing 'climate change'… and all the unnecessary killing that some of you are involved in. It really is the last straw! Earth has finally had enough and called for help. That's why* **you** *are being taken to see Old Woman now'.*

Reuben's attention came back from scary 'aliens' to what Pegasus was saying. "Ooh," he whispered to himself, suddenly remembering all the times recently when he had ignored the Earth, taking for granted all the wonderful gifts she offered him every day.

He knew in his heart that this was wrong. He had heard his parents talking about the harmful way many people behaved towards the planet, causing dangerous things to happen … like climate change. He also remembered that they used a strange name for Earth – Gaia - and that like Pegasus, they always referred to 'her' and 'she'.

He was brought back from his remembering with a start by a sudden jerk that would surely have unseated him had he not been glued to the horse's back. Pegasus had veered sharply to the right.

'Got your attention now have I! You young ones are all the same. Can't be bothered to listen when your elders speak.'

"I'm sorry." said Reuben. "I was thinking about something my Dad said about Earth. What were you saying?"

'Ha! I What I was saying is … that it is exactly because of the condition of your world right now that I've been called out of retirement to do these 'nursery runs' with children like you!'

"Oh," was all Reuben could think of to say.

Pegasus continued anyway: 'Most of our family aren't too keen to work with humans these days. It's very frustrating trying to give messages to Beings who don't believe in your existence… or worse, have never even heard of you!'

He paused, ears flicking backwards and forwards … clearly waiting for a response from Reuben. Reuben, who had never had any reason to consider such things, was at a loss as to what to say but managed to squeak out: "Hmmm … horrid!"

'The younger generation of my family are not very patient. If they try to make contact with a human a couple of times without any luck, they just give up. Say they've got better things to do with their time.'

Another short pause before Pegasus continued: 'You know … none of us are **obliged** to do any of this sort of human contact work - planetary service – it's called. The youngsters don't have much of a sense of duty these days. Why should they when humans are so unappreciative … and behave in such a horrible way to each other … and to the planet herself!'

A strange sadness was threatening to overwhelm Reuben as Pegasus spoke. He felt his heart squeeze tight and tears welled up in his eyes.

'But I remember 'the good old days' as you humans would call them. In those times humans waited impatiently for my appearance in the sky ... and welcomed me like royalty when I arrived. They thought the messages I brought them were important. And they always had plenty of messages - prayers, petitions, thanks - for me to take back to the Gods and Goddesses of those times ...'

Pegasus's voice trailed off at this point and Reuben felt the horse's ribs expand and thought he heard a great long sigh. The sadness the boy was feeling was very powerful. He asked in a choked voice: "How long have you been doing this then?"

'Had my three thousand and seventy-sixth anniversary just last week.'

"Wow ... you serious?" Reuben just couldn't imagine anything being as old as that!

The horse responded with a few quiet words that Reuben couldn't catch. He immediately worried that Pegasus would think he wasn't paying attention again.

But he need not have worried. Pegasus had read his thoughts again and said loudly: *'I said I am grateful for the sadness you are feeling. It shows me that you are a sensitive and caring human.'*

At that Reuben's emotions turned from sadness to embarrassment. He was not sure he wanted to be known as 'sensitive and caring'. 'Brave and strong' would be good.

A horsey chuckle: *'And that too. Do you think you would be with me right now if you were not considered to be strong and brave?'*

Silence from Reuben. Caught out in his thoughts again.

*'And about us communicating with each other. All you have to do is **imagine** catching my words as they reach you. Imagining is another kind of thinkthink. If you imagine often enough it will eventually really happen.'*

"Right!" yelled Reuben to show that he had heard. He then immediately felt silly because he'd forgotten again that he didn't need to speak out loud for Pegasus to understand him. Oh Boy, this was all so confusing!

Pegasus continued 'talking' to Reuben about this and that; and Reuben managed to 'hear' nearly all of it. Without consciously trying he had been doing what he had been told to do. At first he'd actually reached a hand out to grab the words as if they were flying past him in the wind. But of course this physical action hadn't been necessary. All he needed to do was imagine he was catching the words … with his mind!

Reuben's thoughts drifted off to the 'as if' games he sometimes played with his sister. They pretended to do things as if they had special powers. That was a sort of imagining wasn't it? He remembered pretending to be a great singer, standing in the middle of the field, one arm flung wide, the other held over his heart like the hero in a musical he had seen on TV. He opened his mouth wide so that the imaginary voice could pour forth … The budding star was quickly brought right back to the 'here and now'. A great rush of cold air forced its way threateningly into the mouth he hadn't realised he had opened wide, and right down into his throat. He nearly choked before he managed to close his mouth.

'*Concentrate on what you're doing right now.*' Pegasus immediately instructed the startled boy. '*If you think too much about other people and other places, you'll find yourself there instead of here. And you need to be **here** right now!*'

Whoops … In fact that is exactly what happened. Thinking about Esme and their games had taken him right back to awareness of himself – but not the Self he had been so engrossed with seconds before … not the one flying with Pegasus!
He was now back in the Self that was in the field where Mr Nibbs had dumped him. The Self that was sitting next to his sister, half way through telling her where he had been. The Self that was rapidly becoming aware of a physical pain in his body.

His sister looked at him questioningly as he stopped talking and reached to rub his left shoulder.

Suddenly he started laughing out loud. It was so amazingly crazy. Even crazier than the weirdest dreams! What would his sister think about it all?

He fell quiet again and sighed deeply, watching Esme intently, trying to work out what she was thinking.

And ... there was still a lot more to tell and Reuben was scared he would forget it.

Esme said nothing, but her heart was thumping hard.

Finally Reuben said: "So you see, Es, there's an awful lot to remember." He took his gaze away from Esme's dark brown eyes and looked down at the grass, waiting for her to reply.

Esme took a deep breath and chewed on a grass stem she had plucked absentmindedly. But she still didn't say anything.

Neither did Reuben. But he felt somehow relieved that he had told her, even if it did sound crazy. And it did. As each moment passed, the crazier it all sounded.

His shoulder hurt and he realised he felt extraordinarily tired; and a bit silly. Supposing his sister thought he was making it all up. Was he? Perhaps all that had happened was that he had just been bucked off by the horrible little pony. Suddenly he didn't know himself.

His sister was sitting quietly enough. But inside her head all sorts of thoughts were chasing each other, running round and round in circles, tripping each other up and pushing each other over.

These thoughts went something like this: *'He's got con ... concush ... whatever that word is ... a bang on the head ... he looks all right though ... where's he been ... said he'd been somewhere ... he went without me ... what am I thinking ... he hasn't been anywhere ... he'd kidding me ... winding me up ... Old Woman and Pegasus ... don't believe any of it ... that sparkly horse shape ... my dream ... I don't ... I don't know ... I DON'T KNOW!'*

"Reuben if you're kidding me I'll never ever forgive you!" She burst out suddenly, startling her brother.

"Oh, Esme, I promise ... I know it all sounds just crazy ... but I promise I'm not kidding you. I remember it so clearly ... I think! But I do know that it's really important that you believe me. Do you?" His eyes implored her to believe him.

Esme heaved a sigh. "Yes," she muttered. "At least it **feels** like I believe you." another big sigh. "But it just sounds so ... so ... well, you know, like some fairy story. And ... ?" a strange question jumped into her mind.

"And what?" Reuben looked at her quizzically.

"Well ... um ... did you ask Pegasus what we need to do to help?"

'We?' Immediately the sense of rivalry Reuben sometimes felt towards his sister popped up! She had said '**we**'. But it wasn't 'we'. **She** hadn't been there. It was **his** adventure!

As soon as he had the thought, it was as though the voice of Pegasus himself came rushing to him on the wind – even though there wasn't even the gentlest of breezes playing in the field:

'Well young Reuben, there you have it, a perfect example of a human 'out-of-control-angry' thought!' A great neigh of laughter close to his head caused Reuben to jerk his head and blink rapidly several times. He was astounded ... well at least he knew now that it ... whatever 'it' was ... had happened! He looked at Esme cautiously. Had **she** heard?

Apparently not.

But she really startled him by saying: "Look, don't worry Reubs, I know you're feeling really tired and haven't got the energy to tell me any more now ... and aren't even sure it actually happened.
But **I** know it did, and I **know** you won't forget it – any of it; not now you've started to tell it."

"That's what I feel too." Relief that his sister believed him was mingled with a bit of exasperation. How come she could **know** ... anything? "Prruuph." He exhaled noisily, sounding for all the world like a snorting pony. He reached over to pick up the trainer that had been dragged off his foot.

"Ow! my shoulder hurts!" He pulled the shoe on slowly. "I just don't know what to **think**! Only that I **feel** like it really happened." He glanced sideways at his sister questioningly, raising his eyebrows and giving a shrug of his shoulders that caused him to wince and yelp.

"Shoulder will be fine!" She jumped up, brushed off her jeans, smiled down at her befuddled brother and held out her hand. "Come up, let's go home and get some tea, I'm famished!"

He was so surprised, and so so tired, that he could do nothing to protest, even accepting the offer of her outstretched hand to haul himself to his feet.

They started to walk slowly towards the gate and the same thought must have occurred to both of them. They turned around and looked for Mr Nibbs.

And there he was, over in a shady corner of the field, grazing calmly, just an occasional swish from his tail discouraging the late afternoon flies. As though he felt their gaze upon him, he lifted his head and glanced in their direction. But he didn't stop chewing.

The twins climbed over the gate into the lane and set off in the direction of home and tea.

3 - A Good Sister

It was only a few moments' walk between the gate leading into the field and the gate leading into the twins' front garden. Slowly and silently, occasionally scuffing at loose stones in the road, they made their way from field to home.

Such a lot to talk about! But somehow, each time one of them began to say something, the words wouldn't come out. The fact was they just did not know what **to** say. Each child needed time to think about their own experience of 'what had happened'.

Esme pushed open their garden gate. As usual it creaked and as usual three dogs came flying down the path at the side of the house to greet the children. Anyone would think that the twins had been away for days! Frantically wagging tails and barks of pleasure whilst jumping up in delight and trying to sneak in the odd 'in your face' kiss, told the children how much their dogs loved them.
Solo, Mowgli, and Luca were three chocolate Labradors, collectively and affectionately known by the twins and all their friends as The Choccies.

The children responded to the boisterous show of affection from their four-legged friends with less than their usual enthusiasm. Esme was very firm with them: "Down!"
The dogs knew she meant it. They stopped their bouncing and got serious instead, checking out the children's clothing with inquisitive noses. Solo,

getting on in years, suddenly sat down and pawed at Esme's leg, looking up at her with an 'I've got a question for you' expression on his face.

Esme bent down and ruffled behind his ears, mis-understanding what he wanted. "Can you smell that new pony?" she asked.
She could have sworn that the old dog sighed as he got up and set off determinedly down the path towards the back garden. The two younger dogs followed.

She had to giggle as she watched them walk away from her, all in line, doing that Labrador 'wag-gle-bottom' walk all in time with each other. Grand-father Solo in the lead followed by his son Mowgli, and finally Mowgli's son Luca bringing up the rear. But the twins were too tired – and hungry – to pay further attention to The Choccies. Had they done so, they would have noticed that even Luca the ir-repressible youngster was following sedately after his elders as Solo lead the three of them to the far end of the garden and a favourite 'hang-out' spot where they held all their serious dog-discussions.

Esme and Reuben entered the side door of the house quietly, into the little corridor with stairs at its end, and then right into large kitchen. So unusu-ally quiet were they that their mother didn't even notice them come in. She was standing by the sink, putting some flowers into a vase.

Brother and sister automatically headed for two an-cient armchairs placed in a cosy corner of the large kitchen next to an equally ancient Aga cooker. Reuben was so preoccupied with his thoughts, that he didn't even notice Kimber curled up snoozing in the chair. He would have sat on him had not the old cat been just awake enough – or perhaps it was his sixth sense – to become aware of the boy's presence and jump up rapidly with a squawky meow of indignation.

"Sorry Kimber!" muttered Reuben as he flopped down into the depths of the comfy old chair. Kimber gave the boy just enough time to settle before moving onto his lap and making himself comfortable again. Reuben stroked him absently.

The twin's mother jumped, startled by the sound of Kimber's protest, and turned around to see her children.

"You two sneaked in quietly! Tea's ready; there's some salad with goat's cheese, and I've made you some scones. Just need the table laying."

Esme pushed herself up from the depths of her chair and looked pointedly at her brother. He looked back: "What?"

"You can help too!"

Reuben sighed but slid a disgruntled Kimber off his lap and went to help Esme laid plates, cutlery, and kitchen paper napkins on the table. Their mother remarked once more on how unusually silent they were. "You two **are** very quiet."

There was no response. "Is something up?" she asked as she placed a plate full of still warm scones on the table to join a large bowl heaped with salad.

Reuben started to reply but Esme butted in quickly. "Oooh, thanks Mum. These looks yummy. We're starving, aren't we Reuben!" She shoved her brother none too gently towards his seat.

As she sat down she explained to her mother: "We've been to see that new pony Mr Grubble's got. You know, you said his name was Mr Nibbs?"

"I remember. Any good?"

"Don't know Mum. Not very friendly! And he looks a bit old," said Esme vaguely as she put butter onto a scone.

The answer satisfied Eve Montana. She went towards the door that led out into the back garden. "I'll be in the tunnels if you want me," she called over her shoulder as she went out.
The 'tunnels' were where the salady things were grown.

"You weren't going to tell Mum, were you?" Esme spoke through a mouthful of half-chewed leaves and cheese and frowned at her brother.

"Course not, silly! She wouldn't have believed it anyway … she'd just have thought I was joking!" He too began to fork mouthfuls of salad and cheese into his mouth, quickly followed by a huge bite of scone. He concentrated on chewing and said nothing. Several mouthfuls later he stopped eating and looked at his sister. She too stopped chewing immediately and looked straight back at him.

"You do believe me Es? Really, I mean. Not like part of an 'As If' game or anything like that?" Reuben hesitated for a moment as he groped for a memory to do with 'As If' games, then shrugged as nothing came.

"Uhuh, I do." Esme nodded her head in a matter-of-fact sort of way before helping herself to another scone.

"Good!" Reuben was silent again. Then he asked: "Why?"

"Why what?"

"Why do you believe me?"

This time Esme hesitated before saying very quietly: "I believe you because I saw Pegasus … in the field … when you were being bucked off. And anyway …" she felt silent again.

"You **saw** him? You can't have done! What did he look like?"

Esme's description of the great, shimmering, winged horse caused Reuben to put down his fork and stare intently at his sister without saying anything for several moments.

Then he accused: "You're saying that because **I told you** what he looked like."

"No!" Esme shook her head indignantly. "I've ... no I'm not. I really did see him."

Reuben was silent again.

Then he let out a noisy sigh. "Fffff! Well, if you saw him too then it must really have happened mustn't it?"

"Yes." Esme whispered, locking eyes with her brother.

They started eating again, silently, each caught up once more in their own thoughts.

They were still chewing away in silence when their mother returned. She gave them a curious glance. They normally chatted or argued their way through mealtimes. But she didn't say anything this time.

"That was scrummy, Mum, thanks." Esme suddenly jumped up. "I'm going to watch that animal programme on TV."

Reuben didn't follow her, but stayed put at the table. He was still feeling a little sore at his sister and the way she had included herself in his adventure.

His mother, rather unsettled by her children's strange silence, put down the knife she had been using to chop some vegetables, wiped her hands and took the opportunity to go and sit at the table with her son. She put a hand on his shoulder and noticed that he winced slightly.

"Reuben, have you done something to your shoulder? Why do I feel something is up! You both look absolutely exhausted … and it's not like the pair of you to be so quiet. Have you quarrelled?"

Esme, who had come back into the kitchen to get a glass of water, went to stand by her brother. Both children shook their heads.

"We're just really tired, we were playing in the Corner Coppice – you know where the badgers live?" Reuben glanced quickly at his sister. She immediately nodded her head to show agreement.

"I see … and …?" His mother knew all their favourite haunts.

"I was going to climb that old tree but I grabbed a dead branch and it broke. I fell and hurt my shoulder."

His mother looked startled.

Esme admired her brother's quick thinking. She added "But he didn't fall far, Mum."

"And I'm fine really. Honest Mum … look!" Reuben got up from his chair, jumped up and down and twirled around with his arms in the air to show his mother he was not properly 'hurt'.

She laughed at his antics, but the expression on her face remained slightly quizzical. She wasn't sure he'd told her the whole story.

"I'm going upstairs!" Reuben declared.

"Hmmm … me too … that programme's not on after all." Esme yawned. "Night".

"See you in the morning. Sleep well." Eve Montana's gaze followed her children as they left the kitchen and headed upstairs.

Not another word was spoken between the twins. Neither of them felt able to say anything more about what had happened.

Next morning was Sunday, but Esme was up really early. The summer sun was already warming everything when she stepped outside into their back garden. She went through the gate at the left side of the garden into the small field beside their house.
This was where the tomatoes, peppers, chillies and green leafy plants were grown inside a couple of pollytunnels. Her parents sold them to the shop in the village.
She could see her father moving around inside one of the tunnels and went in to say good morning. She loved spending time with her father.

He was half Spanish. His name was Alfonso – Fonso to most of his friends, but Alf to the locals he worked with and occasionally met up with for a beer or two in the village pub.

He was a strong but gentle man who walked with a limp caused by a fall from a horse when he was a boy. He could be very funny, and often made up lovely stories for his children at bedtime. Their favourites were about five monkey friends who had all escaped into southern Spain from The Rock in Gibraltar. They were called Sammy, Sandy, Saucy, Soso and Sausage and were always having adventures.

"Morning Daddy." Esme gave a huge yawn.

"Morning Sleepy Head." Her father stopped tying the tall tomato plants onto their supports, and gave her a big hug before pushing her gently away from him and looking her up and down. "How are you feeling this morning? Mum was worried about the pair of you last night; she said you both looked absolutely exhausted."

Esme grinned at her father, wishing she could tell him all about what had happened. "I'm fine. We just had one of those 'Reuben adventures'."

"Oh?" Her father understood what she meant. Reuben wanted to be an explorer when he grew up, and the children's games often involved one or both of them ending up in 'sticky situations'. "What was it this time?"

Esme decided she would risk telling her father part of the story – even if Reuben was cross when he found out … after all … he really shouldn't have done what he did, even though it had led to 'what had happened'. And probably what had happened to **her** in her dream last night too!

"You know that new pony in Farmer Grubble's field. Well, Reuben decided he was going to ride him, and the pony bucked him off!" She saw the expression on her father's face and added hurriedly "But he wasn't hurt Dad, apart from bruising his shoulder!"

"Oh dear, that boy will get himself into some real trouble one day," sighed her father. "But you know what Esme, sometimes the only way to learn what might hurt you or be dangerous … is to try things out. But always use that common sense of yours!" He tapped his daughter gently on the temple with a grubby finger and then bent down to hug her tight.

Esme stayed helping her father until he stopped suddenly, stretched his arms high above his head and said: "Breakfast! I'm hungry. Let's go."

She followed him back towards the kitchen, a bit anxious about what sort of a mood Reuben would be in, but also excited because this morning she really had a dream worth telling!

"Daddy, don't tell Reuben, or Mummy, that I told you about him being bucked off … please … I promised I wouldn't say anything … and I shouldn't have done …"

Her father stopped and gently took hold of his daughter's arm. He squatted down in front of her.

"All right," he said gently, "I won't say anything ... yet. You will need to let him know you've told me and broken your promise at some point. But I do understand why you told me. Sometimes you know it's better not to make promises you think you'll find difficult to keep!"

Esme smiled her relief "Thanks Daddy; I will tell him, promise ... but later." She reached for his hand and they walked back to the house in companionable silence.

Reuben was already at the table when Esme and her father walked into the kitchen. He was writing or drawing something in a notebook whilst Esme's Mother was busy preparing the big sit-down breakfast they always tried to have together on a Sunday morning no matter how busy they were.

Esme squeezed into a chair beside her brother. He shut his notebook, pushed it aside and asked: "Dreams?" The twins usually remembered their dreams and shared them over breakfast.

Esme gave several tight-mouthed little nods as though desperately wanting to say something but waiting for Reuben to give her the go ahead to do so. She wasn't sure what he would think about the possibility of their parents overhearing, and glanced pointedly towards the sink where their father was washing his hands at the sink and chatting with their mother.

"Go on." He spoke very quietly and indicated she should do the same.

Esme kept her voice very low and started to tell Reuben her dream.

"Well … I dreamed I met this strange person called Old Woman … well … I think she was an 'old' woman … but … sometimes she looked … sort of much younger. She was sitting on the other side of a hearth with a fire in it – sort of like a campfire but not - and I could only see her through the flames and she kept flickering in a strange way … "

Reuben interrupted. His voice was tense and a bit squeaky: "You met an old woman … ?"

"Sort of … but I think 'Old Woman' was, like … her name. And …"

Now he exclaimed – loudly: "What! You met Old Woman?"

"Shhh!" hissed Esme, sneaking a look at their parents. But they were now preoccupied with listening to something on the radio as they prepared fried eggs, mushrooms, tomatoes, toast, coffee and juice for the family. They were used to the twins discussing their dreams during breakfast, and didn't seem to be paying any attention to their children's conversation.

"Well …" Esme continued in a quiet but determined voice, "like I just said … she looked sort of like an 'old' woman … some of the time … really really old, a bit sort of 'witchy'… like from a fairy tale. She wasn't wearing a pointy hat though, and …"

Reuben couldn't contain himself. Even his rivalry with his sister was almost forgotten in his excitement. He cut in ... "That is where Pegasus took me! ... to see Old Woman! ... at the camp fire!"

"Wow!" Esme's eyes widened. Before continuing, she glanced at her brother questioningly. She knew he had been peeved when she had talked about **our** adventure the day before. "Look, I can't help it ... it's just what I dreamed."

"Yeah ... okay! Go on, go on." Reuben realised that as usual his sister had an uncanny ability to know what he was feeling. It had been like that ever since he could remember ... even though they weren't **identical** twins.

"What did she say ... this Old Woman?"

Esme scratched her head and thought for a moment, trying to recall exactly what had happened. And like so often with dreams, as soon as she **tried** to remember, the less she **was able** to remember. All the details seemed to dissolve.

"Wait ... let me catch it." She gently banged her forehead with the heel of her hand and screwed her eyes shut. "Mmmmm ... It wasn't a **camp** fire; It was ... somewhere inside. No ... all I can really remember is that she said it is important to know that all the stuff that they'll tell us doesn't belong to any one person ..."

Reuben interrupted her again, grinning as he suddenly began to feel really happy to have a sister he could share things like this with.

"Yep – I got that too … in fact the more people we tell the better … but only if they **want** to listen … 'cos if they don't want to know they kind of won't hear anyway … something like that."

Esme felt relieved. He wasn't cross with her.

"Hang on Reubs. If you finish telling me what happened to you and where you went, then I might remember more of my dream … and … you can tell me what **your** dreams were last night". But let's wait until we've had breakfast, and go down to safeplace.

"OK." Reuben agreed. He hadn't actually had any dreams – well nothing he could remember anyway. In fact he had fallen asleep almost as soon as he got into bed and didn't recall a thing until he woke up much later than his usual time. He didn't want to admit this to his sister though.

And for a while hunger got the better of both of them as they demolished the Sunday treat with astonishing speed.

"For goodness sake, slow down," exclaimed their father, casting a quick glance towards his wife. "You'll get indigestion! And yes, you can get down," he added as they simultaneously popped last mouthfuls of toast and honey into their mouths, pushed their chairs back and rose from the table.

The pair didn't even appear to have noticed their father's sarcastic comment as they rushed for the back door.

The Choccies all got up to follow them, Solo just managing to get his grey-haired muzzle in the doorway before the door banged shut.

Children and dogs sped down the garden.

"You're right, those two **are** behaving strangely," Alfonso remarked to his wife. "I wonder what they're up to?"

Eve Montana shook her head. "I expect we'll find out eventually."

4 - Old Woman

The bolt hole the twins called safeplace was the twin's favourite spot in the large garden, a wild flower patch tucked away behind some bushes and shrubs. It couldn't be seen from the house. Their father had named it 'the bolt hole' because he thought they looked like little wild animals when they scuttled off down there to have private conversations.

Once the dogs realised this was not going to be a walk or playtime, they scattered, doing their usual patrolling, first around the edges of the garden, and then further afield into the coppice between the garden and the stream that marked the boundary between the Montana's land and more of farmer Grubble's fields.

The twins settled themselves down amongst the tall grasses and wild flowers, automatically plucking tall juicy grass stems to chew on.

Lying on their stomachs, Reuben's dark curly head close to Esme's lighter reddish gold one, they certainly didn't **look** like twins. They were wearing clothes typical of many children their age - jeans and tee-shirts. Their bare feet, now freed from the confines of scuffed trainers, wiggled in delight.
An ordinary girl and her brother - good friends - settling down to tell each other about their adventures.

Once they were comfortably settled Reuben continued telling Esme about 'where he had been'.

53

"Hang on ... let me just remember back to where I stopped telling you yesterday." Reuben pursed his lips and frowned. "Oh gosh, yes! Pegasus saying all that stuff about people knowing what other people are thinking. That's something really weird!" Reuben sighed. "Anyway ... I asked Pegasus where we were going. You'll never believe what he said ..." Reuben paused, waiting for his sister's response.

"Go on then, tell me!"

He said: *"We're going to Cloud Nine of course."*

"Er ... ?" Esme frowned.

"Well that's just what I thought!"

Reuben explained that Pegasus must have realised then that he, Reuben, knew nothing about Cloud Nine ... Ten or Eleven for that matter, and had said to him:

'Look it up on your Internet ... what is that phrase you humans use: 'Google it', that's it ... complicated human mind stuff. Briefly: 'Cloud Nine' is a phrase often used by humans to describe a place where everything is just wonderful. 'I'm on Cloud Nine', they say when something important works out well for them.'

The horse huffed out a little snort and muttered something about how it used to be 'Cloud Seven', and how humans are always changing their minds about things.

Then he fell silent and it was several moments before he continued.

'Hmm… yes … the internet, that's one good human invention anyway. I suppose I'd better tell you a little about The Clouds, hadn't I. The trouble with human schools is that they don't teach children about lots of really important things … like clouds in this case.'

Reuben certainly agreed with Pegasus about school, but couldn't see that knowing about clouds would be that helpful.

'Right then, listen well!' Pegasus assumed a rather teachery sort of voice:
'Those of us who have dealings with clouds often call them 'The Shifties'. This is because they keep shape-shifting. Really tricky characters, never still, always on the move, difficult to catch, changing shape all the time, pretending to be one thing and then another.'

Pegasus paused as though waiting the boy to agree. When there was no response from Reuben he went on:

'I'm sure you know what I mean! Lots of humans spend time watching the clouds changing shape as they move across the sky. First you see a teddy bear and then a battleship, or a castle … isn't that right?'

Reuben was nodding to himself, remembering many occasions lying on his back in their field on warm summer days, staring up at the clouds in a bright blue sky and watching as they changed their shapes.

Pegasus continued: '*Very unreliable they are ... rather like your public transport buses on Earth... none to be seen or masses of them all at once. Not easy for those who need to use them to move around when private transport is not available.*'

Reuben wondered what sort of 'private transport' Pegasus meant.

Of course the winged horse picked up the boy's thought.
'Well, there's my own service, The Pegasus Elite Courier Service. Then there's Dragon Emergency Rescue Services - strictly for emergencies only. Dragons are no longer willing to do much work for Earthlings. Can't say I blame them. Humans have given them such a bad name and persecuted them for so long now ... '

Another snort and pause from Pegasus before he continued:

'*Occasionally the larger birds like Eagles can be pressed into service if they're feeling in an adventurous mood. And then there are the geese. Some of them provide a wonderful long distance service at certain times of the year ... but they only carry messages or packages, not Beings of any sort. There are of course other types of transport systems used on this planet, on the land and in the rivers and seas, but I'm not familiar with them – only Air Services.*
Oh, and let's not forget the pigeons. They have given wonderful service to humans for hundreds of years! But they only carry messages between human beings.'

"Wow!" Reuben was truly impressed by this bit of information, and wondered if chickens could be trained to fly properly and do this sort of work.

The rushing sensation created by moving at high speed suddenly lessened and Reuben realised Pegasus was hardly moving; hovering almost. He wondered what was happening.

'Just stopped to get my breath back,' the horse answered the boy's thought query. *'Now... let me see, which way do we go here. It's always tricky at this spot. It's half way between where we came from and where we're going to. It's never signposted because nobody actually knows where they're going until they've actually got there ... if you see what I mean.'*

Reuben didn't.

'And ... the clouds that one has to catch to get where one is going never stay in one place long enough to be signposted. Never stay the same **shape** *for more than a few moments come to that! Catching a cloud is such an inefficient way to travel.'* Pegasus huffed in what appeared to be exasperation.
'It was much less complicated in the old days when the Pegasus Service was all that was needed to travel from one dimension to another. Today of course humans don't believe such a thing is possible... and when they don't believe ... well then ... it's NOT possible. That children's story of yours, Peter Pan, talks about this when the fairy... what's her name ... Tinker ... something ... speaks of this to the children ... if you don't believe in me I'll die ... something like that... '

The winged horse's voice trailed off. He was obviously concentrating very hard.

'Oh ... you'll learn all about it eventually!' His words brushed aside all the questions going on in Reuben's head. *'Personally ... '* he finished off rather ponderously, *'I think they just enjoy being disruptive! But I won't go into that just now. I have to concentrate or we'll never find Cloud Nine.'*

Back in the bolt hole Reuben paused in his story-telling. He explained to his sister, who was listening intently, that by that time on his journey with the winged horse, he had concluded he was having an extra special dream, so decided to just let it happen like he did with other dreams.

"Pegasus was going on and on about clouds! I can't remember half of what he said. Mostly about their 'shiftiness' and how that had always been part of their nature." Reuben suddenly giggled as he remembered the bit where Pegasus had said: *'Well, can you imagine a cloud just staying put in the sky? That would be like expecting a 10 year old boy to sit still at the dinner table after he's finished eating!'*

"Or girl!" Esme muttered as she pulled her finger from inside her nostril that had suddenly started to itch like crazy because of a grass seed that had crept up into it.

Reuben ignored his sister's comment and continued: "He said that one of the worst things these days was how many more 'bully clouds' around there were than usual. He said they did things like flinging lightening all over the place and setting fire to forests, or dumping buckets full of huge hail stones onto fairgrounds … or just scaring people with extra loud thunder!"

Reuben paused to find another succulent grass stem.

"Crikey!" his sister exclaimed. "I always thought … "

"Yeah, me too." Reuben butted in, knowing what his sister was about to say: "these things 'just happen'… like they're 'just weather'."

Esme was nodding her agreement. "Exactly!"

"Then he said something really weird! I don't quite know what he meant … something about the clouds participating in 'a game' that all humans play. The Blame Game, he called it. Said the idea was something about finding somebody else to blame when something bad happens … and that humans excel at it! I don't think we've got that game at home and I can't remember playing it … can you?" Reuben turned to his sister.

"Nope." She shrugged. "Anyway … go on … what happened next?"

Reuben continued with his story.

They had flown on for ages. Reuben was even almost enjoying all the scary flying sensations when Pegasus slowed right down and hovered again. It reminded Reuben of the hawks he had seen, hanging so still in the sky as they surveyed the landscape below them.

Pegasus' stillness had encouraged Reuben to look down. Not a wise thing to do! Way, way below he could just make out the shape of fields and roads and houses. Suddenly fearful again, he had shivered ... and immediately realised he was cold; very cold indeed.

'*Thinkthink WARM!*' Pegasus instructed a second before turning sharply to the right and shooting off, accelerating to a great speed very quickly. Reuben panicked as the rushing wind pushed him backwards and tore the horse's mane from his fingers.
He was very unsuccessfully trying to lean forward again to clutch another handful of mane when he remembered that he was 'stuck' to Pegasus's back and **couldn't** fall off even if he tried.
Very slowly he sat upright. Yes, he was still glued to the horse's back. He extended his arms out from his sides ... almost as if they were wings. And ... yes, he still felt perfectly safe. In fact it was an amazing feeling!

He let out a whoop of joy ... he was flying! He felt Pegasus chuckle.

And ... having got over his fright he started imagining he had a cosy duvet tucked around him. He **immediately** felt warm!

'*Good, you're getting the hang of it!*' The thought from Pegasus came straight into his mind as they continued at racing-car speed.

In fact the speed they were going at felt so fast to Reuben that he had a sudden thought: He wondered if they might break the sound barrier ... and if they did, would it hurt!

This fast flying went on for quite a while. The wind created was so strong that wind tears were being whipped off Rueben's cheeks as soon as they squeezed out of his tight shut eyes.

As long as he kept his eyes shut, Reuben began to feel 'suspended' – almost as though they weren't moving at all. It was a very strange feeling. Rather pleasant but kind of disorientating, almost as though time was standing still. He had no sense of where he was ... or even what he was!

Finally he had felt the horse slowing down yet again and had opened his eyes a crack. There wasn't much to see though ... just blue sky in every direction. Not a cloud in sight.

Pegasus started speaking again, but none of what he was saying made sense to Reuben.
'*I was called out in such a rush for this job with you that I forgot to borrow some Feminine Intuition from my niece. It helps a lot if you've got a particularly complicated journey to make.*' A horsey sigh. '*It's all right for the young members of my family. These days the boys have*

quite a bit of feminine intuition of their own; as well as the girls!'

Reuben's attention was caught. He realised that he had heard that phrase before. 'Feminine intuition'... when was it? Oh yes, not so long ago. His mother and father had been having quite a heated discussion about something called 'feminine intuition'. Reuben hadn't paid any attention at the time. He wondered what it meant. *'I'll ask Dad'*, he thought vaguely, still feeling 'not really himself'.

Then he heard Pegasus going on about needing to use the old fashioned method and 'tune in' to whatever lesson was waiting for him – Reuben - today before he, Pegasus, could 'set the right course'. Although Reuben heard the winged horse's words clearly, he didn't have a clue what he was talking about.

And with that the horse began to whirl around and around whilst he chanted to himself. Reuben began to feel dizzy. He leant right forward, clasped the horse around the neck and buried his face into the thick mane, as more strange words from Pegasus flowed into his mind.

'East into Fire and Spirit – too hot, too hot. North into Air and Mind – no, we've just come from there. South into Water and Emotions – no, you'd just cry and cry. West into Earth and Body ... maybe ... no ... hmmm ... camp fire? Yes! Camp fire is the place!'

No sooner had the horse made this decision than he shot off at high speed again, once more leaving Reuben gasping for breath.

Almost immediately the boy and the horse were engulfed by thick fog. One moment they were flying through bright blue summer sky; the next Pegasus was breaking rapidly as they entered the thick grey dampness. It became even colder.

'Caught them!' A satisfied thought from Pegasus drifted into Reuben's mind, followed a moment later by the indignant words: *'No warning at all. Should have been much further away. Typical Shifty behaviour!'*

Reuben guessed the winged horse was referring to the cloud – for that is what the 'fog' was. It was so thick that he could no longer see the tips of Pegasus's wings. He was really pleased that he could feel the warm horsy body beneath him, and **so** glad he had managed to create an imaginary duvet to wrap around him.

It was very, very quiet. Reuben felt as though he had ear plugs in. He wondered anxiously what was going to happen next.

As suddenly as they had entered it, they left the cloud, emerging into another patch of bright blue sky. And there, right in the middle of the bright blue, was the most perfect little cotton wool cloud you could imagine.

As Pegasus flew towards this little cloud Reuben could see a flickering light gleaming in its centre. A once-again amazed Reuben noticed that if you concentrated on this flickering light it looked very much like the number nine!

They entered Cloud Nine! It was just as misty as the previous cloud, but quickly the flickering light grew brighter and the mistiness cleared. Reuben blinked in astonishment. They had emerged from the mist to find themselves in what looked like small glade surrounded by large trees!

Back in the bolt hole Reuben stopped speaking, sat up, stretched and then flopped down on the grass again. The expression on his face was one of intense concentration. After a moment he continued speaking.

The clearing had appeared to be empty at first. Pegasus landed on the grassy central area and finally closed his wings with much feather ruffling to get them comfortable. He started walking slowly towards the far side of the clearing and Reuben's attention was attracted by the flickering of small flames in the dark shadow of one of the great trees.

'Ah ... the fire's already alight. That's good, means she's not cross because we're late... wants you to feel her warmth. You're lucky today, Boy.'

The winged horse had come to a halt several metres in front of what appeared to be a camp fire. He stood perfectly still.

But this camp fire was no ordinary camp fire.

Without warning the tiny flames shot upwards, leaping and dancing way above the horse's head.

Reuben cringed away from the fiery light, and his startled expression was lit up by the radiance of the flames. They seemed to move towards him, flickering fingers reaching out to 'feel' him. He felt a strange tingling sensation, but not burning.

'You are late my Equine friend.' The clearly spoken words came from the direction of the flames, which had died back down.

Reuben strained his eyes, peering through the flames as he tried to see who had spoken. He imagined he saw a face … and then a slender hand with a bright ruby red ring on one finger. The face reminded him of his mother's face when she was excited about something. But as soon as he had seen it the face disappeared.

He drew in a sharp breath, puzzled and anxious.

'The harder you look, the less you see.' The voice came from the flames once more.

Pegasus murmured an agreement, and then spoke more loudly to Reuben. *'You'd better get down now Boy. I've got to be going. More messages to deliver before you'll be ready to go home.'*

Reuben was startled. He hadn't known the great horse for more than … well, not long anyway – but at least he knew him a bit. He didn't like the idea of being left in this strange place at all … especially right in the middle of a shifty cloud!

'Off you get.'

Reuben didn't move.

'Remember … thinkthink … glue … unglue!'

Reuben still didn't move. He was scared stiff now. This … horse … this … creature was going to abandon him … on a cloud!

A voice from the other side of the fire said in a calm and gentle tone: *'Welcome boy. I've been looking forward to meeting you. You will be quite safe here, and Pegasus will come back to take you home when we've finished the lesson. He's got lots of other errands to do today, otherwise I expect he'd stay … he says the grass in this meadow is some of the best there is.'*

Despite not wanting to dismount, Reuben found himself standing on the ground between the horse and the fire. Pegasus had done the 'thinkthink' for him.

'You'll be alright. Do as you're told and I'll be back for you when it's time to take you home!' He felt the horse's muzzle in the small of his back, gently nudging him forward. *'Right, I'll be off then.'*
Pegasus snorted, took a few steps backwards and unfurled his great wings. His misty breath enveloped the boy's head as he lifted upwards, his silvery form rapidly melting from sight.

Reuben turned his head to follow the winged horse's departure until he could see him no longer. Then he turned back to face the fire, once again peering through the flames.

He felt his knees begin to tremble and tears begin to prick his eyes. He swallowed hard, desperately wishing he could 'wake-up'... although pride prevented him from letting the tears flow.

The voice soothed. *'See me as your mother if you wish. You can see me as anybody you like if this comforts you.'*

Reuben's eyes widened as the flickering image became more like his sister than his mother ... then quite suddenly it reminded him even more of Rose, a rather strange friend of his sister's that Reuben didn't much like.

He screwed his eyes tight shut for several seconds before looking into the flames again. The face – who's ever it was – had disappeared.

He began to feel very alone ... and no less scared. "He ... hello?" he questioned softly.

'I'm still here.' The voice was gentle and reassuring. *'I don't go away. But when you stop imagining me as another, you don't see me for a while, until it feels safe enough to see me as a truly am. Why don't you sit down? You must be tired after your journey. If you turn around you'll see cushions behind you.'*

The boy turned around quickly, almost tripping over a pile of green and orange cushions. He bent down and touched them, making sure they were real before he gingerly sat down in their midst.

He realised the 'camp' fire had died down low, just glowing embers brightening the light of what seemed to be early evening.

He sighed and tried to make himself comfortable, still anxiously wondering what would happen next.

'I see you are afraid,' the voice continued gently. *'Sometimes it is good to feel fear. Fear protects you from doing many foolish and harmful things. Tell me, what is your Earth name?'*

"Reuben." His own voice came out in a tiny squeak.

The voice from the fire became warm and earthy, comforting the boy as it entered his body through his ears and the hairs of this head. It said:
'You can let your fear go right now. There is no need to fear me at this time. One day, when we know each other better, and you are capable of understanding its purpose, I might show you my fearsome side.'

The young boy gulped, but said nothing.

'Do you wish to see me Reuben?'

Reuben cleared his throat and nodded his head. "Yes please" It was still a squeak.

As he looked at the fire, a face slowly materialised – but not one that reminded Reuben of anybody he had ever seen before.

'I think you're getting sleepy Reuben,' soothed the voice. *'Never mind. Just listen to what I am saying and it won't matter if you go to sleep.'*

How can I listen and go to sleep at the same time? mused one half of Reuben's brain, as the other half heard a soft disembodied voice whispering close to his ear:

'Remember Reuben; remember; remember to tell your sister, Esme isn't it. Tell her Reuben, start to tell her as soon as you wake up. You must start telling her as soon as you see her … as soon as you see her. If you don't, you will forget and she will not be able to remind you. So remember … start telling Esme the minute you see her. Is that clear Reuben?'

"Hmmm" was all Reuben could manage before his eyes drooped closed and he slept.
Not that he felt any different as the strange adventure continued. A vague, distant thought floated through his mind and asked: 'but I was already dreaming wasn't I ... ?' And then all 'thoughts' left his mind and he was left very focussed upon what was happening to him at that very moment.

'Let me introduce myself to you.' The being on the other side of the fire got to its feet, stepped straight into the centre of the fire and came to stand in front of Reuben. For a moment she (for it was a 'she') seemed to be gigantic, towering over Reuben in a

body that seemed to be made from different coloured flickering flames.

Then she shrank, became more solid and about the same size as Reuben. She had long flowing hair made out of flames, skin that was almost golden in colour and eyes that kept changing from blue to green to gold. She wore no shoes and her hands and feet looked as though they had been tattooed with flower and leaf shapes, except that the shapes kept moving! She was wearing a long floaty garment. Perched on top of her head was a tiny little crown made of fine shiny metals shaped like flowers.

Reuben looked at her in astonishment. Might this creature be a fairy?

'No ... I am not a fairy ... though all such beings are my friends.'

She stared at him for a moment, eyes flashing different colours, then suddenly she burst out laughing and plonked herself in a very human way down onto the cushions next to him - just the same way his sister would have done!

'Ah Reuben; I do so enjoy dressing up and surprising my visitors!' As she spoke, all the flashing colours dimmed and she appeared almost like a young girl all dressed up to go to fancy dress party, tinny little crown perched haphazardly on one side of her head.

'You will see me in many forms. But as my dear equine friend Pegasus told you, I am indeed known to most who have dealings with me as Old Woman, as that is the form

I most often take. But my age is of no importance except that my long 'life' on this planet has brought me many experiences. Through these I have gained great wisdom and much understanding of the human race.'

In his sleep state Reuben slipped sideways onto the cushions, his head falling close to the being sitting next to him.

She reached out and gently rested her hand on his head.

'I have many useful things to teach humans if only they desired to listen.'

Reuben heard himself mumble that he did want to listen.

'Indeed. That I know. It is why you are here with me now.' As she said these words, Reuben felt a warm tingling sensation flowing from the hand on his head right through his whole body. It was very pleasant.

'And I am not alone. There are many of us wanting to help, including my 'other half' as you humans might say; my 'partner'. This other half of me is known by most as Young Man. One day you will meet him.'

The sleeping boy had the feeling of being surrounded by thousands of tiny points of bright light. The more attention he gave these the more amazing he felt … like a huge powerful giant who could do just anything!

'Yes, we are all made of Light. We, your older brothers and sisters who have found our Light … who are 'enlightened' as you humans call it, wish to help all humans find that Light that is within each and every one of you. If each one of you does this, each one of you will contribute to a bright bright future.'

She paused for a moment to let that information sink deep into Reuben, before bending close to him and whispering: *'This is white magic child. I gift it to you … as I have already gifted it to your sister.'*

The tiny frown that appeared on Reuben's face as she said these words caused her to chuckle.

The Lights faded and Reuben's sleeping attention was once again directed to the person sitting next to him. 'Old Woman'… it felt weird calling her that when she looked like a young girl.

'So, now that we have met, let me tell you why you are here.'

'Ah,' Reuben's mind offered him a thought as he continued to sleep: 'this is where I get the coded instructions that will take me to the treasure … isn't that what happens in these kinds of adventures.'

Old Woman smiled as she heard his mind's thoughts. So typically human – always seeking hidden treasure. And in some ways he was right. He **would** be given coded instructions, and eventually these **would** take him to the greatest treasure of all – his True Self. She sighed. That was a way to go yet.

Reuben was aware of Old Woman's voice, almost as though she was whispering directly into his ear but at the same time speaking from far away.

'You are one of the many human beings who has chosen to be born at this time to help your human family. The human family on this planet is sick. It is being poisoned by people's beliefs and behaviour. Many changes need to take place for it to be restored to health.'

Again Old Woman paused to allow her words to settle into Reuben's mind.

'You, child, are one of those who has the ability to bring your Light into this darkness that has been created by the fear many humans are feeling right now. Your sister is also one of those humans … and you will work togeth-er.' Again Old woman noted with a gentle smile the tiny frown appearing between Reuben's eyebrows. She sighed and placed two gentle fingers onto the frown before adding: *'It is why you chose to be born together as twins. Representatives from the animal king-doms will also make contact with you. Learn from them, as they will show you the way.'*

'Now dear Reuben, it is time for you to return to your everyday reality. We shall meet again; sometimes here in another reality, sometimes in your everyday reality. Sometimes you will recognise me, sometimes not.' Old Woman – this time in her flickering flame form, bent down again and blew very gentle into Reu-ben's ear.

He vaguely heard a distant whispering in his ear, but none of it made any sense. It was like one of those crazy dreams where all sorts of things become jumbled up together and you're in a place that you know but don't know and meeting people that you know but don't know, and losing something that you didn't know you had.

And that was it.

And thus Reuben had woken up in the field after Mr Nibbs had bucked him off, desperate to tell his sister where he had been.

5 - Weird and More Weird

"Old Woman said Pegasus would come back to get me … but I don't remember that happening."

Reuben had come to the end of his story.

He looked at Esme who had been listening intently and said very quietly: "I don't know, Es, I don't know what to think. It all felt so real … but now that I've said it all out loud, it seems crazy … "

Esme waited patiently for him to continue. She might have dismissed it all and suspected that Reuben was just telling her a tall story; waiting to see how much of it she would believe. She knew her brother was quite capable of playing that sort of a prank.
But she had seen the Pegasus horse with her own eyes. And … she had met Old Woman – sort of – in her own dreams. So she just waited patiently, understanding how he must be feeling.

"Maybe … maybe it **was** just an extraordinary dream." He shrugged and fell silent.

At that point further serious conversation was interrupted by the bouncy arrival of Mowgli and Luca, the two younger Choccies. All three dogs had slipped away earlier to do a smell-inspection around the garden once they realised their humans were not going to pay them any attention.

Wildly wagging tails, paws plonked on legs and arms, noses pushing under chins and other tickly places had the twins rolling over on the grass and laughing helplessly. Grandfather Solo arrived at a more sober pace, gently nosing his son and grandson to the side as he took his turn to check out his humans.

The arrival of the dogs heralded the approach of their father. Always respectful of their privacy when they were in the bold hole, he called out to them from the other side of the shrubs to tell them that lunch was ready.

"Coming!"

Reuben looked at his sister as she mouthed: "Okay, but I need to tell you my dream ... let's come back after lunch. I don't think we're going anywhere this afternoon ... are we?"

Sometimes the twins had to accompany their parents on Sunday-afternoon-outings to visit friends, or very occasionally if it couldn't be helped, accompany their parents to deliver orders to customers. Not that they minded too much; these outings usually yielded something of interest: time spent playing with a new litter of kittens or puppies, large pieces of homemade lemon drizzle cake at one house, a visit to the bee hives at another.

But today nothing would have been as exciting as what they were talking about right then.

They jumped up, and along with the dogs went pelting past their father towards the house where a scrumptious Sunday lunch was waiting for them.

The scent of one of their favourite meals wafted to them as they rushed into the kitchen and scooted towards the table, already laid and …

"Hands!" their mother called.

Immediately changing direction and jostling each other in shared delight at their 'secret', the twins hurried to the little cloakroom situated by the side door into the house.

The small room was so full of 'outdoor things' hanging from the walls and littering the floor that they could only just squeeze their way through to the battered old sink where mucky hands were washed before meals.

They tussled for the towel and rushed back into the kitchen with still wet hands, plonking themselves in their seats just as their father opened the oven door and lifted out 'Dad's old bird'.

The smell was mouth watering. It was a recipe their father remembered from his boyhood in Spain, and it turned even the most ancient hen into the tenderest and tastiest of chicken meals.

"No better way ever to cook an old bird," their father pronounced ceremonially as he lifted the roasted bird from the oven and deeply inhaled the aromatic steam, a satisfied smile on his face.

"You **always** say that Dad!" sighed Esme in mock exasperation, thinking that her desire to become a vegetarian was always halted when she smelled her father's roast chicken!

"I do indeed ... because it's true!" This was a family ritual, and they all laughed.

This 'bird' was accompanied by a mix of roast vegetables, roast potatoes, something green and leafy, and gravy made from the juices left in the roasting tin.

Food on the table, Eve Montana asked for a moments silence as she gave thanks to all who had contributed to the meal: the bird, the veggies and other food stuffs, the energy that had been used to cook it, and the humans who had done the cooking. They all tucked in, ignoring the pleading glances of the Choccies and the disgusting strings of saliva hanging from their lips. Even fast asleep Kimber had opened an eye, stretched and yawned, and nonchalantly sauntered over to sit next to Esme's chair. Although their parents forbade it, the children sometimes managed to slip their friends a scrap or two.

Halfway through the meal, Reuben put his knife and fork down suddenly.
"Es, I forgot to tell you!" Reuben, who had been concentrating on his food until that point, suddenly burst out: "You know when I was riding Pegasus ... well, I was on his ba ... "

Eating stopped and three faces turned towards Reuben. His parents both had encouraging 'go-on-dear,' looks on their faces.

Esme looked aghast, consternation written all over her face. "Reubs ... " she squeaked.

Reuben clamped his mouth closed, cutting off his sentence mid word. Crikey ... he had been about to say something that would lead to lots of awkward questions.

His mind scrabbled for what to say as his hand was rubbing at his lips as though trying to remove some food. '*Oh nothing*' would not do. If his parents had been alerted to him riding an unknown horse or pony they would want to know more.

"Um ... erm ... a dream I had last night. I'd forgotten about it and it suddenly popped into my mind just now. At the end of last term I took this book out of the library ... all about Greek myths ... and there was one story about a horse with wings, called Pegasus."

He could feel Esme relax slightly. She said quickly: "Hmm, I remember you telling me about it. Go on then, let's hear the rest of the dream."

"Well ..." He hesitated, not really wanting to continue but not able to come up with an imaginary story. "I didn't really feel as though I was **riding** Pegasus, more like he was carrying me ... "

He was saved at that moment by the phone ringing. Fons stood up from the table to go an answer it and Eve started collecting up the dirty plates. Both parents were used to hearing their children talking about their dreams – some of which were seriously weird. They didn't feel the need to pay any attention – unless they were asked to!

Reuben had an 'I'm sorry' look on his face as he continued speaking to his sister. His voice had dropped until he was almost whispering. "I just wanted to say that it's not easy to ride a horse with wings! I didn't know where to put my legs. The wings really got in the way! When I sat behind his wings … then I was further back than normal and my legs were sort of under his wings. I had to lean really far forward to get hold of his mane. I was sitting right forward to start with … with my legs in front of his wings. But then they kind of stuck straight out when he lifted his wings up to fly … "
He tailed off, remembering how it had felt. Then he shrugged and added: "I expect I'll get used to it."
He went quiet, chewing at the corner of his lip, having realised that somehow he was expecting to have more rides on the winged horse.

Knowing exactly what he was thinking, Esme said: "I think you're right, there will be more rides … and I shall ride him too!"

The twins looked at each other and both made 'this is scary-exciting' faces.

They said nothing more about it as their mother put a bowlful of raspberries and a jug of cream on the table. Their father returned from the phone and the family resumed their Sunday lunch almost as though nothing had happened.

But both children were itching to get back to the bolt hole. They quietly slid out of their seats and were edging towards the back door when their father said:

"Hey … you two! Help with the washing up please. What are you in such a hurry about … what are you up to?"

"Nothing!" they chorused.

"Nicer outside than in." added Esme with an innocent smile plastered on her face.

After a moment of regarding his children intently, Fons said: "Go on then … and take the dogs with you. Oh, and don't forget you're helping pick tomatoes later … that is, if you want that extra pocket money?"

But they had run off with such speed, he doubted they had heard him. He frowned. Oh yes … they **were** up to something!

Three brown dogs sped ahead of their best friends, delighted to be included.

Settled once more in the seclusion of the bolt hole, Esme was impatient to get back to discussing 'what had happened'.

Her face was serious as she asked Reuben very quietly: "You remember earlier when you said you'd never seen anything like that camp fire?"

Reuben nodded and sighed deeply. He began describing the scene to his sister with a distant look in his eyes: "Beautiful ... it was just beautiful ... almost as though it was alive! It was the same sort of shape as a camp fire, but with all sorts of coloured flames leaping up and down. But it wasn't messy round the bottom like camp fires are - you know with bits of wood and ashes all around it. And what was strangest is that the flames seemed to come up from water ... water that swirled around and had rainbow colours ..." He was still gazing into the distance, chewing in a vague way on the latest grass stem.

"I ... know!"

He shook his head very slowly and emphasised: "Honestly, I have never ever seen anything like it! ... what were you saying Es?"

"Well I have!"

He still looked slightly dreamy. He wasn't really listening to his sister. "Have what ... ?" He finally turned to look at her.

" ... seen a fire like that!" She spoke quietly and very slowly, emphasising each word.

Finally she had her brother's attention. Strangely though, Reuben didn't seem surprised or put-out by her statement. "Dream?" he queried quietly.

Esme nodded her head very slowly. "Not sure why I've not told you about them before ... weird." She made a puzzly face. "But for ... quite a long time now ... I've been having one of those repeat dreams ... you know ... ?"

Reuben nodded encouragingly.

"Well ... I go to this strange round building. It's a house ... sort of ... there's a beautiful bedroom where I sleep sometimes. Then in the centre of the house is a round meeting room kind of place ... and right in the middle of that is this amazing fountain thing ... but it's a fountain that has water at the bottom and rainbow flames coming up from the centre. It's so beautiful!"

"That's it." Reuben's response was almost inaudible. "Wow, Es, this is getting weirder and weirder."

There was quite a long pause as both children contemplated the weirdness of it all.

Esme sighed as she recalled her dream place, sprawling backwards onto the grass and putting her hands behind her head. She spat out the grass stalk still dangling from her mouth and continued, bit by bit telling Reuben about her dream - with lots of dreamy pauses.

"I like being there. You walk into the entrance through a beautiful garden with flowers and veggies ... hmmm the smells ... lovely. And the bedroom is amazing. But the house is not 'finished' in some way. Sometimes when I visit, there are people in the meeting place, sat all around the circle on piles of cushions. But they're not proper people. They're ... more like shadows ... sometimes with colour and bits of 'clothing' that I see clearly for just a few seconds. I can't see any of them properly ... but they all look a little bit like you described 'Old Woman'."

She stopped speaking for a moment, and then added: "I think they know I am there, but they don't say anything to me. And then one time I felt very scared. One of the shadows didn't feel nice."

Esme shivered and remained silent until Reuben prodded her gently. "Go on Es ... "

She sat up quickly and continued much more brightly: "And there are always animals around about this place! Some of them come to greet me as though they know me. There's a beautiful black mare, a very large black dog, sort of like a wolfhound, a black leopard that has bright green eyes and very long legs – a bit strange but lovely. And then there's a very large bird - I think it's a golden eagle - that sometimes appears and circles above us in the sky.
Once I was riding the mare – she had 'told me' her name was Torrela. Didn't have a saddle, or a bridle and we were going really fast ... but I felt safe. The dog was running right alongside us ... and the

strange leopard was running with us too, but a bit further away…

And I know the bird, it **is** an eagle ... from other dreams. It feels like a friend … no, not a 'friend' … more like a part of me."

Esme came to a halt, shook her head and … started to cry! Tears rolled down her face and she sniffed a couple of times before wiping her eyes and smiling at Reuben. "It is **so** beautiful there … and it's almost like another 'home'… you know?" she said with another little sniff. " ... and it feels **so** real!" She finished, and fell silent again.

Reuben was confused! Why was she crying? For once he really didn't know what to say.

Finally Esme broke the silence. "Well … um … this is so weird, seriously weird! You've **been** somewhere weird … and I've had … weird - more weird than usual – dreams. I wonder what's going to happen next … if anything IS going to happen?"

"Well, from what Old Woman said to me, it sounded like there will be more things happening." He heaved a huge sigh. "But what … ?" He gave a resigned 'who knows' shrug.

There didn't seem to be any else to say. It was as though they had both emptied themselves of strange stories and dreams and didn't have anything left to talk about.

After long moments of companiable silence, Reuben got to his feet, not his usual bouncy self at all, and headed towards the gate into the coppice, calling over his shoulder to his sister: "I'm going down to the stream." One by one the Choccies got up and ambled after him. They liked the coppice - always new smells.

Esme knew her brother well enough to interpret that to mean that he wanted to be alone.

That suited her because she too wanted to be alone for a while.
She moved towards the shade of one of the shrubs and laid herself down with her head in the shade. Although it was by now late afternoon, the sun was still hot and freckles and sun don't mix together too well.

Neither of the twins had noticed that Kimber, their old black cat had been present, seated in the shade in a corner of the bolt hole ... away from the boisterous Choccies. As a superior being - a cat - he tolerated the dogs; they were family after all ... but so clingy! He preferred to sit and watch them as they tried to pretend to be human beings. Silly creatures!

Kimber was old; the vet said about 15, but he had only joined the Montana family about three years ago. He had turned up in their garden one day, very very thin, and carrying hoards of fleas. Although he was all black, his long lean body and legs, his small pointed face and rather large ears all pointed to one parent who was Siamese.
At that time they had no other cats and, strangely, the three Labradors accepted him easily. Soon they

even started giving him preference when it came to sleeping places and food.

Both children were really pleased to have a cat come into their household. But it was Esme the cat had particularly taken to; and she to him. They really respected each other those two.

On this occasion, the old cat had heard the whole of the children's conversation, and if a cat could look satisfied, then Kimber did. He flipped the tip of this tail lazily, cleaned both sets of whiskers several times with tongue-wetted paws, and then moved quietly close to Esme as she lay, eyes closed, breathing gently. Somehow she became aware of his presence and reached out a hand, feeling around until she touched him. He stretched out purring with contentment as she tickled behind his ears. '*Yes, some humans were good at tickling*' he conceded.

6 - Mouse ThreeMillionSix

The remaining days of August and summer holidays passed without any further strange happenings.

Mr Nibbs, the scruffy brown pony was no longer in the field next to the twins' house. They didn't know where he'd gone and they didn't try to find out.

In truth Reuben was still trying to make sense of 'where he had been', and wasn't keen on another trip with the flying horse just yet.

And strangely Esme's dream visits to the house and animals she had become very fond of, were almost non-existent. There was just one occasion when she had woken up in the night thinking she had heard someone calling to her: *'Esme … don't forget… don't forget.'* She had opened her eyes and for a moment thought there was somebody in the room with her. A vague shape was sitting at the end of her bed … no … there was nobody there. She closed her eyes and quickly fell asleep again.
Yet in the morning when she awoke the words 'don't forget' were the first things to come into her mind.

She had told Reuben about what she had experienced.

He has said, rather anxiously: "No, we mustn't forget, Es. It's too important."

And they didn't forget exactly, but as 'nothing' happened, they just got on with summer holiday life.

Occasionally one or both of them were invited to spend time at the houses of school friends: birthday parties, summer holiday parties, strawberry and cream teas; that sort of thing.

But mostly, they just pottered around.
They took yet more photographs of local wildlife. They built several dens in the hedgerows and coppice, and a bridge over the coppice stream. They helped their parents in the tunnels, picking tomatoes, peppers and cucumbers. They enjoyed experimenting in the kitchen, inventing new recipes for all the things they picked.

And there were always books to be read, games to be played and sometimes in the evening TV programmes to be enjoyed.

The Choccies were always with them. Kimber sometimes accompanied them, and very occasionally a family of local crows appeared to follow them around - but only when Kimber wasn't there. Crows and Kimber just insulted each other; the crows with extra raucous cawing and diver bombing the cat, and Kimber reacting with murderous but abortive leaps to capture them.

Their antics made the twins laugh.

They were happy. The weather was proper August weather and the freedom from school was something they delighted in. Occasionally when they ran out of things to do, feelings of boredom crept in. But this didn't happen often and when it did being bored actually provided them with 'imagining time'. Esme in particular quite enjoyed just letting her mind wander and following her thoughts to wherever they took her.

They had made a decision not to tell any of their friends about Reuben's adventure. It was just that bit too weird, and they didn't want to lose their friends.

Esme did wish she could share it all with her new friend Rose, though. Rose was a bit odd herself and probably wouldn't have been completely freaked out. But she stuck to the agreement she had made with her brother. Especially as, for some reason, Reuben did not like Rose at all.

Indeed, Esme's other friends all thought that Rose was rather a strange character. She was very tall for her age, and she had spooky hair. It was very fine and straight, and so fair it was almost white – one of the group of friends even said he had seen it glow in the dark! Her pale skin was so fine you could almost imagine seeing through it; and large almond shaped, violet coloured eyes set very wide apart completed her rather other-worldly look.

The twins had met Rose at one of the many summer fairs held in the surrounding villages, where the Montanas sold their fresh produce.

Although Reuben had taken an instant dislike to her, for Esme it was just the opposite. She felt an immediate kinship with the rather odd looking girl. Unlike Esme, who was full of vitality and always had something to say, Rose was a quiet child who said very little. Yet she had a strange charm, and it was as though she and Esme could communicate without using words.

But the strangest thing was that as soon as they were introduced, Esme **knew** she could trust Rose … completely! She would have liked to have seen more of her, but Rose went to a different school from the twins, and her house was too far away for popping in.

And so it was that the twins were spending a whole afternoon at Rose's house, along with several other children … when the story of 'where Reuben had been' nearly came out!

Amongst the other children there was a boy called Peter who went to the twins' school. Neither of them liked Peter! Neither of them actually **knew** Peter. But they had seen him at local gymkhanas on a most beautiful grey show pony. His family were rich and kept several horses and ponies. They were envious of him!

It was mid-afternoon and the children were all exhausted from playing a boisterous game of tag. Rose's mother had brought them out a large tray full of cold drinks and a couple of packets of biscuits.

The small group had sprawled out on the cool stones of a patio that had been built outside French windows leading into the living room. Short flights of steps on either side of the patio led down onto the lawn. Unlike the twins' untidy house and rather neglected garden, Rose's house was 'scared-to-sit on-the-sofa' clean and tidy, and the garden had one of those lawns people referred to as manicured, neatly surrounded by equally well manicured plants.

Animals were not allowed – inside or out! Reuben had even left JasonRat at home just in case he had decided to explore these new surroundings and ventured into the scary clean house.

Rose had told Esme that she had had several 'pets' where she had lived before, and that she missed the company of animals. Esme had not had a chance to ask Rose where she had lived before coming to this house, but sometimes wondered about it. When she had first appeared on the local scene there had been a rumour going around that she was being fostered by Mrs Briggs. Not much was known about Mrs Briggs. Only that she spoke a foreign language that nobody could identify – somebody had heard her speaking on her mobile phone. There was no sign of a Mr Briggs.

None of that bothered Esme though. Maybe because she had a twin brother, she was rather self-contained and didn't have that many friends. If she was going to go to all the effort needed to make a proper friend, then it had to be somebody she really liked. She liked Rose, and that was that.

Esme and Rose, both gasping for breath after the game, had collapsed on the paving stones close to a cluster of shrubs neatly planted beside the steps and along the edge of the patio.

"I'm thirsty!" Finally having caught her breath, Esme got up, went to the tray and got them both a glass of juice.
Rose followed her and picked up one of the packets of biscuits her mother had left on the tray. Back sitting in the spot they had chosen, he discarded its transparent cellophane cover and emptied the biscuits onto a plate between herself and Esme.

There were so many things they wanted to talk about and they needed lots of biscuits to keep them going!

Esme was seriously considering telling Rose about Reuben 'going somewhere', and about her dreams, when Reuben came over to them. He plonked himself down beside them and helped himself to several biscuits. The girls looked at him with disapproving eyes. Not so much as a 'do you mind'. Typical boy their expressions said to each other. There was a bit of an uncomfortable silence as they all munched away. Reuben seemed completely unaware of the girls' disapproval.

The sound of rustling cellophane intruded upon this silence and caught their attention. They all stopped munching to see what had caused the noise.

Rose was first to spot it. She put one finger to her lips to shush them and with the other pointed towards the steps.

There, inside the cellophane biscuit cover, was a tiny mouse that had been chasing crumbs and got trapped. They watched fascinated as the mouse, in panicky efforts to get out of the trap it founds itself in, tumbled over and over down the flight of steps.

Esme put a hand out to stop Rose from getting up to go and rescue the little creature. She knew from experience that tiny creatures become really scared when huge great human hands get involved in their rescue – no matter how well-intentioned!

Finally the mouse managed to remove itself from the biscuit packaging. Most surprisingly, instead of immediately running off, it jumped back up the stairs … to confront the humans!

It was a beautiful mouse: a lovely chestnut brown colour, with huge big ears and bright brown eyes.

"Soooo cute!" whispered Rose, who desperately longed for a pet of her own.

The mouse sat on the top step cleaning its whiskers nervously. But it was clearly so very indignant that it seemed to have lost its fear of humans. It gave a final twitch of its whiskers, lifted its little head high, looked all three children straight in the eye and confronted them with a stream of squeak-grumbling about human behaviour.

'You humans are so thoughtless! Worse than thoughtless … you pretend to be friends and put out tasty food for us … but getting it causes us harm! Look at myself just now … I could have really injured myself. Typical … surely you know better ,.. specially as you're still children!!'

At this point something really strange happened.

Anybody watching the scene would have been surprised at how quiet and motionless the three children were … almost as if they had become frozen on the spot, or were asleep with their eyes wide open.

Rose was crouched on one knee, a hand pointing in the direction of the mouse.
Esme was seated cross-legged at the top of the steps, also watching the mouse.
Reuben was sprawled next to his sister, one hand holding a biscuit that was just about to go into his mouth. He too was looking towards the mouse.

The three children were not 'asleep' though.

Esme and Reuben had both heard a voice inside their heads saying to them: 'Listen to the mouse.' The voice, they somehow knew, was that of Old Woman.

They looked at each other and then the mouse standing defiantly with its back to them and continuing a squeaky muttering to itself. They looked around them and at the giant plants they were standing amongst.

Meanwhile, after a few seconds, Rose, had become unfrozen. She glanced around and moved to sit facing away from the 'frozen' twins. It was almost as though she was on guard, preventing anybody else from intruding upon the scene.

"Oh ..." The tiniest of whispers came from Esme as she realised she and Reuben were only a little bit bigger than the mouse.

It only took that tiny sound to alert the little creature to the presence of another being behind it.
It gave a great jump and whirled around in the air, landing to face the new-comers. As it landed it gave an extra loud squeak in shock at what it saw. But amazingly, instead of scampering off as you would expect, it stood stock still regarding the miniature humans.

Then: *'Oooweeeiioeeooii ... some New Children!'* the tiny brown creature squeaked.

Tiny humans and tiny mouse stared at each other.

'Is that what you are ... 'New Children' ... children who can understand animals?'

Then to Esme's amazement, the tiny Reuben suddenly gained his composure and took a step forward, nodding his head in a little bow to the mouse as he did so.

"Let me introduce you to myself and my twin sister. Reuben and Esme are our names. We were told you could teach us something." As he said the last words he looked at Esme with a 'where did that come from'? expression on his face.

She shook her head and shrugged.

The mouse responded by introducing himself as Mouse ThreeMillionSix.

Once the introductions were over, the three of them 'talked … and talked'. Though in truth it was Mouse ThreeMillionSix who did most of the talking.

They remained hidden amongst the flowers whilst the other Esme and Reuben retained their frozen positions.

The mouse started by saying that amongst his kind, a prophesy had started circulating many mouse lifetimes before he was born. This prophesy told the story of a 'new kind' of human children that would be born on Earth. These children would not only love and respect all animals, but would also be able to communicate with them. *'like you are now with me!'* MTMS suddenly fell silent, sat up on his haunches and began to frantically clean his whiskers, whilst staring at them with his bright, bright eyes.

The twins were fascinated. They could both understand what MTMS was 'saying'!

"But can he understand us?" Reuben whispered, turning his towards his sister, but without taking his eyes of the little creature in front of them.

The rush of excited squeaks told them he could! And in less than a second later he launched into another squeaky story.

'I am a field mouse not a house mouse but house mice are part of my extended family and they in particular are badly treated by humans who think they are 'dirty little things' and even worse fear them and therefore ... '

He paused a fraction of a second to take breath.

' ... and therefore they do all they can to KILL THEM and so all young mice are warned by their elders about the tricky behaviour of humans and brought up to fear them ... and this is much more understandable than the other way round ... isn't it?'

The little creature looked at the children as though waiting for them to answer.

What could they say! They nodded.

'And the most very awful thing is the stories of family members who have been taken in by the pretend kindness and have accepted the pretend 'gifts' and have then been mousenapped and are AND ARE NEVER SEEN AGAIN or sometimes come home but DIE IN PAIN SHORTLY AFTER!'

His whiskers and nose all twisted and twitched as he blinked away the tears that were forming in his eyes. Then he was off again:

'Humans give mixed messages! This is not fair. They leave food lying around everywhere just like a supermarket for mice then BAM they don't like us taking what they offer, set traps to catch us and put poison down to … KILL US!'

The little brown mouse dropped his voice to a whisper. *'Sometimes we get so desperate that we ask the RATSSS to help us … '*

He looked at the children meaningfully as he whispered the word *'ratssss'*.

' … you know… the TERRORATSSS! Sometimes, not often because we don't really trust them, but when our families get really upset … we pay them to set up raiding parties to go and chew through the things you humans call cables … so your film boxes stop working and the see-through objects you use to see in the dark won't go on.'

Esme, who had been holding her hand over her heart as she listened intently to what the mouse was saying suddenly burst in: "And it just serves us right … for being so stupid! I had never thought of that … food left out is like a supermarket for mice! … phooo!" She was remembering all the times she left plates with bits of food on them in her bedroom … for days sometimes!

"I am sooo sorry MouseThreeMillionSix." She glanced over at Reuben.

He was nodding his head very slowly. "I'd never thought ... "

But before he could finish saying what he had never thought, MouseThreeMillionSix froze, twitched its ears, said one word '*Humanadults!*' and leapt away into the bushes.

All in the same instance the twins heard a mousy voice calling out '*Goodbye, so nice to have met you, New Children*' and ...

... felt a strange whooshy sensation and ...

... heard Rose say: "Oh, what a shame, it's run off." And ...

The children heard the voice of Rose's mother. "They are over by the steps Eve," and their mother replying "Ah yes, I see them. Hope they haven't eaten too many biscuits!" And ...

... they felt huge and cumbersome ... like giants ... except Rose was a giant too and so was their mother as she stood over them and smiled. "Hello Rose. You must visit us soon. Come on you two, we've got to get back; Daddy's going to be late back, and the tomato plants need watering. You two can help me if you want."

And then everything felt 'normal' again.

"Ooh yes." said Reuben, quickly jumping to his feet. "I love the smell of the tomato plants in the evening.

Esme was slower to respond, still pondering on what had just happened. She glanced at Rose with a questioning look.

Rose smiled, rather mysteriously, but didn't say anything.

"C'mon Es!" Reuben grabbed his sister's hand and dragged her to her feet.

"I'm coming!" Esme gave her large body a bit of a shake before turning to thank Rose's mother for a 'lovely afternoon'.

"Oh yes, thank you!" Reuben added his thanks before following the two adults into the house.

"Bye Rose ... see you soon?"

"I expect so!" Rose grinned and jumped nimbly to her feet.

The two girls followed slowly.

Esme wondered if they would see MouseThreeMillionSix again.

7 - A Strange Gift

The incident with MouseThreeMillionSix soon went out of the twins' minds as they prepared for the new term at school.

Well, that is not quite accurate.

Later that same evening, Reuben, who wanted to develop his new found ability to communicate with animals, attempted to 'tell' his pet white rat JasonRat, about meeting the mouse.
The reaction from JasonRat was unexpected. He bit the tip of Reuben's ear. Not enough to draw blood but certainly not the usual friendly nibble.

Reuben was so shocked that he nearly missed his pet's other response:

'Don't talk to me about ... MICE! Silly little things ... brainless creatures ... not the faintest idea how to deal with humans!' He leaped off Reuben's shoulder and disappeared under the boy's bed, still chuntering as he went.

Reuben, who was tired, and still had to get school stuff ready for the morning, shrugged and started piling stuff into his school bag.

Last night, Esme had not said anything about their strange experience. This new morning was too full of 'are you sure you've got everything', and 'hurry you're going to miss the bus and 'don't forget your lunch' for either of the twins to talk about the relationship between mice and rats.

The beginning of the new school term was super busy as always: greeting old friends and meeting new ones, meeting new teachers, getting to know a new timetable. And, most challenging of all for the twins, an extra half hours worth of homework each day.

Both Esme and Reuben really resented having to do any sort of homework when there were so many other more interesting things to do at home. But they were good students, so gritted their teeth and got on with it … usually.

Mr Nibbs was no longer in the field they passed each day on their way to and from school. There was nothing to remind them of what had happened, and it was almost as though nothing had.

Until one Monday a few weeks into term.

Reuben had been kept at home because he'd seriously sprained his ankle the day before doing one of his 'stunts'. He had pushed log across the stream at the end of their garden to make a bridge. The log had rolled when he had jumped onto it and he had ended face down in the water … with a sprained ankle.

So coming back from school Esme had been walking alone down their lane from the bus stop on the main road. She saw an elderly woman coming towards her from the opposite direction.

"Good afternoon my dear!" the woman had greeted her warmly.

"Good afternoon." Esme had replied, smiling and walking on. The woman had looked like many of the hikers Esme often saw walking down the lane wearing stout boots and large backpacks.

She had been surprised when the woman had stopped and said: "Wait. I have something for you."

Esme had slowed to a halt and turned around to face the woman, who had taken off her back pack, put it down on the road, and was rummaging in one of the side pockets.

Esme was an open and friendly child, but the constant warnings from adults about not talking to strangers had stuck in her head.

She felt herself tense ever so slightly as what she called her 'danger antennae' automatically came into action. She had had these ever since she could remember and sometimes giggled as she imagined herself as an insect reaching out with lots of waving feelers. She had learned to trust those feelers of hers.

Everything had felt ok … she hadn't felt any sense of there being danger. So she had waited patiently, watching as the woman rummaged through several more of the backpack's pockets before finally straightening up with something in her hand.

She had smiled at Esme, slowly opening up her hand and holding it out for Esme to see. In the palm were two identical little bronze-coloured charms in the shape of an upside down heart resting upon a little 'trunk'. Like a heart-shaped little tree, Esme thought.

"One for you and one for your brother Reuben." The woman had taken Esme's hand, depositing the charms on her palm and gently closing Esme's fingers around them. "Don't lose them. They will come in useful in the future!"

"Er … thank you!" Esme had stammered, not knowing what else to say.

"My pleasure dear." The woman had patted Esme very gently on the cheek before hefting her rucksack up on to her back and continuing on her way.

Esme had been stunned. All the usual warnings about not taking things from strangers had rushed into her head and then straight out again, carried away on the feelers which were saying: 'TAKE THEM' very loudly.

She stood there, watching as the old woman strode away from her, disappearing around a bend in the lane.

'*One for Reuben too*'… how had the woman known she had a brother, and that his name was Reuben? Perhaps she was a friend of their parents.

She shrugged and slowly opened her hand. She smiled and could have sworn that the charms had smiled back. She had placed them gently into the inside pocket of her jacket.

As soon as she opened the gate to the front garden she was swamped, not only by three dogs, as always deliriously happy to see her, but also by an urgent request from Reuben. He had heard the doggie commotion so knew his sister was home from school and had hobbled to the side door to meet her.

"Esme come and see what's in the field!"

"OK ... let me take my backpack off ... and I've got something ... "

"No time!" He grabbed her hand, and with her backpack hanging off one shoulder, she was dragged into the small field where the tunnels were.

"We've got to be quick or it'll move." Reuben was half hopping half limping as fast as he could with his injured ankle.

"What is it?"

"Shhh, or we'll frighten them!" He slowed to a halt and pointed.

Esme could see what looked to be a circle of toadstools some way ahead ... fairy circles some people called them. Inside the circle, right in the centre, were four crows. Reuben was right, they did look odd, almost as though they were having some kind of a conversation.

The two children stood there in the field very quietly for some time, entranced by the birds' strange behaviour and wondering what it might mean

"Come on you two, tea's getting cold!" Their father's voice was loud and clear, startling the birds who immediately launched themselves into the sky.

By the time they were back inside and Esme had taken her jacket off, she had completely forgotten about the charms. She was busy wondering about those crows.

And then a couple of days later, when the family were playing a rare game of cards after tea, she was reminded of them. One of the images on the cards was almost the same shape as the charms. A 'spade' it was called. She had always thought that was an odd name for a symbol on a card.

She could feel excitement rising, but didn't say anything then. She didn't want her parents asking awkward questions.

On their way up to bed she quickly retrieved the charms from her jacket pocket and followed Reuben into his room.

"I've got something to show you!" She showed him the charms, but wouldn't give his to him before he had agreed to listen to the story of where they had come from.

When she had finished telling him about the woman and what she had said, she put one into his hand. He picked it up and scrutinised it carefully. "Oh, look! This one has got 'Esme' written in tiny letters on the back. This one must be yours."
They swapped and sure enough the one Esme had been holding had 'Reuben' written on its back ... the letters so tiny you really had to look hard to see them.

"Wow ... weird ... and weirder!" she whispered.

"Well ... Pegasus must have something to do with it ... or Old Woman!" Reuben exclaimed.

"Hmmmm ... suppose so ... " His sister nodded slowly, and then: "Do you think the woman who gave me these was Old Woman?" she asked excitedly.

"Maybe ... but the person you described didn't sound in any way strange ... ?"

"No ... she looked very ordinary ... sort of boring. But ... " Esme paused. "How did she know I had a brother ... and how come the charms have our names inscribed on them? And Old Woman did say that she could take many shapes."

By this time both children were feeling really sleepy. Reuben shrugged. "'Spect we'll find out! I'm too tired to think."

"Me too … night then." Esme opened the door to go to her own room.

But then she remembered the woman's warning not to lose the charms.

"Don't lose it Reubs!"

"'course not!" he muttered as he pulled back the duvet on his bed.

The following morning and they decided that the only way to keep the charms safe was to wear them around their necks.

So for the next few days they had gone about with the charms attached to pieces of garden twine hanging around their necks.

Eventually their mother had been unable to hide her curiosity and had asked for an explanation.

Without any hesitation, Esme had told their mother that it was to do with a school project that their class was involved with. The charms were a sign of commitment to complete the project.

Reuben stared at his sister, his mouth opening to say something, but turning the words into a little cough as he hastily nodded his agreement.

Esme was quite amazed at how easily she had made up the story and just lied to her mother!

And her mother had made a mental note to check this story out with the children's teacher at some point!

Despite her suspicions, a few days later Mrs Montana had produced two very fine silver chains for the charms, from which the little upside-down hearts hung very nicely.

The only slightly odd thing was that when they forgot to put their amulets on – always around their necks until they were back at school where no jewellery was allowed – something would always remind them. It was as though a tiny internal voice said: *Remember me! Don't leave me behind!*

8 - Mala the Gypsy

It was Sunday, not long after the Autumn term had begun, and many weekends after Reuben had had his first encounter with Pegasus. The whole family – except for Kimber - were spending the day at the county's annual Autumn Fair. This year it took place in the grounds of a large country estate quite close to where the Montanas lived.

For once there had been no rain, no mud … just proper 'fair weather': balmy autumn sun and the hint of a gentle breeze stirring in the branches of the trees.

They had had a wonderful day. Mr and Mrs Montana had met up with a few local friends, they had all stuffed themselves with burgers, sausages, pies, and ice cream. Solo, Mowgli and Luca had been amazingly well behaved, socialising politely with numerous other dogs out for the day with their families.

Reuben had only got lost once.

The family had been slowly wending their way towards the exit, meandering contentedly from stall to stall. The day had been full.
The twins had watched nearly all the horsey events and commented upon the riding skills of several people they knew vaguely. There was that boy Peter, from Reuben's class, who hadn't been able to control his very beautiful show pony. They had

muttered to each other *'shouldn't be allowed to have a pony like that… not fair!'*

The whole family had laughed out loud at the sight of lots of little terriers racing each other to catch a pretend rabbit. It was amazing just how fast the dogs' short little legs could move.

The twins had tasted so many local apples they thought they'd never want to eat an apple again, and their parents were happily mellow after several tastings of the cider made from other local apples.

"Let's sit here for a while and enjoy the last of the sun before we go," their mother had suggested, pointing to a group of straw bales just vacated by another family.

Nobody disagreed, they were all tired. They plonked themselves down on the still warm bales. The Choccies flopped down around their feet.

Esme had become entranced by the huge trees that were dotted all over the estate. She loved trees. Sometimes she imagined they were trying to tell her things. Today, she was fascinated by the way their colourful autumn leaves seemed to shiver as the wind touched them, playfully tugging a few loose to twirl in the air and then drift gently to the ground.
She sighed as she watched them. They looked a bit like fairies when the breeze and sun caught them and made them dance and shimmer as they fell to earth. She began to drift off a little, imagining her-

self becoming a fairy dancing among the branches. She felt so happy! How lucky she was to live in a beautiful place like this.

She had just started imagining what it would be like to be in a desert … no trees … when she was brought back to the fair by her father's laugh.

"Come on all you sleepy heads. We're going to be the last ones here!" He stood up, grabbed Esme round the wait and lifted her to her feet. "There's my girl." He held out a hand to Reuben who allowed himself to be pulled upright.

They were all laughing by the time they had collected their many bags and set off towards the exit once more.

They hadn't progressed that much, taking a last look at the stalls as they went, when suddenly Esme's attention was caught by some bright colours glimpsed between a couple of stalls selling country clothing.

"Ooh, look Reubs, there's a real old-fashioned gypsy caravan! Can we go and have a look. I don't remember seeing it earlier," she puzzled.

Reuben was not convinced – he was tired and wanted to go home.

"Oh come on … just a quick look."

"OK!" he grumbled.

Mr and Mrs Montana agreed ... we'll take the dogs and wait for you in the car. "Don't be too long though."

The twins approached the caravan. It was beautifully painted in dark reds and greens, and golden yellows. The door at the back of the caravan was open. Carved wooden steps led up towards the interior, where a thick dark red curtain prevented anyone from seeing inside.

A notice at the bottom of the steps said. *'Fortune Telling – £1 to Know Your Future!'*
But the twins did not immediately notice the sign.

When they got closer to the caravan, from the corner of her eye Esme noted the swish of a tail from behind the far side of the vehicle. A horse. They bypassed the steps and peered around the corner of the caravan to investigate.

Sure enough two horses were tethered there ... well one pony and one large horse, each resting a hind leg as they dozed in the warmth of the late sun.

"You got sugars?"

"Course!" Reuben felt around in his pocket and withdrew the scrumpled paper bag with its content of sugar lumps and sucky sweets.

The children clicked their tongues to alert the horses to their presence and drew closer slowly. The pony tethered between them and the larger horse was a rather muddy sort of brown. It turned its head to look at them. A piece of half consumed hay dangled from its mouth.

"Oh!" Esme put her hand to her mouth. "Is that … is that Mr Nibbs?" She looked at Reuben.

"Hhmmm … " Reuben cocked his head to one side as he stared. "Could be," he said hesitantly.

At that point the large grey horse tied up loosely on the far side of the pony, stuck its head over the pony's withers and pushed Reuben in the chest with his muzzle.

"Eh! Watch it" said Reuben, putting a hand onto the grey's nose.

This horse too had hay hanging from its mouth, even more than the pony. Neither looked as if they'd been properly groomed for some time.

"What a scruffy pair!" laughed Reuben, scratching the grey's forehead.

'*Do you mind! You'd look scruffy if you'd just travelled through 6 time zones to answer an emergency call!*' The horse then winked, fluttering long eyelashes at Esme, as she stood transfixed … she too had heard the horse 'speak'.

"Pegasus … ?" stuttered Reuben.

'*At your service … as always!*' The horsey voice contained only the slightest hint of sarcasm.

The children looked at each other but said nothing. Had the grey horse really spoken ... right there in the fairground!

Then Esme noticed a white blaze on Mr Nibb's forehead. She had not noticed it previously, but then as a rule the pony's forelock was long enough to keep the mark covered. She traced it gently with her forefinger. It was almost the exact shape of the charms they had around their necks – a heart-shaped 'tree' - though a bit more blurry. She murmured something to herself, reached into the neck-line of her sweater and pulled out the charm.
"I thought so! Look Reubs, check the shape of his blaze!"

Reuben pulled his charm from the inside pocket of his jacket. "Wow!" he whispered as he compared the shape of the charm to the small white blaze on Mr Nibb's forehead.

"That's ... very peculiar!"

Esme nodded – she knew what he was thinking. They had not been wearing the charms for some weeks now. They had been teased at school: Reuben about boys wearing charms; and Esme about the odd shape of her charm: 'not-even-a-proper-heart-shape'.

But today, without consulting with each other, it turned out that they had each decided to bring the charms with them.

A horsy snort interrupted their questioning thoughts.

'Excuse me … but she hasn't got all day you know … !'

"Who hasn't got all day?" Reuben, more used to speaking with Pegasus, was quick to respond.

'Old Woman of course!'

"Old Woman … but where … ?"

'Where do you think … In the caravan!' Both children felt the full force of Pegasus' impatience with human children.

Esme started to query: "… a gypsy?"

At this comment, Mr Nibbs let out a long drawn-out snort, swished his tail and stamped an impatient front leg, clearly as unimpressed by the children's lack of understanding as was Pegasus.

The children took the horsy hints and scurried around to the back of the caravan.

Both hesitated at the bottom of the steps, glancing at each other and each taking a deep breath.

"O.K. ?" Reuben mouthed at his sister.

She nodded and they climbed up the five rather steep little steps. "Hello?" Esme gently drew aside the curtain that prevented them from seeing the interior of the caravan. They peered into the rather dark interior before stepping inside.

The children found themselves in a miniature 'sitting room'. It had a sofa along each side wall, a couple of armchairs at the far end, and was lit by candles and glowing 'fairy lights'. In front of one of the armchairs was a small table covered with a lacy white cloth, and in the centre of the table was ... a large crystal ball.

Sitting in the armchair behind the table was a very young woman, hardly more than a girl. She had long curly chestnut coloured hair held back by a red and yellow scarf, lips that were painted bright red, and green green eyes heavily outlined in black.

This young woman smiled widely at the twins: "Greetings my young friends! I am most pleased to see you. I thought we might miss you." She spoke very fast in a musical voice as she explained: "We arrived so very late, only just in time! Long story ... Cloud 9 got completely caught up in a cloud jam ... dozens of storm clouds piling up and blocking the way! We ended up hitching a lift with some very fast clouds moving at a higher level ... but then they dropped us of further away from this place than we'd planned! Oh the difficulties of transporting a caravan from one dimension to another ... !" She stopped talking, clapped her hands gently, made a wry face and shrugged.

Esme and Reuben were still standing stiffly, chests heaving slightly as their hearts pounded. Neither could take their eyes of this person.

The gypsy girl grinned. "But where are my manners! Welcome. Come in and sit down. You don't need to hear all my excuses! You're here now and that's all that matters." She indicated the sofas.

The gypsy girl's voice had changed in a subtle way. It had become warm and strong … and instantly recognisable to both Reuben - from his trip to Cloud Nine - and to Esme from her dreams.

In almost the same breath, they both stuttered: "Old Woman … is it really you?" Esme's hand went to her mouth and her eyes widened; Reuben had stiffened even more and was as still as a statue.

There was a moment's silence during which the twins felt really uncomfortable. Had they made fools of themselves in front of a young gypsy fortune teller? No, course not. This person had spoken about Cloud Nine!

The young girl's eyes suddenly began to spark with different colours and her laughter filled the caravan.

"Of course it is I! Who else do you think would bring a gypsy caravan and two old reprobate horses along to a fair in this country at this time of the year. I've worked really hard to keep the rain away … did you not notice how unusually warm and bright it was today?"

Esme nodded slowly, remembering how 'taken' she was by the gentle breeze and autumn leaves. "I did." She moved to one of the sofas and tentatively sat down, perching on the edge.

Reuben relaxed slightly and joined his sister. But he was still anxious, remembering his first meeting with Old Woman. He wondered if she would suddenly change shape.

"No," she said aloud. "Whilst in a 'public' human place where other humans are likely to see me, I choose a suitable shape and stick to it. For instance, right now I look exactly like most humans imagine a 'gypsy fortune teller' should look … a very beautiful young woman with flashing eyes (she flashed them again for the twins), luxurious long hair (her hair changed from chestnut and curly to straight and black … and back to red and curly) and white, white teeth, and of course a frilly blouse and skirt!" As she said the last words she stood up, moved from behind the little table into the centre of the room and did a few twirls in front of the children.

"Aren't I just perfect!" she said laughingly before giving the twins a bow and returning to sit behind her table.

They too both burst out laughing, having completely lost their fear. There was something about this person that made them feel completely safe.

"Now, shut the door and come and sit down. Lock it please, I have things to tell you and we don't want any interruptions from fair goers wanting their fortunes told."

Reuben went to the door of the caravan, drew it shut and turned the large key already in the lock.

Esme suddenly made a grimace. "Mum and Dad are waiting for us by the car! They'll be worried if we're long ... "

"No problems! ... as you humans say. For them you will only have been absent for a few minutes."

Esme nodded, finding herself quickly drawn back into this other world of strange beings and happenings.

Once they were seated, Esme coughed slightly and asked in a rather embarrassed voice: "What do we call you? Old Woman just does not feel right when you look like this!"

The gypsy smiled and chuckled sympathetically. "Indeed, it doesn't. You can call me Mala – that's a good gypsy name." She tilted her head slightly to one side as though enquiring if they were happy with this.

Esme nodded slowly and Reuben shrugged in a 'whatever' sort of way.

"Right then, let us start." Mala shifted in her chair, breathed in deeply and looked intently into the eyes of first one and then the other of the children.

"You will not speak to others of what I tell you even when it might be difficult not to do so. This is really important, particularly ... at the beginning. Do you understand?"

The twins, both of whom had felt a strange calming sensation when Mala had looked into their eyes, nodded in unison.

And Mala began to tell them their story.

"Before you were born into your Esme and Reuben human bodies, your spirit-selves had to decide what they wanted your human-selves to do. The decision was taken that you had each reached the point in your development when you could be of great service to the human race and the planet upon which you all live. This was like recognising that as spirit-selves you had 'grown up'.
You were born as twins so that you could help each other right from the start ... as your lives would be full of surprises and challenges."

She told them many more things. The only things they remembered later was that they were somehow different from other children and had a very special task to carry out – a mission. And that would be shown to them step by step.

The twins then came out the trance Mala had put them under.
For a while they sat quietly, sipping at the cups of honey-tea she had given them. Then slowly their curious young minds woke up and started asking questions: who? what? how?

Reuben was the first to open his mouth: "How ... ?"

Mala shook her head gently. "No questions. Not now."

The dozens of questions and all the agitation that accompanied them slipped from their minds and the two children waited to see what more this amazing person was going to say.

"I am glad to see that you are wearing your amulets. These are a gift from those of us whose job it is to help you on your mission. They are made of a special metal that does not rust or tarnish and will let you know where it is if lost."

She paused as each child reached to touch the charm.

"Oh!" Esme had a flash of understanding: the walker who had given her the charms WAS Old Woman … in another disguise.

Mala nodded … and continued: "They are to be used if you wish to speak with me or my partner Young Man at any time … or if you are in danger. Do not use them unless it is exceedingly important or urgent. Do you understand?"

Two heads nodded gravely.

"To call us is very simple. All you have to do is rub the rounded surface gently with your thumb and you will see it begin to glow and shimmer. Hold it in front of your heart and call for one of us – or both."

She looked at Reuben quizzically and asked: "I expect Pegasus has taught you to 'thinkthink'?"

He nodded.

"Explain to your sister how thinkthink works ... sometime within the next few days."

She raised a finger as the twins glanced at each other. "But don't bother to use it when you are in 'everyday life'. It only works when you are about your special tasks."

"But ... how will I know if she's 'got it'... the thinkthink stuff?" quizzed Reuben anxiously.

"All you need to do is explain ... she will remember and know what to do when she needs to. Your sister has a very special memory."

"Please ... repeat to me what I told you about the amulets." she requested as soon as they had finished their drinks.

First Esme and then Reuben repeated what they had heard.

"Good!" said Mala. "Time for you to go. And ... you will have forgotten even these instructions by the time you reach your parent's car."

"But ...?" queried Esme, very aware of the bit Mala had said about 'being in danger'.

"Don't worry. You will remember when you need to."

She smiled so lovingly at them, that any fear they might have had disappeared.

They stepped out from the dim light of the ancient caravan into the autumn afternoon. They were startled to see that large black clouds were building up in the west, threatening to catch and gobble up the sun as it slowly sank behind the local hills. The wind too was no longer the gentle breeze of previously, but a wilder wind … bent on mischief! Both twins felt that mischief and shivered.

They jumped off the caravan's steps and were racing for the car park when Esme stopped so suddenly that Reuben colliding into her from behind.

"We haven't said goodbye to Pegasus and Mr Nibbs!"

"Oh no! Come on then," said Reuben, and they swivelled around to go back.

But the horses were no longer there … neither was the caravan.

"Oh … " exclaimed Esme.

"Look … up there!" Reuben whispered.

Esme looked to where Reuben was pointing and laughed. She waved at a vague shimmery shape in the sky. "That's how I saw him in the field that day."

They both then felt an answering 'wave' in the form of a tingly sensation all over their bodies.

"Come on, we'll get soaked!" yelled Reuben as a streak of lightening shot from the towering dark clouds, which by now were right overhead and letting loose big plump raindrops.

They reached the car and dived inside onto the back seat in a tangle of arms and legs just before the first crack of thunder heralded a heavy storm that was to last for several hours. The Choccies pushed noses against the mesh barrier that confined them to their compartment behind the back seats, whining a greeting to their children.

"Just in time!" said their mother, relieved to have them back so their father could manoeuvre the car over the wet grass before it got churned up into a mud slide.

They made their way slowly to the exit and managed to get out well ahead of most of the other cars. Some of these were not so lucky, slipping and sliding all over the place, some getting well and truly stuck in the mud.

"Haha … look … in that big car over there stuck in the mud. Haha, it's Peter!"

Both children giggled and Esme muttered under her breath so her parents wouldn't hear: "Hope he gets stuck for ever!"

It was the Peter from their school. His family were wealthy and kept several horses. The twins had often seen Peter at the local horse shows. He always rode a very expensive-looking and very beautiful dapple grey show pony. That was bad enough, but what made it worse was that he was a bad rider. He was constantly tugging at his pony's reins as she pranced nervously around. Jabbing at a pony's mouth like that was a sin in the eyes of the twins. They absolutely did not like Peter!

It wasn't far from the site of the fair to their house. Although it was still only late afternoon, within a few minutes of settling into the drive back home, both children were fast asleep. This was not like them at all. Usually they were almost too full of energy and would have been chatting and arguing non-stop about what they had seen.

Once again their parents were puzzled.

"Reminds me of that time some weeks ago. You know, after Reuben was bucked off by that brown pony that was in Mr Grubble's field for a few days … do you remember?" murmured Eve Montana to her husband.

Fonso, his mind already on the tasks that would need to doing when they got home, responded to his wife by nodding slowly. "Hm hm … you're right. Let's keep an eye on them."

With that nobody said anything more until they arrived home and the children had to be gently shaken awake. They stumbled silently out of the car, too tired even to eat any tea. They just found the energy to slurp down a glass of warm milk each before heading for bed. It had only just gone five o'clock.

Their parents let them go without questioning them.

"Just make sure you clean your teeth!" Eve called after them as they staggered up the stairs.
No reply. But a few moments later their mother heard the tap running in the bathroom. The twins had beautiful teeth, small, even and white – inherited from their father – and Eve wanted them to stay that way.

The next morning, energy recovered, the twins bounced into the kitchen, dressed for school and finishing off an animated conversation as they sat down at the table.

"So ... absolutely nobody, not even Rose!" finished off Reuben as he dug his spoon into a bowl of steaming porridge.

"Yep, I know!" replied Esme rather grumpily as she too turned her attention to her breakfast. "Wow I'm hungry!"

"I'm not surprised!" said their mother, taking this opportunity to question them about last night. "... not having any tea last night!"

At his mother's comment, Reuben paused from spooning porridge into his mouth and looked up. "Oh no … we didn't did we! No wonder we're hungry." Another couple of spoonfuls disappeared into his mouth before he continued. "I remember now. I was so tired I could hardly keep my eyes open."

"Me neither," agreed Esme.

"So … why were you so tired?" Their father asked as he joined them at the table, a steaming mug of black coffee clasped in his hands.

No reply.

Fonso took a cautious sip of the steaming liquid before repeating his question: "Why … so tired?"

"Dunno Daddy, we just were." Esme pushed her chair back and stood up. "Hurry up Reubs. We'll miss the bus!" She grabbed her bowl and took it to the sink.

"Not good enough!" Their father's firm voice broke their mad dash to get out of the house.

They came to a halt. A moment's silence before Esme spoke again, saying very brightly: "Perhaps we drank some cider instead of apple juice … by mistake." She could hear Reuben let out the breath he had been holding.

"Ah!" from their father.

"What!" Their Mother's startled voice.

Reuben, finally gathering his wits about him, continued where Esme had left off: "Honest, Dad! We didn't realise! At one of the stalls there were all these little plastic glasses on a tray. They were free ... people were just taking them. So we drank a couple each. Then the woman on the stall said they weren't meant for children."

"OK." Their father again. "So when was this, before or after you went to investigate that gypsy caravan?"

"Er ... " Reuben.

"Just before." Esme got the words in just as Reuben opened his mouth to answer. "Can we go now ... we'll miss the school bus!" She pleaded.

"Right. Off you go then. But we need to talk about why it's not a good idea for children to drink alcohol."

"OK Dad!" from them both in unison as they grabbed their school bags from the floor by the door, scuttled into the hallway and hurriedly pulled on their coats before dashing out of the side door, running down the path, out of the front gate and into the lane.

"What's the time Eve?"

"Just gone ten past eight." replied his wife.

"So … not late for the bus then!"

"No …" Eve Montana was looking very thoughtful and glanced at the glass door that led out to the garden behind which the three Labradors were trying desperately to gain attention. "And not even a word to Kimber or the dogs before they went. Odd … very odd. They seem their usual selves this morning though."

"They do. But like you said yesterday Eve, I have that same strange feeling I had with that pony affair."

His wife rubbed her hands over her face, pushing her hair back from her forehead before she said anything.
"Hmmm, you know Fonso, the more I think about it, the more I think something has changed with them since 'that pony'. They start talking about something and then suddenly stop. Then they go off into a huddle and speak very quietly – as though they don't want me to hear. And … " She paused again. "They're very possessive about those strange little charms they insist on wearing around their necks … well Reuben transferred his to a pin that he attaches to the inside of his trouser pocket … says boys don't wear charms around their necks. Don't you think that's odd?"

"Yes, it is a bit. But didn't they say it was something to do with a school project. Weren't you going to ask their teacher about it?"

"I was. But I never got around to it ... forgot all about it." Eve sighed. "Why are we worrying? We've got two healthy, bright kids, who seem to be very well adjusted and most of the time really enjoy life."

"Eve ... you're right!" Fonso gave his wife a hug. "I too need to get going. That new farm contract I've got starts today and I don't want to turn up late on the first day."

Eve was left sitting alone at the kitchen table. Despite what she had just said, she was puzzled. She really did see some sort of a change in her children ... but she just couldn't put her finger on what it was. And, equally strange was the fact that on every occasion she had been about to phone the school to ask about this 'project' the twins said was linked to the charms, something happened to distract her and she had completely forgotten about it.

She got up from the table. She'd do it right now. But before she could pick up the phone, there was a knock on the front door. As it was only strangers or the post woman who came to the front door, Mrs Montana went to answer it. And sure enough there was the post woman, holding out a parcel for her to sign for. Once again she completely forgot she had been going to phone the school!

"Phew, that was close! You were brilliant, Es!" Reuben affectionately punched his sister on the arm as they strolled slowly along the lane towards the road where the bus stopped.

"Well …" Esme hesitated slightly "The reason I said that is because I did try cider from one of those little plastic glasses!" She looked at the ground and aimed a half hearted kick at a stone in the road.

"You did?" Reuben's expression was a mixture of surprise and disgust. "Yuk, it tastes horrible!"

"How do you know?"

"I tried some once when Dad left some in a glass after some of his friends had been round. It was disgusting."

Esme fell about laughing.

9 - The Joker

Bonfire night was approaching fast!
For the last few years it had been the custom for Mr and Mrs Montana to let the village community use the field next to their house on the Saturday closest to the fifth of November. Though sometimes, if that Saturday was just too wet … it would be postponed until the following Sat.
A village Bonfire Committee organised the bonfire. People brought lots of fireworks and plenty of food for everybody.

All the children from the village looked forward to this event because they had a chance to run a bit wild. Nobody told them off for all the laughing and shouting as they rushed around the field like a herd of wild ponies. The flickering light of the noisy bonfire flames illuminated small groups chasing each other in games of tag. Dark places by the hedge shielded other groups, huddled secretly and plotting mischief of some sort.

The bonfire itself was huge! The villagers had started bringing wood into the field several weeks before the fifth of November and had thrown it in a heap just inside the field gate. There were all sorts: large tree branches, broken chairs, a cupboard without a door, wooden crates, and masses of smaller pieces of wood that the children had collected.

The day before the fire itself, the twins' father and a couple of his friends would drag all this into the centre of the field and expertly pile it up into a great circular tepee shape. It was a heavy task and took several hours. Fonso was very strict about what went where, several times ordering bits of the pile to be pulled apart and rebuilt. Although they grumbled rather a lot, his friends followed his directions. Alfonso Montana had a reputation as an expert fire builder.

A couple years ago, Reuben had asked his father why they didn't put all the wood in the middle of the field to start with!

"Because there are lots of little creatures that like to make their homes in amongst all the wood … "

"Aagh! … I see!" Reuben had got it - he was already imagining dozens of tiny creatures trying to escape death as their homes went up in flames.
At that moment he had felt strangely proud of his father. He had squeezed Fonso's hand tightly before rushing off to find Esme and tell her what he had just learned.

Each year, the local children made a Guy Fawkes just like they used to do when Mrs Montana had been a child. To make the body they stuffed old pillow cases with rags and straw and then fitted these into an old jacket and trousers. The Guy's head was made from a pumpkin that always had a slightly scary face surrounded by spiky straw hair.

On the afternoon of the bonfire, before it had begun to get dark, the children brought the Guy, sitting in a wheelbarrow, from the village to the field. This involved a procession accompanied by much noise and hilarity, with parents attempting half-heartedly to keep control of their rowdy excited children.

Once in the field, the Guy was attached to a wooden pole of some sort and then hoisted up to the very top of the bonfire. This too caused much laughter (as well as a few under-the-breath swearwords) as adults struggled with a Guy that seemed almost alive in its attempts to avoid being propped upright atop the mountain of wood.

A small child watching her father catch the body of the Guy as it toppled down yet again, piped up shrilly: "'Spect he knows he's gonna get burned!"

Reuben and Esme were expected to help. And although they did keep disappearing so they could join in with some of the games, they quite enjoyed having responsibility for their tasks. They helped set up the trestle tables that would hold lots of things to eat and drink. They made sure all the large rubbish and recycling bins were lined with black bags and had notices on them telling people where to put what.

The Choccies and Kimber had been safely shut in the living room of the house well before any of the villagers started arriving. Both children kept popping into the house to check on them though. They knew that only the most well prepared and best trained animals can cope with fire and loud noises. They had both watched in admiration videos of police horses and dogs being trained to ignore fire and loud bangs and just get on with their work.

Certainly the Montana family animals' reaction was pretty typical. As soon as the first firework was let off Kimber disappeared beneath the sofa, whilst Solo, Mowgli and Luca huddled together on top of it.

That Saturday evening was cold and bright. Esme thought how beautiful the star-studded sky looked! It was decorated with lots of little clouds scudding rapidly across it, pushed by a strong wind that could not be felt at ground level.

Once when she looked up, she thought she saw a cloud in the shape of a raggedy number nine rimmed with golden light ... but when she looked again it had changed into another shape. She remembered Reuben saying how Pegasus had called the clouds 'shifties'. She chuckled to herself and wondered if Old Woman was up there watching them.

Now, after everyone had had plenty to eat and drink, it was time to light the bonfire.

There was much cheering as Fonso circled the great stack of wood, ceremoniously pushing a flaming torch into the base of the stack – one in the South, one in the West, one in the North, and finally one in the East. Each time the flames caught, parents as well as children let out a cheer. Some of his friends even chanted "Fonso! ... Fonso!" and the twins felt really proud of their Dad.

As the fire took hold and climbed swiftly up the wooden mountain, fireworks of all sorts were let off. 'Oooohs and aaaahs' came from the crowd. It was getting very late by the time everyone now crowded around the fire waiting for the flames to reach the Guy perched on the very top.

Esme, who was standing with her friend Rose who had been driven over by her mother for the evening, watched as the first flames licked at the feet of the guy. A shiver flowed down her spine and she unexpectedly felt anxious.

Suddenly there was a very loud 'BANG'! The Guy had exploded and burst into thousands of sparks that flew everywhere.

There were more 'ooohs and aaahs' from all around.

But Esme heard one of the adults standing close by say: "What idiot put fireworks into the Guy! That's really dangerous!"

Then the 'ooohs and aaahs' changed from excited exclamations of delight into shouts of anxiety as people moved backwards to get further away from the falling sparks.

But the 'sparks' chased them!

Nearly everybody had at least one spark land on them somewhere, and people were brushing off their clothing to get rid of them. There were lots of cries of alarm and parents calling to their children. Slowly the sparks dispersed and people relaxed again to enjoy the warmth and flickering light of the now dying bonfire.

When the Guy had burst open and the sparks had flown out, Esme had exclaimed: "What's that!" to Rose.

Rose, herself staring intently at the bonfire, pulled a face and said in a very quiet little voice: "It's The Joker and some of the bumblewizards." She sighed and added: "I wondered when that lot would show up."

"It's what ... ?" Esme, eyes still on the fire, was about to ask her friend what she meant, when her attention was drawn to a sudden leap of the flames and what she later described as a strange 'jittery' noise coming from the bonfire.

She stood transfixed as she saw the shape of a figure made of coloured smoke emerge from the Guy.

This figure was very unpleasant! It had a pale face with very red cheeks, nose and chin, and a huge hooked nose and jutting chin. On its head was a funny hat with a bell attached to the pointy end that dangled down the side of its head. Attached to the figure's shoulders was a flowing black cape.

Esme was reminded of the Punch character on television Punch and Judy shows she had watched when she was younger. And even though it was made of smoke, it seemed very real ... and very scary!
And just like the TV Punch character, it wielded a huge stick. Esme shivered again and felt almost sick with fear when she realilsed the figure seemed to be shaking its stick directly at her!

Then as suddenly as it had appeared, the figure disappeared as the gout of smoke sank back down into charred and glowing remains of the guy. There were still some sparks though, sputtering and flying out from the fire.

Esme, aghast by what she had just seen, turned back to her friend, to ask what she had meant. But Rose was no longer there.

Where had Rose gone so suddenly? Esme was puzzled.

She looked around and spotted her friend standing on the opposite side of the fire. She started to shout out to her when she noticed something so odd about Rose that the name died to a whisper as Esme's wide open mouth closed ever so slowly. She blinked, once, twice. Then … the Rose she had been staring at on the other side of the fire was right back at Esme's side. But … this Rose was just her friend … not the Rose she had been gawping at a second before.

But what Esme had just seen remained imprinted on her mind! Her friend … her friend Rose … had looked SO STRANGE. She had looked HUGE … towering over the bonfire. And she seemed to be glowing in a pale unearthly sort of way.

In a flash, Esme's mind added up all sorts of 'odd' things she had noticed about her friend since she had first met her. And a thought just dropped into her mind that should have been really scary but wasn't.

Her friend Rose, her best friend since they had met about a year ago, was not human! As the thought hung there in her mind, her heart understood that it was true. A tingly sensation ran all around her body.

She took a sideways glance at Rose but didn't say anything … she didn't know what to say! How can you say to someone: "You're not human are you!"

Rose glanced back at her and smiled. Esme thought she was going to say something, but at that very moment an excited Reuben arrived and shoved himself between them.

Turning his back on Rose, he grabbed Esme by the arm and dragged her away from Rose. His voice was a loud whisper and full of alarm as he asked her; "did you see that?"

Esme, embarrassed at her brother's show of rudeness towards Rose, pushed him away from her. "Did I see what?"

"That weird horrible … 'thing' on top of the bonfire … ?"

"Yes I did. I'm glad you saw it too." Esme shivered. She had gone from feeling tingly all over to icy cold all over. "Did anybody else see it?"

"Dunno … haven't asked … came straight to you!" Reuben stared at the bonfire. "And look … all those sparks still coming out from the fire … must be 'spitty' wood in there!"

"Maybe ..." Esme paused, looking towards Rose again as she said rather hesitantly, "but I think they might not be sparks. I think they might be something called bumblewizards."

"Mumble whats?" Reuben screwed up his nose.

"Not 'mumble'... bumble ... bumblewizards."

"What are those?"

Esme waggle-waved her hands, scrunched up her shoulders and shook her head violently and said through clenched teeth. "I don't know!" She motioned towards Rose. "Ask Rose. It's what she said!"

"Rose ... ?"

Rose had remained standing where she was. Her attention had been split between observing the twins and observing everything else that was happening.

As Reuben was considering what his sister had just said, Rose pointed and said urgently: "Careful ... look!"

The twins turned to follow her pointing finger and saw that one of the 'sparks' was heading straight for them ... followed by another.

That was when it became obvious that the 'sparks' were not just 'sparks being blown on the wind'.

They were 'sparks' that knew exactly where they were going!

The one in the lead landed on Reuben's woolly hat. There was the sound and smell of singeing. The second one landed on the sleeve of Esme's coat. However, before either child could make a move to brush away the 'sparks' Rose had made a strange motion with her hands, and the 'sparks' had flown off.
She had not said anything as she did this but she was looking at Esme very intently.

Esme looked as though she wanted to say something, but instead suddenly announced: "I'm going inside." Without another word, she turned and set off towards the house.

Reuben, who felt very uncomfortable, marched over to his sister's friend and stared at her questioningly. He demanded aggressively: "Go on then, tell me what you said to Esme!"

Before Rose had a chance to reply, one of Reuben's friends rushed up and grabbed his arm, yelling "Come and help Reubs. They want us to clear the table and ... there's burgers going spare!"

Reuben hesitated. She lifted her chin at him as if telling him to go with his friend. He allowed himself to be dragged away, but not without glancing over his shoulder and glaring pointedly at the still silent Rose.

The girl stood very still for a moment before letting out a great sigh and walking off towards all the adults.

Esme, whose heart was thumping wildly, unlocked the kitchen door, and went straight to the living room. She wanted the comfort of her animals. And they all seemed to know that she was in need of comforting. Luca got down from the sofa and made space for her between the other two. She flopped down between Mowgli and Solo and leant her head on the back of the sofa. Kimber slunk out from beneath the sofa, jumped up onto her knee and then climbed up to sit on the back of the sofa close to her head. Luca plumped his head on her knees, staring up at her face with his most 'hangdog' expression ever, turning his face into a picture of forlornness.

She half laughed and half cried as she stroked them all and whispered '*thank you*' to them.

"What is this all about … what is going to happen next?" she murmured to herself.
The four animals sent her huge waves of 'comfort energy'. It washed over her, and in no time at all she was asleep.

And that is where her father found her some time later: surrounded by the three dogs and with Kimber stretched out on her front, one paw on each shoulder and his head tucked under her chin.
He gently moved the four animals from around his daughter, somehow knowing deep within himself that they had been protecting her from … some-

144

thing. He had no idea what that 'something' could be though.

Shushing a curious Reuben who had poked his head around the door, he lifted the deeply asleep Esme into his arms and took her upstairs to her own bed.

10 - Dogs in Trouble

Esme awoke very late the following morning. She opened her eyes to bright sunlight but struggled to wake properly, so entangled was she with a dream. But try as she might she couldn't catch any of it. The dream kept slipping away from her as she tried to re-enter it so she could remember properly. All she was left with was a horrible feeling of anxiety and a very vague sense of being chased by something … something in the sky. And then … finally she caught hold of a dream fragment … Not good! She had been chased! She had been chased by a cloud … a great black thunder cloud.

Not something she wanted to catch any more of! She scrambled quickly out of bed in an attempt to shake off the scary feeling.

And indeed … a few moments later the feeling was gone as her ears picked up the chit chat from downstairs and her nostrils opened to the smell of Sunday breakfast.

And then all the memories from the previous evening came rushing back to her!

She dressed hurriedly without getting washed and half fell down the stairs in her eagerness to speak with her brother.

Reuben was already halfway through his breakfast as Esme exploded into the kitchen, gave her mother a hurried greeting, and wriggled into the chair next to her brother, whispering as she did so: "Last night ... do you remember ... the weird bits I mean?"

Reuben continued spreading a thick layer of jam on his toast. "Weird? You mean like Rose?"

"No!" Esme looked at him sharply as he took a huge bite of toast. She wasn't ready to tell her suspicions about Rose to her brother. Then: "I 'spose she is a bit odd ... different anyway," she conceded. "But I meant the other stuff ... you know ... those sparks?"

"Yeah, I remember the sparks ... one landed on my hat and burnt it. And ... I remember the guy kind of exploded. That wasn't weird though. Dad said some idiot must have put fireworks inside it."

Esme remained silent as she thought about his answer. Apparently her brother had not seen the horrible figure that had emerged from the exploding guy. 'The Joker', Rose had called it.
"Did you dream last night?" She questioned him.

"Uh uh." He shook his head.

"I did, but I can't remember it properly. Just that it was scary and had something to do with being chased by a cloud ... a big black thunder cloud."

On hearing this, Reuben stopped chewing and looked at her. "A bully cloud, " he murmured to himself as he remembered Pegasus going on about the unreliability of clouds in general, and about the bullying behaviour of some clouds that had started happening recently.

"A what cloud?"

"A bully cloud." It was too complicated to explain bully clouds right now. "Aren't you hungry?" he asked his sister, changing the subject. Her plate was still empty of any of the delicious food on offer.

"Yeah ... I am. But... no I'm not actually." She suddenly became aware of just how unsettled she felt after remembering bits of the dream.

"Okay. But have some breakfast and then we can talk." Reuben had begun to think maybe something 'weird' had happened last night. He did remember noticing that all the stars suddenly disappeared when the Guy had exploded. He'd thought it was just the smoke from the bonfire.

At that very moment they heard their father's voice from outside the kitchen.

"Get inside! All of you inside!" He was clearly angry.

He flung open the kitchen door and repeated: "Inside!"

The three Labradors came through the open door, hustling and shoving each other in order to obey Fons. Their tails were between their legs and their heads held low.

"To your beds!" Fons yelled at the dogs, pointing to the corner of the kitchen where their beds were positioned. "Those ****** dogs!"

Their father swearing …wow! The twins pulled faces at each other. What had the dogs done?

Fons continued: "Anybody would think we didn't feed them!"

Eve Montana, sitting in one of the kitchen armchairs reading the Sunday newspaper, looked up startled. It was a rare thing for Fons to shout in anger.

"What have they done?"

"Emptied all the bins … rubbish all over the field. Would you believe it … they've pulled out all but one of the bags from the bins. I know Labs are greedy, but that beats the biscuit!"

The twin's father turned to them and said brusquely "You two. Finish your breakfast and come out and help me clear up. There's a wind getting up and the rubbish will blow everywhere."

Twins looked at each other and groaned … clearing up the rubbish could take ages and they wanted to talk about last night.

Fons then turned to Reuben: "Did you do what I asked and put the lids on the bins before you came in last night?" He stared accusingly at his son.

"Aagh! Maybe not … can't remember." Reuben looked embarrassed.

His Father grunted in displeasure. "That means you didn't! Tell you what then … you do the clearing up - by yourself!"

Eve Montana gave a big sigh. She folded the newspaper she was obviously enjoying reading. "No Fons. Let's all do it before the wind takes it off into the village."

"Thanks Mum," said Reuben.

Esme kicked him under the table. "It's OK Mum, I'll help him," she said and made a quizzical face at Reuben. He realised immediately. Of course, if they were on their own then they could talk about last night.

"You sure?" their Mother asked.

"Yep … we'll be fine," they chorused.

Their mother smiled in gratitude and opened up her newspaper.

Kimber had been snoozing on Solo's bed. Normally Kimber was 'King of the Beds', choosing whichever bed he preferred at the time, with the three dogs sharing the two remaining beds between them.
Today though he was uprooted by the dogs' sudden arrival. So chastised were they that they almost fell on him in their rush to obey Fons.

The old cat hissed in defiance as he sprang up from between the three doggy forms and landed hunch-backed on the old kitchen tiles, fur along his back standing up on edge in shock. But he quickly lowered his hackles and to show his disdain for their rudeness he cat-stretched with exquisite slowness, and then sauntered casually over to the tiles to jump up onto the empty seat next to Esme.

"Silly old dogs," Esme reached out to stroke the cat as he began to perform an elaborate cleaning ritual.

'Silly indeed!' hissed Kimber in between licks to the paw used to clean his whiskers.

Esme removed her hand from his back, startled. She looked at him intently but he just continued cleaning his whiskers.

Had she heard Kimber speak? No, surely not; she must have been imagining it. But then again … maybe not. She had been able to understand what Mouse ThreeMillionSix had said, hadn't she!

She went back to finishing off her bowl of cereal before joining Reuben in the hallway to get outdoor clothing.

Neither child noticed as Kimber followed them from the house, sauntering along a few feet behind them and slithering under the bottom rung of the gate into the field. They climbed over it, balancing on the top rung and surveying the litter-scattered field in front of them.

"Oh boy! What a mess they've made. They don't usually do this to the bins!"

"Perhaps it's because there were lots of bones from the Barbeque in the bins?"

"I 'spose ... " Esme still wasn't convinced. "Anyway, let's clear up really quickly so we can talk about last night."

"Okay." Reuben jumped down from the gate and shot off towards the furthest bin.

Esme followed her brother more slowly. She stood still for a moment, aware of some sounds that weren't usually part of the 'field sounds'. She was reminded of a group of old people cackling with shrieky laughter.

She turned slowly in a circle trying to identify where the vaguely familiar noise was coming from. Her eyes moved upwards and ... there they were! Perched on the guttering of the roof, four beautiful shiny black crows.

Just like the ones Reuben had been so excited to see in the ring of mushrooms a few weeks ago. The children had taken many photographs of them over the summer. So Esme was very familiar with them.

But today there was something different about them ... she could feel it.

They were all facing in her direction. And they were … laughing! She was convinced that the loudly cackle-cawing that clearly did come from them was laughter. Yes, they were laughing at her!

At that moment she felt Kimber brush against her legs. She looked down, bent to stroke him and said: "What are they laughing at? Do you know Kimber?"

She hadn't really expected a reply. But she got one.

'Of course they laugh! A merry trick they have played.'

 Esme 'heard' Kimber's 'voice' as a kind of hissy purr. The sound had a very 'superior' feel to it. Quickly getting over the surprise of hearing crows laugh at her and Kimber speak to her (after all communicating with beings other than humans had been happening more and more frequently), she wanted to know more.

She squatted down next to Kimber and asked him what the merry trick was.

'Getting those silly dogs their come uppance!'

Esme was aware the Kimber – well cats in general – considered themselves greatly superior to dogs. But to hear the disdain in Kimber's words was quite a shock. She decided she would ask him about that at some point in the future. But right now she wanted to know more about the merry trick.

"What do you mean?"

'Rubbish!'

She was just about to ask the cat what was rubbish, when she suddenly got it. It was the crows, not the dogs, that had pulled all the rubbish out of the bins!

Ah! An image came into her mind from a TV programme she had seen about clever animals. It had actually shown a family of crows working together and using their beaks and claws to lift out black bags from rubbish bins and tip the contents onto the ground. They certainly were clever.

And the dogs had been blamed! No wonder the crows were sitting up on the roof laughing. Poor Choccies ... not fair... she thought to herself.

'Very fair!' Kimber's reply was rapid ... he had obviously picked up on her thoughts.

"Oh ... I see! I suppose they are getting their own back for all the times the dogs have chased them off the field." Esme thought to Kimber. He nuzzled her hand to agree.

"But ... why tell me Cat?" She squatted down and grasped his little black face tightly in both her hands, looking fiercely straight into his golden yellow eyes. "You ... cat ... don't like the dogs ... I get that."
Esme had a strange sensation as she spoke these words. Somehow her relationship with Kimber had changed in that moment. He was no longer her

'pet'. He was another 'being' that she could communicate with … a sort of 'equal'.

Kimber, disconcerted by the unexpectedly rough handling by his favourite human, hissed loudly and wriggled his head free from Esme's grasp before responding in rapid thoughtforms:

'Not for dogs … for you … so you understand … you … other humans … your brother … much to learn. Old Woman says to help. Thus … I help!' He stared at Esme for a few seconds, his eyes round and wide in challenge, before very slowly narrowing them in a gesture of goodwill.

"Oh gosh," breathed Esme. She reached to stroke the cat, but Kimber gave himself a shake and turned his back on her to stalk off towards the house, still full of offended dignity about the way his 'friend' had grabbed and squashed his face.

"Okay … sorry" Esme murmured to his straight-up tail, which gave the very slightest of twitches to show he had heard.

She stood up and started giggling. This is all just crazy! Or … am I crazy? She had remembered the feeling she had felt about Rose the night before: that her best friend wasn't human. Crazy all right! She needed to tell it all to Reuben.

And just as she thought of him he yelled at her to come and help … for goodness sake!

"Coming." She ran over to one of the upended bins and started collecting up all the spilled rubbish. Yuk, she thought ... I should have put some rubber gloves on to do this.

When they had completed their task, the twins headed for the goat shed where it was nice and warm and nobody could see them.
They settled down in the clean straw.

Esme started off by telling her brother about the strange and very scary apparition she had seen the Guy turn into when it had exploded.

"I didn't see that!" Her brother made one of his 'are you sure?' faces. "All I saw were those sparks that almost seemed to chase people ... like those that landed on my hat and your sleeve. Rose said something about them but I didn't hear properly ... ?"
He looked questioningly at his sister.

For some reason Esme was reluctant to tell her brother what Rose had said and tried to brush the question off.

But Reuben insisted: "It was something about Mumble ... no ... bumble ... bumble bees! That was it wasn't it. Didn't look much like bumblebees to me!" He snorted in disdain.

Esme sighed, knowing she'd have to tell him. "No Reuben. It wasn't bumble bees. Rose called the strange Guy thing that I saw 'The Joker', and said the sparks were 'bumble wizards'. And she said that she had been wondering how long it would be before they turned up! There! Now you know!"

Reuben burst out laughing. "Bumble wizards … The Joker! Why do you believe what she says! She's always making things up!" This was true. In the time she had been around, Rose had got herself a bit of a reputation for telling strange stories. Esme had always thought that her friend just had a very vivid imagination … something Esme rather admired.

Now, she wasn't so sure what she thought. Except that Reuben's response didn't encourage her to tell him her thoughts about Rose not being human! She didn't like keeping secrets from her brother. Usually he was the one person she could share everything with. But on this occasion …

They then spent some time going over all the things that had been happening to them since that time Reuben had decided to ride the scruffy brown pony, Mr Nibbs. That first meeting with Mr Nibbs had turned everything upside down. Life was no longer as it used to be. It was part exciting and part very uncomfortable. Not only did they never know what to expect, there was nobody except each other they could tell about … anything! Who would believe them!
And I can't even tell Reuben about what I think about Rose! Esme thought to herself and sighed deeply.

As they talked, they realised that they each felt 'different' from how they had felt a few months ago … sort of 'older'.

"I feel like we've been given a big responsibility ... for things I don't understand." Esme tried to explain her feeling.

"Hmm ... yeah. Es, that's a really good description!" For once Reuben completely agreed with his sister. "And it's sort of exciting and scary at the same time."

Esme nodded. "It is! And what I really don't like is having to tell fibs to Mum and Dad. Like the charms ... I'm sure Mum doesn't believe what we told her! And how do we explain to them that the Choccies are not to blame for tipping out the rubbish?" She paused and then went on quickly: "Because I don't want them to be punished for something they didn't do!"

"What do you mean they didn't do it?" Reuben looked at her sharply.

"It was the crows." Esme realised she hadn't yet said anything about that to her brother. There were so many other strange happenings to be talked about.

"Really? ... oh ... right." A pause. "Okay, let's say that we saw the crows pulling at one of the black bags ... " Another, longer, pause as Reuben looked thoughtfully at his sister who had one of her 'I know something you don't' look on her face. "But hang on, how do you know it was the crows?"

"Kimber told me."

"He spoke to you?"

"Sort of ... in cat language ... and I understood him."

"Can you understand the Choccies?"

"I don't know ... I've never tried ... can you?"

"Same as you ... never tried."

Both children lapsed into silence for several moments before Esme said: "Why is this happening to us? Do you think we have super powers ... there's lots of programmes on TV about humans with super powers."

"Dunno ... " Reuben shook his head and shrugged. "I 'spose sometimes 'things' just happen. Maybe understanding what animals are saying is a sort of super power?"

"Suppose so ... "

Neither child felt very satisfied with that answer. But before they could discuss it any further, they heard their father calling them in for lunch.

They were surprised. Surely they hadn't been outside that long! But tummy rumbles at the mention of 'lunch' assured them it was indeed time for some food.

Back inside the kitchen, lovely aromas greeted them as well as grateful thanks from both their parents.

Esme told them she thought the dogs were innocent ... how she and Reuben had seen she crows picking at a black bag and how that had reminded her of a TV programme about clever crows.

Reuben kept nodding his agreement. "Honest Dad ... I saw that programme too."

Their father looked doubtfully at the three dogs. Their mother gave her support to the twins: "They're right Fons. Crows are known to be very clever, especially when it comes to finding food."

Both children sighed gently, letting out their tension as the explanation was accepted by their parents.

The Choccies were then made a great fuss of with lots of apologies ... They tentatively wagged tails and then slowly began to stand up, all the while watching Fons warily. All morning he has been insistent they stay on their beds, glowering at them each time they moved so much as a paw.

Both children 'felt' the doggie thank yous.

11 - A Nightmare

A couple of weeks after bonfire night and the incident with 'The Joker' and the bumblewizard things, Esme met The Joker's master for the first time.

It was in a dream.

She was walking along the grassy path that led to her dreamtime house. It was a bright sunny day. Her dreamtime animals came running to meet her. he and the black horse, the black dog, and the rather strange-looking black leopard were delightedly greeting each other with pats, strokes and nuzzles. They mussed up of each other's hair and fur, and made a variety of 'it's-so-good-to-see-you' noises.

Esme wondered where her Golden Eagle Gyrre was and expected the great bird to appear any minute.

They were standing a little way off from the entrance to the house's garden when a huge great thunder cloud appeared on the horizon. Although Esme vaguely noticed the cloud, she was much too busy catching up with Torrela, BlackJack, and Esmeralda to really take notice of it. If she thought anything, it was that the cloud was just a summer storm brewing in the distance. She certainly hadn't noticed that it was travelling at tremendous speed in their direction.

All of a sudden a lightning flash shot from the cloud's centre, and this was followed a few seconds later by a clap of thunder so loud it made Esme and her three animal friends quite literally jump in fright. Before they realised what was happening, lightning was shooting all over the place, whilst driving rain and hail stones were being flung in their direction ... even though there was no wind!

Esme and the animals ran towards the shelter of the barn in the orchard at the back of the house; the animals slowing their pace so that she could keep up with them.
But the cloud was upon them before they were even half way there. It surrounded them, its foggy body preventing them from seeing where they were going.

Esme was scared stiff. She stopped running and just stood there with her shoulders hunched up around her ears, head bent forward and her hands covering the top of her head as the power of the cloud engulfed her.

Torrela reared high, lashing out with her front legs and neighing loudly.

Blackjack stood squarely on stiff legs, his hackles raised, barking harshly.

Emeralda crouched down, green eyes flashing, tail lashing, lips drawn back in a snarl.

It felt to Esme as though the cloud was purposely reaching out to touch her with its swirling stormy fingers and breath. She suddenly remembered what Reuben had told her Pegasus had said about 'bully' clouds. This must be one, she thought as she felt herself being buffeted around.

An extra strong gust of moist air pushed her flat to the ground. Lifting her head and protecting her eyes with her hand, she squinted through her fingers, hoping to see a way out from under the cloud.

But what she saw frightened her even more.

Looming over her, in the centre of the cloud was a giant swirling figure in a huge storm-grey hooded cloak. She could see a horrible monster face – a giant mouldy potato covered in knobbles and with potato 'eyes' forming its eyes, nostrils and mouth.
The lightening streaks came from its eyes, and the thunder claps sounded every time it opened its mouth, and the drenching rain and hail were pouring from its nostrils.

She quickly covered her eyes again, wishing she hadn't seen it.

Another strong gust of wind rolled her over onto her back.
Abruptly she was enveloped in the same 'hairs standing on end' feeling that she had experienced that time when it felt like there was an evil presence in the meeting room of her dream house.
The feeling seemed to concentrate itself in her chest and she felt her heart begin to beat wildly. Unthinkingly she reached to cover her pounding heart with her hands. As she did this she touched the amulet she was wearing around her neck. The amulet that the gypsy Mala had told her to keep on her always!

Esme remembered Mala had said to rub is she ever needed help!

She rubbed it frantically and whispered, almost to herself, more a question than a request: "Help ... ?"

Almost as soon as she had whispered the word, the wind died down, the rain and hail changed to drizzle, and the thunder claps and lightning flashes stopped.
At the same time, two shapes appeared high up in the distant sky. Both were moving rapidly towards the place where the thundercloud was situated. One was much bigger than the other – absolutely huge compared to its tiny speck of a companion.

Whatever they were, they were both flying incredibly fast, speeding down towards the thunder cloud.

Esme, still lying on her back with her left hand covering her tight closed eyes, and finger and thumb of her right hand rubbing the charm, was not aware of this. But she was aware that her hairs were no longer standing on end and the beat of her heart had slowed down.

Closer and closer came the shapes.

Had she been looking, Esme would have been able to make out their forms.
She would probably have recognised the smaller creature as it sped past the place where the larger creature had come to a hovering halt in the bright blue sky above the thunder cloud. And she would

have seen flashes of blue-green light coming from the larger creature.

She might, just might, have heard a cry of greeting from the smaller creature as it overtook the larger and continued its downward flight, plummeting right into the centre of the thundercloud.

She would have seen the larger creature send forth what seemed to be a huge golden flame straight at the cloud.
The first 'flame' was followed by second.
And a third.

Had she been looking – but she wasn't – she would have recognised the shape of Gyrre, her Golden Eagle companion, appearing in a sudden break in the cloud's darkness as this was pierced by the golden light.

But … she did hear an eagle-scream as Gyrre swooped towards the eyes of the face in the cloud. Had she been watching, and it was s shame she wasn't, the girl would have seen her winged companion brake speed and push forth his great talons straight into the monster's eyes.

As the eagle's talons sunk into the monster's eyes, first the face, and then the whole cloaked figure began to disappear, sucked into the great hole that was its mouth.
In a moment nothing was left of the monstrous thundercloud – no rain, no hail, no foggy tendrils … just the tiniest white cloud floating alone high in the bright blue sky.

The larger flying creature that had sent forth the flames continued hovering for a while. Then it turned and flew off in the direction it had come.

Of course Esme did not see any of this. But she could feel the rain, wind and hail had stopped pummelling her. And she could clearly hear the familiar harsh eagle chirrup of her winged companion.

Slowly she got up from where she had been pushed into the ground. She stood trembling, looking around the animals. All were standing close by, each looking as exhausted as Esme was feeling.
Gyrre, who had alighted on a tree branch some distance away, left the branch and glided over to her and very gently settled on her shoulder, wings slightly open so that he didn't need to clutch his human friend's shoulder with his great talons in order to balance. His powerful hooked beak nibbled very gently at Esme's ear and then plucked at strands of her hair. Somehow he conveyed to her what he and the other creature had done.

Esme whispered 'thank you!' to the eagle and then turned to check that Torrela, Blackjack and Esmeralda were all OK.

The three were standing very close to each other and she had a sense of them all saying 'Phew … that was close!'

She also had the strange feeling that her dreamtime animal companions knew more about what had just happened than she did!

And at that very moment Gyrre sent a long stream of thought-pictures into her mind. She wasn't able to interpret them all. But she was able to comprehend something about *'the MMMM having noticed that she was 'awake' and using a cloud monster to frighten her so she would 'obey' him ... because 'awake' humans have 'powers' that he wanted to use ... and that she would need to keep vigilant.'*

She was trying to make sense of this rather scary information when another stream of Gyrre's thought-pictures entered her mind: *'He would fly with her constantly from now on, even in the daytime ... she would not often be able to see him, but he would be there. And Et-Evora would always be within calling distance.'*

She was about to ask the Eagle who or what the MMMM and Et-Evora were when something woke her up.

She was drenched in sweat and trembling all over. For a few moments she just lay still, breathing hard without moving and slowly recognising her surroundings and realising she was safe. She was in her bed in her home, coming into her daytime reality.

"Write it down ... now" she muttered to herself.

She managed to sit up and lean over to open the drawer in her bedside table where she kept a pencil and a little book with 'Dreams' written on its cover.

It took her almost an hour to write out all she could remember of the dream. By the time she had finished she was feeling very chilly and very hungry. But she was glad she had done it; it was so easy to forget the detail of dreams, and she was absolutely sure this one was very important.

She'd tell Reuben about it, of course, but not today, she didn't think. She needed to keep it to herself for a while. She knew that, sometimes, if you share dreams, or other 'magic' happenings too early, they lose their power.

Noise from the kitchen below was what had woken her. She dressed and slowly made her way downstairs for breakfast, still feeling exhausted, and hoping she wouldn't be questioned about how she was feeling.

But she was able to slip into her place at the table without anybody taking any notice other than to say a quick 'morning'. A friend of Fonso's had dropped by and there was much hilarious laughter as the three adults discussed one of Farmer Grubble's latest escapades. And although Reuben glanced at her, he too was completely taken up by the story being told.

12 - Just Who *is* Rose?

Esme was excited. Her friend Rose was coming over to spend the day and have a sleep over. They hadn't seen each other since bonfire night and Esme was hoping to get a chance to talk to Rose about what had happened on that night.

She was even hoping to pluck up the courage to ask her 'where she came from'. Funny how this didn't seem such a strange thing to ask her friend now that she herself had had some very odd experiences. She guessed that if she told any of her other friends about any of the things that had happened to her and Reuben over the last few weeks, they would think she was just making it up.

Ever since bonfire night Esme had been remembering odd things about Rose that she had not really taken any notice of before. Things like the way her very fair hair seemed almost to glow when there was not much light around. Her eyes were a very unusual colour too – a sort of pale violet. And, thought Esme to herself, it was most peculiar how the Choccies were with Rose. They seemed very wary of her, not barking and rushing up to greet her like they did to other of the twins' friends, but drooping their tails and sticking close to Esme and Reuben.

Esme had seen this behaviour of theirs on several occasions and noticed how Kimber was just the opposite. He showed his superior cat self with most people by totally ignoring them. But when Rose was around he sat up, preened himself and smiled at her, sometimes even winding his sinuous black body and tail around her legs.

Rose herself didn't appear to take any notice of either the dogs or the cat.

It was about mid morning when Rose arrived. Her Mother had driven her over and was in the kitchen chatting with Mrs Montana, whilst the twins took Rose into the living room. The wood-burning stove had been lit especially for the children and was giving off a bright glow in the cosy room. Some 'elevenses' had been set out for them – hot drinks and biscuits.

Esme had asked Reuben to stay at home with her and Rose, instead of going off to visit one of his own friends. She was hoping that that if he got to know more about her, he wouldn't dislike her so much.

Each of the twins had their own friends, but Esme had been troubled by a nagging feeling that it was important for Reuben to be friends with Rose. She couldn't fathom out why ... but had a tiny inkling that Rose's strangeness was somehow linked with Pegasus and Old Woman.

The three of them settled down and tucked into the elevenses. Nobody was saying much.

The girls knew that something important was to be talked about, but weren't sure how to start the conversation.
Reuben was just feeling uncomfortable.

Esme decided to go for it: "Rose, you remember what happened on bonfire night?"

Rose nodded and looked at her friend encouragingly.

Esme's words tumbled out. "Well, you said something about ... about a ... Joker? ... and ... 'bumblewizards'?" Confusion and anxiety showed on her face. She hesitated for several moments before adding. "And you um ... you ... did something. You looked ... er ... different ... and it looked almost as though you - that different you - put the fire out! You know, after that horrible creature appeared ... so ... um ... ?" Esme's sentence ground to a halt and she shuffled uncomfortably on her cushion.

Reuben seemed more preoccupied by hot chocolate and biscuits than what his sister was saying. Rose smiled slightly as Esme struggled to continue with what she still had to say. But by now Esme felt stupid! "Um ... Oh I dunno ...'spose I just imagined it!" She pulled a face and fell silent.

"What did you imagine? Go on, tell me."

Esme squirmed nervously and finally said: "I know it sounds daft but ... you seemed to move from by my side to the fire and then back again ... without actually moving ... something like that? And ... a thought came into my head ... " Esme's words petered out again.

Rose continued smiling and asked quietly: "And what was that thought?"

By this time Reuben was paying close attention, his hand holding half a biscuit poised to be dunked into his mug of hot chocolate.

Esme had never felt so uncomfortable in her life! She was sweating and even beginning to feel a little scared. Her 'friend' suddenly seemed to be a complete stranger ... not even a child any more, but somebody utterly different to her usual self.

Despite feeling more scared by the minute, Esme found she couldn't help herself. She took a deep breath and then spat it out: "I thought you weren't human!" She gulped, sitting tensely and waiting for Rose to say something.

And with the gentle smile still on her face, Rose said: "You were right. I am not human."

Reuben's biscuit dropped from his fingers into the hot chocolate. He spluttered: "What ... !"

"But I am a friend. And I am here to help you – both of you ... " Rose looked pointedly at Reuben.

Neither twin said anything, eyes wide and glued to Rose.

"There is something that you must begin to understand. It might be difficult. But it is important that you are willing to accept that what I say might be true." As she said this, Rose – Esme's 'friend' – began to glow gently and become larger.

The twins were transfixed … unable to move. They just stared.

"This is who I truly am," said the Rose who was now looking rather like a 'human-shaped' rainbow whose colours were constantly shifting. "Don't be frightened. I am what is known as a Light Being. There are many of us on Earth at this time. I come from a distant planet."

She noted that both children blinked very rapidly and Esme crept out her hand to touch Reuben's. Instead of moving his hand away, he clasped at his sister's, letting out the breath he had been holding in as he did so.

"We are here to help humans understand the changes that will be happening during these times, for there are many. Some of the things that you humans will experience will feel scary unless you understand that they are just a part of changes that need to happen."

She paused to give the two children time to take in what she had said. She noted with satisfaction the intense concentration showing on their faces.

She continued: "So far there are very few humans who are able to understand any of this, or who are even willing to hear about it. And many of these are children – like you.

You are beginning to 'awaken' – as we call it – to what you truly are. You are so much more than you think! And there is so much more happening on Earth than you think … so much more than the great masses of humanity are aware of."

Esme and Reuben hadn't moved, hands still clasped and eyes still fixed on Rose.

In fact, though they were completely unaware of it, they had been entranced! 'Rose' had put them into a state better able to receive all the information she was giving to them.

"There are many things that will be changing … " Rose went on speaking.

But she now spoke very rapidly and in a language they would not have understood had they been in their normal state. She was uploading a huge amount of information into their minds ... just like you do with a computer! However, they would re-member none of it until the time was right for them to do so. And she was pouring Love and comfort into their hearts. This would give them the strength and courage they would need.

The strange words she used could more or less be translated in this way: "*We – those of us whose job it is to aid this Earth-changing process - need those humans who are already 'awakening' to help other humans to 'wake up' and understand what is happening … so that they in their turn can do the same again.*"

The information that 'Rose' gave them entered their minds mostly in images that told a whole 'story', plus a few key words.

"This task is being asked of you now that you have had your 10th birthday, and it is something you both agreed do before you were born. You have known each other for a very, very long time, and your Souls agreed to be born as twins so that you could help each other."

As she said this, Rose smiled lovingly and reached out to touch each twin gently on the middle of the forehead. "But for now that is enough!"

As once again both children blinked rapidly and took several deep breaths, the rainbow form of herself that 'Rose' had shown them quickly dimmed and she changed back into the Rose that they both recognised.

This Rose clapped her hands and shivered. "Ooh, I'm hungry!" she exclaimed, as she reached for a biscuit and her mug of hot chocolate.

The twins both shook their heads several times as though trying to get rid of an insect that had landed on their hair. They looked at each other wordlessly. Then they noticed they were holding hands. Reuben snatched his hand from his sister's as though it had burnt him, and Esme looked at her brother with a 'what the ... ?' expression on her face and then shrugged.

"Lesson finished for today," grinned Esme's-friend-Rose.

And without giving Esme or Reuben a chance to say anything, she clapped her hands once and continued: "But … there are all sorts of practical things that you two will need to do that most of your friends would find very odd. Like right now … I have a feeling that there is a something in your garden that needs attending to. Let's go … "

But Esme had something important to ask her 'friend'. She found her tongue and interrupted her friend: "But Rose, can we still be just 'friends'? You know, like we have been 'til now?"

Rose smiled warmly before she replied slowly. "Well … maybe not quite the same. You know who I am now! But almost the same if you want. We can still do human children things together. I really enjoy those sort of things … and remember my 'mother' is human. She doesn't know who I truly am … she just thinks I can be a little strange. She 'adopted' me you know when I was in my 'baby form'."

Once again, the twins gazed at this Being-who-looked-like-Esme's-friend-Rose with astonishment. How was it possible that Rose's mother didn't know that 'her daughter' was not human!

Reuben gulped, and Esme realised that her brother had been quite right when he thought that Rose was weird.

Rose stopped speaking and moved her hands to tell them to 'wait'. "Oh … I forgot to say … you can't tell anybody else about me. In fact you won't be able to tell anyone else about me! Do you understand?"

The expressions on the twins' faces showed their bewilderment about the situation they now found themselves in.
In fact, Reuben had already been imagining what it would be like to be surrounded by a group of admiring school friends as he told them he was friends with an Alien!

Rose shook her head and chuckled, clearly aware of this temptation.

"Because I know how difficult that would be for you both, especially you Reuben, I used a little 'enchantment' just now during the lesson I was giving you, to prevent that from happening. If you forget and start to tell anybody about what has happened or will happen in the future, you will just start coughing until the urge to tell had gone away!"
Disappointment showed on Reuben's face; relief on Esme's – who had also wondered if she would be able to keep such an amazing secret!

"Sorry … but it's got to be like that. Can you imagine what people would think of you if you actually started telling them you had a friend who was 'an alien' – for indeed that is the name that Earthlings have for those like me? And, what do you think would happen to me?" She raised her eyebrows.
"Oh, and one more thing: I would prefer it if you didn't think of me as an 'Alien'. That word brings

to human's minds fearful thoughts … of enemies. Think of me as an Extra-Terrestrial … or even better as an 'Off-Earth Friend.'"

Reuben was the first to respond. "I understand." This Rose was very different to the one who was just 'Esme's friend', and now that he understood why he had felt there was something weird about her, he was able to like her. She was exciting … another of the strange Beings he had met recently. Clearly, he thought to himself, there really is more to life than meets the eye!

He suddenly started to laugh – loudly. And he laughed and he laughed. And soon both Esme and Rose had joined him, all laughing their heads off!

Moments later the door to the living room was pushed open and Mrs Montana pocked her head around it. "I'm glad to hear you three are enjoying yourselves," she said. "You were so quiet earlier on, I wondered what was happening. Do you want more biscuits?"

The three children all shook their heads in unison. "No thank you!" they gasped as their laughing died down.

Esme said to her mother. "Thanks Mum. We're going into the garden now. There's something there I want to show Rose … it's a rose bush that is still flowering!" As the completely unexpected words tumbled out of her mouth, Esme remembered that she had indeed noticed a hedge rose that had quite a lot of flowers on it even though it was December. And hadn't Rose started to say something about 'something in the garden that needed attending to' before she had interrupted her? She glanced quizzically at Rose, who nodded her acknowledgement as though able to read Esme's thoughts.

"Really?" Her mother raised her eyebrows in surprise. "I'll go and have a look later. Wrap up well. It's horribly cold outside!"

"We will!" the three children chorused.

Esme led the way out of the warm cosy living room into the hallway where all the coats and outdoor shoes were kept.

The Choccies, who had been kept out of the living room, followed the children as they went out through the side door and down into the back garden. But … they still kept a distance between themselves and Rose.

Esme noticed this and called them to her. She fussed them all in turn and said softly: "It's all right you know. She's a friend."

The dogs responded unenthusiastically with little wags of their dipped tails.

"Now I know why they've never fussed over you." They usually jump all over my friends. But … why … actually?" She looked at Rose.

"They are frightened of me ... they can't 'understand me' like they can a human. The energy I give off – the vibration you might call it – is totally different from a human's. They find it disturbing. But they will be fine once they get used to it. Most animals are frightened by me to start with." Rose paused and gave a big sigh. "Except for birds," she added in a low voice. "They seem to be OK with me."

There was another pause, longer this time. The twins waited for her to continue. They had come to a halt at the beginning of the hedge where Esme thought she remembered the 'rose-bush-she-known-nothing-about-until-a-few-moments-ago' was.

Rose had a wistful look upon her face as she said: "I sometimes miss my own companions – animal pets you would call them. I have three in my home."

"Are there animals on your planet then?" Esme asked excitedly.

Rose sighed again, looked intensely at the boy and girl standing staring at her. Suddenly she laughed. She was feeling happy because these two human children had accepted her. This was not always the case when she revealed her TrueSelf to humans. "I've got so much to tell. But not now. Let's go to the rose bush."

And sure enough down towards the far end of the garden, several white blooms could be seen amongst the dark foliage of the hedge rose.

Whilst they were still several yards away from the bush, Rose put up her hand to stop them. "Listen carefully," she said. "Can you hear anything?"

They all kept very quiet, the twins listening intently. The three dogs still keeping their distance from Rose. They sat in a quiet group in the centre of the lawn instead of rushing around doing their usual frantic sniffing for smell messages in the hedgerow.

Just as Esme thought she could hear a strange sound, Reuben spoke. Esme could see him listening intently, just as she was. He looked startled. "Sounds like there's a wasp's nest in there!"

Esme too had heard what seemed to be a very loud buzzing noise that had suddenly started up. She nodded to her brother in agreement.

"Close!" said Rose.

The twins looked at her puzzled. "Um ... what is it then?" asked Esme anxiously. "Had we better move away? We might get stung."

But Rose just marched up to the bush and peered into its depths. Then she beckoned to the children. "Just as I thought! Don't worry, it won't hurt you. Come and have a look."

Reuben bounced forward, eager to investigate, whilst his sister approached much more slowly, still not convinced they weren't in danger of upsetting a nest of angry wasps.

"Come on … it's quite safe!" Rose encouraged them. "It's stuck. It wants rescuing. That's why it's buzzing so loudly. Says it's been trying to attract your attention for days."

"It?" The twins mouthed, looking at each other and pulling 'I-don't-like-this' faces.

At that moment the Choccies came rushing over, noses in the air, tails up, 'interest' all over their faces. Their fear of Rose seemed forgotten and Luca let out a little yip of excitement. Solo pushed his nose into Esme's hand, then grabbed her wrist (as he did when he wanted to take her somewhere) and pulled her towards the rose bush, suddenly unafraid of Rose.

"Ouch!" she exclaimed. "Be gentle!" Solo immediately lessened the grip of his teeth, but continued tugging her closer to the bush.

Mowgli, head cocked to one side stood very close to the bush, peering intently at something.

Esme now remembered some days back when the dogs had seemed really interested in something in the hedge row. Solo kept taking her into the garden and down to that spot. But although Esme had tried hard to work out what the old dog wanted her to know, she was unable to understand. She imagined that they had smelt the scent of a fox that had come through the hedge. She hadn't heard the strange buzzing sound she was hearing now.

The buzzing grew even angrier, and Rose motioned for the dogs to move away. They did so, immediately.

Rose then put her hand slowly into the centre of the hedge rose. Esme and Reuben looked on silently, amazed that she didn't once get caught up by the thorns. Gently she began to withdraw her arm, and as her hand emerged, the twins could see she had something loosely contained within it.

She spoke to the thing in her hand – sounds that made no sense to the children – then very slowly opened up her fingers to show a 'creature' resting in the palm of her hand. Whatever she had 'said' to it, had resulted in immediate cessation of the buzzing noise.

"It's a Bumblewizard," she told the children. "It has a tear in one of its wings that is preventing it from flying. It needs healing."

She held her open hand out towards the twins. "It will need to be kept warm and fed honey-water for a few days. Then it will heal and be able to fly again. Look."

'Bumblewizard'! Esme took a couple of steps back. She was remembering her encounter with the nasty little sparks that had tried to set them on fire during bonfire night. Rose had mentioned 'bumblewizards'... and a ... Joker ... when all that was happening.

Even Reuben had backed away when he saw what Rose was holding.

But their curiosity quickly overcame their fear and they moved closer and peered cautiously into Rose's hand.

"Aaaah!" murmured Esme as she put her hand to her mouth in amazement.

The creature lying in Rose's hand was the size of a giant beetle. It was furry though, black, brown and yellow - rather like a bumble bee. But it's 'wings' looked more like a kind of split cape attached to its front and back legs. From what they could see it appeared to have four legs only … but not insect legs, actually a set of miniature human legs … and arms. Its head had a tiny pointy hat on it … just like wizards in picture books. And showing under the hat was a little face that was almost human but a bit like an insect too. The expression on its face was very fierce and grumpy looking.

Reuben, no longer scared, reached out a pointed finger to touch the creature … until Rose stopped him. "Careful! He does have tiny poisonous darts. If you frighten him he will use them. They are stored in his hat."

Reuben quickly snatched back his finger.

After a quick discussion about what to do next, they all trooped back to the house through the side door, sneaking past the kitchen door on tip toe and up into Esme's bedroom.

The Choccies, who were very well trained, had obeyed Esme when she told them to 'stay' in the garden. They wouldn't stay there indefinitely of course, but long enough so that their noisy approach didn't draw the attention of the children's parents' to the children as they had crept into the house.

They had decided it would be safest to keep the bumblewizard in Esme's room. Reuben's room would not be so good because Jason his pet rat, lived there. JasonRat might try to eat the bumblewizard ... and then get stung if he did!

Reuben went to fetch a small cardboard box. He had lots of these scattered around his room because Jason loved to spend time in dark little boxes.
Esme looked through her drawers and brought out a pair of old socks. These were used to line the box before Rose very gently deposited the Bumblewizard into it.

"Honey water! I'll get it." said Esme. "How much?"
"Just a thimbleful ... they hardly need to eat anything at all." explained Rose, "only when they've used up too much energy."

"Er ... how much?" Esme, who didn't know what a thimble was, frowned her question at Rose.

"The smallest container you can find ... with a few drops in the bottom ... mix half a teaspoon of honey with one teaspoon of water. And ... do you have one of those little squeegee dropper things?"

Esme nodded, knowing exactly where several of these were kept – in case they were needed to hand-rear baby rabbits. She ran downstairs and burst into the kitchen intent on her task. She came to a halt suddenly when she saw her parents. Unusually they were taking some time off to relax, and each sat in one of the armchairs by the Aga holding steaming cups in their hands. "You're in a hurry ... anything wrong?" queried her father whilst both parents contemplating their young daughter with questioning looks.

Whoops, this could be difficult! She thought quickly. "I need some honey-water and one of those eye droppers" she looked at her Mother questioningly ... and suddenly knew what to say:
"JasonRat isn't very well, and Reuben thinks feeding him some water and honey will help."

"Honey and water ... for the rat?" Esme's Father looked quizzically at his wife?

"Er ... yes ... Reuben read about it in the rodent magazine he sometimes gets." Esme was amazed to discover how easy she found it to lie when important things were at stake.

"OK, if you say so!" Fons smiled indulgently at his daughter.

Eve Montana raised an eyebrow. She knew her children well and thought it unlikely the honey-water was for the rat.

She had seen them all trooping down to a spot in the hedge and suspected they had found some little wild creature in the garden whose life they were trying to save. But apart from finding it a little odd that they didn't want to admit to this, she didn't see any reason to question Esme further.

"You know where they are don't you?" She was loathe to get up from her warm comfy spot by the stove.

"Yep ... I'll get it," reassured Esme quickly. She fished the honey pot out of the cupboard, stirred the half teaspoon of honey into a little bit of warm water at the bottom of a teacup, and grabbed a dropper from a drawer in the sideboard. She rushed for the door, and tripped on the corner of an old rug. Luckily her balance was good and she managed to save herself from falling flat on her face without dropping the teacup and dropper.

"Careful!" exclaimed her father. "I'm sure that rat can wait a couple more minutes."

But Esme was already halfway up the stairs, three disappointed Labradors sitting at the bottom, once again having been told to "STAY!"

Fons shook his head in amusement. "Kids!"

His wife said nothing, but continued taking small sips of her hot drink with a thoughtful look on her face. "Yes ... kids ... I do wonder" she murmured to herself, recalling the rather odd way her own two had been behaving for some months now.

Upstairs in Esme's bedroom, the two human children and Rose the ET, were all grouped around the box containing the bumblewizard. The children watching intently as Rose carefully allowed a tiny drop of honey water to gather on the end of the dropper before holding it close to the little creature's face. It reached out its tiny arms and held the dropper steady whilst it sipped at the liquid. It consumed about three drops of the honey water before sinking back into the sock at the bottom of the box. It uttered a funny little buzz.

"It says 'thank you'" interpreted Rose.

By this time, both children had decided that the bumblewizard lying in the shoebox was actually rather cute. The closer they looked at it, the more captivated they became.

And something really strange happened to the little creature as the two children began to like it. The grumpy look on its tiny face began to change into a much happier expression. And ... a thin band of pulsing light began to show around its little body.

When Esme pointed this out, Rose nodded and explained that bumblewizards weren't used to being liked! But ... when they felt that somebody did like them, they became very loving themselves. The band of light - that pulsed in rhythm to the creature's heartbeat – was their way of showing this love.

"Wow ... how beautiful ... " murmured Esme.

Reuben though couldn't contain himself any longer. "Yeah … cute. But what are they? And where do they come from?" he burst out.

"Well, if you are really interested, I shall tell you all about them …" Rose paused… "But you will need to open your mind to ideas that you might find strange."

Since their first meeting with Mr Nibbs, The twins had become really familiar with 'strange things', so they nodded their heads eagerly to Rose.

Then Rose told them the story of Bumblewizards.

13 - Merlin's blunder

"Once upon a time ..." Rose began the story in the way these kind of stories have been told since time began.

"Yes ... once upon a time humans believed in the existence of Fairies, and Elves, Gnomes and all sorts of Beings that were mostly invisible to the human eye. They didn't understand what jobs these Beings do, but enough humans had seen them to make many others believe they existed ... which of course they did ... and still do!" Rose cocked an eye at the girl and boy sat on cushions in front of her.

"And they also believed strongly in magic. In those times it was common for wizards to roam the land ... "

The two children were listening so intently that they were holding their breath. Rose laughed. "It's OK to breathe you know!"

The children laughed too and relaxed.

Rose continued: "So a long time ago in this land that you now call England, Wales and Scotland, in the times of the famous King Arthur ... have you heard of him?"

"Yes," They both nodded. " ... And the Round Table ... " Esme added in a hushed voice. The story of King Arthur and the Knights of the Round Table was one of her favourite history stories.

Rose continued: "This King – Arthur – had a lot of help and support from a well-known wizard of those times … "

"Merlin!" Both children exclaimed excitedly.

"Yes … Merlin." Rose gave a little sigh. "One of the greatest human wizards of all times." She fell silent, almost as though she was remembering something.

"Merlin … ?" prompted Reuben.

Rose took a deep breath and continued with the story: "Perhaps you know that Wizards are Alchemists … no? ... never mind. Let's just say that part of the job of a wizard is to 'change things' … to turn one thing into something else. This is called alchemy. Most humans wanted to use this process to turn lead into gold, though this is not what it was ever really intended for … " Rose gave her head a quick shake. "Oof … I'm getting distracted. Back to the bit about Bumblewizards."

Esme was mulling over the word 'Alchemist'. She knew she'd heard it somewhere and that it was an important word … she'd google it later, she promised herself.

"Esme?" Rose's voice brought her back to the story.

"One of the 'changing' experiments that Merlin carried out was to try and make lots of copies of himself – 'clones' you humans call them. It was at a time in his life when he was confined to living alone in a cave for many years. He was lonely ... wanted someone to talk to, to argue with, to share a meal with. So he decided to make several clones of himself so that they could have interesting conversations – as they would all be interested in the same things."

At this point Rose gave a little shrug and raised her eyebrows as if to say that might have been a rather nutty idea.

"Anyway ... that was his thinking!" She looked a bit sad as she said this, and sighed again.

The twins giggled at the idea of somebody wanting to do such a strange thing. But they were clearly enthralled by the story, so Rose carried on:

"Merlin needed something he could change into clones of himself. For some reason – it has never been discovered why; perhaps it was summer and there were lots of them around - he chose a bumble bee."

"Crikey!" exclaimed Reuben.

"Oh boy!" whispered Esme.

Both children had immediately seen the connection.

"So ... the experiment went wrong?" Reuben's eyes were wide.

"It did!" agreed Rose. "It went very wrong. Not that it was unusual for a wizard's experiments to go wrong. But this was a mega mess-up. The first thing to go wrong was the numbers.
He had intended to create three or four 'friends' to sit around the fire with him and enjoy the discussions. So he thought he'd make about 10 to start with. He presumed that they wouldn't all work, so a few spares would be useful."

The twins were following the story intently.

"What must have been going on in his brilliant wizard mind - for it was absolutely brilliant - at that moment, I can't imagine." Rose shook her head gently and was quiet for a few moments.

She started again: "So ... instead of making ten 'first stage clones' he got his zeros mixed up and with a tiny slip of his wand finger, ended up making ... thousands of them!"

Esme's hand went to her mouth ... "Wow!" She sometimes had problems with zeros and felt sorry for him. "So ... did they escape?" she asked.

"Patience," said Rose. "Of course with all these thousands of tiny 'fist- stage clones' coming to life, Merlin was unable to do anything but try and catch as many as possible. He didn't want them getting loose. But of course as we now know, lots of them did. The thing was that these 'first stage clones' were mostly still in their insect form; still able to fly, and ... worst of all, they still had their stings!"

Rose looked at the twins and could see from the expressions on their faces that they had realised what had happened … mostly anyway.

"So there was Merlin, one of the most brilliant Wizards ever, chasing around with a net trying to catch as many 'bee wizard clones' as he could. Can you imagine it!" Even Rose had to smile at the vision.

"But the bee-wizards did not want to be caught. So lots of them attacked him by stinging him, and then flew off … out into the world!"

Another "Crikey!" came from Reuben, but he didn't try to interrupt.

"Merlin received so many stings from the tiny creatures that he became unconscious. Indeed, he might never have recovered if his assistant had not come on her weekly visit to his cave. She found him lying on the floor of the cave, his face all swollen up, and mumbling to himself about 'bungling the job'. He managed to tell her what had happened and she was able to find the insect-sting antidote he kept amongst all his other magic potions."

"She gave it to him and once he had recovered, she was very cross with him. She agreed with him in no uncertain terms that he had indeed bungled the job. This is why the little creatures Merlin had created by mistake were first called Bunglewizards. But slowly over time the name changed into Bumblewizards, for after all they were still part bumble bees."

"Anyway, the result was that several thousands of these immortal little creatures were let loose on the world by mistake. The wizard part of them is what makes them immortal."

"So what did they do?" interrupted Reuben, who couldn't keep quiet any longer.

"For the first few years of their existence they were content with exploring the world they found themselves in. They travelled around, all together, in what looked like a huge great cloud, like swarms of honey bees. But then it seems they discovered they could frighten humans and animals alike! ... And even worse, they found this to be fun! They just delighting in stinging people and making them yell and dance around in pain."

Esme looked aghast, not wanting to believe such behaviour of the tiny creature now resting peacefully in the shoebox.

"Yes, it's sad isn't it." Rose shook her head in a gesture of despair before continuing. "But this seems to be the way with some creatures, including human beings. And what must be remembered is that these 'bees' did not die when they used their stings – unlike the bees that you two are familiar with today."

"Aagh scary!" Esme was imagining being chased by a swarm of tiny stinging creatures out to get her.

"That is how they became to be so disliked ... and feared in the world. Of course people tried to kill them! And indeed did manage to kill their bodies, by swatting them to the ground and stamping on them. But because they are immortal, their 'essence' was never killed and remained in the ground."

Another 'crikey' from Reuben, who thought he could see where this story was going.

"Crikey indeed!" agreed Rose, making a wry face. "So ... what happened was that when people stepped on that precise bit of ground they would feel a sharp pain in their foot. The foot would swell up and the pain that would last several days, preventing them from walking. They would put honey on the swelling and say *'Bumble Bumble wizz away, hurt me not, this I pray.'*"

"But over the generations humans forgot that Bumblewizards had actually existed. They have become a myth, or an old wives tale. To this day if country folk feel a sudden pain in a foot they will often exclaim: 'wizz fizz bumble bizz!'"

Both children were looking really worried now. They both really enjoyed running around outside barefoot.

"But you needn't worry!" Rose soothed. "That was many hundreds of years ago and the Bumblewizard essence has long been absorbed by the soil."

"You sure?" Reuben wasn't convinced.

"I am. And if you let me finish the story, you will understand why."

"Okay."

"Well, Merlin of course was devastated by what he had let loose upon the planet. So although he didn't feel it right to kill all these tiny creatures he had created, he did try to come up with a magic that would change their aggressive behaviour. And he was partly successful. As time went by more and more of the creatures became 'sleepy' – unconscious almost, in a permanent state of hibernation. But he hadn't reckoned with their intelligence – something they had inherited from him of course!" Rose chuckled and shook her head, musing at the foolishness of such a great wizard.

"Some of the Bumblewizards were less affected by the sleep magic and remained more 'alert'. These decided they needed to find a way of keeping this way – because they were really enjoying the experience of 'being alive'!
This is when they discovered eating and drinking and found that this activity, which seemed very strange to them at first, would keep them alive and alert.
And it wasn't long before the 'bee' part of themselves found out that the nectar and the pollen to be found in some flowers, was the very best thing for keeping them healthy."

Rose paused for a moment, taking a couple of deep breaths and checking that the twins were still interested. She had been talking for some time now.

They were. Indeed Reuben prompted with an impatient "And ... ?"

"Well ... " continued Rose, " ... because they were intelligent, they realised that if they split into smaller groups about twenty or so and explored different places they would be more likely to find enough of the 'food' they needed.
Some of them even tried to join honey bee colonies, but the honey bees didn't want anything to do with them and kicked them out.
Others of the groups soon discovered places where the plants they needed were most numerous. Eventually they had done all the world exploration that was possible, and they settled down to established their colonies and lead ordinary bee-like lives. And then ... guess what?"

Rose looked at the two children expectantly, indicating they answer.

For a moment there was complete silence and then boy and girl burst out at the same time:

"They got bored!"

Rose clapped her hands in delight. "Yes ... the wizard part of them, which was just like humans ... got bored!"

Then she pulled a face. "And ... just like humans, that was when the trouble started. That was when they discovered that they could interact with humans and animals."

The twins were nodding their heads and sighing as Rose spoke. They too, human children that they were, knew the sort of things that can happen when a group of children get bored.

"I can see that you can imagine the kind of things that happened … ?" She looked at them.

"Yeah," said Rueben slowly, feeling a bit embarrassed as he recalled some of the fun tricks he and his friends had played on people. "Things like knocking on people's doors and running away, and hiding somebody's pen, and … "

"Posting nasty things on Face Book!" Esme jumped in. She had done that a couple of times, as well as joining her brother in some of his pranks.

"Exactly those sorts of things," agreed Rose, "The sort of things that make people unhappy, scared or anxious. But … there was a huge difference with the bumblewizards. They don't have any parents or teachers to tell them what is right or wrong. And although they are tiny and cannot do a lot of the physical things that humans can, they have their stings, and … " She paused here dramatically: "They can do minor magic!"

"Aaaaa!" exclaimed Esme, her mind racing. "So that is why they tried to set us alight on bonfire night!"

"Yes, that's it. The trouble is they didn't realise that they can cause a lot of harm. They don't understand the kind of things that really frighten humans or cause them pain. It was never their intention to cause serious damage when they first started looking for things to do to amuse themselves.

So when the kind of things they did caused humans – and animals – to dislike them … and to try and kill them instead of playing with them – which is what they had wanted - they eventually became very resentful of humans …"

"What other sort of things do they do?" asked Reuben, suddenly feeling rather anxious about having a bumblewizard on the loose in the house.

"Will this one … I'm going to call it Buzzchat, don't you think that's a great name?" He looked at Esme. "Will this Buzzchat do harmful things when it's better?"

Rose was about to answer when Esme started to speak quietly and rather slowly as though not quite sure what she wanted to say.

"I … I don't think it will … I just get a feeling … I'm getting a feeling from it right now … almost as though it's speaking to me and trying to reassure me that it won't hurt me … not sure … ?" She grimaced and looked questioningly at Rose.

Rose smiled. "That's great … you are picking up its meaning pretty well. You know how I said that a bumblewizard will start to glow with light when it feels it is loved?"

Nods from the twins.

"As well as 'glowing' it will actually *feel* very loving towards the 'being', whether it's a human or an animal, that shows it love. So you have absolutely no need to worry about er … Buzzchat (she suppressed a laugh as she said this name out loud) being loose in the house – not that it will want to live inside. In fact, it will do all it can to protect such a being … in its own manner." She chuckled as she said this and the children looked at her quizzically.

"Well … there might be the odd occasion when it has a go at your parents, or the dogs, or even your cat Kimber - though mostly he is wise enough to avoid having any contact with it at all. That is of course if it thinks they are being unkind to you!"

There was a moments silence and then all three of them burst into laughter. The 'Esme's-friend-Rose' enjoyed this idea just as much as the twins.

Esme was the first to stop laughing. She suddenly looked serious. "It won't be anything really harmful will it?" she asked Rose anxiously.

"Very unlikely." Rose too became serious – the 'teacher' once again.

"A bumblewizard will only do serious harm if it feels seriously threatened itself – which is not often – or if its 'friend' is being threatened. Most often it will be pranks like buzzing around and around a light bulb making lots of noise; or around somebody's head. Part of their magic is to become invisible and to fly without making any noise. So they might untie shoelaces – remember they have hands

– or drop flies and spiders into people's food. Or they might pull at a person's or an animal's hair. Occasionally they move small objects from one place to another … or push them onto the floor. Those are the kind of things they get up to"

Esme, who had been holding her breath, let it out in a big sigh. She hadn't liked the idea of any of their animals – or even their parents – being hurt.

Reuben, who had been very quiet, asked "Can you teach them tricks?"

"Good question," replied Rose, "I don't know!" She turned in the direction of the little box containing Buzzchat and a stream of unintelligible noises came from her mouth.

A couple of seconds later, similar sounds came from the box.

"Buzzchat says that if the 'tricks' appeal to it, then of course it can learn … what do you take it for! … but if the tricks do not appeal, then there is no reason to learn."

The twins started to laugh at this until Rose put a finger to her lips: "Shhh, they take offence very easily."

There was silence for a few moments until Rose broke it by saying she thought it was time she went home and left them to get on with the rest of the day. They knew how to care for Buzzchat – a few drops of honey water for a couple of weeks until its wing had completely mended … and to spend time with it and try to learn how to understand its language even if not to actually speak it.

"If you have any trouble, call me."

Just as she finished speaking the twins' father's voice came floating up the stairs:

"Are you three hungry? Lunch is ready… "

"Coming!" yelled Reuben loudly enough to provoke an agitated series of buzzing noises from the box. Buzzchat was obviously sensitive to loud noise also!

Esme looked at Rose questioningly.

She shook her head. "I need to get back. I told my mother (she smiled wryly as she said this word) I'd be back in time to have lunch, and she's cooking my favourite meal – mushrooms stuffed with pine nuts and herbs. There's a bus from the end of the lane in about fifteen minutes."

"Okay then, see you soon." Esme gave her friend a big hug.

Reuben gave a cheeky grin, then said seriously: "I'm glad I've met you now!" before rushing off downstairs, followed more slowly by the two girls.

Rose put her head around the kitchen door to thank Mrs Montana for having her, then put on her outdoor clothes, opened the side door and stepped outside into the cold winter air.

But before she had taken a couple of steps along the path, Reuben poked his head around the door: "Rose … where exactly do you come from?" he asked rather awkwardly.

"Reuben!" shushed Esme "don't be rude!"… though in fact she too wanted to know exactly this!

Rose turned and smiled at them both enigmatically. "I'll tell you … when the time is right!" she said gently and continued on her way.

Strangely this answer seemed to satisfy both of them.

Once its wing had completely mended and its strength had returned, Buzzchat took up permanent residence in the very same rosebush where the children had found it. And much to the dogs' interest it invited several of its family to join it. The children were never quite sure how many of the little creatures lived in the rose bush.

Although the Choccies were very curious at first, they soon learned that bumblewizards like nothing better than to tease dogs. Whenever any of the dogs started to poke its nose into the rose bush, they would rush out and buzz around under the dog's tail, sending it rushing around in circles trying to catch them. They never actually stung them though.

Esme felt a bit anxious when she heard her mother asking their father if he had noticed the dogs chasing their tails like crazy over the last few days ... Perhaps they'd better check for worms.

Fonso, who had been working away from the house quite a lot, said he hadn't noticed them doing that, and they all seemed healthy enough. So no need to worm them for the moment anyway.

"I'll keep an eye on them anyway." Said Eve Montana, noting to herself that quite a few strange things had been happening in their household over the last months.

One of these strange things, was Esme going to school wearing a very unusual hair slide. Buzzchat would position itself just above and behind one of her ears so that from a distance it looked as though she was wearing a fancy hair slide.

The first few times this happened, it felt very strange because she could feel tiny vibrations as Buzzchat breathed ... almost like a minute cat purring. But she soon got used to it.

She never knew why Buzzchat chose to accompany her on some days and not others ... but she did notice that it was usually on days when she was likely to meet up with one of the school bullies who was in the same class as Esme for art.

14 - A Christmas Present

The twins had each been given a Smartphone for Christmas - not the latest 'be all do all' version, but 'smart enough' for Reuben and Esme to feel one of the gang with their school mates.

Eve and Fonso Montana had talked long and hard about whether to get their children smartphones. Eventually they had fallen prey to pressure; partly from the twins themselves who complained about feeling really left out and partly by vague feelings of anxiety. There was so much talk of keeping children safe these days; and the twins were becoming more and more adventurous as they got older. Finally their parents decided that knowing their children could phone them if they needed to would lessen their anxiety.

So on this morning of the first day back to school after Christmas, Esme and Reuben were walking down their lane to catch the school bus from the main road. And already they looked just like most other kids with smartphones: heads down, attention focussed on the phone screens.

And because they were looking at their phones, they didn't see that the gate into Mr Grubble's field had somehow swung open, and that the small brown pony had walked through it into the lane.

Although the pony was standing in the lane facing the children, a strand of grass dangling from his lips, the children had been so engrossed with their phones, that they were completely unaware of his presence.

Then Reuben, who was slightly in the lead, had suddenly become aware of two hooves planted on the ground a few steps ahead of him. Startled, he looked up and almost knocked heads with the pony. Esme, as intent upon whatever messages her smart phone was giving her as her brother, walked straight into Reuben. Bump!

"Ruebs!"

"Esme!"

They both fell silent as they observed the familiar form of the pony blocking their way.

Esme was first to speak: "Mr Nibbs … ?" she questioned quietly.

The pony huffed: "I do wish you wouldn't call me by that name … so undignified."

Esme could hardly contain her laughter as she looked the scruffy pony over. His dark brown coat was caked in mud where he had been rolling, his mane tangled with a few old thistle heads stuck in it, long straggly tail dragging a length of dried bramble, and of course his trade-mark grass stems hanging from his lips.

"Laugh away!" the pony snorted. "Personally I think this is a brilliant disguise – nobody's going to bother with me when I look like this!"

"I'm sorry!" Esme was contrite and reached out a hand to rub the pony between his eyes. "What do you want us to call you?"

"Pegasus of course!"

Reuben, who hadn't yet spoken, took a deep breath. "But you're not Pegasus. He's much bigger than you and ... different ... "

"Like this you mean?" If a pony could smirk, this one did as his physical form began to glow and shimmer. A large transparent horse took shape around the small brown pony.

"Yeah ... okay!" For some reason Reuben did not appear to be pleased by what was happening. Actually ... he felt annoyed!
He had been entirely engrossed in a game he was playing on his new phone. He had been about to get a high score that would allow him to play at a higher level.
And he certainly didn't want to 'go anywhere'! Not even with the amazing theatrical looking Pegasus that had materialised around Mr Nibbs. This Pegasus was different from the other Pegasus though. He was green in colour, not silver like the first one.

Reuben stood there silently whilst his sister continued to pet the scruffy Mr Nibbs pony.

'Hmmph!' A very loud snort as the great shimmering greenness separated itself from Mr Nibbs. '*The Boss – my grandfather - did say that the boy might be difficult and not want to go with you. If so, to take the gir,l and the boy can go with Nibbsy. There are lessons to be learned and it's your job to make sure these children learn them.'*

On saying this, the great green horse tossed its head in the air and stamped hard with its right leg, letting out what sounded almost like a squeal of delight.

Both children backed away, rather intimidated by this show of physical strength. But Esme was bold enough to observe that the Pegasus she had seen before was silver. "And you are very green!"

'Yes, of course! We can't all be the same colour, can we! I'm GreenZap, a Pegasus Junior ... one of the many. My grandfather couldn't be here today ... busy with ... something or other important ... but he wanted to 'send you a message' and asked me to deliver it. So ... pleased to meet the two of you I'm sure.'

The Green Pegasus was prancing around in the road ... skittishly, just like any young horse might ... but unlike any other young horse, it was also lifting and ruffling its huge feathered wings.

Esme stood her ground despite all the prancing. "Greenzap is a funny name."

'Oh, is it! What is your name?'

"Esme."

'Well that's a funny name to me! What does it mean?'

"I don't know. It's just my name."

'Well, there you are then! At least my name describes me: green and zappy!'

The winged horse swished his tail wildly, half unfurled his great wings and pranced some more, twitching his ears back and forth and snorting loudly.

Esme couldn't help laughing ... even though she did feel rather nervous. This beautiful creature that was strutting around just in front of her was huge and more than a little bit intimidating.

As though he had recognised her fear, GreenZap completed his antics by coming to an abrupt halt in front of Esme and bowing his head almost to the ground.

'So ... Esme ... Greenzap at your service. But my friends call me GZee!'

"Cheesy!"

'Not Cheesy ... Gee ... Zee; GZee!' He shook himself all over as though trying to shake off any cheesy bits that might have stuck to him.

'*Anyway ... to get to the point. Seems like Old Woman has been observing you two with your phones ... what's the boy's name?'* The horse looked in the direction of Reuben, who was still fiddling with his phone.

"Reuben."
On hearing his name spoken out loud, Reuben finally started paying attention. He went to stand next to his sister.

*'Ah, right … Reuben … another very funny sounding name without a meaning! Anyway, as I was saying, Old Woman, who has her spies just **everywhere**, so knows what **everybody** is up to **all the time**, asked us to do her a favour and sort the pair of you out. So … Esme girl child, you're to come with me!'*

"Sort us out? Me … to go with you … where?" Esme was seriously startled and backed away.

'You'll find out soon enough. Up you get. Don't worry you'll be safe with me.' Greenzap stopped his prancing and sort of 'shivered' into stillness next to Esme. He nudged her in the chest and said: *'Come on then, on my back and we'll be off.'*

Finally Reuben, who had reluctantly switched off his phone and pocketed it, seemed to wake up to what was happening.
He looked a little unsurely from his sister to the great green shimmery 'Pegasus'. "You sure? She's to go with you? Not me?"

'The girl … Esme … she's to come. You stay with … him.' Greenzap nudged Esme in the chest again and then flicked his ears and head in the direction

of Mr Nibs. *'Up you get.'* A slightly rougher nudge pushed Esme towards his side.

Reuben sprang to life. "It's OK Es ... I'll show you how ... "

'No need; she'll work it out for herself.'

"I will?" asked Esme out loud as she approached the side of a horse that if anything was even taller than the original Pegasus.

'Remember what Pegasus told Reuben that first time?'

"Umm ... thinkthink ... ?"

A cloud of greenish mist streamed from the horse's nostrils as he nodded his head and huffed his approval.

Esme looked tiny as she stood close to the horse's left shoulder and tentatively reached her left hand up to just touch the top of his withers. She seemed completely daunted and slowly let her hand slide back down to her side "Can't!" she murmured to herself.

"I'll show you!" Reuben rushed up to her.

'No! She will do it herself.' Quietly Greenzap said to Esme *'There's another word you humans use to do thinkthink, as well as 'imagine'. It's 'visualise' ...'*

Almost as soon as he had said it Esme found herself sitting on his back. She was always visualising things, so as soon as she heard that word she knew exactly what to do. "Ooooh!" she whispered "this feels ... amazing."

'OK, are you ready ... remember 'glue'... let's get going.' This 'imaginary' creature tossed its head and gave a very real-feeling buck – real enough for Esme to squeak in surprise, clamp her legs into its sides and reach out to grab a handful of mane.
Luckily, she was prepared by Reuben's account of his first adventure to know what to do when the great wings began to unfurl.

They rose so quickly into the air that her shout to Reuben was lost in the wind.

Reuben gaped as he watched his sister and the Green Pegasus disappear in the blink of an eye. He was left standing in the middle of the wintery lane, mouth hanging open with the beginnings of a 'but?' still inside, and with only Mr Nibbs for company.

There was a gravelly cough from Mr Nibbs. *'You are to come with me ...'*

15 - Esme in Tears

Esme, atop Greenzap, had got over her initial fear. Having already heard about Reuben's trip with Pegasus Senior ('the Boss' Greenzap had called him), had really helped. She sort of knew what to expect.

Strangely, she didn't feel the need to thinkthink 'glue' to feel safe. She always had really good balance and had ridden lots of ponies and horses bareback. And she felt perfectly balanced on this flying horse.

As though he had read her thought (he had of course), Greenzap send her the message that it was good to balance, but that she might need 'glue' on occasion … and so to be prepared.

Esme nodded, but was too exhilarated with all that was happening to really pay attention. They were whizzing at high speed, though not terribly high over fields, woods, roads and villages.

Esme wondered what people would think if they looked up and saw them. Would they think Greenzap, or GZee as he had said his friends called him, was a dragon? Of course not, she reminded herself. Dragons don't really exist. She sighed.

'Nobody can see us. And … don't be too sure!' GZee's thoughts - or were they words - flew into her mind. She remembered Reuben telling how he had reached out a hand to catch Pegasus's thoughts when this had happened to him. She vaguely won-

dered what the words 'don't be too sure' meant. But she was too taken by the experience of riding through the air on a winged horse to ask.

A while later Esme felt the great wings slowing their beating. She realised the horse was now descending. She looked down on what appeared to be a large park of some sort.

Then GZee began to fly in tighter and tighter circles. Esme felt herself losing her balance as they whirled around and around, down and down.Her heart jumped into her throat and she felt suddenly terrified. Aagh … GLUE!

It worked … she wasn't flung off. But … she had almost left the glue thinkthink too late! She had glued herself into the tilted position she had slipped into when GZee had suddenly executed the tightest of the tight turns just before they landed. Esme couldn't be certain, but she suspected that GZee had done this just to show off. There didn't seem to be any reason to spiral down instead of doing an ordinary landing! Although there were many trees in the area, there were none close to the spot where GZee had touched ground - on the upper part of a huge grassy slope with a path running along its top.

Esme, still glued halfway down the winged horse's right side was reluctant to unglue, knowing she would fall to the ground. GZee was obviously aware of her predicament because he very gently partly unfurled his rightwing so she could lean on it before she did an unglue thinkthink.

"Thank you," she said aloud as she slid tentatively off the wing and onto the ground.

'My pleasure!' the horse huffed noisily.

About twenty yards from where they had landed was one of several park benches. It was occupied by what appeared to be a young girl, who lifted her head and looked briefly in their direction. But she gave no indication that she had seen them.

Esme now spotted a dog lying on the ground next to the girl. She noted with interest that it was a chocolate Labrador.

'We'll move closer so that you can see her through my eyes. She won't notice us, though the dog might,' said GZ.

And so it was. A moment later the dog stood up. It looked in their direction and whined very gently as its dipped tail made the slightest of wags. It tugged at the leash attaching it to the leg of the bench.

The girl though, who looked to be several of years older than Esme.
She was looking down at her left hand. It was resting in her lap and cradling a mobile phone – new and shiny. Her right hand was tap-tapping and swipe-swiping at the images on phone's screen … definitely a very smart Smartphone! Apparently.
She appeared to remain in complete ignorance of the presence of a girl accompanied by a huge green winged horse!

As GZee and Esmel moved slightly closer, the dog pricked its ears and began to scent the air. It whined again. The girl on the bench absentmindedly reached out her right hand to touch its head for a second. That seemed to settle the dog and it sat down. But it kept its tail tucked close to its haunches and its muzzle on the bench, just touching the girl's leg. It was clearly feeling unsettled by what it could sense but not see.

In this place that GZee had brought Esme to, it was a most beautiful summer's day. The sun was shining brightly, and there were a few fluff clouds in the sky drifting along gently on the whisper of a breeze. It was early enough in the day for the birds to be still singing.

From where she was sitting the girl on the bench had the most wonderful view of parkland stretching away in front of her towards sun-sparkled blue sea in the distance. If she had been looking! But she wasn't. All her attention on the phone in her lap.

Esme's first thought was for the dog. "Poor dog, it's scared and needs some attention." She whispered and looked at GZee.

'Good, you are an observant child. What else do you see?'

"You mean this beautiful day and that fantastic view?"

'That is so … and I am pleased to hear that you notice and appreciate it! But, no that is not what I meant.'

"Can we go closer?"

'A little. Stand in front of me.'

As soon as she moved from the side of the horse to in front of its head, Esme could see – through GZ's eyes! What the horse saw was very different from what Esme herself saw.

It was very odd. Through the eyes of GZee, the girl on the bench had only a vague body outline and instead of clothes she 'wore' colours. And Esme could tell that her colours were strange … wrong even … because she, Esme, suddenly felt nauseous and only just managed to prevent herself from throwing up! The main colour for the body area of the girl on the bench was a sickly yellowish grey. In the centre of her chest, where her heart was, a tiny patch of bright green pulsated, and masses of brownish red flames kept flaring up from inside her head.

Then Esme observed something even stranger. The girl seemed to be attached, bound almost, to her phone by myriads of super fine threads that emerged from various places within her body and her head and entered the phone.

As Esme watched, she realised that not only did the girl have strange colours, she was also feeling anxiety and fear. She knew this because she was feeling the girl's emotions! And they were not pleasant!
She quickly moved away from her position in front of GZee. With relief, her eyes again saw the girl as … a girl sitting on a bench.

She was breathing very rapidly though and Green-zap, recognising his charge's fear, commented rather off-handedly that she needn't worry, as the feelings didn't belong to her, well not yet anyway.

"How do you mean, 'not yet'?"

'Take a closer look, if you like.'

"Won't she see me?"

'Nope, 'course not! You're in your spirit form ... like when you're dreaming!' The slight irritation in GZee's voice indicated that he was still finding it difficult to believe just how ignorant most human beings were. Patience had never been a quality that members of the Family of Pegasus were known for.

"Oh ..." Esme wanted to ask more about this but GZ's obvious impatience didn't encourage questions. She'd ask Rose, she decided.

After a moment's hesitation, she inched her way even closer the girl, who really did seem completely unaware of Esme's presence. Still unconvinced, Esme cleared her throat gently.
No response from the girl, but huge interest from the dog who stood up and moved as far as the leash would allow, reaching its head out in Esme's direction, seeking the source of a familiar smell. It was a smell that removed the dog's anxiety, and its tail lifted, a slight wag beginning at the very tip. It whined again and added a little yip of excitement. The seated girl yanked on the dog's lead impatient-

ly. "Sit!" her voice was harsh, her eyes still fixated by the piece of metal in her lap.

The dog obeyed, dropping to its haunches again. But its gaze remained fixed in Esme's direction, and another little whine escaped its throat.

This time the seated girl did take notice. "What's the matter with you, you stupid dog!" She was annoyed! But at least she did look up and peer all around her to see if she could see why her dog was so agitated. But she couldn't … even though Esme was now right in front of her and was waving a hand in front of her face! At this, the girl on the bench made a brushing away movement in front of her face as though trying to shoo away an insect.

This allowed Esme to see the girl's face.

"Oh!" Her hand went to her mouth to stifle a cry of alarm.

The girl was herself!

But several years older!

'Esme's heart began to pound and she felt very, very scared. She slowly backed away from her future self, hand still to her mouth.

The Esme-on-the-bench still remained engrossed in the device on her lap, apparently completely unaware of what her dog was doing as it stood up and whined again. its tail now wagging furiously as it 'felt' a familiar spirit presence.

Now young Esme focussed on the dog. She gasped. It was Mowgli ... an older grey-whiskered Mowgli. "Oh Mowgs," she whispered, approaching the dog and kneeling down to cuddle him. "I am so, so sorry."

She was most confused by being in this 'spirit form'. How could the dog know she was there when her own physical self did not? But was that 'other' older Esme actually physical ... or another spirit form? Esme's mind was working overtime, trying to understand what was happening. And ... her heart was full of sorrow. It was all too much to bear.

At this very point a loud snort from GZee attracted her attention. The young Pegasus was prancing around, tail swishing, looking really pleased with himself. *'You see, you see!'* Esme felt the force of his determination to make her 'see'.

Still kneeling by Mowgli, tears running down her face, she sobbed: "Yes, I see: I do see; I understand what you are showing me. It is just too horrible." She gasped for breath as the sobs continued. "But GZee, what can I do?"

By this time the dog was going crazy, attempting to put his paws on spirit Esme's shoulders and lick her face. He gave a sharp bark and jumped so hard towards her, that had she been solidly physical, she would have been knocked off her feet.

"Huh! What was that?" Something had got through to the Esme-on-the- bench. Startled, she looked around her, blinked rapidly and rubbed her eyes before stretching her arms up behind her head. She felt as though she was waking from sleep. She looked around in puzzlement.

The dog's excited bark had caught her attention and she turned to look at him. "Okay, okay! I guess it's time to go home." Reluctantly she made some final swipes on her phone, flipped it shut, slipped it into her pocket and got to her feet. She untied Mowgli from the bench and then unhooked his lead. She didn't notice that the phone had missed her pocket and had instead slipped between the slats on the bench. It hit the soft ground below soundlessly.

The dog took one look at the girl and then shot off down into the park, running as though his life depended upon it. His yips of delight could be heard as he circled, coming back to the bench and shooting off again, time after time. Finally he exhausted himself and flopped down in front of the older Esme, bright pink tongue lolling from the side of his mouth and eyes bright,

"Crikey!" The older girl surveyed her dog in amazement. "Haven't seen you run like that for months!" She actually crouched down next to him, and ruffled behind his ears.
He gave her several lick-kisses before jumping up, giving himself a good shake, titling his head to one side and giving her the look she knew so well: *'Come on, let's go … there's scents to be followed,*

birds to scare, and splash water to be found!' A forceful whine accompanied the look.

"Okay. You win. We'll go home through the wood where the badgers live." She started walking.

It was not until they had entered the wood that the girl remembered her phone. 'My phone! Aaagh!' She turned and rushed back towards the bench.
She quickly spotted the phone on the ground and felt a huge rush of relief. As soon as she picked it up she felt the urge to check … just see if any messages had come through. But its battery was dead. 'Hmmm … that's odd' she murmured to herself, wondering just how long she had 'slept' on that bench.

But Mowgli came bounding up to her and regained her attention. She shrugged and put the dead phone into her pocket and jogged after the dog back towards home via badgers and other smells … to the obvious delight of Mowgli. He had finally got his 'mistress' back. After all these months of her belonging to that 'thing' she now carried with her!

Despite herself, young Esme, who had been quietly observing all this, couldn't help a laugh burbling up through her tears. Seeing Mowgli running around like crazy had been just wonderful. Watching animals play was one of the things she enjoyed most.

She turned to GZee, who had stopped his prancing now and had come to stand beside her, muzzle resting gently on her shoulder. She put her hand up to touch his soft nostrils.

Another snort and he moved back a step. *'Hey, that tickles!'*

"Sorry." Esme turned to him, stood on tiptoe in an attempt to hug him. "Thank you GZee, for showing me this. But … but … what can I do to change it?"

GreenZap, wanting to oblige this human child, dipped his head so that Esme could reach both arms around his neck. After a couple of moments, he squinted down his long cheeks at the girl clinging to his neck. This was not something he was used to … or very comfortable with. He lifted his head, hoisting Esme off her feet.

Esme took the hint and let go, dropping to the ground.

As she did so she heard: *'You have **already** done something about it. You have become aware. What I have shown you has made you aware that you have choices to make, choices that will change your future and that of the dog. Remember. You always have a choice!'*

What did he mean by that? Esme's mind was still jumping all over the place, trying to make sense of the things that had just happened.

*'I meant **exactly** what I said. You **always** have a choice.'*

This time the power of the great horse's thought 'poke' almost knocked Esme over. Her mind slowed right down, releasing some of her inner questions so that she could give her attention to what the winged horse was telling her.

'That's better!' A gentler thought-poke. *'This is one of the most important things you will ever learn ...'* GZee paused, waiting for Esme to calm her mind even more before he continued. His words came very slowly, each one emphasised.

'Right! As I have just said ... and others wills ay to you many more times: You always have a choice ... and every choice you make will have a consequence! Do you understand?'

"Sort of ..."

'For example ... what you have just seen is the conse-quence of you deciding that you prefer playing with your 'device' (GZee snorted in disgust as he used the word) *to playing with your dog. Does this consequence feel good to you?'*

"No ... sniff ... course not!"

'Well then, blow your nose and give me your attention again.'

Esme did her best to do as he said.

GZee continued – with the same exaggeratedly slow speech: *'And you do this - make choices - thou-sands of times each day. It's a bit like the 'thinkthink' process. You make happen what you have just 'chosen'.* That is how life 'happens'. Do you understand?'

"Umm ... not really ... maybe ... sort of." Esme shook her head in bewilderment. Then she took a deep breath and said: "But I do know that I don't want to be like THAT when I get older!" She pointed to the now empty bench where the other Esme had been seated, tap-tapping away on the screen of her mobile phone.

'*Good! So now you can practice ... and make a different choice.*'

"How do I do that?" Esme was flummoxed.

'*Well ... just **imagine** yourself – sat on that bench - doing something different!*' GZee blew out strongly through his nostrils and stamped once with a forefoot. He was seriously running out of patience with this human child who didn't seem to know even the basics of 'creation'.

Feeling a bit daunted by the winged horse's obvious impatience with her, Esme shut her eyes – because you have to do that, she thought. You have to shut your eyes to visualise things.
Nothing happened. Her mind was racing, filled with fearful thoughts about how awful it would be to become that Esme she had seen sitting on the bench.

As GZee continued to snort and began to prance around impatiently, and as Esme unsuccessfully attempted to use her imagination, help arrived unexpectedly. A much older Green Pegasus who had the task of keeping an eye on the younger members of his green family, had become aware of the situation. He chuckled to himself as he observed what was happening. He was remembering how impatient he had been with humans when he started his training as a young apprentice in the Elite Pegasus Messenger Corps.

This wise old Pegasus telepathically sent GZee a blast of patience.

The young Pegasus received it with gratitude. It brought relief from the tension he had been feeling. He knew he still had much to learn if he was to be accepted as a member of the elite team of winged horses dedicated to assisting humanity.

His stompy prancing stopped. And so did the snorting, ... which was a good thing as it had not been proving helpful to Esme.

He now felt calm. A delightful tingling sensation rippled through his whole body and then his wings. This sensation allowed him to feel just how upset his young human charge was.
'*Amazing!*' he thought to himself as he felt his heart swell with Love for the child!

He moved close to her and gently rested his muzzle on the top of her head. He nickered quietly and sent a gentle calming thought to her: '*No need to pay any attention to those nasty fearful thoughts ... just let them float out of your mind ... then you will be able to 'see' a different image of your older self. Think about how much you love your dog*'.

Esme took heart from what was now a very loving, supporting horsey presence. And … sure enough … a vapoury image of 'another girl on the bench' began to tremble into existence. Esme gasped in amazement. "Magic!" she whispered to herself.

'Kind of … just you playing with creativity.' The thought words were accompanied by a gentle horsey chuckle from GZee. He had actually succeeded in teaching this human child something. He was pleased with himself and his pupil.

The vapoury vision on the bench began to take on a more solid form and yet another older Esme now sat there. This one was very different from the first bench girl. Light shone from her body, with a beautiful green and turquoise light in the area of her heart. Her head was surrounded by a gentle violet colour.

The old Mowgli was sat leaning against her legs, and the girl's hand rested on his head. She was looking out over the vista spread before her. She heaved a sigh of contentment.
A noise from her pocket alerted her to her phone's desire for attention. She pulled it out and flipped it open for a quick glance. "I'll get that later," she said to the dog, ruffling behind his ear.

Young Esme watched entranced as this older Esme flipped the phone shut again before putting it back into her skirt pocket.

What happened next was a bit different to what had happened before … not a lot different, but more fun!

The Older Esme stood up, stretched her arms wide, picked up the dog's lead from the bench and smiled to herself before she moved off down the hill, gathering speed and calling to the dog as she went. Mowgli was hot on her heels, rushing in excited circles around her. So excited were they both that on one occasion they tripped each other up, falling down and rolling over several times before stopping for long enough to pick themselves up again and continue their game.

The chasing game continued for several minutes until the dog suddenly came to a stop under the canopy of a huge oak tree. His head went down and he pulled and tugged, and pulled and tugged some more until he had freed a large branch that had been stuck in the ground. Proudly he dragged it towards the Esme girl. She was laughing out loud as she stooped down and patted her thighs to encourage the heavily laden dog to come to her.

"Oh … thank you Mowgs!" she exclaimed when he reached her, in that 'guudboyee voice that humans use with children and animals. The dog deposited the branch at her feet. "Silly old fella," she added lovingly to him and tousled his head as he flung his old body down, exhausted.

Young Esme watched as the older Esme girl and the dog sat side by side, the girl's arm flung over the dog's shoulder … much in the way that she, young Esme, did with all the Choccies.

She reached her hand up to the side of her and ran it down the warm hairy neck of the amazing creature standing beside her. "Thank you so much GZee" she whispered, wondering as she spoke the words aloud how it could be that this mythical creature actually felt like a real live horse!

GreenZap shimmered his greenness in a great ripple all over his body and huffed delightedly onto Esme's head.
And that was the moment when this young Pegasus decided he would continue with his training and become the very best GreenZap he could possibly be!

By now more tears were streaming down Esme's face as she watched the vision of the older Esme and the older Mowgli become vapoury once more and gently fade away. But this time the tears were of a strange kind of happiness. She felt very trembly as she reached into her pocket for her hankie to wipe them away.

Then a movement in the sky above her made her look up and she gave a little gasp.

"Look GZee!" her voice was a bit squeaky and sniffy as she pointed upwards to a great bird that seemed to be hovering high above. "Isn't that an Eagle … a Golden Eagle? How can that be?"

She had been attracted by birds of prey, especially Eagles, ever since she had first seen one at a Centre for Birds of Prey when she was about five. She knew that Eagles didn't live in England ...

'*Aha,*' responded GZee, '*A friend of yours I believe?*'

Esme was silent for several moments, before she said: "You mean ... you mean ... my dreamtime eagle? Is that ... Gyrre?"

'*Could be.*'

'Oh ...'

Esme squinted her eyes and peered intensely at the sky as the flying form drifted round and round, higher and higher on a hot air thermal until it was nothing more than a tiny speck.

"No ... I think it's a buzzard."

'*Perhaps.*'

And then, in a small voice Esme asked: "GZee, can we go home? I'm really, really tired."

'*At your command! Home it is!*'

The winged horse, who had managed to keep very still until that point, gave a little prance before standing straight up on his hind legs and unfurling his great wings, creating quite a wind as he undulated them several times. He towered over Esme, and the wind created by his wings nearly made her lose her balance. But strangely she felt no fear, even when for a moment his front hooves were hovering only inches in front of her face.

Indeed those hooves stayed in front of her face just long enough for her to see, very clearly, two tiny wings attached to each of his fetlocks.

She was entranced and a wide smile appeared on her face.

'Up you get. As you're so tired I'll help you this time.'
And before she even had time to consider it, Esme was on his back, 'glued' into place and they were off, flying at speed. Had she not been so exhausted and taken aback by her experience, Esme would have been terrified by the speed they were travelling at.

As it was she was completely unaware of any of the journey home.

It was as though she had been deep asleep and woken up to find herself standing in the lane – her lane - completely alone. There was no sign of the great green winged horse … he had just disappeared … into thin air.

Esme slowly looked around her and saw her new smart phone at her feet on the ground. Without thought she raised a foot to stamp on it. In that instant a clear but distant voice called out: *'No need, it is a useful tool, as long as it remains a tool and does not become … 'the boss'! Just remain aware!'*

A great neigh of horsey laughter filled the air as Esme collapsed into a heap on the road in the middle of the lane. She had been truly shaken and was left with feelings of so much sadness that tears streamed down her face.

16 - Peter Sees

Esme was still in this same position when Reuben emerged from Mr Grubble's field, looking pretty glum himself. He was running his hands though his hair and muttering "Oh boy ... that was awful!"

Then he saw Esme. Her face was streaked with tears and she was blowing her nose into a scrumpled up paper bag.

For a moment he forgot his own woes.

"Es, what's happened? Why are you crying?"

Hearing her brother's voice brought Esme back to her current situation. "Oh ... Reuben ...!" she wailed "it was awful!"

Reuben was so taken aback by his sister's distress that he plonked himself down next to her and actually put an arm around her shoulders.

And there and then, both of them sitting in the middle of the lane oblivious to the cold of the winter's day, Esme told her brother what had happened to her after she had flown off with GZee, leaving Reuben in the lane with Mr Nibbs.

She has just reached the bit where GZee tells her that she can choose to 'make it better' when a tractor came trundling down the lane and they were forced to move. Moving made them aware of two things: they were freezing cold, and they were completely disoriented. What time of day was it anyway? Last time they had been together they had been on their way to school … hadn't they?

They decided to go home.

They reached the house and were on their way straight up to Esme's bedroom, giving only the briefest greetings to the Choccies … until Esme remembered just why she was so upset! She got on her knees and put her arms tight around a rather startled Mowgli.

"I promise you I'll never love my phone more than I love you!"

The patient dog put up with the very tight hug, knowing his mistress was upset about something. They were watched intently by Solo and Luca, who both sat quietly, aware that something 'serious' was happening.

Reuben, who was watching from the top of the stairs, called to his sister: "Come on Es, I want to know the rest of the story. Then I'll tell you what happened to me!

Esme nodded, but continued to focus on the dog, taking his head into her hands and rubbing her forehead against his. Slowly she released her hold on Mowgli and got to her feet. The dog looked at her, head on one side and whined gently.

"Sorry Reubs. My room?"

He nodded: "It's a good thing Mum and Dad are out!"

After Esme had grabbed a handful of tissues to wipe the tears from her face and to blow her nose, they settled themselves on cushions on the floor in her bedroom. She was about to start speaking when her brother suddenly jumped up. "Just got to go and check JasonRat is OK. Can I bring him in here?"

"Okay … I 'spose …" The pet rat was not allowed in Esme's room. It wasn't that she didn't like the little creature. It was just that he had a tendency to chew things up … all sorts of things, some of them precious to Esme!

Reuben returned with JasonRat in his hand. "He's okay!" he said as he sunk down onto the cushion next to his sister.

Esme wondered why the rat wouldn't be OK … but didn't say anything. Too many other things going round in her mind!

She finished recounting what had happened to her. She looked at her brother intently and repeated what he had heard her say in the lane: "It was just so awful!" She heaved a huge great sigh as she added: "And … well … I really really like my phone! So you see, Reubs … having smart phones is really good … but …" She shrugged and fell silent.

Amazingly Reuben had let his sister finish her story without saying a single word other than a few grunts of encouragement. But alongside listening intently, his mind was in a whirl. He could hardly believe what he was hearing!

For once almost lost for words, it was several moments before he managed to blurt out: "Me too … It was awful! Not exactly the same, but very nearly."

"What?" a sniff from Esme. "What do you mean?"

"Well, after you left on the green Pegasus, something happened to me too!"

"What!" Esme peered round into her brother's face. "Tell me … tell me!" she whispered.

Reuben was about to tell Esme his story when a sound in the distance caught his attention – was it the church clock? – anyway, he suddenly remembered 'time' and 'place'.

"Oh!" he said.

"Oh!" said Esme, also suddenly becoming aware of her surroundings and all the rest of normal day things.

"School!" they looked at each other and then at their watches.

"Ahhh time's gone all weird" exclaimed Reuben.

"If we run we might just catch the late bus?" queried Esme, reluctantly getting up from her cushion.

Both were silent for a moment, each considering the possibility of not going to school at all. But without having to say so out loud they both knew that not going to school would not be a good idea … there would be just too many questions asked!

"We'd better go. Come on … I'll tell you later!"

They almost threw themselves downstairs, slammed the door in the faces of three disappointed dogs, bolted out through the front gate and shot off down the lane.

They emerged onto the main road just in time to see their school bus about to pull away from the bust stop.

Reuben began to yell, waving his arms; and Esme found some extra energy to sprint after the bus, also waving an arm.

The bus driver saw them in his mirror, his brake lights came on, and when the twins reached the bus, its door was already open for them to pile on board.

"Not like you two to be late?" said the driver, who drove this route regularly.

They were too puffed to do anything but gasp out a 'thank you', bending over and try to catch their breath, before going to find empty seats.

Esme sat down next to a class mate, and Reuben also sat next to a boy from his class. This boy was sitting on the verge side of the bus and as Reuben sat down next to him the boy looked at him strangely and asked "What was all that about?"

"All what?" Reuben was still breathing deeply.

The boy, whose name was Peter, looked at Reuben even more strangely.
"You know, … you being dumped at the bus stop by that pony!"

Reuben, utterly confused now as to **what** had happened **when**, ignored the question and bent down as though to tie up his shoelace – giving himself time to think. Peter had seen him on Mr Nibs! How many of the other kids on the bus had seen **that version** of what had happened to him this morning?

What could he say that would explain it … when he didn't even know himself how it had all happened, only that he had 'been somewhere' once again. How could he explain it?

He decided to bluff. "What pony?"

"I don't know!" said Peter, raising his eyebrows, "a scruffy little brown thing … and you were bareback!" Peter's parents kept a couple of hunters and he had his own show pony.

"I wasn't on a pony; why would I come on a pony to catch the bus, stupid!" Reuben was still fiddling with his shoelace.

"I don't know … you tell me!" from an exasperated Peter.

"Stop messing around," grumbled Reuben, determined enough now to stick to his story. "You're nuts. Why would you want to make up something like that?"

"I didn't make it up. I saw you." Peter turned around to the two girls sitting behind him. "You saw him, didn't you?"

"Saw him what?" asked one of them, not really paying attention, her eyes focussed on her mobile.

"Reuben cantering up to the bus stop on that pony … and then being dumped by it!"

"What! Don't be daft! What are you on?"

"But I saw him; I did." exclaimed Peter loudly. "Scruffy pony and Reuben here riding bareback up to the bus stop … ?"

The girl, irritated now … stood up and turned to the rest of the busload of children. "You hear that … Peter says he saw Reuben riding up to the bus stop on a pony … anybody else see it?"

Blank looks and shaking heads.

The girl turned back to Peter and smirked. "What sort of eyes are you wearing this morning?" She scoffed. "Not sharp ones that's for sure!"

Peter slouched back down into his seat, his face bright pink, thoroughly embarrassed. "I did see you on a pony!" he muttered.

Reuben, who quite liked Peter despite his family being really snobby, and who now felt much more confident as nobody else on the bus seemed to have seen that version of his catching the bus, said kindly:

"I often think I've seen something weird and then it turns out that I didn't."

"You do …?" Peter pulled a face.

"Yeah" answered Reuben cheerfully. "My dad says I've got an 'over-active imagination'."
At that the matter was dropped, though both boys were much quieter than their usual selves.

Although Esme had heard Peter calling out to ask if anybody else had seen Reuben coming to the bus stop on a pony, she was already feeling confused enough by what had happened to her this morning, to want to get involved with her brother's situation. She just kept looking at the school book she had taken out, with a muttered "got to check my homework" when she sat down. She didn't want her classmate to start asking questions.

The bus arrived at the school and disgorged its load of noisy children.
Reuben quickly found Esme and arranged to meet during lunch break, then set off at a run to catch up with some mates. As they all pushed their way

through the main entrance doors, a girl, who was a friend of the boy Peter, and who was in the year above Reuben, came up and walked next to him. She whispered in his ear:

"I saw that pony, you know. And it looked a lot like a pony I know called Mr Nibbs?"

Reuben stopped dead in his tracks, biting his tongue as he did so. Several children bumped into him, causing a bit of a children traffic jam.

"Ouch!" exclaimed Reuben, freaked out for the second time that morning.

"Don't worry, I won't tell," smiled the girl, whose name Reuben didn't know."But it would be good to talk with you." She lifted quizzical eyebrows and hurried off to catch up with some friends.

"Come on, Montana, no loitering!"

The teacher's voice broke into the messy thoughts swirling around in Reuben's mind, and he set off for his first lesson.

He had real trouble concentrating during the morning's lessons, and was twice reprimanded for not paying attention. He was also aware that Peter kept looking at him.

Finally it was time for lunch break and the twins met up where they had arranged, in a 'hangout' area of the playground not much used during the winter. But although Esme was longing to hear what had happened to him, Reuben couldn't bring himself to tell her. All he would say was that it was all just too freaky, that he wasn't feeling well and that he hoped JasonRat was alright.

It was clear that whatever had happened to him earlier that morning after she had left with GZee had upset him a lot. His hunched shoulders and arms wrapped around himself were far from his usual boisterous behaviour.

Esme, empathising with her brother as she often did … and having had her own adventure from which she was just beginning to recover, suggested he say he was sick and go home. They could catch up with each other when she got home later in the afternoon.

Reuben gave her a weak smile, sniffing and shifting from foot to foot uncertainly before agreeing to take her advice. "Okay."

Esme went back into the school to find a warm spot where she could be on her own for a while because in truth she too was still feeling the effect of her adventure and didn't have the energy to be with her friends.

Reuben went to find the school nurse. She took one look at him, his flushed face and sweaty tousled hair, and, having checked with him that his parents would be available, phoned for somebody to drive him home.

This task fell to the school caretaker, who very re-luctantly agreed to leave him at the front gate without reporting to his parents. Reuben, surrounded by tail wagging Choccies, thanked him very politely and managed to persuade him it was absolutely fine; that his father was out in the pollytunnels. This was true. Fonso remained there until tea time, completely unaware that his son had returned home.

Reuben didn't want to speak to anybody! He had grabbed a glass of water and some biscuits from the kitchen and gone straight up to his room, shutting the door properly so the dogs couldn't get in – much to their confusion.

Although the three dogs were unable to communicate directly with their children, they absolutely knew that 'things' were not the same as before … as before that pony had come to live in the field next to their house! Even wise old Solo was unable to sniff out exactly what had changed. He, along with Mowgli and Luca, just experienced the children as smelling somehow different. All three were worried!

The first thing Reuben did was to check on Jason-Rat. Much to his relief, he found the white rat sleeping peacefully, almost buried in the deep shavings that filled his shoe box bed.

After gulping some water and eating two biscuits, he threw himself onto his bed and burst into tears. This morning's adventure – or adventures in plural - had been just too much.

He fell into a deep and dreamless sleep, only waking when Esme crept into his room and gently shook his shoulder.

"Reubs … you'd better get up and come down for tea. Mum thinks we've both just got back from school together. Are you feeling better? You looked awful at lunch."

Reuben sat up and realised that he was feeling physically fine, full of energy, and very hungry. But … still very confused by all that had happened. He desperately wanted to tell Esme all about it, but knew the story would be long in the telling.

"O.K. Tea. Then we talk … right?"

Esme nodded eagerly.

Tea over, they asked if they could be excused washing up and clearing away because they had to 'sort some stuff out' for school tomorrow on top of their usual homework.

Instead of going into the sitting room where they usually did their homework in the winter, they scuttled quietly upstairs and went into Esme's bedroom. Esme closed the door behind them as quietly as she could and then turned to Reuben who had thrown himself down onto her bed and was starting to tell his story in a loud voice.

She put a finger to her lips and whispered "Shush … don't speak so loudly; don't want Mum and Dad to hear." She plonked down on the bed next to him and he continued in a quiet almost whispery voice.

She could tell he was still really upset by whatever had happened. Sensing her brother's fear reminded Esme of her own experience and how frightened she had been. A shiver ran up and down her spine.

Then she remembered what GreenZap had said about the main reason for showing her the picture of older versions of herself.
She had choices ... and was able to decide how her future was going to be!

She settled down to hear her brother's story.

17 - Reuben in Shock

After Esme and the green Pegasus had flown out of sight, Reuben was left alone standing in the lane, next to the small brown pony. He was feeling pretty angry. Why hadn't he been asked to go with them!

The pony gave himself a great shake, sending dust flying in all directions.

"Eh!" Reuben put his arms up to protect his face.

After one last shake, the pony stretched out his neck towards Reuben, and with soft hairy muzzle and rubbery lips began to nuzzle and pluck at the boy's hands and then his coat pocket. '*Sugar?*' An image of sugar lumps with fluff sticking to them flooded Reuben's mind.

Still feeling distinctly put out by what had just happened, the boy absentmindedly fished around in his pocket and produced a sugar lump and held it out to the pony. Mr Nibbs - for indeed it was he – took it from his open palm and scrunched it noisily.

Reuben was feeling … abandoned. He didn't know what to do with himself.
But for sure Mr Nibbs couldn't be allowed to wander around the lane, so he grabbed the pony's forelock and tugged, hoping to get the pony to follow him back into the field he had obviously escaped from.

Mr Nibbs had other ideas though. He straightened his front legs and dug in, leaning back against Reuben's pull.

'Uh uh!' He shook his head quite roughly and dislodged Reuben's grasp. *'You're to come with me.'*

Reuben stood stock still, cocked his head to one said and looked quizzically at the pony. Had Mr Nibbs just said something?

'Yes. You could 'hear' Pegasus couldn't you? So you can 'hear' me if you decide to. As I said: You're to come with me. Hop on.'

Given that the last time Reuben had 'hopped on' to Mr Nibbs was the beginning of what Reuben thought of as 'adventures with Pegasus', the boy felt both wary and excited about following the pony's instructions.

'Come on, we haven't got all day. If you don't hurry, we'll be too late. Got to get there in time for lunch break.'

Reuben approached the pony with some trepidation. Where did they have to be before lunch time? What was going to happen?

He got up onto Mr Nibb/s back – not as elegantly as his first time vault … with a bit of a scramble in fact – and grabbed a handful of dusty mane. He waited for the pony to explode into Pegasus …

… and waited.

Nothing happened, except that the pony set off at a bone shaking trot down the lane in the direction of the road.

Reuben, not having anything to control the pony with, just sat there, legs slightly lifted to help him balance, wondering when the 'transformation' was going to take place.

It didn't. They just kept trotting right on down to the main road, turned left and kept going along the verge towards the bus stop where the twins always caught the school bus. As they turned, Reuben just caught a glimpse of the bus coming into view back down the road.

"What the …?" thought Reuben, feeling very embarrassed as the bus slowly passed them before coming to a halt at the bus stop.

The pony broke into a canter for the last few yards and then came to an abrupt halt at the same time as lowering his head to the ground. Reuben, unprepared for this manoeuvre, was tipped forward and slid head first down the pony's neck and onto the ground right in front of the opening doors of the bus.

He had never felt so undignified in his life. He scrambled to his feet and brushed down his slightly muddy trousers and jacket.

"You all right son?" called the driver.

"I'm fine!" Reuben muttered, before stepping up into the bus, wondering how he could explain what had happened. But the bus driver just smiled and said: "You need to watch it running along the verge like that when it's so muddy. Easy to slip!"

Reuben turned around just in time to see Mr Nibbs cantering back the way they had come. As he did so, Reuben heard what could be called a horsey version of a chuckle. The words: 'see you later in the playground!' floated back into his mind.

It seemed though, that the driver had not even seen the pony! Nor, it appeared had any of the children travelling on the bus. Reuben had felt relieved and puzzled at the same time.

"It was really weird, Es," Reuben said to his sister, pausing in his storytelling. "It was a bit like nobody could actually see me … 'cept the driver … and he didn't see Nibbs."

Esme nodded. "Know what you mean … is sounds a bit like me and the older Esme … but not quite the same …?"

"Hmm." Reuben remained silent for several moments, puzzling over it.

"So what happened then?" his sister prompted.

"Well … I can't remember anything about the bus journey!"

He shrugged and continued with the story.

The next thing he had been aware of after catching the bus was lunch time at school.

Even though it was winter, the children were encouraged to go outside - unless the weather was too awful - after they had had their lunch and before starting afternoon classes.

Reuben was standing at the top of the steps leading down to the playground. He had started to walk down them to join the other children, but had felt very odd and had come to a halt.

A couple of his friends had run down the steps right next to him without saying anything … almost as if he was invisible … or not really there.

And then he realised that the rest of the children looked really strange – as though they weren't really there either. It was a very weird feeling.

As he recounted this bit, Esme started nodding. "Yes, yes … that's it!"

"I was scared, Es!" he admitted.

Then he had heard a whooshing sort of sound, and Pegasus, in his great silvery form, gently landed on the steps next to him. Reuben had felt such a relief. Somehow the presence of Pegasus made him feel safe, even when such strange things were happening to him. And … if the other children couldn't see him, then they wouldn't be able to see a huge great silver winged horse either!

He had turned to Pegasus and began to ask: "What has happened to …?" But Pegasus had stopped him finishing his question. *'Not now. I'll explain some time … you'll get used to being in spirit form and others not being able to see you. And you'll get used to being in more than one place at the same time. But right now, I'm short on time … got another appointment and I don't want to be late for that. What I want you to do now is look around the playground and tell me what you see.'*

Once Reuben had felt the connection between himself and the great horse, he had been more or less able to accept the very strange situation he found himself in.

He did what Pegasus had asked of him and looked around the playground below. Once again he became aware that what he was observing was not the usual noisy scene of lots of children playing, rushing around and yelling at each, or standing huddled together in deep conversation.

No. The younger children and several small groups were playing the usual sort of games. But dotted amongst this 'normality' were individual children standing or sitting completely alone.
These children were quite still, apart from their fingers which were tap-tapping on the screens of their mobile phones! And even stranger, they all seemed to be shadowy grey looking – a bit like Reuben imagined a ghost might look - except for when brownish reddish colours flared out from their heads.

Reuben had shuddered as he suddenly 'felt' the fear and anger these colours gave off. It felt almost as though he had been punched in the gut.

"Ugh! What is that?" He rubbed his solar plexus and inched closer to Pegasus.

'Don't fear, nothing can harm you. Now... you see that older boy over there in the corner ... go over to him and ...'

Esme was nodding frantically. "I know what's going to happen!"

"Yep! It was like you had in your story. It was me – only older!"

Reuben explained how he had felt scared to do what Pegasus had told him to do, and how the horse had given him an 'energy push' in the small of his back so that he had reluctantly set off towards the boy in the corner.

As he did so, JasonRat, who had been nestling quietly in the boy's inner coat pocket, gave a sudden squeak and moved out of the pocket up onto Reuben's shoulder, nestling down close to the boy's ear, long whiskers twitching and tickling his neck. Reuben had put a hand up to touch the rat and at that moment felt the tiny creature begin to tremble as it squeaked: *'Horrid, horrid, horrid!'*

Slightly startled, but not very – he was beginning to accept strange happens like animals speaking to him – Reuben asked: "What's horrid?"

'... *metal ... dead ... robots ... traps ... ugh!*' Jason's little furry body shivered all over as Reuben continued to make his way towards the boy in the far corner of the playground.

This boy was sitting on part of a climbing frame, peering intently at the screen of the brightly coloured Smartphone held in his left hand. Reuben could see that the boy's breathing was very fast and shallow, making a loud noise as though he was out of breath. A string of swear word that the twins were encouraged not to use came tumbling out of his mouth. Suddenly he had shut his phone and looked up, staring into the distance.

Reuben described to Esme how he had kept inching closer to the boy – with encouragement from Pegasus - and how it was clear he was very very upset about something.
The words 'cyber bullying' had popped into Reuben's mind. He wondered if somebody had posted something horrible on the boy's phone.

"It was really weird him not seeing me!"

"I know Ruebs ... really weird!" agreed Esme.

"So anyway ..." Reuben continued with his story:

The boy had put his phone away and pulled his coat closely around him. And at that moment JasonRat had started squeaking like crazy: '*look ... look ... escaping ... danger.*'

Reuben was startled to see the head of a white rat emerging from the older boy's jacket pocket. The boy had taken no notice of it at all. The rat had run down the side of his trouser leg onto the ground and very quickly through the fence into the playing field next to the playground. The boy seemed completely unaware of what had happened.

Then JasonRat got really upset. *'Weeeh,'* he squeaked, *'danger ... danger ...'* His little squeak trailed off into nothing and Reuben had felt the rat tense up his tiny body and nestle even closer into his neck. He had put a hand up to comfort the little creature, and had begun to edge his way in front of the boy, whose own rat had just escaped and run off into the dangerous 'wild' of the playing field.

But before Reuben had taken more than a few steps a series of terrified *'eeek, eeek, eeek ... loook'* shrilled by JasonRat, had stopped him in his tracks. If a rat could point, then JasonRat pointed with his whole little body towards the playing field.

Reuben had turned his gaze in that direction and watched mesmerised as the boy's rat rapidly snaked its way across the very green grass. Its white colour made it stand out like a bandaged thumb.

Reuben described how a horrifying scene had played out in front of his eyes whilst the boy who was his older self remained unaware, just staring blankly in front of him.

A dark speck in the sky had grown larger and larger and Reuben could make out the form of a large bird plummeting earthwards, its great talons stretching out ahead of it.

"No!" he had cried out loud … for he knew what was going to happen!

And it did. He stood helplessly watching as the great bird swooped down on the rodent, plucking it from the grass and carrying it skywards, clasped in its talons.

JasonRat, who, strangely enough, had already understood that the rat was in fact himself in the future, completely lost it. He burrowed his way downwards - out of site - causing Reuben to choke as he had squeezed his way between Reuben's throat and his shirt collar. He had finally come to a halt in Reuben's armpit – a safe space he hoped!

Reuben had just stood there, heart thumping, right hand under his left armpit as he cradled his terrified pet, telling himself there was absolutely nothing he could have done to save that 'other' rat.

And yet … Into his mind, as though from a huge distance, had come the words: *'I am Gyrre … Lord of the Air … keep you children safe!'*

Esme's eyebrows went up. "What! Did you say Gyrre?"

"Well, that's what it sounded like … that's what I thought I heard!" shrugged Reuben and went back to his story.

The Eagle, for that is what Reuben had realised it was, with the rat held tightly within its talons, had once again become nothing but a distant speck in the sky.

Reuben, very conscious of the warm breathing furriness in his left armpit, had slowly unbuttoned his shirt and caressed Jason with his right hand. "It's safe now, you can come out." he had murmured.

Jason's response had been very clear, though not 'spoken': *'No way! I'm staying here for now!'*

Reuben's mind had been swirling with questions: "An Eagle ... here? Can't be, they live in the mountains ... where am I ... school? ... who is this boy?"

At that last thought, he had felt a distinct 'mind-prod' from Pegasus who had been standing very, very patiently to the side of him all the while this had been happening.

'Check the boy, Reuben.'

So finally Reuben had gone to stand right in front of the older boy – who had still paid him no heed at all - his blank eyes staring into the distance, his forehead screwed up into a deep frown.

"I'll never forget that moment Es ... when I saw he was an older version of me! But ... he couldn't see me!"

His sister smiled in sympathy. "Me too ... never forget it! And she couldn't see me either."

Confronted by this older version of himself, Reuben had found himself completely paralysed. He had not been able to understand what was happening.

And he had been truly shocked by all that he had seen: the grey robot-like children sitting alone and silent with their mobile phones; the fate of the other white rat and JasonRat's fear.

The blood had drained from his face and he was visibly trembling. He was obviously in such a state of shock that even Pegasus - who had brought him here in the first place - felt pity for him.

So the great horse moved to stand so that the boy was encompassed by his giant silvery transparent form ... so that the boy's heart and his were close together. Anyone who had been able to 'see' would have thought that the horse was giving the boy a 'heart to heart' transfusion of light.

Whatever it was that was happening, after a few moments Reuben had regained his colour and had almost stopped trembling.

At this point in the story, Reuben gave a huge shiver and fell silent.

Esme prompted him: "So what happened then?"

He told how he had heard Pegasus say very gently: *'There is a message for you from Old Woman. Listen carefully.'*

So Reuben had tried to 'listen'. After some moments, and with the steadying presence of Pegasus,

258

the boy had felt the flickering fiery presence of that Being who had introduced herself to him as Old Woman.

He had then 'felt' her words as they had streamed into his mind: *'Reuben child, I am sorry that you have had to experience this fear. However, you have been shown this scene because it is very important that you understand how your own future ... and that of all humans ... is determined by the choices each of you makes.'*

'You were given a Smartphone as a Christmas present. Most of your friends have these wonderful pieces of technology, so it feels good for you to have one also. This is natural.
'Humans can use technology to provide useful and beneficial tools. And ... some of this technology can also be very dangerous and harmful. A tool such as a Smartphone can become your 'master' instead of a 'useful friend.'
'Do you understand why you have been shown these things?'

Reuben was not at all sure that he did, so had responded with a rather tentative 'think so'.

'That's all right ... no need to worry yourself. When you return to your usual consciousness, tell your sister about this experience. She will understand.'

Reuben had only had time to vaguely wonder what Old Woman had meant by 'usual consciousness' before he had found himself back in the lane where his sister had been about to stamp on her mobile phone.

So this was the story Reuben told his sister as they sat side by side on cushions in Esme's bedroom.

And of course his adventure made perfect sense to her, having had such a similar experience herself. She felt excited and confused all at the same time – as though she had learned something of mind-boggling importance ... but didn't really know what it was! There was so much to talk about ... so much she didn't understand.

And one of the biggest questions going round in her mind was about that bird of prey that had taken the 'other' rat. Reuben had said he had heard something like '*I am Gyrre Lord of the Sky ... or of the Air*' ... ? If this was so then maybe the bird that had appeared when she was in the park with her older self was Gyrre. And if it was ... then what was her eagle doing in one of her brother's dreams ... visions ... experiences ... adventures? She didn't know what to call the things that were happening to them.

But the first question she had for her brother was:

"Is JasonRat okay?"

A tiny squeak from within Reuben's jacket pocket gave her the answer. She had never particularly liked the rat but suddenly she felt a great surge of love for him.

They spent the next hour discussing all this craziness that had come into their lives.

"I can understand 'dreams'… well, I mean I know what they are … they're dreams!"

"Yeah … but these last things weren't dreams were they? We were awake when they happened … "

"That time at the fair with Old Woman Gypsy … she was the one who 'moved'."

"But this morning … we were in two places at once … and two different times as well …"

"And invisible to other people!"

In the end they gave up trying to work it all out.

"It's just weird … and that's it!" sighed Esme.

"And it's just happening … and that's how it is!" added Reuben with an attempt to laugh. "And I'm zonked … going to bed."

"Me too."

Not long afterwards, Eve Montana, who had gone to check if the twins had finished their homework and wanted a hot drink before bed, was surprised to find them both in their bedrooms and already sound asleep.
In the kitchen, she reported this to Fonso.

"Hm! I think you're right, Eve. There's something odd going on with those two. But you know what … they're happy … they're healthy … and they're getting good marks at school. Perhaps it's all just part of growing up. I know I kept lots of secrets from my parents when I was their age. Let's not worry about it."

"Maybe you're right Fonso." She sank down into one the armchairs by the Aga, with one of those great big 'end-of-the-day' sighs. She waited for Kimber to settle himself on her lap before reaching for the book she was reading.

18 - A Trip to the Zoo

Mr and Mrs Montana had decided to take the twins to the zoo. There was a zoo in Bristol. It would take them about an hour and a half to drive from home to Bristol, and if they set off really early there would be time for a trip to a big shopping centre after the zoo visit.

Neither of the twins had been to a zoo before, though they had watched television programmes about them. And what is more, they had never been to a large shopping centre either. So they were very excited about the trip.

There had been a lot of talk recently – on TV programmes, and at school - about whether zoos were a good thing or a bad thing. Was it better for animals to be bred in zoos and kept there in captivity than for their species to become extinct? Some people said it was really important to prevent species from becoming extinct; some people said that there was always a time for 'extinction'… think of the dinosaurs.

The twins had come to the conclusion that perhaps zoos were a fairly good thing – as long as the animals were kept properly and loved by their keepers. They had always enjoyed the company of animals and deeply loved their own animal companions.
Esme had even considered being a zoo keeper when she got older. But when she realised that

none of the animals could actually leave the zoo ... even if they wanted to, she changed her mind.

It was hearing their children seriously discussing zoos that had decided their parents to let them spend time in a zoo for themselves.

The trip to the shopping centre was to give the children - and their parents – the chance to choose some new summer clothes, particularly shoes, for themselves. Because the Montanas were kept so busy, what with growing and selling vegetables and Fons' work on the farms, they rarely had time to shop for anything other than daily necessities. Often their clothes were bought from catalogues and they didn't always fit well.

In fact, the whole family were all excited about the trip! Even Fons, who was reluctant to take time away from preparing the tunnels for the salad leaf seedlings he had waiting to be planted out! He was not looking forward to the clothes shopping bit, but had been promised an hour on his own to look around the bookshop Waterstones to see if he could find a book about growing chilli peppers that had been recommended to him.

In the end the family set off so early that the zoo had only just opened when they arrived. They left their car in the parking lot and walked slowly towards the entrance, enjoying the feelings of anticipation and listening intently to the animal sounds coming from inside the zoo's grounds.

"That's a lion!" whispered Reuben to his sister.

She waited for the sound again and said: "No, I think it's an elephant!"

"No way!" insisted Reuben. "That's a roar!"

The sound came again, and Esme was about to argue that Elephants sometimes sound like lions when the 'roar' was drowned out by a sudden cacophony of bird noises. "Crikey! I wonder what caused that!" she said instead.

The children's excitement was palpable as they fidgeted in the small queue to buy their tickets.

Where to go first?

Reuben wanted to see the chimpanzees and gorillas. "Pleeeeze!" He was bouncing up and down.

"Must see the raptors ... birds of prey!" Esme determined quietly, to which Reuben added: "Yes we must ... but after the chimps!"

Fonso expressed a preference for starting off at the wolf enclosure.

Eve Montana said she really didn't care ... she was interested in everything but could they please make up their minds ... unless they wanted to spend most of their time arguing! How about they pulled straws and the person who got the long straw chose where to go first? As she spoke she was busy pulling up long strands of grass to act as straws.

She held out the grass stalks ... and it was their father who pulled the long stalk. "Right ... wolves!"

Although the twins whinged a little, he stood his ground, laughing out loud.

"Wolves it is! I want you to see wolves 'in the flesh'".

Alfonso Montana had often told the children stories of his boyhood in Cazorla, a huge nature reserve in South Eastern Spain, and the wild animals that used to roam free. One of their favourite stories was of how he had found a tiny wolf cub with a broken leg that had been abandoned by its family. He told them that he had taken it home and cared for it and that it had lived with them until it died many years later. The twins were not sure they believed their father ... but it was a good story!

By the middle of the day they all agreed that they couldn't take in any more zoo sights and sounds.

"We'll come back again in the summer holidays." their mother promised.

Esme in particular was exhausted. She had been trying so hard to understand what the animals were saying! After all, she could 'speak with animals' couldn't she! What she didn't then know, is that not all animals either want to or can communicate with humans.

Reuben had not been trying to 'understand' anything! He had just been totally absorbed by the way the zoo animals looked and behaved. Seeing them live, even being able to touch some of them was very different from seeing them on the TV. At one point he realised that his parents had been right when they refused to let him bring JasonRat. Supposing the rat had decided to leave the safety of Reuben's pockets and explore ... just imagine what could have happened to him!

But what had really caught his attention was a very large, very brightly coloured parrot. The bird was intelligent indeed! Its clever antics were captivating a large audience.

The bird's keeper had asked all the children in the crowd to come to the rail that separated the audience from the bird and its keeper. Each child had then been given two small handfuls of food that parrots are supposed to like. They were then asked to put their hands behind their backs and wait to see who the parrot, whose name was Billy, would choose to take food from.
Next, the bird would fly around a few times before alighting and perching on the wooden rail in front of its chosen child, who was then asked to hold out one of its hands and offer Bill the food.
If the parrot was pleased with what was offered it bobbed its head up and down, gently took a beak full, and said to the child in its very distinct parrotty voice: 'Clever girl!' or 'Clever boy!'
If the food offered was not to its liking is shook its head from side to side and said 'Silly boy!' or 'Silly girl'!

The children loved it.

Reuben, who had always been fascinated by parrots and had wanted one of his own for a long time, hoped Billy would choose him.

He did.

Reuben opened one of his hands and held it out to the bird. The parrot did not take the food. Neither did it nod or shake its head. It just cocked its head to one side and stared intently at Reuben with a bright black eye for several seconds. Then before anybody had realised what was happening, Billy hopped up onto Reuben's shoulder and started pecking at his ear.

"Billy! Stop!" The keeper grabbed at the leather thong attached to one of the parrot's legs and tugged.

Reuben was startled and confused … and happy! The parrot wasn't really pecking his ear, but very gently nibbling with its enormous beak and emitting odd little clicketty-click sounds as it did so.

It resisted the tug on its leg for several seconds before opening its wings and flying off Reuben's shoulder with an almighty squawk that had the audience covering their ears with their hands. The squawks continued for several minutes as the bird tugged free of the keeper's hold and flew round and round the enclosure before eventually coming to land on the keeper's shoulder.

The keeper who really loved his birds, could tell that Billy was mighty upset about something. He called out that the session was over, and the children and their parents began moving away from the display area, off to find another animal to entertain them.

Reuben stayed though, looking at the bird still sitting on its keeper's shoulder and rapidly bobbing its head up and down.

"Off you go son, we've finished now!" called the keeper.

Reuben turned to move away and as he did so his mind was filled with images of many parrots flying high above tree tops. The image made him feel really sad. He looked back towards the parrot once more and muttered under his breath: "What's the matter parrot? What did I do to upset you?"

Immediately Billy stopped the bobbing. And just as immediately Reuben's mind was filled once again with the image of many flying parrots. He could almost feel his heart squeeze with immense sorrow, and he felt tears welling up in his eyes.

Not knowing what else to do he went to find his family where they were waiting for him in the zoo's café.

He was unusually quiet on the journey between the zoo and the shopping centre. But his sister and parents were chatting animatedly about all the animals they had seen.

"Weren't those wolves wonderful ... "

"Did you see that little elephant kick the even smaller one … "

"That huge male Orang-utan was just spectacular … those jowls … "

"That Golden Eagle was so very special." Esme sighed.

They chatted on and on, not even Esme noticing how quiet Reuben was.

Several hours later, having successfully bought all they were looking for, the family were wending their way towards the exit of the shopping centre. Each was carrying several shopping bags.

They were passing a pet shop with a window full of small animals and birds in cages. Through the open shop doorway a large brightly coloured parrot chained to a perch could be seen.

Reuben, who in the excitement of buying stuff, had finally forgotten the unsettling incident with the zoo parrot, was startled back into remembering when he spotted the bird at the back of the shop.

He started walking slowly backwards after his parents, his gaze fixed on the pet shop.

Esme had been dawdling along, finishing off an ice cream and looking in the window of a shop that sold crafty things from around the world. She caught up with Reuben and looked to see what he was watching.

"Wow, those colours are just amazing!" she whispered.

Reuben nodded without saying anything. He stopped moving. Then he started walking slowly towards the pet shop. He looked a bit as though he had been hypnotised.

Esme, who knew how fascinated her brother was by parrots, realised he wanted to go into the pet shop to see the bird close up.

"I'll get Mum and Dad to wait for you over there in that seating area by the cafes."

Reuben, nodded again. "Thanks Es."

Then something unexpected happened.

Before she had time to move off to catch up with their parents, Esme saw a figure walking quickly towards her brother. Realising that Rueben's attention was totally focused on the parrot and he was probably going to bump into this person, she started to call out to him.

Too late!

Reuben did indeed bump straight into the person. Or perhaps the person bumped into him?

Esme was startled. A very strange looking person, she observed.

The person was a young man, tall, slim and broad shouldered. The most immediately noticeable thing about him was his hair, dark red with orange streaks. And it stood straight out for several inches all around his head.

Unaware of what was happening, the twin's parents kept on walking slowly towards the shopping centre's exit, chatting intently with each other as they went.

Esme hesitated, not knowing whether to chase after her parents and ask them to wait, or stay and see what happened. She stayed. Not only was she fascinated by the young man; she felt as if she was living in a world of slow motion ... and that made the idea of running anywhere seem impossible!

Reuben, startled out of his reverie, backed away and looked up to face the person who had blocked his passage. He was ready to apologise.

But no words left his mouth as he stared at the young man, who had moved away from him slightly but was regarding him with interest as a slow smile crept across a face the colour of a ginger biscuit.

Before the smile the face had been rather fearsome, reminding Esme of the piercing fierce look that was her Eagle Gyrre's normal expression.
She was just close enough to hear the young man say to Reuben: "Ah, I do apologise for stopping you, but I have the feeling you might be able to help me. I am looking for the cloud with the copper lining, and something tells me you might now where to find it."

Reuben stared into the young man's face, a little frown of puzzlement appearing between his eyebrows as though trying to remember something.

Esme had managed to float (or so it felt to her) to her brother's side - just in case he might need help. She saw earrings in each of the young man's ears, one jewel flashing ruby red and the other emerald green. His clothes were most unusual - shirt and trousers made of soft 'almost patterned' deep brown cloth. Over the shirt was a sleeveless jacket that appeared to be made entirely of feathers. They were iridescent black feathers and they shimmered with just a hint of dark blue, almost as though they were part of a live bird. His feet, she noticed, were bare, with long brown toes and toenails painted a deep shimmering blue – the same colour that glinted in the feathers.

Esme drew in her breath ready to speak, and reached out a hand to touch her brother's shoulder.

But he was no longer there. Neither was the young man.

She was left standing there, hand reaching out into thin air … and back in 'normal' time.
She turned a complete circle, scanning everywhere for Reuben as she did so. She noticed her parents, now some distance away, had stopped and turned around, checking to see where their children were. She saw her father lift his hand and call out: "Come on you two!"

She waved back at him to show she had heard.

Then ... from the corner of her eye she saw Reuben hurrying towards her ... from the direction of pet shop. He caught up with her, a strange puzzled look on his face.

"What ...?" Esme was about to ask what had happened when the penny dropped: He had just 'been somewhere'.

She gave her brother a shove and said urgently: "Tell me when we get home. We'd better catch up with Mum and Dad."

His puzzled look was replaced by a look of relief. "Ooof! ... OK."

When they caught up with their parents, their father said to Reuben:

"I saw you looking at that parrot in the pet shop. If you are serious about keeping a parrot you need to start saving. They cost a lot of money. And you'd better learn all you can about the ... they live for a very long time you know ... "

Reuben didn't answer his father immediately. When he finally replied it was to say very quietly: "No Dad, I don't. I don't ever want to keep a parrot!"

Fons looked down at his son in surprise and noticed what seemed to be a tear running down his cheek. He put a hand gently on his son's shoulder. "Okay ... tell me about it later ... we need to hurry now if we don't want to get caught up in the rush hour."

After a raised eyebrow glance at his wife who had been following the conversation intently, he took hold of Reuben's hand and started walking really fast towards the exit.

Reuben didn't even object to his father holding his hand, and just allowed himself to be pulled along. He remained unusually quiet all the way home, apparently lost in thought. Esme too was quiet, letting her brother be, now knowing for herself how strange it felt when you got back from having 'been somewhere'.

It was just beginning to get dark when they arrived home. The twins, loaded down with parcels, were first out of the car. They walked tiredly up the path to the side door of the house.
Suddenly a huge cackling and cawing erupted from some of the trees at the bottom of the garden and five black shapes came swooping towards the house, alighting on the guttering of the roof. It was the family of crows who lived close by; the same ones who had emptied out the rubbish bins on bonfire night!
They perched in a line right above the door at the side of the house, cackling and cawing non-stop.

Reuben slowly let his parcels slider to the ground and looked up at the birds. Quietly he said "I'm really sorry!" Their chatter stopped apart from some low level beak clicks. Then, as suddenly as they had arrived, they flew off the guttering and back to their tree.

Esme looked at her brother quizzically but he just shook his head and muttered "Later."

By this time the dogs had been alerted to something strange happening and were barking frantically and scrabbling at the inside of the door.
Eve Montana arrived, loaded with packages. She handed the door key to Reuben, who opened the door and was almost bowled over by three Choccies pushing their way out. The dogs greeted Mrs Montana briefly and then clustered around the two children.

"What on earth is going on?" Demanded Fons, also laden with packages, as he strode down the path towards the rest of his family. "What were those crows on about? They're not usually around at this time! Is everybody OK?"

Eve Montana was standing there, her arms full of bags, waiting for the twins to untangle themselves from the Choccies. She was looking very puzzled. "I don't know …?" She replied to her husband's question, "They seemed upset about something but they've gone now … can we get in please!" This addressed to the twins who had sunk down onto the doorstep and were making only vague attempts to push the dogs away.

Finally they all managed to tumble in … Esme, dogs, Mrs Montana, Mr Montana, and finally … Reuben. Apart from greeting the dogs he had not said a word. He followed the rest of his family into the kitchen, dumped his packages on the floor and sank into one of the old armchairs.

The others were too busy to notice …

"Let's get those dogs fed … they're making such a fuss … you sure they were fed this morning?"

"I'll feed them, Mum." said Esme, knowing that it was not food the dogs were clamouring for. Feeding them gave her a chance to be with them and assure them that she and Reuben were all right.

While all this had been going on, Kimber had been sitting on his 'escape' perch – the top of the tall cupboard where all the china was kept. His tail was whipping from side to side, his ears flat to his head and eyes shimmering with anger.
Esme could feel the cat's anger. She stopped fussing the agitated Luca and looked around for the cat. He let her know where he was by hissing from his perch.
Although Esme could tell he was upset, she didn't know why. She sighed and went to put food into his dish. This 'understanding animals' was really tiring. Was the cat upset because the dogs were getting all the attention? Or was it because the dogs were upset about something?

She showed him his food bowl and asked him to come down and be fussed. Slowly his body relaxed and his tail stopped whipping. He jumped down and stalked over to where Esme had put his bowl on the floor. To reach it he had to pass the dogs, all now busy eating from their own bowls. As he passed, he hissed loudly and took a swipe at a hairy brown leg.

He only picked at his food before leaving a half full bowl and leaping to sit on the back of the chair Reuben was sitting in. Esme noticed Kimber move his head away from Reuben's hand as the boy reach up behind him to touch the cat.

Weird! Esme guessed that the crows' strange behaviour was something to do with Reuben and the parrot, but no more than that. And obviously whatever it was had upset the dogs ... but she couldn't imagine why. And now Kimber! Was the cat just cross about the dogs getting all the attention ... or was there something more?

A little while later, when Fons got back from shutting up the tunnels and attending to the chickens, he reported that these birds too had appeared to be upset, all huddled in a corner of their shed and clucking more than normal. He wondered aloud if the animals had been upset by a fox doing the rounds.
Before she could help herself Esme said: "No, Daddy, it's not that ... " and then tailed off into silence, turning away from her Father and catching a quick glance at Reuben.

But her brother's eyes were closed and he seemed unaware of the exchange.

Esme shrugged off what she had said by exclaiming "I'm famished! What's for tea Mum?"

"I've got some pasta to heat up. It'll take five minutes if you can wait." She was relieved to turn her attention to the more ordinary needs of her family … something had been very unsettled and strange earlier on!

Over the evening meal Reuben told his parents about how seeing the parrots - first at the zoo and then in the pet shop – had made him realise that can be really cruel to keep a bird in a cage or even in captivity … especially birds like parrots that usually live in big groups like families and fly freely for long distances.

Ah! Esme got it!

Both parents responded by telling Reuben that they were pleased that he had come to that conclusion for himself. It was just what they had wanted to tell him, but knew that if they tried to dissuade him he would have been even more determined.

So that was that!

What Reuben had not told his parents was about the trip he had been taken on by the 'strange person' he had bumped into at the shopping centre.

He was so exhausted by the experience that he didn't even have the energy to tell Esme about it, but went to bed as soon as he had finished his meal. Esme had followed her brother upstairs as soon as she could without risking making her parents suspicious, but by the time she peered around the open door of Reuben's bedroom, she could see that he was fast asleep.

And anyway she too felt extraordinarily sleepy. It had after all been a very busy day for all of the family!

19 - A Strange Young Man

Both children were up late the following Sunday morning. Their parents were out already, working in the tunnels. They had left a note for the twins to get their own breakfast.

They served themselves bowls of cereal and sat close together at a corner of the table.

"Go on then, tell me where you went with that strange looking person?"

Reuben started telling the story, speaking quietly just in case their parents entered the kitchen unexpectedly. But he hadn't got any further than saying that the strange person had turned out to be ... 'YoungMan', when he suggested they go up to Esme's bedroom.

"It's a long story," he explained ... "And some of it might be difficult to tell. I don't want Mum and Dad barging in ..."

"OK, come on then."

Taking their bowls with them, they scrambled upstairs to Esme room. She was feeling very exciting, anticipating the telling of an adventure. She didn't notice how quiet Reuben was.

They settled themselves on the floor of Esme's room. Reuben picked up the story where he had left off:

"I looked into that man's rather strange face ... really weird ... I saw a kind of bird, not a man ... his nose looked like a great beak. I was really scared" Reuben shivered slightly "Then he said: 'Greetings to you from Old Woman. She has suggested that the time is right for me to introduce myself to you. So let me introduce myself. I am Young Man. I believe she mentioned me to you ...?' He cocked his head in a most birdlike manner.' I am her other half. And you, I believe are called Reuben in the human realm ... is that not so?'"

At this revelation Reuben had felt his hairs stand on end and a shiver run down his spine ... but with anticipation, not fear. He managed a slight nod.

'Good, so now we know each other. I am taking you to meet some birds. Apparently you like birds? Do you give your permission for me to take you on a journey?'

Again Reuben managed a slight nod, very unsure of what to expect. He did indeed remember Old Woman mentioning Young Man on that first occasion he had been taken to see her by Pegasus.
But this was in the middle of a family shopping trip and they were on their way home.

Of course Young Man knew what Reuben was thinking and said: *'Don't worry. In human terms you'll only be gone for the blink of an eye!'*

At that, Reuben could have sworn the bird man winked, before taking him by the hand.

In that moment al Reuben's doubts vanished, and the strange adult and the child entered another dimension!

Reuben described to his sister how he had found himself in the shape of a large brightly coloured parrot, was flying alongside YoungMan who was also in the form of a bird!
"Talk about weird! I was flying like a bird … and my eyesight was like a bird … I think anyway … but I was thinking like me … you know, like a human … and … I wasn't frightened!" Reuben stopped to breath and looked at his sister.

"Go on then!" she said impatiently, perfectly at home with the idea of her brother turning into a parrot.

The bird form that YoungMan had taken was one that Reuben had never seen before. He tried to describe it to his sister: "It was sort of the same colours as when he was a man … but not quite. His head and neck feathers were all glowing orangy red and yellow … and the rest of his feathers were the same colour as before but more glowing. He had a long tail a bit like a pheasant's and then he had sort of feathery plumes coming out of his head. Very beautiful!" finished Reuben with a wide smile.

Esme nodded encouragingly at her brother, trying to envisage this beautiful bird as she waited for him to continue.

Reuben, who by that time was no longer totally surprised by the strange things that kept happening to him, described how he had began to feel more curiosity than fright. He had done what he had learned to do with Pegasus and 'opened his mind' to the thoughts of this strange YoungMan Bird.

'The cloud with the copper lining will take us where we are going the quickest … if we can find it! Clouds are the trickiest beings to work with you know. When the air and the water get together to form clouds The Winds seem to enjoy nothing more than confusing all other beings by constantly moving the 'Cloudpoints' – meeting places you would call them – around the sky … and that's without the clouds themselves constantly changing shape!'

This all sounded most familiar to Reuben, who distinctly remembered Pegasus going on about the unreliability of clouds.

Reuben turned to ask Esme: "Remember I told you how Pegasus went on about unreliable clouds?"

She shrugged. "A bit."

"Well, YoungMan must have heard a thought I was having about how strange it was that these amazing Magical Beings that I kept meeting were bamboozled by … clouds! He went into this long explanation about the 'power of the elements' and how they need to be treated with respect … otherwise they become unwilling to co-operate in activities such as providing rain for crops … something about humans having disturbed the weather. I didn't understand half of it but he said that didn't matter because I would understand when I needed to." Reuben pulled a frowny face. "I hope I do."

"Anyway…" Reuben returned to his story.

All this time they had been flying along in a bright blue sky with not a cloud in sight. At last they found themselves at the beginnings of a vapour trail – rather like those left by some aeroplanes.
'Ah, here we are. This will lead us to the cloud we need … see how the path shimmers copper?'

Reuben did see. There was a distinct pinkish colour to the vapour they had entered into.

Then, as if no time at all had passed, they were right close up to an enormous dark grey cloud. It looked rather ominous and Reuben had felt scared again. But his bird-Self seemed quite undeterred, plunging straight into the cloud alongside Young-Man-Bird.

And once inside the cloud, all Reuben's fear was gone. This cloud really did have a warm coppery-coloured lining and its gentle shimmer surrounded them with feelings of peace and contentment.
But this had only lasted for a few moments. Reuben heard YoungMan think: *'Here we go!'* and they exited from the cloud with the copper lining into … another world.

Reuben had gasped as he had looked down onto treetops … and more treetops. As far as he could see there was nothing but treetops below them.

'Well Parrot, this is your homeland. Let's go find your family!' They began to fly downwards towards the great carpet of trees below them.

Excitement welled up within Reuben-Parrot. If he had been in his human form he would have been crying with happiness. But in his parrot form, crying was not possible … instead he felt his little bird heart swell up and begin to pound with happiness.'

His Parrot-Self let out a tiny squawk … 'Home!'

The squawks became louder and louder and he could only just hear YoungMan-Bird answer 'Yes! I've brought you home, Parrot!'

As the two of them come closer to the trees they could see groups of brightly coloured birds flying here and there, in and out of the tree tops. Reuben-parrot could feel their delight in their freedom. He could 'hear' them gossiping amongst each other … telling each other where to find the best fruit … where there was a wonderful sand bath on the banks of the river … and less happily, where there were groups of humans and machines cutting down the trees – their trees – making horrible noise and sending horrible smells into the air!

Reuben-Parrot could hardly control his excitement, squawking and squawking, and flapping and flapping – all over the place as the human part of him tried to get the hang of using his wings to swoop and swirl and twist and turn.

YoungMan-Bird flew tightly by his side, following each twist and turn.
'Is this not beautiful … to fly freely in the ai r… to survey the world from on high. Let's visit your family … follow me.'

Reuben-Parrot, still confused about whether he was human or bird, managed to nod his feathery head up and down up and down in between squawks.

He followed Young-Man-Bird in a spiral down, and down, towards the tree tops.
As they got close, a group of about eight large parrots emerged from where they had been perching in the top branches of a particularly high tree. They came flying directly towards the two adventurers.

During their flight down from the cloud to the forest below, YoungMan had explained to Reuben that these very large, red, yellow, blue and green 'parrots' were called 'Macaws' by humans, and that they lived in the tropical forests of South and Central America.

These welcoming Macaws flew around and about Reuben-Parrot and YoungMan-Bird. They flew in front of them, between them and alongside them, making so much noise that had Rueben had hands he would have covered his ears.

Finally the family – for that is who they were - guided the two strangers down into the trees and onto branches where they could all perch close together. Individual parrots were all trying to get as close as possible to Reuben-Parrot, jostling each other out of the way so they could touch beaks. Although he couldn't actually understand what they were saying, he sort of 'knew' that they were asking him questions.

All these birds seemed to have great respect for YoungMan-Bird, not jostling him once. He remained close to Reuben through all the manoeuvrings, and sent the boy thoughts telling him what the family of Macaws were saying:

'We missed you …'
'It has been a long time …'
'Where have you been? …'
'Why have you not come back before?'

Suddenly Reuben parrot realised something. He, the human Reuben had taken on the form of Billy – the parrot from the zoo!

The human Reuben, sitting with his sister, telling her this story, suddenly stopped talking. He sighed deeply and remained silent. Esme saw that a couple of tears had started to run down his cheeks.

What! Reuben crying? Her brother never cried!

Reuben hurriedly brushed the tears away and began to speak again, very quietly: "The next part was horrible Es; I don't really want to talk about it much …"

"But … what was so horrible?"

"Well ... it was as though I was suddenly filled with lots of memories from lots of different parrots that were in captivity ... and they were such sad memories. I realised that Macaws ... well parrots ... are very sociable creatures. I saw ... and heard ... how they had been captured when tiny and taken from their families ... lots of them had died! Then some of them had been cruelly treated, kept in tiny cages, never let loose to fly free!

And ... all this because people pay lots of money for them! Because they are beautiful and because they are clever!"

Reuben paused before adding: "You know Es, when I was there it felt like I was actually part of that family ... it really did! I could never want to have a 'pet' parrot now! It would be just too awful!"

"You didn't know ... !" Esme reached out to touch her brother.

"No. I didn't. But I do now!"

Esme said nothing. Reuben was staring into the distance ... not really there ... remembering the memories of Reuben–Parrot.

His next words came out in a rush: "But not all the memories were so awful. Some of them weren't so sad. Some parrots had lived with a loving human for many years and quite enjoyed the company, enjoyed learning how to 'speak human'; not having to go looking for food ... and other things like that. And ... there were some who all lived together in groups in 'parrot sanctuaries' – which they seemed to quite enjoy … but still they wished they could fly free."

He looked at his sister; "I actually felt what it was like to be Billy – you know, the parrot in the zoo, and then Redcap – that was the parrot in the pet shop. I actually felt what it was like to have to perform for humans all day long, and what it was like to attached to a perch …" his voice trailed off " … all … day … long … "

Esme felt so much misery coming from Reuben, that she could feel tears welling up in her own eyes and spilling down her cheeks.

That seemed to give Reuben permission to cry too, and he did … arms crossed and hugging his shoulders, he started to sob.

Esme didn't know what to do. She felt embarrassed. Her brother sometimes called her a cry baby when she cried because something had caused her to feel sad. And now here was her brother 'crying his heart out' in front of her.

She decided that the best thing to do was leave him to it. She got up from the floor, gave him a slight touch on the shoulder, crept to the door, let herself out and shut it gently. Just before it shut she thought she heard him mutter to himself "'spose I could have a parrot if I had rescued it from a cruel home."

She went downstairs just as her father opened the kitchen door, pushed off his wellingtons with a sigh and said: "Time for a cuppa, Eve; that was hard work."

Mrs Montana nodded an agreement as she followed her husband into the kitchen and went over to the Aga for the kettle of hot water sitting there, ready to produce cups of tea at short notice on occasions like this.

By this time Esme had managed to clear the dishes from the table and move them over to the sink where she washed them quickly before either of her parents could make any comments about it being time their children learned to clear up after themselves.

20 - Birds in Cages

It was several days after Reuben's 'parrot trip' and Esme was getting a bit worried about her brother. He had been so unlike his usual self: really quiet instead of talkative. He sighed rather a lot and spent strange amounts of time just sitting in the old armchair by the Aga, absentmindedly twiddling Kimber's fur.

The cat of course, took advantage of this unusual access to a warm lap and some rather haphazard grooming. He dozed contentedly. And this worried Esme too. She even felt slightly jealous, because **she** was supposed to be Kimber's special human friend!

Her brother was also spending ages in his room, apparently talking to JasonRat, though even when Esme listened at the door, she couldn't make out what he was saying.

Or sometimes he just spent ages outside with the Choccies. They of course were more than happy to have his company and on a couple of occasions Esme saw Solo grasp her brother's wrist and take him off somewhere.

But he wasn't talking to her! Well only 'hurry up!' or 'pass the salt' sort of talk. He wasn't sharing what he was thinking with her! She felt lonely. It was almost as though she had lost her twin.

She did realise though that he was trying to work stuff out … stuff to do with the parrot trip. So she tried not to feel too upset about being ignored.

Eve and Alfonso Montana were once again concerned by the unusual behaviour of their children. There had never been a time when the two hadn't communicated continuously, but now …

They discussed it, listened to fierce denials from each twin that 'anything was wrong', and … as both children were eating well and seemed to be happily getting on with homework and such like … they put it down to 'growing up'.

And because Reuben was so preoccupied with his own thoughts, Esme had time to spare. She started to pay more attention to her frequent dreams than she had previously. Even when nothing particular happened in them, she began to realise that her 'dreamtime animals' were in some strange way teaching her stuff.

It wasn't always obvious what they were teaching her, but she just knew that she could learn from them if she allowed herself to do so. It was almost as though in some strange way during dreams they became a part of her and showed her how they experienced the world. At least, that's how she explained it to herself … even though it seemed a little weird and she didn't think she could explain it to anybody else, even Reuben. For instance when she saw the world through the eyes of the eagle Gyrre, she could see so much all at once and how one thing was connected to another. But when she used her human eyes only she lost sight of all the connections and couldn't work out how things fitted together.

And because of this she began to observe her own pets and the animals and birds she saw every day with more attention as well.

Then one afternoon, about a couple of weeks after their Bristol trip, on their way back from school, when they were walking silently home down the lane, Reuben burst out: "I think I know how to fix it."

"Fix what?" Esme asked vaguely, her mind on some homework she had to finish.

"The parrot thing! Well the bird thing really ... 'cos it's not only parrots you know!"

That caught Esme's attention. She turned to look at him. "What's not only parrots? Tell me."

"Well ..., I've been wondering how I tell other people not to keep birds in cages!" The words all came out in a rush. "I've wanted to have a parrot of my own since I was little ... you know that don't you?"

"corse I do! ... you've even talked about saving up your pocket money!"

"Well ... I can't do that now, can I!" It was a statement, not a question.

"Well ... s'pose not." She shrugged, still cross with him for having ignored her for all these days.

"It really is important Es ... you know! I mean I can't just go around telling people not to keep birds in cages, can I!" He flung his hands out in frustration. "Anyway, today at school we were given English homework to write a story about something that happened during half term. I'm going to write about the parrot in the zoo ... I think his name was Billy".

"Why not." His sister shrugged yet again in an off-hand sort of way.

Reuben caught hold of his sister's arm. "Es! I'm serious!"

"Ok ... I didn't say you weren't!" With a sharp gesture she moved her arm away from his hand, annoyed that he now wanted her full attention ... immediately.

Reuben suddenly clocked why his sister was responding in such an off-hand way. "Sorry, Es." he muttered. "I know I've been a bit weird recently. But I've been so worried. You see, I promised that bird ... the pet shop one ... or was it Billy, the one on the zoo? ..." He hesitated here and shook his head. "Whichever one, I don't know ... anyway the one that took me to the Amazon forests ... or the one that I became! I did become a parrot you know." He glanced at his sister to check her reaction.

She just nodded. "Yep, you said ... I remember. Go on."

"Well, I promised that bird that I would tell people – 'humans' it said - that they shouldn't keep birds in cages! Birds have wings because they fly … and if they are in cages they can't fly properly!"

"Of course!" Esme's face suddenly lit up as she shrugged off her rucksack and stood stock still with her arms held straight down her sides. She was suddenly experiencing all sorts of sensations. She was remembering the amazing feeling of flying she had when Gyrre took her places in her dreams … or sometimes just when she was daydreaming. She remembered how wonderful it felt. And she found herself imagining being shut in a cage that was so small she could only just flap her wings … or even being in a huge cage where she flew up and up and then … hit the roof of the cage.

"Aw wow … yes … it is important, isn't it!" She turned to face Reuben. "Ah … I understand why you've been so worried. And you're going to fix it by writing a story and reading it out at school?"

Reuben looked at his sister in amazement. "Exactly!" he exclaimed.

"But how do you know you will be asked to read it out loud to the class?"

Reuben frowned and started hitting the knuckles of one hand with the palm of the other … something he did when he was agitated. "I don't. But it must work. It's the only thing I can think of!" He looked deflated.

"You know what …" said Esme, a smile slowly appearing on her face. "Of course it will work. If the

Parrot man ... YoungMan, and therefore Old Woman, want you to do it, then they'll help somehow."

Reuben stopped his agitating and let out a huge sigh. A tiny smile crept into the corners of his mouth as he slowly nodded his head. "Yeah ... I think you're right Es!"
And with that he took off down the lane, yelling "Race you home! I'm famished!"

"But what about canaries and budgerigars?" Esme called after him as she picked up her rucksack and ran after her him.

The twins parents were immensely relieved to see that their children were once again back to their usual selves, wolfing down their tea whilst talking excitedly between mouthfuls. Eve and Fons looked at each other with raised eyebrows as the words 'the parrot story' were repeated several times.

"It's homework!" Reuben laughed gleefully, seeing his mother's questioning look. He scrubbed tomato sauce from around his mouth with a piece of kitchen towel, pushed back his chair and got to his feet. "Come on Es! Can't you bring that with you ...?" pointing at his sister's plate, still half full of pasta.

 "No ... she cannot!" Fons moved to the table and put a gentle hand on his daughter's shoulder, preventing her from rising from the table. "Let your sister finish her tea in peace. She'll join you when she's ready."

By the time his father had finished talking, Reuben had already left the kitchen. Esme could hear him shuffling around in the corridor changing into his slippers. His voice was muffled as he called: "I'll get started. You think up some names for other parrots. It's going to be about how Billy is kidnapped … well 'chicknapped'!" … Exuberant laughter reached the kitchen and then Reuben poked his head around the kitchen door: "Ha…did you hear that, good innit … 'chicknapped'… you finished yet?"

"Reuben!" His mother this time: "Let her finish her tea! Just what is so urgent about this piece of homework anyway?"

Esme looked at Reuben with an expression that told him to answer. She didn't know why he was so anxious to get started immediately … he had a whole week to write it in. She scooped up the last few mouthfuls of her meal, wiped her mouth and hands slowly.

"That was really good Mum. I like that sauce made from our own tomatoes."

"Thank you darling!" Eve Montana smiled. It was good to know that her children, well one of them anyway, appreciated fresh food. She turned to Reuben still in the doorway. "So….? Just why is this homework so urgent?"

Reuben had been hoping she wouldn't ask a second time. He tried to shrug nonchalantly. "Well … it's important I get it right … it's about that parrot … er

Billy was his name ... the one in the zoo. If I leave it ... I might forget what happened." He finished off rather lamely, realising too late that his parents didn't know that 'something had happened'.

Luckily his mother didn't seem to notice. "But it's already a couple of weeks since we went to the zoo. If you haven't forgotten it by now, surely a few more days won't make a difference?" she probed. She was still slightly suspicious about the sudden turn-around in her son's mood.

Reuben looked at the floor and scuffed his feet. His mother could see that he was feeling uncomfortable. And to make it worse, Fons had now joined his wife and was looking at Reuben quizzically.

Reuben had a brainwave and took a risk. "Well actually I had a dream about a parrot last night ... that's why I thought it would make a good homework story ... you know how easy it is to forget dreams!" He gave an offhand sort of shrug.

"Ah ... okay ... okay."

By now Esme had joined her brother in the doorway. They waited to be released from their parents' questioning gaze.

"Off you go then!"

They fled into the cosy little front room they all called The Snug. The twins liked to use it instead of their bedrooms when they were working on schoolwork together.

"Phew … that was close!" Esme blew out a sigh of relief. "You know, Reubs, I think they're getting a bit suspicious!" She reached for the charm she was wearing around her neck. "Mum spotted this the other day when I left it in the bathroom. She brought it to me and asked me to remind her how I had got it."

"Hmm. I think you're right. What do we do?"

"Dunno. Hope for the best I spose. If they keep asking praps we can tell them about some of it … like how I actually got the charms."

That seemed to satisfy Reuben. He rarely worried about what might happen.
Esme though, did worry about what might happen, and decided she had better have a story ready just in case.

Once they settled down to plan the parrot story, it didn't take too long for the beginnings of a good story to emerge. Esme thought up lots of names for wild parrots. Squawk, Flute, Flap and Glide were some they chose. They had loads of ideas and some of things they imagined young parrots might get up to had them shrieking with laughter.

But then when they got to the 'chick-knapping' part they both fell silent, each imagining how awful it must be to be captured and taken away from your parents.

"And … there's something else … what about pet budgies and canaries?"

She had visited an old people's home with her class the previous year and had seen how one of the old ladies had so loved a little blue budgie. It had been let out of its cage when the children were there. After flying around the large room for a few minutes it had landed on the old lady's shoulder and gently clicked its beak at against her ear. It had chattered and chirped non-stop, sometimes saying actual English language words in a strange whistly sort of way. The scene had stayed in Esme's mind.

"Oh gosh ... I'd forgotten about them …" Reuben's expression showed he was thinking hard.
They both realised it wouldn't be fair to make children - or old ladies - feel bad about having pet birds. They knew that some of these little birds are actually bred to be pets and kept in cages from the moment they hatch. These birds wouldn't know how to look after themselves if they were suddenly let free. So it would not be a good thing to encourage people to free their caged birds.

"I'll think of something!" Reuben sat up straight and stretched. "Good thing you reminded me though! I don't have to hand it in until Friday so I've got plenty of time to add something about that. Can't think straight now; too tired ... I'm going to bed."

He stood up and stretched, grinning widely at his sister. "These things are exciting … don't you think so Es?"

Esme stifled a huge yawn so she could answer. "Yea … it has been exciting … but a bit scary as well!" She was thinking of her dream when the great black cloud that had tried to swallow her. The yawn overtook her. "… night" she mumbled and headed out of the sitting room and upstairs to bed.

"Girls!" her brother muttered, … "always scared of something!" He stretched again, suddenly feeling … just a little bit superior! Happily for him, he had absolutely no inkling that this confidence would be severely tested within the next few weeks.

By that Friday Reuben, with Esme's help, had written what they both thought was a pretty good parrot story. They had even shown what they had written to their parents. Their father had actually expressed astonishment at what an amazingly thoughtful story it was.

21 - Peter 's Secret

It was Monday afternoon. Esme had arrived home first.

Reuben had not been around when the earliest of the school buses had pulled in through the school gates. Usually the twins travelled home together and she had been a little disappointed he hadn't appeared before the bus left.
Today was the day for him to read out his parrot story to the class and she wanted to know how it had gone.

But she had caught the first bus without him because she wanted to get home quickly. Luca, the youngest of the Choccies, had been taken to the vet earlier in the day with a huge great thorn stuck between the pads of a front paw. Neither he nor any of 'his humans' had been able to get it out. She wanted to see how he was.

So she was really pleased to see him rushing down the garden path to meet her. She – stupid! she thought as she did it! - crouched down and opened her arms to him. His boisterous greeting sent her flying backwards, and he jumped up and down on top of her for several minutes, managing to get in lots of loving licks all over her face before she managed to fend him off and scramble to her feet.

"Okay … okay … calm down … really glad your paw's not hurting anymore." She laughed as she watched him rushing back down the path towards

Solo and Mowgli who were coming to greet Esme at a more sedate pace. The younger dog bounced into and over his elders with no sign of the sore paw that had so bothered him for several days previously.

The children's tea was all laid out on the kitchen table, so as soon as she had changed into her indoor clothes and given Kimber a chin tickle, she settled herself at the table and piled a plate high with tasty food.

She had nearly finished by the time she heard the Choccies' *'hello hello family'* greeting. The side door rattled open and Reuben called out "Thanks for bringing me home!" to someone.

A few moments later he burst into the kitchen … really excited.

"Peter's father brought me home in their car," he said in answer to her unspoken query.

"Peter … ?

"Hmmmhm!" Her brother nodded his head rapidly several times whilst plonking himself down at the table with his outdoor clothes still on. "I'm famished … they asked me to stay to tea … but that would have been too much … his father and mother and older brothers and sisters … and things!"

Esme was trying to be as patient as possible. She desperately wanted to know what had happened, but she knew she'd get no sense out of her brother until he had at least half filled his stomach.

After several minutes of concentrated eating, Reuben lifted his head from his plate, wiped a hand across his mouth, sniffed loudly, and sighed contentedly.

"Well?" Esme was just about at the end of her patience. "What happened?"

So Reuben recounted to his sister all the things that had happened to him that day.

He had indeed been asked to read out his story to the class. It went down well … so well that the class had decided that the topic of keeping pets of any sort would be a good subject for one of their discussion circles.
These 'circles' were something new that the school had started at the beginning of term. They consisted of a half hour space one afternoon a week where pupils could discuss amongst themselves things they found important. They actually sat in a large circle, with a teacher to facilitate … but not teach. The children loved it!

Reuben was feeling very pleased with this outcome to telling his parrot story. But … that wasn't all. He took a deep breath. "You'll never guess!"

"No, I won't … so tell me!"

"After the class … Peter grabbed hold of me out in the corridor and asked where I'd got the story from. He said it wasn't right to pretend the story was mine when actually it was from a book ..." Reuben paused for affect, giving Esme a wide-eyed stare.

She responded as he had hoped: "Peter...? What, the Peter?"

Her brother gave a series of slow and exaggerated nods. "Yep ... the Peter!"

"Uh!" Esme's face was one great question mark. She knew that Reuben didn't like this Peter. He, well she too, was envious of him because his family were well-off, owned several horses and Peter had his own show pony – a beautiful dapple grey welsh mountain/new forest cross named Mickleton. "Cheek!" she muttered under her breath.

"Yeah." Reuben continued his story. "I told him I hadn't nicked the story from anywhere and went to push him off me. But ... I saw he was upset about something. I asked him what was the matter?"

"He said he had read almost that same story a few years ago. And at the time he had had a pet budgie that he was very fond of. He said it was more of a friend than a pet ... used to sit on his shoulder and talk to him ... spent most of its time out of the cage."

"Oh no" ... Esme could see where this was going.

Reuben nodded his head: "Uha. So ... after reading that story, Peter had 'let it free', 'cos in the book there was nothing about that not being a good thing to do.

"He said he took it out into some woods near his house and let it go. The next days he had seen it a couple of times flying around in their garden, but he ignored it. And that was that; he had never seen it again. Until today he had thought that was just fine and that the little bird would have been enjoying its freedom. Now he thought he might just have left it to be killed or die from starvation ... or cold ... or something."

"Wow ... that's really sad," murmured Esme, imagining that poor little bird trying to get back into the safety of its home. "I can see why he was upset ... I expect he's feeling really guilty now."

"Hmm ... expect he is. Well, it's a good thing there was something in my story about not setting them free!" Reuben stopped talking and shrugged.

Esme resisted the temptation to remind him it was she who had suggested he wrote that part of it. "And ... ?"

"And ... then he said he wanted to ask me something - after school finished. I didn't really expect him to follow up ... but he was waiting for me by the school gate. He seemed a bit anxious ... said a few things about having wanted to ask me this for ages ...'cos he thought he might be going nuts ... and that I might understand."

"He said what?" Esme pulled a questioning face.

"Exactly! He said he thought he might be going nuts. Well, when he said that, I thought I'd better listen to what he had to say. I could see you getting on the early bus ... I did wave to catch your attention ... but you didn't see me." He looked at Esme.

"I believe you."

Reuben paused for affect before carrying on: "He said he wanted to ask me something about that scruffy brown pony that had dumped me at the bus stop the other week."

"Oh boy!" Esme gasped.

"Yep." First thing I said was "Maybe you are nuts. But as soon as I'd said it ... that Pegassy voice came into my head. It was really weird ... well not so weird now ... I'm getting used to it ..."

"What did he say - Pegasus?" Esme was getting impatient.

Reuben scrunched up his face as he tried to remember what he had heard. "Well, he didn't actually say anything ... I just sort of ... 'got a big feeling' that told me Peter is OK ... and to let him become my friend ... well our friend." He glanced at his sister, knowing that she didn't like Peter either. "I knew that feeling was sent by Pegasus though. I sort of saw him in my head ... and felt his huffy breath. And then I'm sure I heard the actual words: 'Take him under your wing'."

"Ha ha ha … a Pegasus joke! I wonder how we do that!" Esme couldn't help laughing slightly hysterically.

"I think that maybe … maybe … Pegasus … or Old Women/Young Man set it up. I think that's why Peter got his father to give me a lift home. When we were in the car Peter asked his Dad if I could go to his for tea some time."

"Wow … that would be weird!" said Esme, not yet convinced.

Both children had always thought that Peter was just the sort of person they shouldn't be friends with. His parents were wealthy; the family lived in a very large house and kept several horses and ponies in fields adjacent to their house that also belonged to them. They were what Esme had heard her parents call 'privileged'. And anyway, Peter was 'stuck-up'. And worst of all he had that very beautiful show pony called Mickleton that won rosettes at gymkhanas and horse shows.

In other words, the twins were envious.

So the thought of him becoming a friend of theirs was indeed weird. At least it was for Esme. But she could see that Reuben, who before today felt like she did, now seemed to be okay with it.

'This is really peculiar' thought Esme to herself. But then … all sorts of things had been peculiar since the flying horse had come into their lives.

And so began a strange friendship between Reuben and Peter; and it wasn't long before Reuben was indeed invited to go and have tea at Peter's house.

In truth Esme was a little upset that she hadn't been invited too. But she pretended not to be.

And of course, Reuben reported back to Esme all that had happened.

It seemed that Peter was not happy. He had two sisters, both older than him, who were very sporty, loved hunting to hounds in winter and competing in as many shows as possible in the summer. Then there was the eldest son ... much older than the others and at University. Apparently he was very clever. He was studying economics because he wanted to become a banker and make loads of money... like the father. They were a very competitive family ... both parents always nagging at the children to 'do better'.... to make a success of it – whatever 'it' was!

"They don't seem to care about anything but 'winning'. Win ... win ... win was all they talked about over tea. Prizes, money, awards, places at 'good' schools!" Reuben sighed. "The way they think, our school is not good enough. They went on and on about wishing Peter went to the same prep school as his sisters. But for some reason he had just refused and became ill when they tried to force him. Mother, father, and sisters all shook their heads in unison, whilst Peter said nothing and looked down at the table whilst his Father told the story.

"And" Rueben added, "they didn't seem to realise that what they were saying about my school, might upset me!"

"They sound rather horrible." As she listened, Esme even began to feel a little bit sorry for Peter.

When they had finished tea, Reuben explained, he was then taken out to the stables to see the horses. "Four huge hunters!" Reuben emphasised the 'huge'. "One beautiful black stallion that does dressage … he was just awesome. And then there were a couple of other horses, and … Mickleton … that's Peter's show pony. They must be sooo rich!" finished Reuben.

"What's he like ... the show pony?" asked Esme, really interested despite her determination NOT to show she was in any way impressed.

"It's a mare actually," replied Reuben, lifting his eyebrows to show surprise. "Dark dapple grey … hmmm … she seemed very nervy … I couldn't see too much … she kept to the back of the loose box. Peter was going to take me in to the box, but his father called us right then. Said he had an appointment later and needed to take me home first."

After that first visit to Peter's home, Reuben decided they had been wrong about Peter and that he was OK. The two boys began spending time together during school lunch breaks.

It was the first time in her life that Esme had felt really jealous!

In her mind, her twin brother 'belonged' to her. Even though they bickered with each other, she and Reuben were seriously good friends. Although each twin had several friends they spent time with at school, they nearly always spent found time in the school day to catch up with each other.
But now Reuben was now spending so much time with this 'Peter' that he didn't have much time for his other friends … or her!

Deep down, Esme suspected that Reuben wanted to be Peter's friend so he would get invited to ride Mickleton. And she didn't like that!

As it turned out, she was both right and wrong. Reuben did want to ride Mickleton, but he also genuinely liked Peter when he got to know him better. And he felt sorry for him … a rich boy who was unhappy! Reuben had always thought that if you had plenty of money there would be nothing to be unhappy about.

And even though he had rather enjoyed knowing his sister was jealous, he eventually realised that she was actually feeling very hurt, no matter how she desperately tried to pretend she didn't care.

Over the next few weeks, Reuben discovered that Peter was a 'dreamer' like them. So he finally introduced Peter to his sister, and then it was the three of them who huddled together at lunch break - much to the annoyance of some of their other friends.

Mostly they talked about school stuff, pony stuff; and they shared their dreams.

Very occasionally one of the twins would make an offhand comment like: "Wouldn't it be great if we could understand what our animals are saying ... or know what they are thinking ... or event speak to them!"

Peter would always agree with them. And sometimes it looked as though he really wanted to say something more about it. But though the twins waited expectantly, he would just shrug.

One day during lunch break the three of them were talking about different breeds of horses. Some of the twins' remarks made it clear just how envious they felt of Peter for having a beautiful, clever pony and all the other horses his family owned.

Peter suddenly burst out: "Oh stop going on about it! You don't understand! I don't enjoy competing ... I just don't!"

There was a stunned silence.

"All my parents care about is me winning. If I don't get at least a second prize they start talking about getting a special tutor for me to improve my riding ... or getting a 'better' pony for me!"

Peter was clearly upset ... angry and sad at the same time. He took a deep breath and continued: "Mickleton's a great pony. She could win lots of classes..." He paused again for several moments obviously trying to find words to say what he wanted. Eventually he shrugged his shoulders and muttered: "I think I kind of let her down ..." His shoulders lifted again as he fell silent.

"How do you do that?" Esme asked quietly. She could see how upset Peter was. She put a restraining hand on her brother's arm as he was about to burst in. "Let him finish!"

"Dunno really ..." Peter mumbled, embarrassed now. "Thing is ... she's very nervous and I'm not a very good rider so I get nervous too and that only makes her worse ... and then I can't control her and sometimes ... sometimes she throws me!" All this came out in a huge rush.

Neither twin knew what to say to this, so they kept quiet.

Peter then went on in a much calmer tone: "But I do enjoy taking her out into the countryside along paths I know. I take some sandwiches and we have a picnic. She grazes whilst I eat my sandwiches and listen to music. There's a couple of places I know where there's a fantastic view ... all across the valley to the Black Mountains."

"Isn't that boring?" interjected Reuben, no longer able to keep quiet.

"Hmmm, maybe. But I really enjoy it. You see ..." Peter's words tailed off into another silence and his eyes had that 'faraway' expression in them.

"I know what you mean." Esme nodded her head. "I'd like to do that too … go find nice picnic places … if I had a pony."

"But you do have a pony!" Peter's attention came back to the 'there and then'. He looked at Esme and then Reuben in surprise. "… the small brown pony that I saw you riding to the bus stop that day … even though you said you hadn't!" Peter challenged Reuben to disagree.

Reuben was about to speak when Esme elbowed him in the ribs. Her mind was racing and she said quickly: "Ah … no … that's not our pony. He belongs to a local Farmer – Mr Grubble!"

"Oh, I see. I thought when I saw Reuben riding him to the bus stop the other day that he was yours. I thought it was really funny when he dumped you like that. Makes a change to see somebody else come off!" An embarrassed smile flitted across his mouth. "I did wonder though … who took the pony home … was there somebody else with you?"

To this, Esme could find no answer. Neither could Reuben.

Luckily the lesson bell rang at that moment.

The twins decided to invite Peter for tea at their place. Esme suggested to Reuben that they ask Rose too - to see what she thought of Peter and Rueben was okay with that. The more time Esme spent with Peter, the more she felt that he was 'strange' in some way; and it was a strangeness that she liked.

Peter got permission from his parents, the twins' parents were very happy for them to bring a school friend home, and Fonso offered to take Peter home.

And so it was that Rose met the twins' new friend Peter. She was pleased by what they had done, and she and Peter seemed to get on well.

After Peter had left to go home with Fonso, Rose – who of course could 'see' many things about people that ordinary humans couldn't – told them that that Peter was what was sometimes called 'sensitive'.

"What … you mean … like a girl?" Reuben's expression showed his scorn.

Before Esme could thump her brother, Rose lifted a calming hand and explained that this meant being aware of things that most humans aren't aware of. Both children had puzzled looks on their faces.

"Like you two!" She laughed out loud at the look of dawning understanding on their faces.

"Oh!" from both of them.

It was at that moment that Esme and Reuben finally realised that they themselves were very 'different' indeed.
Until that moment they had somehow just 'gone along' with strange things happening to them. For each of them, odd things, sometimes scary things, a bit like dreams, had happened. They had dealt

with it, reported these things to each other ... and got on with ordinary life. But now ... now, suddenly the boy and the girl experienced something rather ... solemn about these happenings.

Rose told them it would it would be good for them to include Peter more in their lives. He was, she said, somebody who would understand and learn ... quickly. And he would be really useful in helping them do their special work.

"What special work?" asked Esme.

"You mean join us on our adventures?" queried her brother.

"Yes ... yes!" Rose smiled. "The adventures you have show you examples of this very special work you are being asked to do. Do you understand that?"

Slowly the twins began to nod. Each was remembering, and realising that they had learned things during their adventures. They had learned that there is much more to the world than most people know. They had been shown how it is wise to be careful when using modern technology. They had been shown that wild birds kept in cages and unable to fly freely can feel sad.
And ... of course they did actually realise, when they thought about it, that having a rather wise extraterrestrial person - an 'Alien' – for a friend, was probably rather unusual.

But there were other things that were not so clear. What about the bumblewizards and … Esme shuddered as she remembered her encounter with The Joker.

"Don't worry. All these things will become clear to you at the right time." Rose smiled as she got up to go. "Next thing is to introduce Mr Nibs to Peter and Mickleton."

"How do we do that?" frowned Reuben.

"Ah, you'll see. Surely you know by now that when a thing is meant to happen it will happen."

She shut the door behind her as she left the room, leaving two silent children to think things over.

22 - Three Ponies for Three Children

Needless to say, as always happens when 'things are meant to happen', it wasn't long before Peter had the opportunity to meet Mr Nibbs.

It was a couple of weeks later, one Saturday.

The twins had been invited to spend the day at Peter's place. For some reason Peter's father had taken a liking to the twins and thought they would be a 'good influence' on Peter. It appeared that he had temporarily 'acquired' another couple of ponies so the children could all ride together.

"Dad has borrowed a couple of ponies from a friend of his. Let's go get them. They're in the field … been out at grass for a while Dad says. Spect we'll have to give them a good clean!" Peter's excitement was catching. "I think you're in for a surprise!" He laughed.

The stable yard behind Peter's house gave onto the field in question and the children could see a couple of ponies in a far corner. One bay and one black.

Peter rattled a bucket with pony nuts in it … a trusted way to get ponies to come to you. Sure enough both ponies paused from their grass munching, lifted their heads, pricked their ears and looked towards the gate. After a couple of moments they decided the bucket was worth investigating and began to amble slowly in the direction of the gate.

"What ... !" Exclaimed Reuben as they got closer. "That looks like ... ?" He broke off as the unmistakeably scruffy brown shape drew closer. It could be none other than Mr Nibbs.

Peter laughed out loud. "See! I said you'd be in for a surprise. That Farmer Grubble said he wouldn't charge my Dad for their hire if we pastured them and fed them a few buckets of oats."

Esme, who had already recognised Mr Nibbs and wasn't too surprised to see him, was staring at the slightly larger black pony. It was a mare and looked very different from Mr Nibbs. It was rather beautiful even though it was as dirty as the brown pony. But ... what was it about this other pony that made her heart lurch?

She kept staring.

Whilst Mr Nibbs thrust his head into the bucket, obviously enjoying the pony nuts, the black mare thrust her head over the gate towards Esme.

Tentatively Esme reached out a hand for the pony to sniff. And ... as soon as her hand was touched by the velvety muzzle she understood. Torrela!

But how could it be? Torrela, black and beautiful, was her dream companion, not a real flesh and blood pony. And ... she was much larger than this black pony. How could this be happening!

A flood of horse-thought streamed into Esme's mind: *'That Pegasus … clever … said you would need my help … given me a body … had to be smaller because of the brown one!'*

As if to show off her physical body, the black pony lifted her head, let out a shrill whinny and took off around the field. She gave a display of amazing bronco bucks before settling down into the most wonderful high stepping, dancing trot, head and tail held high. She circuited the field about four times before returning to the gate.

"Wow … what's that about Pony?" Reuben and Peter had both taken their attention away from Mr Nibbs to watch the black pony.

Mr Nibbs kept his head stuck deep in the bucket.

Esme chuckled as she reached for the pony's head and offered her face for a breathy greeting. "I think she's jealous of Mr Nibbs!"

Well impressed by her display, both boys left Mr Nibbs to get on with his nuts and moved over to touch the black pony. But she declined their touch, moving her head away from their reaching hands.

"Not so friendly though!" remarked Peter.

"Oh, she'll be fine," smiled Esme. "I've come across her before … she just likes to take her time getting to know people."

Reuben looked at his sister. "Where?" he demanded, puzzled, for he didn't remember ever having seen this pony before.

Whoops! Esme's mind raced. She wasn't sure it was the right time to bring up her dreams. "Er … you know that time you were ill … months ago … erm … it was a weekend and I went to spend a night with Rose …" She was desperately groping for some story Reuben would believe. "Well … this pony was in a field just down from Rose's house and we …"

Esme could see that Reuben wasn't too convinced and was about to question her.
But at that moment the children heard the voice of Peter's father, shouting a question from the house: "You've found those ponies then! There's some tack for them in the tack room. Get them cleaned up before you get Mickleton out!" He disappeared back into the house.

Peter led Reuben over to the tack room and they disappeared inside to find pony-cleaning kit.

Esme who had remained with Torrela, gently rubbing the pony's forehead, let out a sigh of relief.

Torrela sent more forceful thoughts to Esme about not wanting 'those boys' riding her. *'They won't stay on my back for long if they manage to get on!'*
She snorted, tossed her head, twizzled around and gave a couple of bucks to demonstrate what she meant.

Esme laughed out loud. She had never seen this side of her beautiful dream companion's character before.

'*No! Well, I've never had to fit myself into a physical shape before! And it doesn't feel good – I feel heavy ... and clumsy ... and ... dirty!*' The pony snorted again, turned back to the gate, thrust her head over it and leaned heavily on Esme's shoulder. '*But that Pegasus is very persuasive.*' A huge horsy sigh followed that statement.

The boys came back with brushes and curry combs; and the children set to their task. The boys worked on Mr Nibbs removing as much mud as they could and picking off burrs and twigs from his mane and tale. To Reuben's amazement the pony tolerated all the attention with good humour, remaining still and even giving the impression he was half asleep.

Esme worked on Torrela – who indicated that she rather enjoyed the sensation of being brushed.

As soon as the two ponies where clean and had been tacked up, Peter went to get Mickleton from her loosebox.
It was obvious to both Esme and Reuben that Peter was very nervous of this extremely beautiful pony. She had been immaculately groomed, her sleek tail swishing and her oiled hooves making small prancing movements as she emerged from her stable.
Peter tugged as her bridle as a loud voice called from the house: "Keep that pony under control Son. Don't let her get the better of you!" Mr Young had returned to check on the children.

Peter tugged and Mickleton pranced more.

Esme's heart went out to both Peter and his pony. She could 'feel' just how uncomfortable they were in each other's company.

Mickleton suddenly noticed the two new ponies and stopped her prancing. She stood stock still, ears pricking in their direction.

"Take them into the field!" boomed Peter's father.

The children obeyed. Reuben opened the gate wide and stood aside, holding Mr Nibbs as Mickleton almost dragged Peter into the field.

Despite Mickleton's non-stop prancing and Peter's nervousness, he was soon mounted on the pony, showing an unexpected physical agility. Strangely the pony calmed down with a rider on her back.

The field was a large one and the three children rode their ponies slowly around its perimeter several times. Both Reuben and Esme - and their mounts - needed to get used to the feeling of a saddle and bridle.

When they were comfortable they began to move faster. Mr Nibbs struggled a bit to keep up with the other two swifter ponies and snorted to Reuben that *'if he was his real self, he'd show them what it meant to 'fly across the ground'*. Reuben let himself imagine just what that might feel like.

Peter pulled up and asked Reuben if he wanted to ride Mickleton.

Reuben was quick to accept ... even though he did feel a little anxious.He had seen what a tight control Peter had kept of his pony, riding in a style that Reuben was unused to.

As soon as he was mounted on Mickleton, Rueben knew his anxiety had been well founded!

His easy going riding style allowed Mickleton her head. It only took a couple of seconds. Feeling no pressure from the reins, the pony flicked her head up a couple of times ... testing. Then with a huge toss of her head that snatched the reins from Reuben's fingers, they were off!

Reuben felt the shriek '*f~~ r~~ e ~~ e~~ d~~o~~m*' enter his head as the pony accelerated at unbelievable speed. There was very little Reuben could do about it except cling on for all he was worth.

Mickleton stretched her neck low, extended her legs to move faster than ever before and galloped around and around the field. She skidded as she went round the corners, and it was as much as Reuben could do to stay in the saddle. There was no way he could stop her. She kept sending him the 'freedom' feeling and was obviously delighting in being able to run ... and run ... and run. Reuben was later to find out that she was never let out of her stable: too valuable to risk injury out in the field.

A memory lodged itself in Reuben's mind, followed by a familiar huffy voice. '*Let her run, let her run.'* Reuben felt the presence of Pegasus and remembered the 'thinkthink' instructions. He relaxed then, finding a good balance and imagining the runaway pony coming to a gentle stop next to the other two ponies.

Peter and Esme were watching wide eyed - Peter with a hand to his mouth! Esme felt calm though because Torrela had communicated to her that it would be just fine.

Mickleton made one more round of the field and then came to a trembling halt beside the other ponies. Her neck and chest were covered in foamy sweat, her sides heaved, and her head dropped towards the ground in exhaustion.

Reuben, just as exhausted as the pony, managed to slide to the ground himself, where he remained sitting on the grass.

Peter rushed up to grab his pony before she ran off again, but Reuben waved him away. "It's OK … it's OK … she's not going anywhere …"

Nobody said anything until Reuben slowly stood up, and gave Mickleton hearty pats on her shoulder and neck. He gathered up her reins and said to Peter: "Wow, that's some pony! I think she needs a bit more exercise!" Then he started to laugh and laugh. "Don't think I've ever been as fast as that."

Peter was unsure how to respond. He was actually rather pleased that his new friend had not been able to control Mickleton, but he had also been really worried in case Reuben had come off and been badly hurt. He glanced round back to the house, wondering if his father that seen what had happened, but there was no sign of him.

By this time Mr Nibbs had manoeuvred close to Reuben, who he prodded gently in the chest. Reuben knuckled the brown pony's forehead and whispered 'thanks'.

"Thanks for what?" asked Peter.

Reuben was startled out of his communication with his four-legged friend. "What …? Oh … er well, thanks for letting me ride Mickleton!" He grinned at Peter.

"I think she needs drying off". Esme nodded towards the sweaty pony, all the prance now run out of her.

This was a sensible suggestion and the children took the tack off Mr Nibbs and Torrela, turning them loose in the field. As they trotted off together, Reuben and Esme both 'heard' their friends' exclamations of relief at being freed from the cumbersome restraints of the saddles and bridles.
They both chuckled.

Peter looked at them strangely. "What's funny?"

"Nothing really. Just looks like those two have become good friends," explained Esme.

"Hmm … I thought I …" Peter didn't finish his sentence.

He turned instead towards Mickleton who was looking longingly after the rapidly disappearing shapes of the scruffy little brown pony trotting along next to the elegant black pony. He put his hand on her neck and said very very quietly: "Sorry Mick."

Mickleton huffed out a very long sigh.

After that first day, the three children decided that they'd like to spend more time riding together.

Mr Young also thought this was a good idea. Unseen, he had been watching as Reuben had ridden Mickleton and realised the boy had a natural talent that his own son seemed to be missing. As he said to his wife, who had also been observing events from inside the house: "I think riding with those two youngsters might put some backbone into our boy!"

This all happened a couple of weeks after Peter's parents had finally given up on the idea that their son would join his sisters in winning prizes all around the country. They had even discussed selling Mickleton. "Clearly Peter isn't cut out for competing," his mother had sadly acknowledged. "We might as well sell that pony!"

But Peter had pleaded to be able to keep Mickleton. Although he felt nervous when riding her, he was very fond of her. He had always imagined that if he and she had been able to get to know each other slowly, without her being stuffed full of buck-inducing oats, and away from the critical eyes of his family, they would have got on well together.

And since he had watched Reuben ride her, Peter thought that maybe his new friends could help him in this.

His father had eventually relented. "Oh for goodness sake boy … if you must … anything to stop your whining! But don't blame me if something awful happens to you or that pony!" He had thrown the words over his shoulder as he had stomped off to 'do something important'.

The outcome of this day at Peter's was that Mr Young arranged with Farmer Grubble and the twin's parents for the two ponies, Mr Nibbs and 'Blackie', to be moved permanently into the field next to the twins' house. Initially he was fiercely against the idea of allowing the valuable show pony to join them there.

But then, a few days later he said to Peter at breakfast: "I've changed my mind. Maybe it would do that pony of yours good to rough it a bit. She's been too mollycoddled for her own good. And she costs a fortune in oats! You can keep her over to the Montana's."

Peter looked at his father in amazement. "But … ?"

"No 'buts', Son. I've decided. I'll give Montana money to build a shed big enough for the three of them."

With that he got up from the table and headed for his office. As he went he called out: "There's some spare tack as well for those two ponies if you need it."

Peter couldn't believe his luck.
'Luck had nothing to do with it!' The whispery thought entered his head at the same time as the vague image of a horse with wings.

But Peter was too excited to pay much attention to that fleeting experience. He rushed for the phone to tell his friends the news.

23 - Never Make Assumptions

All this had come about because Pegasus had suggested to Mr Nibbs (not quite an order) that he – Mr Nibbs - should teach Peter to ride 'properly' and at the same time help the pony Mickleton to overcome her anxiety around humans.

It had absolutely not been Mr Nibb's own idea!

He had made this very clear to Reuben during a dream when they had spent some time together just messing around in a sunny meadow where the grass was orange but the tastiest ever!

As Reuben remembered it, it went something like this:

'I didn't like this 'suggestion' at all and complained to 'the boss' (this is how Mr Nibbs referred to Pegasus). Why was he now asking me to play nursemaid to yet another human child. Wasn't it enough being known to humans as 'that scruffy little brown pony'. What next for horseheaven's sake?'

At this point Reuben had rubbed the pony's forehead with his knuckles to let him know that he understood perfectly … for indeed he did. He guiltily remembered that time of the 'smart phone adventure' when Esme had flown off on GZee and he, Reuben, had been carted off to the bus stop on 'the scruffy little brown pony'!

As Mr Nibbs had spoken, Reuben had felt a sudden overwhelming love for the pony. And Mr Nibbs had allowed his grumpy self to enjoy the sensations of being groomed. He had decided that he could develop a fondness for this human child. Boy and pony had spent a few quiet moments savouring their thoughts and feelings.

Rueben had continued brushing the pony's tickly bits, and gently teasing off little chunks of mud.

It was Mr Nibbs who had broken the silence. *'Do you know what The Boss replied?'*

He hadn't waited for a response from Reuben.
'He said to me: we do whatever is needed, dear friend, to enable children to understand just how important animals are, and how to communicate with them respectfully and lovingly.'

"Oh … gosh." The boy could think of nothing else to say. But it was at that very moment they had both realised just how important their 'special work' was.

The pony turned his head to the boy at his side and gently snuffed his cheek … and Reuben woke up.
He stayed quite still in bed for some time, carefully recalling as much as he could of the dream.

In the same way that Esme had not yet told her brother that the elegant black pony was actually her dream companion, Torrela, Reuben chose not to tell his sister about this dream. He would tell her eventually, he knew that.But not yet.

Whereas Esme was still feeling unsettled by Torrela turning up in this way, and thought Reuben might scoff at the idea, Reuben wanted to keep the rather strange feelings of affection he was feeling for Mr Nibbs to himself. He wasn't sure why, except that it was something about needing to make these new feelings properly 'a part of himself' before telling anybody else about them.

Later that same day, at school, the teacher had asked the class about the importance of 'friendship'.
Reuben had been right in the middle of answering this when something had happened that made him stop in mid-sentence. Mr Nibbs' voice was bouncing words around in his head: '*don't make assumptions ... about ... anything ... or... anybody!*'

Embarrassed, he had said: "I've forgotten what I was going to say!"

"It happens," the teacher had said with a smile. She had waited a few moments, giving him a chance to continue. But he shook his head, and she asked another child to speak.

Reuben had sat down, trying to make sense of the words in his head.

Suddenly he had got it!

He had made assumptions about Mr Nibbs: just a scruffy non-descript common little brown pony not worth bothering with. How wrong he had been!

And … he had made assumptions about Peter too! His family was wealthy; and posh; and Peter had an expensive show pony of his own! Therefore he must be snooty and 'not nice' mustn't he? Again, a wrong assumption!

Reuben realised that he had just learned something really important.

"Huh!" He had exclaimed to himself … but loudly enough for the teacher to give him a questioning look.
"Have you remembered what you wanted to say?" she had asked him.

"No." He shook his head.

24 - Three Become Four

Since his son had become such good friends with the Montana twins, Mr Young had been forced to realise that winning competitions was of absolutely no interest to Peter.

To his way of thinking this meant that Mickleton was no longer valuable and didn't need the special treatment she had been given up to that point. He realised it would save him money if she joined the other ponies permanently in the field next to the twins' house – Nibbs Field, the children now called it.

And so it was that three special children and three special ponies were brought together.

Over the next few weeks, as the days became longer and the weather warmer, Peter began to spend a lot of his time at the twins' house. He was warmly welcomed by their parents and invited to join the family for the lovely teas Mrs Montana produced. And he was enthralled by their father's stories about his childhood in Cortona, a huge nature reserve in the southern part of Spain.

"Do you speak Spanish?" Peter asked the twins one afternoon after a story from Fonso that had been sprinkled with unfamiliar words.

"Un poquito - a little bit" mumbled Esme, mouth full of pasta.

"Not really." Reuben's mouth turned down. "I'd like to though … shame we don't do languages at school!"

"Hmm, it is isn't it ... I'd never thought about it before." Peter looked thoughtful.

"Right you three ... four!" Mrs Montana amended looking pointedly at Alfonso. "Out of the kitchen! I need the table to sort the herbs for drying.And those ponies are waiting!" She began to clear the table.

Remaining food was quickly polished off and all four trooped out into the back garden and through the gate into the tunnel field.
The children had stored the saddles and bridles Mr Young had given them in an unused part of one of the polly tunnels. But bridles were all they were after. Mr Nibbs had been very firm with Reuben, insisting that Peter needed to learn to ride bareback, and therefore he and Esme should also ride bareback.

Esme didn't mind this as she had always ridden Torrela bareback in dreamtime, and was now really enjoying the feeling of a real warm pony beneath her. And Torrela was indeed 'a dream to ride'. Her gait was smooth and she responded instantly to Esme's directions ... as though the horse knew what her rider wanted a second or two before physical aids were given.

Reuben had grumbled a bit, wanting to feel he was riding 'properly'.

Although Peter had been very nervous at first about riding bareback, he found that he too was enjoying feeling the warmth of a pony underneath him. His balance was improving dramatically now that he didn't have stirrups to rely on.

And Esme had put a thick strap around Mr Nibbs' neck so that if Peter did lose his balance he would have something to hang on to other than the reins. This made him feel extra secure and better able to relax.

Not that Mr Nibbs was planning to do anything that was likely to make the boy lose his balance. He was taking his teaching duties very seriously.

The three children went to the field and called the ponies, who came eagerly, knowing there would be a handful of treaty things for each of them.

Peter had now had several sessions on Mr Nibbs, and Reuben on Mickleton. This had given the boys and the ponies a chance to get to know each other. Mr Nibbs was teaching Peter to balance and communicate with his mount through a variety of subtle body movements … and … telepathy.

Not that this word was used. Mr Nibbs just communicated the 'idea' to Peter that he should 'pretend' he could 'thinktalk' to the pony in his head. Peter had started doing this and as it was turning out, he had a natural talent for this manner of communication.

As a result he was learning to change his riding style completely.

And Reuben was discovering just how little 'telling' an intelligent and well trained pony like Mickleton needed.

He had been very anxious when he first rode Peter's pony – 'Mick' as the children now called her. He remembered his first experience all too well! But without Peter's anxious hands tugging at the bit in her mouth, Mickleton had quickly come to trust her new rider. Reuben was absolutely delighted. He had never had the chance to ride such a responsive pony. "She's just fabulous to ride," he enthused to his sister.

Meantime Esme was stuck with Torrela. Not that she minded of course, loving this beautiful black horse as she did. But she did want to have a chance to ride the other two ponies as well!
But for some strange unfathomable reason, Torrela would not tolerate either of the boys on her back. Each time one of them had approached her, she had jiggled and pranced, laid her ears back and made it very clear to all the children that the boys riding her was not going to happen.

Esme had asked 'why?' but all she got back was a vague *'it's for the best'*. Eventually she came to understand. There was a slight risk that Torrela's physical body would begin to disappear if anybody other than Esme – who had 'created' her in dream time in the first place - touched her.

The more time the three children spent together at the twin's home the more they found out about each other; and the closer they became as a threesome.

But at school it was very different.

Reuben, and particularly Peter, had always been popular. And since they had teamed up they were usually surrounded by other children wanting to be mates with them. Of course the boys rather enjoyed this!

But for Esme it was different. She began to feel left out. She had a few friends of her own to hang out with if she wanted to, but none of them were really close.
Even though she saw plenty of both boys anyway and was not too fussed about her brother's extra popularity, she did find it was irritating when she needed to talk to him and he was surrounded by 'fans' as she started calling them.

After a few weeks of this, Esme noticed that she was not the only one being left out. Before he and Reuben had become friends, Peter had often hung out with a girl called Hannelore, who had always struck Esme as kind of beautiful but standoffish.
This was why she hasn't got many other friends, Esme had thought to herself. But ... she began to feel a bit sorry for her when it became obvious that this girl didn't fit in with the group that had began to surround Peter and Reuben any more than she did herself.

She began to wonder if Hannelore might be willing to be friends with her, but found it difficult to approach the other girl. So she decided to just keep an eye on her for a while.

Meanwhile during the time he spent with Esme and Reuben at their place,
usually when grooming the ponies, Peter revealed bit by bit, just how unhappy he was at home.

One day he began: "I want to tell you something … please don't laugh".

The twins nodded their agreement.

"Well … sometimes I hear voices and see things that other people can't …" Peter paused and looked anxiously at the twins.

"Do you!" Reuben exclaimed, a big grin appearing on his face, while Esme tried not to smile.

"You said you wouldn't laugh!" muttered Peter, brushing Mickleton's mane furiously.

"Is a smile a laugh?" asked Esme quickly, head to one side. "Go on, tell us more. I think it's really important we know."

Reuben was nodding his head crazily, lips clamped together to prevent the happy laughter within him from bursting out and upsetting Peter.

Very hesitantly Peter started speaking again … and then the words began to tumble out: "I'm sure I can 'hear' Mick speaking to me … in my head though, not out loud. … I have these weird weird dreams sometimes! And I think I see things that aren't actually there … !"

He stopped talking and just looked at the twins. "Spect you think I'm nuts now ... just like my parents do! I told my Mum when it all started a few years ago because ... because ... I was scared. She told my Dad and they gave me a lecture about trying to avoid homework by making up stupid stories. They told me to stop imagining stupid things and get on with my school work ... they ..." He gave a huge sigh and stopped talking again.

"Look, don't worry about your parents!" Reuben burst in, no longer able to contain himself and clearly excited. "They don't have to know about anything ... but we do! We need to know all about it" He glanced at Esme.

She nodded vigorously. "We do!"

"Our Mum and Dad don't know about lots of stuff that happens to us," continued Reuben. "We don't tell them because if we did they would worry about us and prevent us from 'doing things'... and ...," he hesitated. "I guess they might think we're just making it all up!"

Again Esme nodded. "Look, let's finish cleaning the ponies and we'll go to our safe place and tell you what has been happening to us ... right?" She looked to Reuben for agreement.

"Yeah ... let's do that ... that's a good idea!"

They hastily completed the ponies' grooming (much to Torrela's annoyance, who was enjoying the physical sensation of being brushed), put Mickleton's blanket back on - as she was still not used to living outdoors and too delicate to cope with 'weather' – and shooed them off to continue their grazing. Led by Torrela, there was a lot of bucking and capering around before they settled down in the centre of the field.

"I just love watching them mess around like that!" Esme let out a huge sigh of pleasure. She realised she was speaking to herself and hurriedly followed the boys, who had already set off back to the house and their safe place at the bottom of the garden.

A couple of hours later, Eve Montana was surprised the children had not yet shown up ravenously hungry. She decided to look for them with the help of The Choccies who had been shut up in the kitchen for several hours after Fonso had caught them hassling a fledgling crow.

Within minutes an 'invasion by chocolate Labrador', split the huddled group of three children, sending them tumbling over as paws were planted on chests, tongues licked faces and tails wagged like crazy.

"Okay, okay … enough, enough!" Reuben managed to extricate himself from underneath Luca and get to his feet. "Gosh … I'm famished! What time is it?"

"Past teatime!" His mother had followed the dogs, knowing they would take her to the twins. "What are all you up to? It must be something important for you to forget tea!"

Silence

Then Esme jumped in: "Peter's been telling us all about the competing his sisters do with their horses."

"Er … yeh, that's right Mrs Montana." Peter, an arm around Solo's neck, nodded his agreement. "Gosh, I wish I had a dog like these three. The only dog we have is Jack Russell my Dad keeps for ratting. He's not so friendly."

Esme and Reuben sent admiring glances towards him, noting the way he had so cleverly changed the subject.

"Come on then." Eve Montana looked at her children and their new friend curiously, but said nothing. Yet again she had that funny little feeling that things weren't quite as they seemed.

Over the next couple of weeks the twins began sharing with Peter some of what had been happening to them since last summer.

One afternoon after school when Peter had gone with the twins to their place, Reuben casually mentioned that they had been told 'by someone they trusted and who was very wise' that he, Peter, was like them … one of the children who was waking up to things that other people did not know about.

"You know what I mean ..." Reuben asked in a nonchalant sort of a way, looking at a piece of grass he was fiddling with.

Peter was quiet, without responding for several moments before answering very slowly. "Err ... I don't know ... but I sort of do know?" His questioning look begged for understanding.

"Yes! That's just how we felt at first, isn't Es?"

His sister nodded. "And it was sort of scary but not actually scary ... only scary when we thought about it 'cos the things that were happening were not what other people think are 'normal'. So we can't really talk about it to our parents, or our teachers ... or our friends!"

"Except now we can with you!" Reuben high-fived Peter.

"Don't forget Rose!" interrupted Esme, giving Reuben a stern look.

"Yeah well ... Rose. She's a weird one herself ..."

"Rose?" Peter questioned.

"She's a friend of Esme's. Doesn't go to our school!" explained Reuben."She's very different, that's for sure!"

"Yes ... she is ... very different!" agreed Esme vigorously but without any further explanation as to what 'different' meant. "And she's really really cool! I expect you'll meet her soon."

She paused before adding: "All the Beings we've met have been really kind ... well mostly ..." She gave a deep frown but decided not to say any more and quickly changed the subject to the riding lessons they were giving themselves.

Even though Peter did begin to accept that perhaps he too was 'different', he found some of what the twins told him a bit too much to believe. Or perhaps he didn't want to believe it.

One Friday evening when they told him about the 'smart phone adventure', he actually got angry and stomped off to walk home without waiting for his mother to come and collect him, yelling over his shoulder: "You're just making that up!"

He even refused to answer their texts over the weekend. He had been given his first smart phone for his 10th birthday and was very, very attached to it!

Then early Monday morning he texted Reuben, apologising and saying he needed to tell them something.

The three of them managed to sneak off together during lunch and Peter told them his news.

"On Saturday night I had this dream. I met up with you two at some strange place ... ?"

"Oh!" from both twins at once. Neither of them could remember this!

"And … Pegasus was there … well it must have been him, a huge silvery horse with wings … ?"

"Hmhm, that sounds like him." Reuben agreed.

"And … there was another flying horse there too … a bit smaller and a greeny colour … and … I'm sure he 'told' me his name was Cheesie!"

To Peter's consternation the twins burst into laughter. They laughed and laughed … and clapped their hands. They were so happy to hear that Peter had had an 'experience' of his own. Now there was no way he would think they were making it all up.

When she could stop laughing Esme hugged Peter. "That was GZee! He's one of Pegasus' young relations."

As she spoke, she realised just how strange their discussion would sound to most people. And as she realised this, her mood changed from happiness to doubt. A nasty spiteful little voice inside her head was telling her that all the amazing things she and Reuben had experienced over the last months were nothing but imagination.

"He's a bit of a show-off." she added lamely.

Peter's look of consternation had turned to one of relief and he too started laughing. "Crazy, crazy … I'm going crazy!"

'Well, if I'm imagining it, then so are the others!' The thought cheered Esme up again and all three of

them started bouncing up and down and yelling: "Crazy … crazy … we're going crazy!"

Then suddenly Esme noticed that the girl called Hannelore was standing quite still a little way off. She was clearly watching them.

Esme stopped laughing and bouncing. "Look, there's what's her name … Hanna something."

"Oh … gosh!" Peter turned towards the staring girl and said under his breath: "I don't know what to do about her."

"Is she a friend of yours?" Esme asked a practical question.

"Yeah … she is actually. She's very nice … and … I wonder … ?"

"What?"

"Well … I don't know but … like I feel bad about ignoring her a lot since we've been friends …" He hesitated before plunging on. "Well … she's a bit strange herself, she says some funny things … and … she's got a pony ...?"

He shrugged with a questioning look to Reuben to Esme.

"What? … you saying she could join us?" Reuben frowned at Peter.

"Why not? I think that might be a good idea!" Esme's eyes widened as though something had just occurred to her. "Not sure 'why'… but I'm getting a feeling about her … ah! … it's from Rose!"

"Rose!" Reuben looked startled and Peter looked confused.

"Ye … ye … I can feel her telling me that this girl is 'good to go'."

"Why would Rose know!" Reuben sounded exasperated.

"Is that the Rose you told me about before?" asked Peter.

"That's her … Esme's 'special' friend. She knows … e v e r y t h i n g!" Reuben pulled a face.

"Well she does know lots of things, doesn't she!"

"'Spose so … weird things though." Reuben looked down and scuffed the gravel.

"I don't understand why you don't like her, Ruebs?" Esme looked crestfallen.

"Well … I don't actually, not like her. But she is seriously weird. 'Spose I find her a bit scary … the way she 'teaches' us things. Anyway … whatever … you will have to meet her. And … what about her?" Peter pointed with his head towards Hannelore.

Always practical, Esme suggested they invite her for tea one day. "That way we can check out if she would 'fit'."

"Okay." Both boys agreed. It was decided Peter should ask her if she wanted to come to the twins' place for tea on Friday.

And so it was that Hannelore was invited to make the three a four.

25 - Hannelore

So the next Friday afternoon, Hannelore rather hesitantly joined Peter and the twins on their after - school journey to the twins' house.

They had made Peter promise not to tell her about any of the strange things that were happening to them. So he had told her only that they wanted to show her their ponies after he had told them she too had a pony and didn't know many people in the area to ride with.

Hannelore didn't know what to expect. She felt rather nervous as the twins rushed up to the gate into the field and pointed out the three ponies grazing in a far corner.

Reuben said excitedly: "The black is called Torrela. She belongs to Esme and won't let anybody else ride her. The grey is Peter's show pony Mickleton; she's a fabulous ride. And that scruffy little brown one ... that's Mr Nibbs ... and he's very special, isn't he Es?" The boy's voice was full of love as he spoke the last pony's name.

"He sure is! Come on, let's get tea first. Then we can introduce Hannelore to them."

That left Hannelore feeling even more nervous. Meeting the ponies was one thing. Meeting the twins' parents was another.

But she need not have worried.

As soon as they heard the click of the garden gate, the three Labradors came rushing to greet their children. They checked for a moment upon seeing yet another new person before sniffing every bit of the 'new girl' they could. Within seconds their approval was given with enthusiastic tail wags and pleading 'can we jump up and give her a kiss' looks on their faces.

Hannelore was delighted and before the twins could give their permission for the dogs to jump up, she herself had patted her thighs and invited them to do just that.

"Oh … how lovely you are!" She laughed whilst trying to fuss all three of them at once.

And thus she gained a first mark of approval from the twins.

Once their new friend had been introduced to the Choccies the four children trooped indoors for tea and chat.

The twins' mother soon put their newest friend at ease, and Hannelore's anxiety completely disappeared. By the time their father arrived, shaking straw bits from his head, and happily demanding to know what was on the menu, she was so engrossed in discussion with the three other children that she didn't even notice as he grabbed a plate full of food and rushed out again, calling over his shoulder: "I'm going to put in another couple of hours in the field whilst this weather lasts."

Hanni, as they realised her friends called her, was telling them all about her pony Barnaby. "He's a Welsh cob mixed with something or other. So he's quite chunky, but also beautiful … well I think he is! He's a kind of dirty palomino colour. His main and tail are blondie grey. And …" Hanni hesitated. "And he has a short tail … it's been docked."

The three other all children raised their eyebrows as this.

"I thought docking was illegal?" muttered Esme.

"It is … you're right. But Barnaby's about 15 years old, and over in the Welsh valleys, all sorts happens that's not supposed to. He's a rescue pony. I've only had him for a few months, and already I love him lots. We get on really well together." She stopped speaking and glanced at Peter again.

"Tell them," he encouraged her.

"Well … perhaps it sounds silly but … Barnaby seems to know what I'm thinking!" She blurted it out hurriedly and stared defiantly at Reuben and Esme whilst a deep blush crept into her face.

"You see! Rose was right!" Unexpectedly Esme found herself going over to the new girl and giving her a quick hug. "We know exactly what you mean … and it would be lovely to meet Barnaby."

Hannelore smiled with relief.

More talk revealed that Hannelore was a year older than the other three. She had been kept down a year at school.

"I'm dyslexic. All the academic stuff does my head in and I get really low marks for English. I'm sort of okay with maths as long as it's only numbers … But I love drawing and painting." She screwed up her face as she said this last and glanced at Peter.

"Yeh, she's super artistic and does beautiful pictures. Some of them are really strange." Her friend supported what she had said. "And she can do proper cartwheels!" He added with a grin.

He explained to the twins that Hanni's parents were business friends of his parents – which is how he had come to be meet her. "Her Mum is German and her Dad comes from Nigeria. Hannelore is a German name and her surname is Ado … ?" He couldn't finish the name and looked questioningly at Hanni.

"Adebisi. My dad came to England years before I was born … he's quite old. There was a horrible civil war in Nigeria and his life was in danger, so he had to leave his family … I think most of them had been killed anyway. He came to England as a refugee … I think he was about fifteen."

"Oh, how awful!" Esme's heart felt really sad. She had never been able to see what good wars did, or understand why humans did such horrible things to each other (even though sometimes she did want to do horrible things to her brother!).

Hannelore inclined her head in agreement. "It must have been just too terrible. My dad doesn't talk about it often … I expect it makes him sad to think about it." She gave a little shrug and smiled at them. "But he's okay now, he's got Mum and Me … that must be good mustn't it."

Esme grinned and gave Hanni another hug. "Yes it must!" She was thinking of how she and Reuben had ignored Hanni at school, thinking she was really stand-offish. Now, although she still felt envious of the girl's unusual good looks, she was surprised at how happy she felt to think that they would be friends.

Hanni was quite a bit taller than Esme, and very slim. Her skin was the most beautiful colour that reminded Esme of a perfectly toasted biscuit. She wished her skin was that colour instead of fair and covered with freckles that got bigger and more numerous when it was sunny. 'But my hair's just as nice as hers' she thought to herself as she surreptitiously examined Hanni's outrageously curly hair. It was dark brown with gold threads running through it, almost an Afro, but almost. Hanni kept it fiercely controlled for school, but let it stand up and float around her head out of class.

And that same Friday afternoon Hannelore began to understand that these new friends, 'the twins', were extremely unusual.

Some of the things they told her seemed unbelievable and she wondered if they were making it all up.

But when they asked her if she ever remembered her dreams and noticed how intensely they were gazing at her, she suddenly found herself remembering her childhood.

She had always told her dad about her dreams then. In the place where he had been born, he had said, dreams were an important part of life and always shared with others.

"My dad used to say to me when I was little that I remembered my dreams so well that in his country I would probably have become a famous 'dream teller'".

As she said this her eyes flew wide open and her hand went to her mouth.

Bits and pieces of all sorts of weird dreams were streaming into her mind, including one that had a flying horse in it!

She held her breath for a long time before letting it out in an explosive sigh. Then, in a very, very low voice, almost a whisper, she said: "Pegasus ... 'praps that was him then ... ?" She looked from Esme, to Reuben to Peter.

Peter shrugged. "Could be I 'spose ... I've never seen this Pegasus ... except in that dream I had".

The twins continued to stare intensely at Hanni. "Go on ... what happened ... tell us." Reuben sounded impatient.

"Er ... this will sound nuts ... and it was a dream I had months ago ... but ... I was riding this ... er ...

horse with wings ... in the sky ... you know? I can't remember properly ... but he was talking to me ..." she shrugged. "I think he said something about going to a cloud called nine ... but it was probably something else he said ... it was very windy and I couldn't hear anything too well." She stopped speaking and looked apologetic.

Reuben, who was feeling quite shaken up at hearing this news - after all, Pegasus was his friend! - frowned a question at Esme, who was still staring at Hannelore. "Es ..." he began.

Esme, without taking her eyes off their new friend stopped him from continuing with a movement of her hand and then reached out to touch Hannelore on the arm.

"It's okay Hanni. Dreaming is what happens. There are lots of Beings that are usually only visible in dreams ... but that seems to be changing ... doesn't it Reubs?" As she spoke, she vaguely wondered how she knew this and where the words came from.

Her brother nodded uncertainly.

All this time Peter had been sitting quite still without saying anything; just listening to the conversation.
Suddenly he cleared his throat and said: "I sometimes remember bits of very strange dreams when I wake up ... but then just forget them completely until something reminds me of them ... like now! I

think we are meant to be together … the four of us … I think 'somebody' has planned it".

The four children slowly looked at each other. Nothing was said but each of them made the same movement as they took a very deep breath and then let it out in a tiny sigh.

Peter's face showed a bit of anxiety as he searched the twins' faces for approval of his bold suggestion.

Hannelore kept as still as a mouse, almost frozen in anticipation.

Reuben remained deadpan, eyes cast downwards as he tried to get used to the idea of sharing his 'specialness' with anybody other than his twin.

Esme slowly began to nod, a big smile creeping onto her face. She looked at Peter: "I think you just might be right … and … it would be really good to have back-up!"

The tension was broken.

Reuben suddenly recognised the benefit of 'being four' instead of 'being two'. "Yes … it … would!" he exclaimed and clapped his hands together.

Peter was utterly relieved and felt he had made his first proper contribution to the 'work of the group'.

And Hannelore felt that finally she had met people she could be proper friends with.

Esme, grinning like the Cheshire Cat in the Alice in Wonderland story, felt that 'everything was falling into place'. This feeling was confirmed by the 'agreement from Rose feeling' that filled her thoughts for a second.

From that point onwards it became difficult to separate the four children during their free time.

Hannelore rode Barnaby over to the twins place and he was introduced to the other three ponies. These, after a long 'horsey discussion' involving snuffing, snorting, rearing, galloping around the field several times and finally settling to graze close to each other … agreed that he could 'join the gang'. What was particularly interesting to the children about this process was that Mr Nibbs was quite clearly 'the boss'.

The children managed to persuade all parents concerned that Barnaby should come to live with the other three in Nibbs' Field – at least until the end of the summer holidays.

"I do hope that field will be able to provide enough grass for all four ponies," remarked Mr Montana. "I'll have to keep an eye on it. But it's amazing how well all four of them seem to get on together … that's quite unusual!" He shook his head in puzzlement.

Later on, Esme was tucked up in bed, eyes beginning to droop as she finished the last chapter of the book she was reading. The bedroom door was pushed open and a very wide awake Reuben came bouncing in and plonked himself on her bed.

"Isn't it funny," he burst out "How people you think you really don't like can become friends if you let them think you do like them … sort of."

26 - Buzzchat meets Hannelore

A few weekends later, after the various parents had spoken to each other on the phone (after much pleading from their offspring), it was organised for the twins' two new friends to spend the whole weekend at the Montana's with a sleep-over on Saturday night.

Rose was also contacted and agreed to join them, though not for the sleepovers.

All the visitors arrived just after breakfast on Saturday.

Peter and Hannelore were introduced to Rose. "I'm really glad you two have arrived," she said brightly and glanced towards Esme with a slight nod of her head. "Yes, it's good."

The May weather was surprisingly warm and dry so the twins took their three visitors down to the 'safe place' at the bottom of the garden.
The Choccies bounced around them as they went and even Kimber sauntered nonchalantly after them.

Esme noticed that the three crows who had been perching on their roof now flew over to perch in a tree in the coppice at the end of the garden. 'Like they want to listen,' she thought to herself.

On their way down the garden, Hannelore, who noticed these kind of things, pointed to the bush full of white roses in the hedge. "Gosh, it's early for roses to be blooming. I can smell their scent from here ... hmmm lovely." She veered over towards the bush.

"No, don't go to it!" Esme grabbed the girl's arm.

Hannelore looked startled.

"It's ... 'special'. We'll tell you about it later."

"Oh ... kay!" a gleam of excitement shone in Hanni's eyes.

The children got themselves settled, throwing onto the grass the rugs they had brought with them. The drinks and snacks Mrs Montana had provided were arranged in the middle of their circle.

Each of the Choccies chose a child to sit by or lean on: Young Luca the bounciest of the bunch threw himself onto Reuben, insisting on a quick game before settling down with his head on the boy's lap. Solo, the eldest sat sedately next to Peter, and Mowgli, the middle in age lay down close to Hanni.

Kimber had sneaked onto Esme's lap before the dogs could make their choices.

None of the animals approached Rose. But she pointed to them one by one, and then to the three crows perched on a low bough in the tree. "You see ... they know you're special."

"You think so?" asked Peter.

"I know so."

Peter let out a sigh of contentment and draped an arm over Solo's back.

A couple of hours later, long after all the snacks and drinks had been consumed, and after many tales had been told, an exhausted silence fell over the group of children.

Rose, who had not said too much so far (just enough for Peter and Hannelore to realise she wasn't an 'ordinary' child), asked: "Perhaps that's a good stopping point. What has been happening to Esme and Reuben is difficult for a human to understand!"

Hanni raised an eyebrow when she heard the last bit. "How do you mean 'for a human'?"

Rose's huge violet grey eyes peered into Hanni's pale green ones. The green eyes went blank and the human child 'slept' for a couple of seconds.

The twins observed this and were made aware once again that Rose had strange powers.

Peter did not notice. His attention had been taken by Solo, who was enjoying having his tummy tickled by the new child who had been spending so much time with his family.

Hanni 'came to', blinked and then stretched. "I'm hungry!"

"Let's go and have lunch then. Mum said she'd leave us some sandwiches in the kitchen."

"Good idea." Rose smiled and got up.

Peter and Esme followed, collecting empty bottles and plates to take back into the house.
They moved up the garden and once again Hannelore was distracted by the bush of white roses. Rose noticed and said to them all: "After lunch there is one more person that we need to introduce Hanni and Peter to."

Reuben looked puzzled, but Esme clocked immediately and pointed her chin towards the hedge.

"Of course!" Reuben grinned. "How could I have forgotten about him."

Hanni pulled a face at Peter that said 'this is weird'.

He shrugged back at her. The shrug said 'what's one more strange thing on top of the rest!' "'Spect we'll find out." He muttered to her.

Rumbling tummies took their attention, telling them it was important to get some food into them.

Apart from Rose, who always ate very little and very slowly, the children wolfed down plates of freshly made sandwiches and emptied a litre bottle of cold goat milk. Mouths were wiped clean with the backs of hands, and satisfied sighs heard around the table ... plus a rather large burp from Peter, who grinned and said: "That was good!"

Then silence again as the children slumped back in their chairs and Reuben let out a huge yawn. As yawns are catching, the other three soon followed with great yawns of their own.

"I feel sleepy!" Esme sounded surprised.

"Good idea!" said Rose. "Let's have a quick zizz ... a siesta ... that's what they call it in Spain, don't they?"

"What ... sleep?" exclaimed Reuben. "No way!"

"I think that's a very good idea," mumbled Esme as another yawn split her mouth open.

Reuben looked at Peter, who just shrugged. "Not bothered. What about you, Hanni?"

"Just show me a bed!" Hannelore was following Esme who was already halfway upstairs.

So, much to Reuben's disgust, snooze it was. Yet after a couple of minutes of resentful resistance, he was fast asleep. So were the other three.

Rose, however, had stayed downstairs, sitting wide awake in one of the old armchairs by the Aga. Kimber, stretched along the top of the other chair, kept a close watch upon this strange person who had started visiting his house. He was giving her the wide-eyed stare that says 'I don't trust you' and his tail twitched slowly, showing his annoyance.

Rose, slowly half blinking her eyes at him to put him at ease, spoke a few quiet words in a language that none of the other children would have been able to understand, ... and he too fell asleep.

Rose, being Rose, and therefore knowing things that other people did not, realised that Peter and Hannelore needed to sleep in order to absorb all the information they had received from Reuben and Esme that morning. And she knew that Reuben and Esme needed to sleep to create strong energy links to these new friends.
These energy links would serve them well in the future.

It didn't need to be a long sleep though. Fifteen minutes later she heard the children stirring upstairs.

Hanni's head was the first to peer around the kitchen door. She spotted Rose and the empty chair opposite and flopped in to it, waking Kimber as she did so.

"What a lovely cat!" She twisted around in her chair to watch as he cat-stretched his long black body and made a little noise that was a grumbly sort of a meow before twitching his whiskers a couple of times at the girl's mass of curly hair.
He then jumped from the back of the chair onto Hanni's lap, made himself comfortable and promptly went asleep again.

"He likes you ... he trusts you." Rose smiled.

"That's good. I really like cats ... a lot!" Hanni's fingers were gently playing with the cat's shoulder fur.

The three other children entered the kitchen in a group.

"Is it only two o'clock? Crikey, I feel like I've been asleep for days!" Reuben gave a huge stretch.

Peter and Esme nodded. "Yeah, feels like ages ... except that my tummy still feels full." Peter patted his belly.

"Hanni has met Kimber now." Rose's voice turned their attention to where cat and girl were nestled together in the deep armchair.

"Oh good ... and I can see he likes you!" Esme looked surprised as she spotted the black cat on her new friend's lap. "He's really fussy about who he makes friends with ... so that's a good sign."

Rose stood up. "Come on, let's take Peter and Hanni to meet Buzzchat."

"Buzzchat ... ?" Peter's nose and eyebrows frown-crinkled his question.

"He's a Bumblewizard," laughed Esme as she followed Rose out of the kitchen into the garden.

"Bumblewizard ... ?" Peter and Hannelore queried in unison, looking at each other with 'what on earth?' expressions on their faces.

366

"Come on, hurry up you two!" Reuben was holding the kitchen door open for them. "Buzzchat is just one of our new ... friends!" A wide grin accompanied a great big shrug that said 'don't ask me'.

Rose and Esme were waiting for them at the white rose bush.
There was a buzzing sound coming from it, and both Peter and Hannelore hesitated when they heard the loud noise.

"It's OK. He won't sting you ... as long as you don't hurt him. His wing is nearly healed but not quite, so be gentle with him.
As she spoke, Esme put her hand deep into the centre of the rose bush, careful to avoid the thorns. She made a few little buzzy noises herself and then carefully withdrew her hand.

The twins' new friends were silent and stood rather tensely as she opened her hand and they saw she had some kind of ... large insect in her hand.

"Come closer and meet him." Esme giggled.

"What is that?" a look of repulsion was on Peter's face.

"It's huge ... what did you say it was?" Hannelore had crept closer and was peering at the creature in Esme's hand.

"He's a Bumblewizard." Esme smiled a bit smugly, clearly pleased with the affect Bzzzzchzzzcht (his real name ... but humans couldn't say that easily so he had given permission for them to call him Buzz-chat) was having on her new friends.

"Look how beautiful he is." She held her hand towards Peter who was still looking dubious.

The 'insect', which had been hunkered down in the palm of her hand, slowly unravelled itself and stood up. Its little face topped with a pointy hat, brown and black striped leggings could now be seen clearly as he opened his leathery wings wide ...

"It's a miniature bat!" exclaimed Peter.

"No, not a bat ... a Bumblewizard. Come on, let's go down to the bottom of the garden and I'll tell you all about him." Rose set off.

Much to Hannelore and Peter's startlement, Buzz-chat took that moment to launch from Esme hand and start a noisy bzzzzzyy flight around all the children's heads.

Peter and Hannelore ducked.

"No ... it's okay ... let him check you out." Reuben grinned widely. Like his sister, he was feeling rather smug that they had been able to amaze their two new friends yet again.

Still very unsure about it, Peter and Hannelore followed Rose, Esme and Reuben towards the end of the garden. They tried desperately to control their reflex ducking movements whenever the flying creature came close.

Eventually Buzzchat alighted on Esme's head and settled in her hair just above her ear. Esme appeared to be listening ... then she laughed and said to Hanni: "He really likes your hair."

"What!" Hanni gave an exclamation and her hands went to her head.

"Don't worry. He says he never enters any human hair without their permission. To do so would be much too dangerous ... er ..." Esme paused, obviously trying to make sense of the suddenly extra loud bbzzzs and chttss that were coming from the little creature. "Oh! Yes ... nasty. Definitely not!"

She pulled a face and turned to the waiting children. "An image of a squashed bug came into my mind".
"I was going to say ... before Buzzchat interrupted me" She giggled. "I was going to ask if either of you were around that day at school when that boy got chased all around the playground by a 'wasp'?"

Peter remembered but not Hanni. "Yeah ... he looked really funny ... oh ... was that this ... er... Bumblewizard?"

Esme nodded. "Yep it was. That boy is a bully and he was trying to bully me. Doubt he'll try again." Her grin had more than a touch of satisfaction.

Peter and Hannelore were looking at her in amazement, not sure what to say.

Reuben's voice broke into the silence: "My sister can speak 'bug'" he announced with a mixture of pride and envy in his voice.

"That's almost correct." Rose, who had said very little whilst all this was going on, spoke in a quiet voice. "Esme doesn't exactly 'speak bug' … or 'cat'… or 'dog'. But she does have the ability to understand what they mean …
"… as does Peter." She looked at the boy who blushed a bright pink. "And I suspect that Hanni will also discover she can communicate very easily with the animals. It is a fact that all humans could do this, but very few make the effort required to do so … often because they do not believe it is possible." She paused before adding "And girls usually find it easier than boys."

All four children began to speak at once, but Rose raised her hand gently in a 'not now' sort of way. The twins realised that their friend had gone into 'teacher mode' as they called it, and shushed the other two.

When Rose had spoken Reuben had felt as though he was being chastised. How could girls be better at all these 'magicky' sort of things? Surely that wasn't right. Boys had to be better, hadn't they? After all, boys were just … better than girls! And … wizards were much more powerful than witches, weren't they! He was feeling really put out until he suddenly remembered that if it hadn't been for him deciding to ride Mr Nibbs, none of this would have happened! His self esteem immediately rose. Okay. So maybe girls were better at communicating with animals, but boys were the ones who took risk ... who did the adventurous things. And that was really important.

Rose's voice broke into his thoughts.

"Right! Let's sit down and I shall tell you very briefly the story of how the great wizard Merlin created Bumblewizards by mistake. Reuben and Esme have already heard the story but it won't hurt them to hear it again." She looked at the four human children sitting around her in a small circle on the grass and repeated the story she had told the twins just a few short weeks ago.
As had been the case then, she put them into a very light trance so that they would not be distracted by each other or any of the things that were happening around them.

When she had finished and had lifted the trance there was a low "Crikey!" from Peter. But otherwise they were silent, all thinking their own thoughts.
The silence was broken by some sudden and very irate bbzzz chttts.

Esme listened and then burst into laughter. "Buzzchat says it's all very telling his story but what about getting permission for him to visit 'the beautiful hair'! Can he, Hanni?" She looked hopefully at the other girl.

"Hanni scrunched her shoulders up a bit and pulled a face but said; "I suppose ... "

No sooner said than done! The Bumblewizard, until then still perched on a cluster of Esme's curls, flew with 'hardly saw it move' speed over to Hanni.

Still very tense, Hanni managed to keep still whilst Buzzchat circled her head very rapidly several times before coming to rest right on the very top of the swirl of curly hair that gently stood up from her head.
There were some very loud bbzzs and chtts, and Hanni's curls waved from side to side ... then all was quiet.

Hanni, who was the picture of anxiety as all this was happening (and who wouldn't feel rather nervous if a very large bumble bee started to make a nest in their hair, never mind a BumbleWizard!), suddenly opened wide her screwed-shut eyes, let out a huge sigh and un-hunched her shoulders.

"Ooh! ... that feels nice ... just like somebody's tickling my head ever so gently." she looked as Esme. "Is that what you feel?"

"Sort of ... I forget he's there," agreed Esme. "I think it's his way of relaxing humans. 'Spose the wizardy bit of him's kinda ... wise?" She shrugged her uncertainty.

There were some extra loud buzzy noises from the Bumblewizard and she chuckled. "He says something like it being about time we realised that!"

This made all the children laugh; with even Rose joining in.

As her other worldly friend joined in with their laughter, Esme observed how something about her changed. The 'teacher person' disappeared and she became a child again ... just like them.

"I'm hungry now!" she exclaimed. "Do you think tea will be ready soon?"

"Let's go and find out!" Reuben jumped to his feet, causing Luca to bounce around in excitement hoping for a game of chase.

Kimber, unexpectedly disturbed from his own dreaming, swiped at the young dog's tail and hissed loudly, lips drawn back to show some impressive teeth. Rose scrambled to her feet, keeping the cat in her arms as she did so. She could have sworn he muttered something along the lines of *'why on earth would a creator make dogs!'*
Much to the cat's disgust, she lifted him high, looked intensely into his eyes and said loudly: "I like dogs. And I want you to like dogs you miserable old cat." She then lowered him and dropped him gently on the ground.

The cat shook himself and stalked off towards the house with tail held high.

Esme couldn't help chuckling as Hannelore came up to her side. "He's such an old grump sometimes. But I do love him so much! My parents had had him for some years before Reuben and I were born. They thought he might be jealous of us, but he's been really good with us. Mum used to say she thought he wanted to protect us."

"You're so lucky. I wish I had a cat or a dog … well one of each really, to be proper friends with. Barnaby is great and we do get on really well, but I can't take him to bed with me." She sighed.

"Well, it's obvious that our animals like you a lot." Esme smiled at her friend.

Tea over and washing up done super quickly with so many hands to help, the children went to Nibb's field to show Rose the ponies whilst they waited for her mother to come and collect her.

Rose complimented each pony in turn as she looked at them from some way off. It was clear that although she was not 'an animal person' (as Reuben had observed with some disdain), she really did appreciate their beauty.

They were just coming out of the field into the lane when Rose's mother pulled up in her car.

She delicately emerged from behind the steering wheel and stood rather uncertainly in the lane, clearly not wanting to step into any 'dirt' with her shiny high-heeled shoes.

"Hello children. Come on Rose, time to go home. Have you been in that field? You really should be careful."

Rose smiled a sad little smile at the four children and went towards the car. "Coming mother."

Hannelore, Peter, Esme and Reuben followed and clustered around Rose to say goodbye.

Suddenly Rose's mother let out a shriek. She pointed at Hannelore.

"What's that ... that thing in your hair?" She shrieked again "Ugh ... get it off!"

A very angry buzzing reminded the children that Buzzchat was still with them. *'That **THING**! Humans! What do they know about anything!'*

Hanni covered her mouth, trying not to laugh; and glanced at Esme. They had both got the gist of what the Bumblewizard had said.

The angry buzzing continued as the Bumblewizard opened his wings and lifted off from Hannelore's hair. He flew straight for Rose's mother, who covered her face with one hand and flapped at the creature with the other, yelling all the time.

The children's faces were a picture as they desperately tried not to laugh.

Rose caught hold of her mother's flapping hand and said in a very quiet voice: "It's gone, Mother. Shall we go home now."

"We shall! Get in the car." Her mother had become aware of how silly she must have looked and was trying to retain her dignity. She gave a shiver and quickly got back into the driving seat, and without a word of goodbye to the four children standing by the roadside she drove off.

Rose lifted a hand to wave and mouthed: "see you soon."

The four children went to bed early that night, Peter with a mattress in Reuben's room, and Hannelore with a mattress in Esme's room.
Each wanted to talk with the other about all that had happened today, but it was as though some of Rose's 'trance' remained attached to them. They all fell deeply asleep within five minutes of laying heads on pillows.

Sunday morning was a rush. The children were so eager to get out with their ponies that breakfast was gobbled up with huge haste, much to the amazement of Mr and Mrs Montana, who were used to the twins lingering over Sunday breakfasts.

There had been much discussion between parents about how safe it was to let four children, four ponies and three dogs out for several hours on their own.

Mr & Mrs Young and Mr & Mrs Adebisi had spent an evening with Mr & Mrs Montana sorting out all the pros and cons of allowing their children to do what they wanted. This involved much reminiscing about how when they were children they would often go off for a whole day with a bottle of water and some sandwiches.

Peter's parents had been all for it. "Might toughen him up ... time he took responsibility ... no mobile phones in those days, but nobody thought twice about it."
"I think our parents were glad to get rid of us for the day ... it let them get on with their own work," added Peter's mother.

Hannelore's parents had eventually agreed, saying that because the twins knew the area well and as long as they had their mobiles with them, it should be just fine. "It's good that they learn by making a few mistakes when it's fairly safe to do so," offered Mrs Adebisi.
Her father didn't say much, secretly thinking that children in this society had no idea what 'dangerous' meant. But he didn't want to offend so he just supported his wife's view.

Mr and Mrs Montana had also given it much thought, feeling responsible not only for their own children, but for the two as well. So they decided to set some 'rules':
The children must all know how to read a map and how to use a compass - Mr Montana said he would teach them.
They must show their parents where they planned to go – more or less.
They must make sure their mobiles were fully charged before they set off. They must agree to be

back by a certain time, and if they thought they might be late, they must phone all the parents.

"Phew … that's a lot of 'musts' Dad!" Reuben had started to argue with his father.

"Do you want to do this … or not?" This from his mother.

"Okay … if we must."

The rest of the day was spent preparing themselves and the ponies for the trip.

The next morning, each with charged phone, a packet of sandwiches and a bottle of water, Esme, Reuben, Hannelore and Peter set off on their first trip to find good riding tracks.
The track they chose that first morning was an easy one, a bridle path that started a few hundred meters past their house towards the village and on the other side of the lane. They had walked the first parts of it on many occasions with the dogs.

They chatted about all sorts of ordinary things: school, parents, upcoming local fairs, TV characters. The bridle path was wide enough for two to ride abreast. Reuben and Peter were leading the way, Hanni and Esme trailing behind a little. The Choccies were doing the usual doggie things when in the woods: rushing off to follow up scents, rushing back to check on their children and then rushing off again after another scent. Sometimes they were away for minutes at a time, the elderly Solo usually the first to return.

As they came around a bend the children could see somebody in the distance, walking towards them. As it was not unusual for walkers to use this bridle path, none of them took notice other than to call the Choccies close to hand so that they wouldn't be likely to frighten the walker.

As the figure came closer the children could see that it was an old man. He was carrying a long stave and wearing some odd clothing that looked like monks robes.

They moved into single file so he could pass them easily. But to their surprise he lifted his stave and held it out across the path.
Mickleton, who was in the lead, startled and shied backwards into Mr Nibbs who was right behind her. She started prancing and Peter immediately tensed up ... which made her act up even more.

The old man lowered the stave and approached the jittery pony with his hand outstretched. "Now there, my fine young pony, nothing to worry about," he said as he held out his hand. Strangely the nervous pony reached out to get his scent ... and immediately calmed down.

"Good day to you all, my fine young people." The man, whose face was as wrinkled as the proverbial walnut and as brown as the proverbial berry, smiled widely at them, showing very white teeth.

Hesitantly the children returned his greeting.

"I'm visiting a friend of mine, not seen for many a year. I am led to believe that he lives in a cottage to be found over a lane that lies yonder. Would you be so kind as to tell me if I am headed in the right direction?"

The children were slightly intrigued by his rather odd way of speaking. Reuben was the first to answer. "Well, this track does take you to a lane, and I think that if you turn left and walk for a little way, there is an old cottage on the other side of the road. But I'm not sure … you can't see it very well from the lane, but I've been told it's there, in a large orchard."
He glanced at Esme for confirmation.

She nodded her head. "That's what we've been told anyway."

The old man slowly nodded his head a couple of times. "That sounds to be my friend, finding himself a cottage in the middle of an orchard. Thank you young people, you have been most helpful." He looked intently at each of them in turn. "May you enjoy the rest of your ride with these most lovely creatures. And you too." He turned towards the three dogs who were sat in a row by the side of the track.

He moved to pass them and be on his way. But after a few steps, stopped and said to them all very clearly: "My name is Sirus Ganda. I hope we meet again." Then off he went moving up the track in long strides. As he went Esme caught a glimpse of his shoes. Or were they sandals, she couldn't tell, only that they were bright emerald green.

"Crikey, he's a bit odd," said Peter quietly as he kicked Mickleton to move forward. "But Mick seemed to like him, so he must be okay."

"Yeah … and the dogs ... well they behaved very well." said Esme.

"Hmm." Reuben said nothing but looked thoughtful.

"What a strange name. What was it? ... Sirus Ganda?" Hanni looked nonplussed.

"Come on, let's get going. Torrela's getting fidgety!" As she said this, the beautiful black horse tossed her head, swirling her long mane and taking small leaps forward. "Wheee!" Esme exclaimed in delight and let her mount set off down the long empty path ahead of them at quite a pace.

The others followed. After several minutes of enjoying being able to allow their ponies to speed along without check, the bridleway entered a little valley. It was part of a well-known walk, known locally as the bluebell walk because of the masses of these flowers that grew under the shady trees that clothed the valley's sides. Neither Peter nor Hanni had ever been there before and thought it was very beautiful.

They decided the flat grassy centre of the valley would be a great place to stop and have their picnic, especially as there was a tiny stream than ran all the way through it. This would provide water for the ponies and the Choccies.

The children dismounted, unloosened girths, let the ponies drink and got out their food, which had all been stored in a saddle bag carried by Barnaby and lent to them for the occasion by the twins' father.
The Choccies, who had drunk their fill from the stream had all flopped down for several minutes, tired out after the long run. But they were soon up again, rushing around all over the place, excited to have some wonderful new scents to follow.

They were just finishing their sandwiches when Peter pointed to the sky.
"Look! There's a buzzard ... Or ... ?"

The four children looked upwards.

"Oooh, yes, I see it. Gosh ... it's huge!" exclaimed Hanni.

The bird circled several times and then spiralled higher and higher until it was just a speck in the sky.

But Esme's heart missed a beat and a shiver ran through her body. She said nothing. But she knew the bird was no buzzard. It was Gyrre!

"Phew ... for a moment I thought it was an eagle!" Peter laughed nervously.

"Eagles don't live in this kind of countryside, do they?" Reuben sounded puzzled, as he too had thought it looked like an eagle. He gave a quick glance at his sister – he knew about her dreamtime Eagle friend.

But Esme had turned to say something to Torrela.

"No they don't!" Hanni was very sure of this. "Well ... not unless it was one that has escaped from that Birds of Prey Centre in Newbridge.

"It's gone now anyway. I want to get going, I'm chilly!" Esme tightened Torrela's girth. The pony showed her disgust at 'being belted up' by a tail swish and ear twitch. "Sorry." Esme patted her friend.

Using proper saddles and bridles was another thing the parents had insisted upon if the children wanted to ride outside of Nibbs Field.

The other three followed her quickly. Esme was right; it had got colder. The sun that had warmed them as they had their lunch was now covered by a mass of grey clouds.

They kept up a gentle trot for most of the way back, suddenly eager to get home.

Once again, Esme felt a shiver run all over her body. She wondered why Gyrre had appeared in non-dreamtime ... as though he was patrolling the sky. She knew he was a sort of 'protector' and felt a slight apprehension. What did they need protecting from?

But nothing happened and they reached home just in time to avoid getting a soaking from the heavy rain that had been dumped where they had been riding just 15 minutes earlier.

27 - Saved by a Dragon

After that first outing, the four children spent most of their weekends together, doing things they all enjoyed.

Unless the weather was really unhappy, a lot of time was spent continuing exploring the local countryside. They found lots of 'special places' for picnics and 'conferences'; even a couple of places where they let the ponies graze untied. The Choccies were always with them. Gyrre sometimes patrolled the skies above them.

"Look, there's that large buzzard again." Reuben would sometimes say and look at Esme with a question in his eyes. Eventually she did tell him that it was Gyrre. They decided not to say anything to the other two though.

The three sets of parents had met and it had been agreed that the children were responsible enough to be allowed out with their ponies for the whole day …
… as long as they told the twins' parents where they were going …
… as long as they were back by tea time …
… as long as they didn't take stupid risks …
… as long as they made sure any fires they had lit to cook sausages on were well and truly out…
… as long as …

The four children were actually very self-responsible, and they were happy to agree to all the conditions set by the parents. They were sensible conditions!

It was a Saturday not long before the beginning of the summer holidays when the little group of four children, four ponies and three dogs set off once again, this time for their first whole day out exploring.

Locally there were stories about an ancient oak tree that had been used for pagan ceremonies in the past. And perhaps still was, some of the local people said! It was called the White Leaf Oak.

When they looked on the map of their area they had actually found it marked.

They began imagining all sorts of things about this tree.

"I wonder if we could all get inside it ... like that famous one in Sherwood Forest where Robin Hood used to hide?"

"praps we can store provisions in it."

"praps we could build a tree house ...?"

They were sitting around the kitchen table with the map laid out on the middle. They were looking for the best riding route to the tree, which was several miles away from the twins' house.

"Oh look, there's us ... our house!" Reuben pointed delightedly to a tiny house icon with the words Enfield Cottage written next to it.

"Remember that it is possible that people still meet there," cautioned the twins' mother. She always did some research about the places her children and their friends were likely to be before they were given permission to go on these 'jaunts' as she called them. "Somebody told me there's a group been set up recently by a couple of witches. They would probably use the tree as one of their meeting places."

"Witches!" All the children turned towards the adult, questioning looks on their faces.

"Huhu … don't look so surprised!" Mrs Montana laughed. "Being a witch is quite trendy these days!"

"Oooh perhaps that's what we are!" Hanni giggled and looked at Esme.

"Yep … I guess we are. And the boys are the … wizards!"

The children laughed uproariously at this suggestion until Esme paused for breath and then said quietly: "Maybe we are!"

At that all four fell silent, suddenly aware that Mrs Montana was observing them.

After a moment of uncomfortable silence, Reuben said innocently: "Come on you lot … mustn't keep Harry Potter waiting."
Esme threw her brother a glance of thanks and a joint sigh of relief might have been heard.

Finally, picnic prepared and route decided - with Hanni in charge of navigation for the day - they went to get the ponies. The Choccies bounded and bounced around them, even old Solo. The dogs just loved these jaunts … so many new smells, and occasionally things to chase! Not that they had ever caught anything … so far.

The ponies seemed to know there was an adventure planned and they were all waiting quietly by the gate of their field.
The children tacked them up quickly, all now experts at the intricacies of saddle and bridle.
They managed to follow the route on the map fairly easily, only getting a little lost once. After about an hour they reached the part of their ride that went along a high ridge. The views of the surrounding valleys and hills were stupendous and the children halted their ponies so they could take it all in.

"Feels like we're all alone in the world up here," said Hanni, breaking the awed silence.

There were murmurs of assent from the others.

It was tempting to all of them to stop right there for their picnic.
Even the Choccies has stopped their noses-to-ground-scent-following-investigations and plonked themselves down close to the ponies, tongues lolling out as they panted themselves cool after their exertions.

Esme was noticing how reluctant to move she was feeling. She just wanted to go get off Torrela, lie down on the grass to sleep. This is weird, she thought to herself. She looked at the others. They were all sitting slumped, heads drooping.

Suddenly Peter lifted his head and said; almost shouted: "No! Not here! We'll never find the tree if we stop here now."
The three others turned to look at him, surprised at how adamant he sounded.

"Yeah, you're right. Let's go." Hanni gathered up Barnaby's reins, pulled his head up from the grass he was steadily cropping, turned his head in the direction they needed to go and gave him a little kick. "Come on!" she called over her shoulder.

Everyone surged forward to follow her … it was as if somehow a spell had been broken.

A streak of light and a sharp crack of thunder came from out of the bright blue sky, causing all the humans and the four-leggeds to jump with fright.

"That's odd!"
"Lightning … and thunder?"
"Hope there's not going to be a storm!"
"Praps we should go back!"

After some moments of hesitation wondering what was best to do, the children decided to keep going – after all the sun was shining with not a cloud in sight.

After several hundred yards, the ridge narrowed. It was still just wide enough for all four to ride alongside each other, but its sides dropped away quite sharply and they decided that riding in single file would be safer. They moved slowly, allowing the ponies to pick their way carefully along the stony track.

Although the sun was indeed shining in a clear blue sky, the wind began to pick up. It started to blow quite fiercely from the direction they were heading in. It brought a chill to the warm day.

There was a real air of seriousness and concentration about the small group moving slowly along the ridge. Even the dogs remained close to the group, not rushing around after scents like they usually did.

Esme shivered and reached out a hand to rest on Torrela's warm neck.
They trudged forward, children's and ponies' heads tucked down into the wind.

After a little while later they were happy to see the ridge was opening out again into a wider flatter area of grass. The wind had died down to a gentle breeze. Over to the left of them a little copse of shrubby trees peeked up from the side of the ridge.

"Gosh ... that was a bit scary!" Esme let out a huge sigh of relief. "I thought ..."

Before she could finish, Hanni called out: "Oh look ... those flowers ... they're amazing ... see ... over there." She was pointing and wiggling her fingers towards a shrub that appeared to be bright pink all over.

"Gosh, how strange … and … wow … can you smell that scent?" Reuben was standing up in his stirrups, sniffing the air.

"Hmm … I can … lovely smell! Come on, let's look!"

Barnaby, followed by Mr Nibbs, trotted Hanni and Reuben towards the pink shrub. Hanni jumped off Barnaby to get close enough to push her nose into the mass of flowers. "Hmmm … just gorgeous!"

Peter, Mickleton, Esme and Torrela and the dogs – who had all been quite a way behind Hanni and Rueben - came to a halt in the centre of the flat area. They had watched as the other two had trotted over to the bushes.

"Why have they gone over there?"

"They must have spotted something interesting. Let's go and see." They turned their ponies towards their friends.

But Esme pulled up. "Wait!" she called to Peter. The distant cry of a bird carried on the air and a tiny speck in the sky grew rapidly larger. Esme knew it was Gyrre. As soon as it arrived above them, the eagle began circling around and around, repeating a piercing cry again and again.

Esme knew Gyrre was sending them a warning! But about what? She reached for Gyrre with her mind like she did when they were in dreamtime. "What is it?" But there was no reply. They were not in dreamtime now, and Esme didn't know how to contact her feathered companion.

"What's happening?" Peter looked over at Esme.

"I don't know!" But Peter could see she was nervous.

And then they noticed: huge dark clouds had appeared on the horizon, and closer by wispy clouds had appeared out of nowhere and were beginning to veil the sun.

Esme looked around anxiously ... there was nowhere to take shelter.

The wind had got up again and was rolling the clouds towards them at a terrific speed. These had grown darker and bigger and were no longer distant. Grey streaks descending from them meant heavy rain.

The storm was approaching with crazy speed.

The circling eagle was overtaken and swallowed up by black swirling clouds that now filled the sky, blotting out the light and warmth of that beautiful day.

A great flash of lightning, followed by an ear splitting crack of thunder rent the silence! The streaming rain curtain advanced was almost upon them.

Peter and Esme looked at each other in horror.
What to do ... where could they go to escape.

"Come on ... over to the shrubs!" Peter's voice
broke into her panic and she watched as he and
Mickleton took off towards Hanni and Reuben.
She kicked Torrela, who was shivering all over,
into movement.

As they began to move towards the shrubs, there
was another bright flash of many fingered lightning. One of the shrubs close to Reuben and Hanni
burst into flames and immediately a great thunder-
clap followed.

To the horror of the watching Peter and Esme, the
shrubby trees and a whole chunk of the side of the
ridge began to move as a crack appeared in the
land just in front of the shrubs.

The piece of land was slipping out of sight. And it
wanted to carry two children and their ponies with
it!

A panicked Barnaby jumped backwards and pulled
his reins out of Hanni's hand! With a great leap,
he jumped over the crack and raced towards the
other two ponies and their riders. They had halted
in their tracks and were staring in horrified fasci-
nation as Reuben on Mr Nibbs and Hanni disap-

peared from their view as the land continued its slide, sinking beyond their sight.

The rain was carried on a howling wind. It drenched Esme and Peter, the ponies and the dogs in an instant as they huddled together in a forlorn group.

Almost blinded by the windswept rain, they appeared to be rooted to the spot. What could they do? What they had looked to for shelter had turned into a landslide that was carrying their companions down the side of the ridge!

Amongst the scrub, Hannelore's terrified voice calling to Reuben was carried away on the howling wind ... a wind that seemed to be shrieking something: 'Maawaawaaaa ... ma ... ma ... ma ... ma ...' it whined.

Hannelore watched Mr Nibbs slip-slithering down the steep shaking slope, Reuben still balancing precariously in the saddle. Then pony and boy disappeared over the edge of the precipice that hadn't been there a few moments ago!

The girl clung to a thorny branch of the pink flowering shrub that was the only thing preventing her from following her friend. The pain in her hand was intense as the thorns bit into her skin, but she dared not let go.

She yelled out Reuben's name again and again. But there was no reply.

What was going on? What had happened? One panicky thought after another rushed through her mind.

Meanwhile, Esme, who had flung her free hand up to her heart to try and stop it pounding, had encountered the hard little shape of her amulet, nestling among several other pretty little things she always wore around her neck.

And in that moment she remembered Old Woman's instructions: '*Rub it if you need help!*' She desperately pulled the necklace and its charms up through the neck of her soaking tee-shirt and started rubbing the amulet between her thumb and forefinger.

"What are you doing?" Peter's shaky voice ...

Esme didn't answer; just kept rubbing the amulet and muttering 'help us!' under her breath.

A few seconds later, just as suddenly as it had started, the land stopped shaking, the howling wind dropped to a gentle breeze, and the lashing rain had become a rather miserable drizzle.

Now that the ground by the bushes was no longer shaking, Hanni managed to get to her feet and scramble down into the mini ravine left by the ground splitting, and up the other side onto the flat part of the ridge.
She called out and waved frantically at the three ponies and two children who were still huddled in a bunch some distance away.

Still dazed from the wind and rain battering, Esme slowly raised her head and looked towards the call. She saw a figure emerging from the bushes.

One figure alone.

"Hanni!" She cried and kicked the still trembling Torrela towards the figure of her friend.
Peter, who had dismounted from a spooked Mickleton, scared he might not stop her from bolting, dragged the still jumpy pony after them.

The riderless Barnaby stuck close to Torrela.

Hanni stumbled to meet them flung her arms around a rather startled Barnaby's neck. Tears were streaming down her face.
"Reuben went over, down the steep side ... on Nibbs" she blurted out. "I saw them both slip over the edge. We've got to go and find them."

"Right! Come on then!" Peter felt his fear disappear and was all set for action.

"No ... wait" Esme suddenly felt very calm, almost as though she was contained within a very quiet bubble. The voice was in her head again, the same voice telling her the same thing as it had done all those weeks ago: 'Reuben is all right ... Reuben is all right.' This time, after a slight pause it added: 'He will join you soon.'

She came out of the bubble to see the other two staring at her expectantly. She took a deep breath and blurted out: "Reuben and Mr Nibbs are fine."

Peter's mouth fell open, and Hanni gasped.

"Really. We don't need to worry about them. We just need to wait here."

"But … I saw them …"

"What! How do you know they're OK?"

Esme shook her head slowly from side to side. "I don't know how I know … just do … know! We need to stay here."

A moment later the attention of the three anxious children was caught by a flash of light coming from the centre of the dark clouds that were still hanging scarily low in the sky even though the wind and rain had almost stopped.

"Oh no …" Esme whispered to herself.

"What is it Esme?" Peter's sharp hearing had caught the whisper.

Hanni was pointing and gaping open-mouthed at the clouds. They seemed to be turning blacker and heavier by the minute. She said in a strained voice: "I think ... I think we should be going home … or going to find Reuben ... that storm ... it hasn't finished. Esme are you sure Reuben and Nibbs will be OK?"

Esme, who had now slipped off Torrela to stand by the pony's head, nodded her head vigorously, still rubbing the amulet between her forefinger and thumb. "Mmm! And we can't go home without Reuben and Nibbs anyway."

"Awesome ..." Peter's voice was hushed as he too realised what was happening with the clouds.

They watched in silence as the clouds began to roil and boil. It was as if they were alive. They ceaselessly changed shape, splitting into myriads of small clouds and scattering over the sky before rushing back together as though drawn by magnetism. Flashes of what seemed like sparkling multi-coloured flames blazoned forth from the very centre of the seething mass.

It was beautiful ... and absolutely terrifying.

The three children seemed to be hypnotized by the horrible beauty of an amazing battle of light and dark that was happening in the sky. All thoughts of 'going home' had vanished.

Even the ponies and dogs were still, standing with their heads turned to the sky ... watching.

The children could only look on in wonderment. Without being aware of it, ponies' reins had been dropped and each child had moved their hands to clasp them over their midriffs. Instinctively they wanted to protect that sensitive area from the vibrations caused by the forces battling for power overhead.

For that is what they realised it was – a battle for power.

And they could see that things were changing with the clouds. Each time the small scattered clouds re-formed as one, the main cloud grew smaller and lost a little of the deep blackness that made it so scary.

Then two things happened at the same time.

From the centre of the cloud mass a tiny shape emerged, falling like a stone, dropping towards them. Esme put a hand to her mouth and took in a sharp breath. "No!" she whispered to herself. For a fleeting second she had felt the presence of Gyrre, whirling around and down …

But before she could say anything more …

"Look! What's that?" Peter pointed to one side of the mass of clouds.

Another shape could be seen, moving rapidly in their direction.

Hannelore, still hunkered up close to Barnaby, looked in the direction he was pointing. "Is that … it is … it's a horse … in the sky … a horse with wings!"

She heard Esme breathe a huge sigh of relief and whisper "We're safe now!"

The creature approached rapidly, its wings beating powerfully as it covered the distance with amazing speed.

As Esme spoke both Torrela and Mickleton stopped shivering. Their gaze turned away from the clouds and towards the oncoming flying creature.

Barnaby, so far unfazed by all that was happening, pricked up his ears and lifted his head. Hanni felt a shiver go all through him. He watched the approaching creature intently for a few seconds before trumpeting a loud neigh and ... rearing up on his hind legs.

The other two ponies followed suit, the noise of their combined neighing so loud that Esme covered her ears in protest.

The three children looked at the ponies in astonishment.

"What the ...!" Peter muttered to himself.

As the flying horse came in to land, Esme turned to the other two children and said quietly: "This is Pegasus ... and ... he's got Reuben with him." Tears started to roll down her face.

It was only then, utterly astounded by the great size of the 'horse' that had just landed, that Hannelore and Peter spotted a small figure on its back. As soon as the creature had allowed its wings to sink slowly to its sides and had ruffled them into a comfortable position, Reuben – for indeed it was he

– commented offhandedly: "Phew that was awesome!"

None of the children moved ... but Esme, with tears running into a little smile just twitching up the corners of her mouth, managed to blurt out: "Go on then!" she said loudly, "tell us what happened."

"I'll tell you all later." He grinned at their astonished faces. "Pegasus says it's not quite finished yet."

"What's not finished?" Peter was frowning, not liking the feeling of not understanding a single thing that was happening!

"The fight of course!" Reuben jabbed upwards with a finger to where the clouds still roiled and boiled fiercely, and continued to spit forth flashes of rainbow light.

He then appeared to just float off the broad back of the huge horse and slip gently to the ground by the creature's shoulder before moving to stand under its head and allowing it to snuffle his hair for several moments.

Hannelore, completely shaken up by what had just happened to her could only stand and stare. This 'horse' was huge ... and it had wings. She was feeling really scared by what was happening.

Peter reacted to it all by flinging an arm over Mickleton's neck and whispering something towards the still jittery pony's left ear, which was cocked in his direction while the right one was cocked to-wards Pegasus.

Reuben, feeling really pleased by the affect his re-appearance was having, gave the winged horse's nose a last stroke and walked rather cockily to-wards his sister and friends.

He threw out his arm in the direction of the animal. "Let me introduce you.This is Pegasus – my friend. Pegasus, this is Peter and this is Hannelore – also my friends."

Esme's feelings were seriously confused between huge relief that her brother had turned up alive and well ... and annoyance as she was reminded how insufferably obnoxious he could be sometimes.

As though he agreed with her, Pegasus gave a great snort. It was such a powerful snort that it blew Reu-ben off his feet, knocked him face down onto the grass.

Esme started to laugh ... a bit hysterically.

Hanni could have sworn she saw the great horse wink at her.

Reuben got to his feet. He looked a little chastised ... but then grinned. "Well, that was an adventure!"

At that point, the children came out of their amaze-ment and clustered around Reuben asking if he was alright, what had happened ...

Then Hanni suddenly remembered! She put her hand to her mouth and frowned at Reuben. "What about Mr Nibbs? I ... I saw both of you go over the edge of that precipice!"

Peter too stopped talking for a moment before looking quizzically at Reuben. "No need to worry about him, is there?" he asked rather tentatively. "He's with us now, isn't he?" Peter reached out a hand in the direction of the huge winged horse.

Esme glanced at Peter in surprise: "You know?"

"Know what?" asked Hanni looking even more confused.

"About Mr Nibbs," Esme sounded tense and looked quickly to her brother: "Peter's right isn't he? Mr Nibbs is just fine ... isn't he?"

Reuben laughed out loud. "Yep ... he sure is." He turned and walked over to the winged horse, who had been standing very quietly, observing the children.

"Can you show Peter and Hanni your other self?"

"Humph ... if I have to! But for a moment only ... I need to stay as I am right now – for things are not complete!" Reuben was so caught up in the excitement of showing his two friends who Mr Nibbs really was that he did not hear the last part of what Pegasus had just said to him.

"Watch ... watch Pegasus!" he called out, enjoying the puzzled expression on Hanni's face.

And ... just as he had hoped, the puzzlement turned to utter amazement as Pegasus obligingly shape-shifted – very briefly - into the form of a scruffy little brown pony.

"What ...? ... But ... how ...?" Hanni's face was a picture.

Peter though was nodding his head slightly. "So ... I was right!"

Mr Nibbs disappeared as once again the shimmering shape of the winged horse materialised in front of them.

It was now Reuben's turn to laugh rather hysterically. Although he wasn't going to admit it, he had been absolutely terrified by what had happened earlier!

Pegasus snorted loudly and obviously did 'something' that calmed the boy down. He became very serious and ran a hand through his soaking curls, pushing them back off his face. He walked slowly over to stand by his sister. He looked at Peter and Hannelore and said quietly: "I'm sorry."

"Sorry ... for what?" asked Hanni.

"For not warning you that being friends with us might not be easy!"

It was Peter who was first to respond: "Well I'm not that surprised. That first time I saw Mr Nibbs when he dumped you at the bus stop ... it seemed to me then that his shape changed as he trotted off ... became sort of transparent and shimmery and ... he rose into the air. I didn't really pay much attention at the time ... I was anxious about a test in class ... and anyway, I often see things that aren't really there." He shrugged.

Esme's expression showed that a light had dawned. "Ah ... now I understand why Nibbs insisted we make friends with you! He said ..."

She stopped talking and her gaze returned to the part of the sky from where Pegasus had emerged.

A tiny dot became larger and larger and Esme breathed. "Is that ... is that GZee?" She glanced over at Reuben who followed her gaze.

"Yeah I think it is ... it's Cheesie!"

"Reuben ... don't call him that! Yes ... it is him ... how wonderful."

Then she began to move slowly in the direction of the new arrival, calling to Reuben and Pegasus as she passed them: "I'm going to meet him."

A muttered *'better late than never'* drifted into her mind from the direction of Pegasus.

To Hannelore's utter astonishment ... but no longer fear, another great winged horse landed a little way off. This one was a shimmery greenish colour, and it greeted Esme as she approached with a loud high-pitched whinny and a lot of showy prancing.

A very short but sharp neigh from Pegasus caused the young winged horse to calm down, come to a standstill and lower his head as Esme reached him and put a hand up to stroke him between the eyes. Then, wings still wide open, he lowered his head even more, so that Esme could fling her arms around his neck. He immediately whickered and lifted his head high in the air, leaving Esme hanging several inches from the ground before she loosened her arms and dropped onto the grass.

GZee nuzzled her hair and 'apologised' with another little wicker, letting her know that he was just excited. The words '*I've never been called out on a rescue job before ...*' entered her head as he rather reluctantly lowered his wings and followed Esme back to the others.

When she was within speaking distance: "I sent for help!" She explained to the others, looking at Reuben whilst groping around her neck and pulling out the amulet to show them.

Reuben exclaimed: "Oh Es ... I didn't bring mine ... stupid, stupid!"

Hanni looked from one to the other with a frown on her face. What were they talking about now. She turned to Peter and asked: "What is all this about? Do you know?"

"No ... I don't I expect they'll tell us though ... when the fight is over."

"What fight?"

Peter lifted a hand to the sky. "Looks like a fight to me."

All the children had been totally absorbed by the arrival of two flying horses. They had more or less forgotten about 'the battling clouds'. These were still overhead but had moved much higher into the sky so that the grumbling and growling that had been going on above their heads all the time had become less noticeable.

Hannelore had moved to stand close to Peter, still slightly wary of the huge winged horses, especially the one Reuben had called 'Cheesie'. This one kept abruptly swinging around in a way that could easily have knocked her over. Esme didn't seem afraid though, despite being so tiny compared to the creature she was standing close to.

Now that Peter had reminded them of 'the clouds', they all looked skywards. Although those overwhelming black thunder clouds were still swirling around a great deal, the children could see that they seemed to be breaking up into smaller clouds and turning rapidly from black to dark grey and then light grey. The flashes of bright lights still shot through them.

"I'm not sure ... but I think it's a fight between the light and the dark." Peter hesitated a moment before adding: "Between good and evil."

Hannelore felt a shiver run though her. Could this be true? She didn't know what to say.

"I'm sure they will tell us all about it ..." Peter nodded towards Esme, Reuben, and the two giant horses, "... now that this has happened!"

But 'this' wasn't the end of it!

All of a sudden there was an almighty great shriek and an explosion of sound and colour that made the ponies lay their ears flat back, the dogs crouch with tails between their legs, and the children clap their hands over their ears.
They saw the remaining clouds disintegrate into what looked like little puffs of smoke and then disappear completely.
Left behind in the bright blue sky was something that looked a bit like one of those glitter ball things. Ever-changing multi-coloured lights were streaming from it as it fell from the sky, plummeted downwards.

Not a word was said, not a sound from dogs or horses ... and GZee stopped prancing.

Abruptly, as though a parachute had opened, the glitter ball came to a halt. For several seconds it oscillated sideways before splitting apart into a myriad tiny shining pieces that hovered in the air, seeming to be suspended in time. It couldn't have been more than a few seconds but to the children it seemed a lifetime.

A second ear-splitting shriek rent the air.
The children pushed their hands tighter over their ears, the dogs hunched closer to the ground, and the ponies, whites of eyes showing, squeezed their ears even tighter against their heads. Had they not had such a strong bond with their humans they would have fled.

As they watched, a pattern formed in the sky from the pieces of glitter ball. It was like watching pieces of a jigsaw being slotted into place and gradually revealing a shape.

The shape became recognisable to Esme.

"Aaah ... the dragon!" She gasped! Images from one of her nightmares flashed through her mind: great thunder clouds with a nightmare monster face at their centre ... coming to kill her … The Joker! And … a brief flash of 'Dragon Light' that chased the clouds away.

And sure enough it was soon clear to all the children that the shape in the sky was indeed that of a dragon ... a dragon that had now opened a pair of powerful wings and was flying fast ... in their direction!

Four children, three ponies, and three dogs stood as still as stone; all heads turned in one direction.

They ought to have been afraid. So afraid that they took to their heels to run as fast as possible away from the giant flying creature that was very rapidly approaching the very place where they were standing.

But they could not move, not even to look at each other.

But none of them felt fear. Mind numbing awe yes, but not fear. As Hanni said later, much later when it was all over: "I just knew she (for the dragon turned out to be a 'she') wasn't going to hurt us even though she did look very fierce.

The Dragon landed, her enormous wings creating such a rush of wind, that had they not been immobilised by some strange force, the children would have been knocked off their two feet.

She came to a halt, resting those great outspread wings with their tips just touching the ground for several long moments before slowly folding them to her sides.

She glowed. Her multi-coloured scales seemed to pulse with dark red and orange as she took one deep breath after another, eventually lowering her head and resting the tip of her snout on the grass. Steam issued from her nostrils, mouth and ears.

Esme realised that this enormous creature was ... exhausted.

Rather than feeling afraid of the fearsome looking beast the girl felt a strange sensation of great love. She realised that this amazing mythical creature had come to their rescue, doing battle with those great life-threatening clouds.

She took a couple of steps forwards, intent upon going to the dragon to thank it.

GZee squealed and pranced around in front of her. 'No ... no ... no ... NO ... HOT!'

Esme came to a halt.

Although they could all now move again and the ponies and dogs had relaxed, everybody remained standing still ... waiting to see what would happen.

Peter suddenly glanced all around them, checking to see if there were any other people in sight. A thought had popped into his mind: 'what would happen if some other people saw them?'

Though ... of course, even if other walkers had happened upon the children and their animal companions, they would have seen nothing more than four children, four ponies and three dogs. They might have noticed an odd smell, rather like when a very wet dog sits in front of an open fire, but probably not given it much attention ... after all, lots of unusual smells get carried around on the wind in the countryside.

But to Peter's relief, they were all alone: four children, three ponies, three dogs, two very large winged horses and one enormous dragon.

Finally the dragon lifted her head and surveyed the small group. Her dragon eyes seemed to have a life of their own, sending off little flashes and sparks.

She nodded her great head slowly a couple of times, 'said' something and began to walk towards them.

'Careful My Lady Dragon ... you're still very hot!' Pegasus moved to place himself between the advancing dragon and the children.

The dragon halted and then very slowly lowered her huge body to the ground.

Again she 'said' something. None of the children could understand. Her speech sounded like a mixture of the noise made by a sparkler as it burns and pebbles being jumbled against each other by rushing water.

Pegasus, who could obviously understand Dragonaish, translated:

'Hot ... tired ... devil of a battle ... must be watchful ... still danger ... Magnificent Master of Malicious Magic determined to stop these ...

Pegasus interrupted her and said something that sounded a bit like the Dragon's way of speaking.

She listened and then nodded her great head a couple of times before getting to her feet and directing another spurt of 'hzztzrrbleblezzzzz' sounds towards Pegasus.

Then she began once more to walk very slowly towards the group of children, ponies and dogs.

All three ponies flattened their ears again and began shifting backwards. The Choccies remained in a huddle, tails back between legs.

Pegasus, a quietened Gzee at his side, walked in front of the dragon towards the waiting group. His words reached into all their minds:

'Do not be afraid. The dragon means you no harm. She is here to help you. She is right now programming herself to speak Human'.

Pegasus' words had a calming effect and everybody visibly relaxed. None of them any longer felt even the teeniest desire to run as far away as possible from this great beast that was getting closer and closer.

The dragon finally stopped - close enough for them to feel the heat that was coming off her body. They could make out the beautiful patterning of her scales – now mostly different shades of green - and the little puffs of steam that issued from her wide nostrils.

She sank to the ground once again, but even so she dwarfed even Pegasus and Gzee.

At this point, Luca, still young enough to be curious and foolish all at the same time, left the dog huddle and slunk towards the dragon on his belly ... he wanted to get close enough to catch her scent.

A sharp 'ruuff!' from old Solo, brought him scurrying back.

The dragon lifted her long neck and held her head high. As she spoke little tongues of flame to flickered from her mouth. She said with a voice that commanded attention and in words that were just Human enough for them to understand:

'I am The Dragon of The West. I am The Dragon Et-Evora'

Her eyes had stopped their swirling, and she directed her gaze at the group with an intensity that left them all feeling as though she knew everything there was to know about each one of them.

'I have chosen. I have chosen to serve humans who show their love and respect for this planet that you call Earth. I come in response to the cry of help from the girl child there – the one you call Esme'.

And then, if a dragon could be said to smile, this one did just that. She lowered her head and her long neck reached out towards Esme. *'Dragon Emergency Services ... at your service!'*

Reuben, Hanni and Peter all turned to look at Esme. She was standing there with eyes wide and her right hand touching the amulet around her neck.

414

"Wow!" breathed Hanni.

Suddenly, Reuben started to move slowly forward, almost as though hypnotised. He walked towards the dragon and halted several meters in front of her. After several long seconds he bowed his head, and spoke.

"I greet you Great Dragon Et-Evora. I thank you for saving us from The Magnificent Master of Malicious Magic. You are ever welcome in our company."
Looking most surprised at hearing himself speak these words, the boy lifted his head to gaze at the great creature he had just addressed, and then began to move backwards as fast as he could.

Watching this happen, the other three children looked at each other with 'What the ...?' expressions on their faces.

Esme shook her head in bewilderment, lifted her shoulders and gave that palms up sign that said 'not a clue!'
When Reuben was back by her side once more, she mouthed at him "What was that ... what did you just do?"

Reuben looked at his sister with confusion. "Don't know ... just happened! Those words ... they just came out of my mouth!"
Esme could see he was struggling to say something else. She looked at the other two and made a sign for them to stay silent.

When Reuben finally began to speak again, the eyes of his sister, Hannelore and Peter were all directed straight at him.

"I ... she's ... I ... I wanted to thank her. She is soooo beautiful ... I ... I love her. I have known her before ... she is ... a friend." He blurted all this out in a jumble and tapped the knuckles of one hand against his chest several times before turning away from them.

They knew why he turned away. As he was speaking the other three had each taken long, long breaths and nodded their heads very slowly. Three more sets of eyes filled with tears as three more human children FELT their hearts being filled with something that had been missing for eons of time: a connection with Dragon Kind.

On hearing the sounds of muffled sobs, the Choccies sprung into movement, running up to their children and whining loudly.

They got no response from the children until old Solo sat directly in front of Esme and spoke loudly three times:

'Grwoof! ... Grwoof! ... Grwoof!

At this Esme, sniffed loudly, wiped her eyes and then her nose with the backs of her hands. She sat down on the wet grass and motioned the three dogs to come to her. They jumped all over her in their enthusiasm and relief at finding she was alright and then went to each of the other children in turn to receive stroked, pats and cuddles.

"Look!" called Reuben, pointing in the direction of the dragon.

All eyes turned towards The Dragon Et-Evora.

The great creature was … fading. The deep green colours of the scales that had pulsed all over her body were fading into a light yellowy-green and she seemed to be almost merging with the grass she was sitting on.

The children watched in amazement.

At the moment before she disappeared completely, a strange sound filled the air. It was a little bit like the sound of a melancholy wind instrument and sent shivers down their spines.

The two winged horses opened their wings, stood on their hind legs and neighed their answer to her.

After several moments of stunned silence, the children all started talking at once. The Choccies ran to where the dragon had been, frantically sniffing the air and snuffling the ground for her scent. The ponies, after giving little whickers to each other, started doing ordinary 'pony-things'- mostly getting their heads down and tearing off mouthfuls of the grass that tasted so much better than that in their own paddock!

A rather loud high-pitched squeak caught the children's attention.

"Rattie!" exclaimed Reuben. "Sorry ... I had forgotten you were there!"Reuben reached inside his jacket and undid the button that was holding shut the pocket containing JasonRat. Reuben had buttoned him in for safety when things started to kick off.

A long pair of quivering whiskers attached to a little pink nose appeared from around the opening to Reuben's jacket, quickly followed by a little white head. The tiny creature's eyes – one black and one pink – darted around for several seconds before JasonRat dared to reveal himself completely and climb up onto Reuben's shoulder – where he sat and started to groom himself.

Peter and Hannelore, who had not met Jason previously, were entranced.

"Ooh ... aaah ... cute ..." and other similar exclamations issued forth.

Reuben, happy to find himself the centre of attention, hammed it up:
"JasonRat, let me introduce you to my friends Peter and Hannelore ... and of course you know my sister, Esme."

Any remaining tension was broken when all the children burst out laughing.

Until suddenly Esme put a hand to her mouth: "Oh my goodness!"

"What is it Es?" asked her brother anxiously. Peter and Hanni stopped talking and all three looked anxiously at Esme. What now?

"Gyrre! I'd forgotten him! … My eagle" she explained to Hannelore and Peter, who were looking at her questioningly.

"Eagle … what eagle?" Hanni looked even more confused. But Peter nodded slowly. "Er … you mean … the large buzzard?"

"Yeah, yeah yeah … I saw him fall from those clouds just after the storm began. I meant to go find him … then I forgot because it all got so scary!"

Whilst Peter turned to Hanni and mouthed: "Dreamtime … I think …?" the distraught girl began running in the direction she remembered having seen the eagle falling from the sky.

Pegasus, who had been observing the children and 'listening' to their conversation, watched the girl for a few moments. Then, with a few half-flaps of his great wings, he overtook her and planted himself directly in front of her, wings slightly open so that she could not easily run past him.

She veered off to the side to get around him.

He also moved to the side, blocking her again.

She shouted at the winged horse. "Let me pass ... I've got to find Gyrre ... he must be hurt."

'STOP!' The word entered her mind so forcefully that her head was thrown backwards.
The great horse moved closer to her and huffed on her head. The girl was sobbing uncontrollably.
The next words she heard were: *'You humans ... so much panic!'*

"But ..."

'No buts child. Just find some common sense in that clever mind of yours.'

Esme sobs lessened and the back of her hand became a handkerchief once again as she sniffed hard and wiped her nose.

The powerful energy that Pegasus surrounded her with calmed her down and she was indeed able to find some common sense.

"Oh ... I see ... I think ... you mean ...?"

'Indeed,' huffed Pegasus – for he knew what she was thinking without her having to say anything.

"So he's not been hurt?" She asked, just to check that her common sense had been telling the truth.

'Precisely so. He will 'tell' you his part in it all when you next meet'.

Esme heaved a sigh of relief and walked back to the others. "I think we should be going home. I don't know what the time is but I'm really cold and it must be getting late. We promised Mum we'd be back for tea."

This comment from Esme brought them all back to their present reality: soaking wet, exhausted ... and with several miles to ride back home.

"Where are they ... the flying horses?" asked Hannelore, wanting to thank Pegasus and Gzee for rescuing them even though the creatures had scared her a little.
But all that was left of the two winged horses was a slight shimmering in the air – rather like a mirage. The creatures had disappeared, just like the dragon had earlier.

In their place Mr Nibbs moved ever so solely towards the children, head down, tearing off mouthfuls of grass as he came.

"Oh, they'll be around," said Reuben with the 'I don't understand but ... that's the way it is' sort of gesture. He went to Mr Nibbs and climbed aboard.

So without further ado the children, ponies and dogs set off for home.

They were all very subdued during the rather uncomfortable ride home, each one immersed in her or his own thoughts.

Hanni was trying to not to notice the sharp pain in the thorn torn palm of her hand. It was looking very red and beginning to swell a little.

28 - What Will Be Next?

All of them were pleased to see Enfield Cottage come into view as they turned from the track into the lane.

The three dogs rushed ahead and stood with their noses pressed to the garden gate.

"Let's tie the ponies here for the moment and let Mum and Dad know we're home."
Four children slid off the four ponies and tied their mounts to the sturdy front fence. Although the fence was set back quite a way off the road, they were not supposed to do this. Any sort of accident could be caused.
But on this occasion, they all agreed with Reuben's suggestion instead of spending extra time turning them out into their field.

No sooner had they opened the gate leading down the side of the house, than Mrs Montana appeared at the side door.

"Ah, there you all are. That friend of yours Esme ... Rose ... she's waiting for you ..." She broke off, taking in the bedraggled group. "What ... on ... earth! You're all soaked! What's happened?" She reached out and cupped Reuben's chin in her hand, turning his face towards her. "Reuben ... tell me!" She knew her son's adventurous spirit often led him into trouble.

"It rained Mum, that's all." He shrugged.

Mrs Montana turned her attention towards her daughter. "Esme … ?"

"It's all right Mum," Esme reassured her mother. "We got caught in a storm up on the ridge. And it really did rain bucketsful!" she added.

"How very odd! We've had bright sun all day here. But now I come to think of it though … I did notice some black clouds over to the west. Looked like there were lightning strikes too … just for a very short while though. The clouds seemed to disappear rather suddenly. You were unlucky to get caught in it."

"We were," said Reuben … and all four children gravely nodded their agreement.

"Anyway, as soon as you've let Rose know you're back, come in and change into some dry clothes. I'm sure I can find something that will fit Peter and Hanni. And there's homemade pizza for tea."

"Oooh … great!"

"Thank you Mrs Montana."

"Yes … thank you so much."

"Is there enough for Rose?"

"Of course … if you four eat less! She's been here for about half an hour … down by that strange rose bush I think … said she needed to speak to you about …"

But they were already heading off down into the back garden.

"Rose, Rose!" Esme called loudly, as her friend was nowhere to be seen.

Rose emerged … that was the only word to describe how she seemed to appear from the very inside of that strange rose bush … once again festooned in beautiful white flowers.

"Ah! You're back. Good. I was a bit worried. Are you all okay?"

"We are okay, but … why do you think we might not be? And … how did you get here?"

Rose grinned. "You know … ways and means. My mother thinks I'm playing in the garden." She shrugged it off. "It's just that I heard from …"

She broke off and turned towards Hanni and Peter, as though suddenly becoming aware of their presence. "Hello again" she said, and cocked her head questioningly at Esme.

"They've met Pegasus and Gzee now … and …"

Esme was going to add that they had all met a dragon. But Rose held up her hands and waggled them gently. "Okay. Esme, stop!"

All the while she was smiling at Peter and Hanni but was clearly unsure how to continue.

Then: "Hello again Rose." Peter's natural courtesy took hold, and he offered Rose his hand to shake. She didn't take it, but bowed very slightly to him instead. "Thank you Peter."

There was an uncomfortable pause, and Esme thought once again that the way Rose behaved sometimes was very odd.

"Yes ... me too ... pleased to meet you again that is!" added Hanni, dipping her head slightly in the direction of Rose. "Err ..." she pointed a finger in the direction of Rose's hair. "I think ..." she giggled a bit. "I think you're wearing a live hair slide."

At this, Rose seemed to relax, as though recalling what she knew about these two 'new' children. She smiled at them all. "I'm sorry; I was a bit distracted when you all arrived."

She then lifted a finger to her hair for Buzzchat to climb on to. "His torn wing is completely healed now ... look." She stretched the wing right out for the children to look at. "He can fly well enough to leave now. But he's told me he's going to stay here instead of going back to his group."

"Oh?" Esme lifted her eyebrows in surprise and reached out to gently touch the tiny creature. Buzzchat Bzzzzzd in pleasure.

"Says he wants to stay close to you humans ... keep an eye on you."

"Oh ... that's ... er ... good. Thank you Buzzchat! Esme nodded at the tiny creature. "Rose ... you asked if we were okay. Why did you think we might not be?"

"Well you see Bumble Wizards have amazing networks spread out all over the country. And news travels very quickly between them! Local connections of Buzzchat's informed him that a group of children, ponies and dogs up on the hills over there (Rose pointed over to the west) had been storm-attacked by The Joker and a bunch of Bully Clouds ..."

"Yeah, yeah, yeah, we sure were!" Reuben nodded vehemently to emphasise the point.

"What are those?" Hanni whispered to Peter.

"Dunno ... not heard of them before."

"We'll explain later," Esme whispered back. When she had heard the word 'Joker' an image of the horrid face in the bonfire came to her immediately. She shivered.

Rose continued: "He said the group had been in great danger of their lives." Her serious expression as she said this caused various looks of consternation.

"Yes ... in danger of your lives. You could have been killed; you probably would have been killed, or at the very least hurt badly ... by lightning ... or perhaps large hail stones." She paused for affect and waited to see that all four children were paying attention.

They were, each one holding his or her breath.

"Yes ... you could have been KILLED!
"If Esme had not remembered she could call for help ... only just in time as it turned out!" She looked intently at Esme, who grimaced and let her breath out between her clenched teeth.
"But at least Esme had her amulet with her." She now turned a stern gaze upon Reuben, who squirmed with embarrassment.

"Sorry." The others could just hear his voice as he stood in front of Rose, eyes cast to the ground.

Peter and Hanni looked at each other, feelings of embarrassment for their friend added to all the other confused emotions they were experiencing. Each was thinking that this girl, Rose, was behaving more like a head teacher than a friend!

Rose dropped the stern look and instantaneously changed her tone. She said cheerfully: "You were lucky on this occasion that The Dragon Et-Evora was not only in the neighbourhood, but willing to lend her strength to fight your battle for you. But you'll learn ... all of you." She glanced towards Hanni and Peter and lifted her eyebrows at them. "But come now ... I believe the twins' mother has prepared tea and dry clothes for you all … and agreed that there is plenty for me too … as long as you four eat a little less?"

Esme looked at her friend aghast. She couldn't keep up with this switching from talk of magical things to talk of having tea! She was about to protest; but Rose said quickly: "We mustn't keep her waiting, must we!" and set off towards the kitchen with the others following.

Buzzchat flew from Rose's hand up into Hanni's hair, quickly nestling into her mass of curls. Hanni giggled. It wasn't often she was happy about having super curly hair.

After changing into dry clothes, enjoying a wonderful tea and telling their mother – vaguely – about the storm that had left them so wet, they had all fallen silent, each with his or her own thoughts.

A loud shrieky neigh broke the silence.

Startled, the children looked at each other.

"The ponies!" Hannelore exclaimed. "We've left them tied to the fence!"

"Oh we did!"

"Crikey!"

"Poor things!"

The children jumped up from the table, and in his hurry, Reuben knocked his chair over and it clattered to the ground. A startled Kimber awoke from his nap. The cat flattened his ears, extend his claws and hissed *'clumsy humans'*.

All five children stopped in their tracks and turned to look at him.

"Did he say what I thought he said?" asked Peter.

"Well, I heard 'clumsy humans'." said Esme and laughed, before mouthing at the cat "Sorry".

Peter smiled widely. Having friends who understood his ability to know what animals were saying instead of thinking he was nuts, was … just the very best!

"Silly old cat!" Reuben threw Kimber an affectionate glance … be rewarded with another hiss.

All four ponies had been taught to stand still – or at least stay in the same place - when tied or left with reins hanging. The twins' father thought it important they learn this if the children were intending to out for long rides and wanting to stop for picnics, or to explore.

But after standing very patiently for over an hour Mr Nibbs had had enough. He had muttered *'selfish creatures humans'* to his three companions before letting out the ear splitting neigh that reminded the children of their obligations!

Mr Montana, whose turn it was to run the visiting children home, called after Rose as she followed the others: "And you Rose? Do you need a lift or is your mother coming for you?"

Rose hesitated briefly before answering. "I am hoping to stay for the night." She touched Esme on the shoulder. "Isn't that so?"

Esme, surprised, turned to her friend and nodded. "Umm … er … yep, that's right … er … your mum said yes did she?"

"She's fine with it." Rose winked at Esme.

"Right then, I'll start the car whilst you take the ponies to the field." Mr Montana followed the children down the path and then headed for the garage, whilst the children untied the ponies from the front fence.

'*About time!*' muttered Mr Nibbs. He shook his head and gave Reuben a gentle nip on the arm.

"Owe! … Nibbs!"

Mr Nibbs gave another gentle nip.
"Owe! … okay … I'm sorry. We shouldn't have forgotten about you!"
Accepting the apology, the pony placed his muzzle on the boy's head and let out a huffy breath that ruffled his hair.

The ponies were taken into the field and stripped of their saddles and bridles. Each one gave a vigorous shake as soon as the tack came off.

Torrela, Mickleton, and Barnaby all shot off at high speed, giving a few bucks on the way before getting down for a good roll. Mr Nibbs left the gate more sedately, having stopped behind to accept a grubby sugar lump from Reuben. He headed at a leisurely pace towards the coppice in the far corner of the field before getting down for his roll.

Esme noticed that just for a couple of seconds, Torrela become semi-transparent when she bucked. She hoped this didn't mean the beautiful mare had been harmed by the battling energies they had all experienced.

Peter turned to Reuben and said: "I'm sure I heard Mr Nibbs say: '*Until next time then children*'."

Hanni grinned "Well that's good!" Of the four children, she seemed the most physically resilient and the least affected by what had happened to them.

"That sounds like him." Reuben, who had hardly said anything since Rose had 'ticked him' off, suddenly came to life. "See you both tomorrow … mid morning? … got a lot to talk about … and … things to do … don't we Es?"

"Yeah … we sure do don't we."

"Indeed we do!" agreed Rose in her teachery voice.

Hanni and Peter looked surprised but nodded in agreement.

"I'll have to ask my Dad," demurred Peter and looked at Hanni.

"Me too ... I'll have to ask my parents. Let's text in the morning if we can't come. Otherwise ... see you all about eleven?"

And so it was agreed that the five of them should try and meet up the next day to talk over their adventure.

Esme, who was making sure the gate was properly shut muttered something about expecting these summer holidays would be full of 'going places'.

As they walked back down the lane to the cottage, Hanni remarked in a nonchalant manner: "What a shame we can't tell anybody about all this!Imagine saying to our parents: I've made some really interesting new friends since I met Reuben and Esme ... there's two winged horses, an eagle that doesn't really exist, and a dragon."

The four children were still laughing their heads off when they parted company, Peter and Hanni being taken home by Mr Montana, and Rose accompanying Reuben and Esme back into the cottage.

All four went to bed exceptionally early that night. Each was going over memories of their scary adventure. Each had finally realised that what Rose had said was actually true. They could have died had it not been for that dragon – *The Dragon Et-Evora* as she had introduced herself. Finally sleep came, with each child wondering what the next morning's meeting with Rose would bring.

Esme was the only one who remembered her dream when she awoke next day. As Pegasus had predicted, she had met up with Gyrre and he had explained to her what had happened to him.

***

I hope you have enjoyed the book and ask you to take a moment to make a brief review on your favourite retail website or send it to the publsiher.
Hint: You may write it down now and share it later.

Thanks in advance, *SPW*.

E-mails will reach the author if you use this address: eip@erikistrup.dk and refer to the book title.

Acknowledgements

I've had support and encouragement from many people during the long drawn out process of producing this book, but without the input from many of the story's own characters I would never have put pen to paper in the first place. Some of these characters badger me within my mind or dreams, demanding I tell a story about them. Others are actual animal personalities I have lived with or known, who have brought joy and on occasion sadness into my life and caused me to wish that I could speak dog, cat, horse, eagle, crow or mouse.

And I thank those 10-year olds who read the first two chapters and asked me to write more; and the adults who read the story and told me how much they enjoyed it; and my twin daughters who helped in various ways with getting the story ready for publication. And I thank those members of the Shaumbra family who responded to my request for advice on how to 'get this book out into the world', and started me off on my steps towards publication by putting me in touch with Erik my oh so patient publisher, and Stella who created the lovely image of Mr Nibbs and Pegasus that adorns the front cover. And I thank earth angel Belara.

Author's note

Although I have always enjoyed writing, it had never occurred to me to write a book. Articles were what I enjoyed: researching a topic, including through experience where possible. I was good at that. And then one day a character from this book popped into my head and asked that I write a story about him. This of course was Pegasus. I wrote the first two chapters with ease, and having received constructive criticism and approval from a couple of 10-year olds, blithely carried on with chapter three. I completed it and hit a blank wall: the story lines completely dried up and I had no idea where to go next.

That was over 25 years ago. Life was busy at the time and I forgot all about Adventures with Pegasus ... until a few years ago when a clear-out of my old writings led me to handwritten sheets of those first two chapters. I read through them, felt enthusiasm rising and ended up having to say 'Woa' to the numerous characters and their stories that were clamouring to get out of my head and onto the page.

And Pegasus, bless his beautiful wings, although not the main protagonist in the stories, remains a key character in the background, ready to rather grumpily lead the children into new adventures when they are in danger of becoming complacent, and stop questioning whether 'how things are' is the best way they can be.

The main theme running through the adventures that Pegasus initiates for the twins and their friends is that of our human relationships: with each other and with all the other sentient beings with whom we share life on this beautiful planet Earth, including those Beings who are invisible to most people. The more adventures the children have, the more they learn to be ever curious and open to other realities.